'With great sensitivity and psychological subtlety, Freudenberger charts the misunderstandings experienced by the couple in their first years together' *Observer*

'The richness and restraint recall Vikram Seth's epic of pragmatism, *A Suitable Boy*' Sunday Telegraph

'Freudenberger has rare humanity, and talent great enough to command not only a vast landscape of imbalance and misunderstanding, but also a tender sphere of tiny intimacy, hidden yearning . . . A marvellous book' Kiran Desai, author of *The Inheritance of Loss*

'A fresh and modern look at relationships, told with heart' *Elle*

'A big, complicated portrait of marriage, culture, family and love. Freudenberger never settles for an easy answer, and what she delivers is a story that feels absolutely true' Ann Patchett, author of *State of Wonder*

'Genuinely moving. Freudenberger demonstrates her assurance as a novelist and her knowledge of the complicated arithmetic of familial love and the mathematics of romantic passion' *The New York Times*

'The most remarkable accomplishment of this hugely satisfying novel is Freudenberger's subtle exploration of the stage of adulthood at the heart of *The Newlyweds*, and all the compromises with selfhood those early years of love and marriage entail' *Los Angeles Times*

'Powerful . . . in its clear-eyed openness and compassion toward the world, in its nuanced and human representation of Muslim characters and their varying Islams, and in the understanding and sympathy it displays for the nostalgia of migrants – which is to say, for all human beings' *The New York Times Book Review*

'A delight, one of the easiest book recommendations of the year. Freudenberger knows Amina as well as Jane Austen knows Emma, and despite its globe-spanning set changes, *The Newlyweds* offers a reading experience redolent of Janeite charms: gentle touches of social satire, subtly drawn characters and dialogue that expresses far more than its polite surface' *Washington Post*

'Like Lahiri, Franzen and Eugenides, Freudenberger excels at chronicling her character's emotional lives' *San Francisco Chronicle*

'It's really, really good. A luscious and intelligent novel that will stick with you' *NPR*

'Exceptional . . . Here is an honest depiction of life as most people actually live it: Americans and Asians, Christians and Muslims, liberals and conservatives. Freudenberger writes with a cultural fluency that is remarkable and in a prose that is clean, intelligent, and very witty' David Bezmozgis, author of *The Free World*

'Wise, timely, ripe with humour and complexity, *The Newlyweds* is one of the most believable love stories of our young century' Gary Shteyngart, author of *Super Sad True Love Story*

'Like writers such as Jhumpa Lahiri and Ha Jin, she deftly shows how strange the rituals of suburban America seem to an observant outsider' *Wall Street Journal*

'*The Newlyweds* is about all sorts of complex relationships: between parents and children; with first loves; with the places we depart and those we adopt, and "the many selves" this fluidity creates. Freudenberger does an especially lovely job creating Amina's worlds – her emotional terrain, her wonder and bewilderment adjusting to America, her life in Bangladesh' *Seattle Times*

'*The Newlyweds* crosses continents, cultures and generations . . . It's funny, gracefully written and full of loneliness and yearning. It's also a candid, recognizable story about love – the real-life kind, which is often hard and sustained by hope, kindness and pure effort' *USA Today*

'As the tale traces their tumultuous first years together, George and Amina's union is revealed as hardly standard, but at once idiosyncratic and universal. . . . Fluid and utterly confident' *Time Out New York*

'Freudenberger's masterful prose makes comprehensible how someone can become a stranger in two places at once' *New York Observer*

'Captivating . . . Freudenberger's latest novel explores the unexpected consequences when two distinct cultures collide . . . This engaging story, with its page after page of effortless prose, ultimately offers up a deeper narrative of the protagonist's yearning' *Boston Globe*

'Freudenberger has created an unforgettable character: Amina's determination, intelligence and resilience make her a heroine for any culture and any time' *Marie Claire*

'Generous and moving . . . In this remarkably clear-eyed novel, the hopes and pretensions of Americans and Bangladeshis alike are laid bare, and what they end up with may be both more than and less than they deserve, and certainly not what they planned' *The Times Literary Supplement*

ABOUT THE AUTHOR

Nell Freudenberger is the author of the novel *The Dissident*, longlisted for the Orange Prize and a *New York Times Review* Notable Book, and the story collection *Lucky Girls*, shortlisted for the Orange New Writers' Award and winner of the PEN/Malamud Award and the Sue Kaufman Prize for First Fiction from the American Academy of Arts and Letters, and also a *New York Times Book Review* Notable Book. She was named a *New Yorker* '20 Under 40' writer and one of *Granta*'s Best Young American Novelists. She lives in Brooklyn.

The Newlyweds

A NOVEL

Nell Freudenberger

PENGUIN BOOKS

PENGUIN BOOKS

Published by the Penguin Group
Penguin Books Ltd, 80 Strand, London WC2R 0RL, England
Penguin Group (USA) Inc., 375 Hudson Street, New York, New York 10014, USA
Penguin Group (Canada), 90 Eglinton Avenue East, Suite 700, Toronto, Ontario, Canada M4P 2Y3
(a division of Pearson Penguin Canada Inc.)
Penguin Ireland, 25 St Stephen's Green, Dublin 2, Ireland (a division of Penguin Books Ltd)
Penguin Group (Australia), 707 Collins Street, Melbourne, Victoria 3008, Australia
(a division of Pearson Australia Group Pty Ltd)
Penguin Books India Pvt Ltd, 11 Community Centre, Panchsheel Park, New Delhi – 110 017, India
Penguin Group (NZ), 67 Apollo Drive, Rosedale, Auckland 0632, New Zealand
(a division of Pearson New Zealand Ltd)
Penguin Books (South Africa) (Pty) Ltd, Block D, Rosebank Office Park,
181 Jan Smuts Avenue, Parktown North, Gauteng 2193, South Africa

Penguin Books Ltd, Registered Offices: 80 Strand, London WC2R 0RL, England

www.penguin.com

First published in the United States of America by Alfred A. Knopf 2012
First published in Great Britain by Viking 2012
Published in Penguin Books 2013
001

Printed in Great Britain by Clays Ltd, St Ives plc

A CIP catalogue record for this book is available from the British Library

ISBN: 978-0-241-96270-1

www.greenpenguin.co.uk

Penguin Books is committed to a sustainable
future for our business, our readers and our planet.
This book is made from Forest Stewardship
Council™ certified paper.

ALWAYS LEARNING   **PEARSON**

For Paul

In a courtyard
She is waiting,
Wearing a Dacca sari, vermilion in her parting.

RABINDRANATH TAGORE, *"Flute Music"*

An Arranged Marriage

1 She hadn't heard the mailman, but Amina decided to go out and check. Just in case. If anyone saw her, they would know that there was someone in the house now during the day while George was at work. They would watch Amina hurrying coatless to the mailbox, still wearing her bedroom slippers, and would conclude that this was her home. She had come to stay.

The mailbox was new. She had ordered it herself with George's credit card, from mailboxes.com, and she had not chosen the cheapest one. George had said that they needed something sturdy, and so Amina had turned off the Deshi part of her brain and ordered the heavy-duty rural model, in glossy black, for $90. She had not done the conversion into taka, and when it arrived, wrapped in plastic, surrounded by Styrofoam chips, and carefully tucked into its corrugated cardboard box—a box that most Americans would simply throw away but that Amina could not help storing in the basement, in a growing pile behind George's Bowflex—she had taken pleasure in its size and solidity. She showed George the detachable red flag that you could move up or down to indicate whether you had letters for collection.

"That wasn't even in the picture," she told him. "It just came with it, free."

The old mailbox had been bashed in by thugs. The first time had been right after Amina arrived from Bangladesh, one Thursday night in March. George had left for work on Friday morning, but he hadn't gotten even as far as his car when he came back through the kitchen door, uncharacteristically furious.

"Goddamn thugs. Potheads. Smoking weed and destroying private property. And the police don't do a fucking thing."

"Thugs are here? In Pittsford?" She couldn't understand it, and that made him angrier.

"Thugs! Vandals. Hooligans—whatever you want to call them. Uneducated pieces of human garbage." Then he went down to the basement to get his tools, because you had to take the mailbox off its post and repair the damage right away. If the thugs saw that you hadn't fixed it, that was an invitation.

The flag was still raised, and when she double-checked, sticking her hand all the way into its black depths, there was only the stack of bills George had left on his way to work. The thugs did not actually steal the mail, and so her green card, which was supposed to arrive this month, would have been safe even if she could have forgotten to check. "Thugs" had a different meaning in America, and that was why she'd been confused. George had been talking about kids, trouble-makers from East Rochester High, while Amina had been thinking of dacoits: bandits who haunted the highways and made it unsafe to take the bus. She had lived in Rochester six months now—long enough to know that there were no bandits on Pittsford roads at night.

American English was different from the language she'd learned at Maple Leaf International in Dhaka, but she was lucky because George corrected her and kept her from making embarrassing mistakes. Americans always went to the bathroom, never the loo. They did not live in flats or stow anything in the boot of the car, and under no circumstances did they ever pop outside to smoke a fag.

Maple Leaf was where she first learned to use the computer, and the computer was how she met George, a thirty-four-year-old SWM who was looking for a wife. George had explained to her that he had always wanted to get married. He had dated women in Rochester, but often found them silly, and had such a strong aversion to perfume that he couldn't sit across the table from a woman who was wearing it. George's cousin Kim had called him "picky," and had suggested that he might have better luck on the Internet, where he could clarify his requirements from the beginning.

George told Amina that he had been waiting for a special connection. He was a romantic, and he didn't want to compromise on just anyone. It wasn't until his colleague Ed told him that he'd met his wife, Min, on AsianEuro.com that he had thought of trying that particular site. When he had received the first e-mail from Amina, he said that he'd "had a feeling." When Amina asked what had given him the feeling, he said that she was "straightforward" and that she did not play games, unlike some women he knew. Which women were those, she had asked, but George said he was talking about women he'd known a long time ago, when he was in college.

She hadn't been testing him: she had really wanted to know, only because her own experience had been so different. She had been contacted by several men before George, and each time she'd wondered if this was the person she would marry. Once she and George had started e-mailing each other exclusively, she had wondered the same thing about him, and she'd continued wondering even after he booked the flight to Dhaka in order to meet her. She had wondered that first night when he ate with her parents at the wobbly table covered by the plasticized map of the world—which her father discreetly steadied by placing his elbow somewhere in the neighborhood of Sudan—and during the agonizing hours they had spent in the homes of their Dhaka friends and relatives, talking to each other in English while everyone sat around them and watched. It wasn't until she was actually on the plane to Washington, D.C., wearing the University of Rochester sweatshirt he'd given her, that she had finally become convinced it was going to happen.

It was the first week of September, but the leaves were already starting to turn yellow. George said that the fall was coming early, making up for the fact that last spring had been unusually warm: a gift to Amina from the year 2005—her first in America. By the time she arrived in March most of the snow was gone, and so she had not yet experienced a real Rochester winter.

In those first weeks she had been pleased to notice that her husband had a large collection of books: biographies (Abraham Lincoln, Anne Frank, Cary Grant, Mary Queen of Scots, John Lennon, and Napoléon) as well as classic novels by Charles Dickens, Cervantes, Tolstoy, Ernest Hemingway, and Jane Austen. George told Amina that he was a reader but that he couldn't understand people who waded through all of the garbage they published these days, when it was possible to spend your whole life reading books the greatness of which had already been established.

George did have some books from his childhood, when he'd been interested in fantasy novels, especially retellings of the Arthurian legend and anything to do with dragons. There was also a book his mother had given him, *1001 Facts for Kids,* which he claimed had "basically got him through the stupidity of elementary school." In high school he had put away the *1001 Facts* in favor of a game called Dungeons & Dragons, but there were now websites that served the same purpose, and George retained a storehouse of interesting tidbits that he periodically related to Amina.

"Did you know that there is an actual society made up of people who believe the earth is flat?"

"Did you know that one out of twenty people has an extra rib?"

"Did you know that most lipstick contains fish scales?"

For several weeks Amina had answered "No" to each of these questions, until she gradually understood that this was another colloquialism—perhaps more typical of her husband than of the English language—simply a way of introducing a new subject that did not demand an actual response.

"Did you know that seventy percent of men and sixty percent of women admit to having been unfaithful to their spouse, but that eighty percent of men say they would marry the same woman if they had the chance to live their lives over again?"

"What do the women say?" Amina had asked, but George's website hadn't cited that statistic.

George had said that they could use the money he'd been saving for a rainy day for her to begin studying at Monroe Community College next year, and as soon as her green card arrived, Amina planned to start looking for a job. She wanted to contribute to the cost of her education, even if it was just a small amount. George supported the idea of her continuing her studies, but only once she had a specific goal in mind. It wasn't the degree that counted but what you did with it; he believed that too many Americans wasted time and money on college simply for the sake of a fancy piece of paper. And so Amina told him that she'd always dreamed of becoming a real teacher. This was not untrue, in the sense that she had hoped her tutoring jobs at home might one day lead to a more sustained and distinguished kind of work. What she didn't mention to George was how important the

U.S. college diploma would be to everyone she knew at home—a tangible symbol of what she had accomplished halfway across the world.

She was standing at the sink, chopping eggplant for dinner, when she saw their neighbor Annie Snyder coming up Skytop Lane, pushing an infant in a stroller and talking to her little boy, Lawson, who was pedaling a low plastic bike. The garish colors and balloon-like shapes of that toy reminded Amina of a commercial she had seen on TV soon after she'd arrived in Rochester, in which real people were eating breakfast in a cartoon house. Annie had introduced herself when Amina had moved in and invited her out for coffee. Then she'd asked if Amina had any babysitting experience, because she was always looking for someone to watch the kids for an hour or two while she did the shopping or went to the gym.

She asks that because you're from someplace else, George had said. She sees brown skin and all she can think of is housecleaning or babysitting. He told her she was welcome to go to Starbucks with Annie, but under no circumstances was she to take care of Annie's children, even for an hour. Amina was desperate to find a job, but secretly she was glad of George's prohibition. American babies made her nervous, the way they traveled in their padded strollers, wrapped up in blankets like precious goods from UPS.

She had never worried about motherhood before, since she'd always known she would have her own mother to help her. When she and George had become serious, Amina and her parents had decided that she would do everything she could to bring them to America with her. Only once they'd arrived did she want to have her first child. They'd talked their plan through again and again at home, researching the green card and citizenship requirements—determining that if all went well, it would be three years from the time she arrived before her parents could hope to join her. Just before she left, her cousin Ghaniyah had shown her an article in *Femina* called "After the Honeymoon," which said that a couple remained newlyweds for a year and a day after marriage. In her case, Amina thought, the newlywed period would last three times that long, because she wouldn't feel truly settled until her parents had arrived.

In spite of all the preparation, there was something surprising about actually finding herself in Rochester, waiting for a green card in the mail. The sight of Annie squatting down and retrieving something from the netting underneath the stroller reminded her that she had been here six months already and had not yet found an opportunity to discuss her thoughts about children or her parents' emigration with George.

2 Theirs was the second-to-last house on the road. The road ended in an asphalt circle called a cul-de-sac, and beyond the cul-de-sac was a field of corn. That field had startled Amina when she first arrived—had made her wonder, just for a moment, if she had not been tricked (as everyone had predicted) and found herself in a sort of American village. She'd had to remind herself of the clean and modern Rochester airport and of the Pittsford Wegmans—a grocery store that was the first thing she described to her mother during their first conversation on the phone. When she asked about the field, George had explained that there were power lines that couldn't be moved, and so no one could build a house there.

After she understood its purpose, Amina liked the cornfield, which reminded her of Haibatpur, her grandmother's village. She had been born there. That was when the house was still a hut, with a thatched roof and a fired-dung floor. After she was born, when her parents were struggling to feed even themselves in Dhaka, they had done as many people did and sent their child back to live with her grandparents in the village. Because of a land dispute between Amina's father and his cousins, it was her mother's village to which they habitually returned. And so Amina had stayed with Nanu and her Parveen Aunty and Parveen's daughter—her favorite cousin, Micki—until she was six years old. Her first memory was of climbing up the stone steps from the pond with her hand in Nanu's, watching a funny pattern of light and dark splotches turn into a frog, holding still in the ragged shade of a coconut palm.

Her nanu had had four daughters and two sons, but both of Amina's uncles had died too young for Amina to remember them. The elder, Khokon, had been Mukti Bahini like her father, a Freedom Fighter against the Pakistanis, while the younger one, Emdad, had stayed in the village so that her grandmother wouldn't worry too much. Even though he was younger, it was Emdad her grandmother loved the best: that was why she'd kept him with her. When you tried to trick God that way, bad things could happen. Khokon had been killed by General Yahya's soldiers only two weeks after he'd enlisted, but Emdad had lived long enough to marry. Her mother said that Nanu had often congratulated herself on her foresight in convincing Emdad to stay at home, and so it had been almost impossible for her to believe the news, ten years after the war had ended, that her younger son had been killed in a motorbike accident on his way to Shyamnagar, delivering prescription medicines to the family pharmacy. For months afterward, whenever people offered condolences, her grandmother would correct them:

"You're thinking of Khokon, my elder son. He was killed in the war."

By the time Amina was grown up, her grandmother had recovered her wits. But by then she had only daughters, and that was the reason she'd become the way she was now, very quiet and heavy, like a stone.

Little by little, over the eleven months they had written to each other, Amina had told George about her life. She'd said that she came from a good family and that her parents had sacrificed to send her to an English medium school, but she had not exaggerated her father's financial situation or the extent of her formal education. She'd said that she had learned to speak English at Maple Leaf International in Dhaka but that she'd been forced to drop out when she was thirteen, when her father could no longer pay the fees. She'd tried to explain that it wasn't arriving in a rickshaw every day, when everyone else came by car or taxi, or borrowing the books other girls owned, or even working twice as hard because everyone else had a private tutor after school. What she couldn't stand, she wrote to George, was having to leave school a few months after her thirteenth birthday, waking up in the morning and knowing that today she was falling six hours behind, tomorrow twelve, and the next day eighteen. What she couldn't stand was all the waste.

She'd also confessed that she was twenty-four rather than twenty-three that year: her parents had waited to file her birth certificate, as many families did, so that she might one day have extra time to qualify for university or the civil-service exam. Her mother had warned her to be careful about what she revealed in her e-mails, but Amina found that once she got started writing, it was difficult to stop.

She told George how her father's business plans had a tendency to fail, and how each time one of those schemes had foundered, they had lost their apartment. She told him about the year they had spent living in Tejgaon, after losing the apartment in the building called Moti Mahal, and how during that time her father had bought a single egg every day, which her mother would cook for her because Amina was still growing and needed the protein. One night, when she had tried to share the egg with her parents, dividing it up into three parts, her father had gotten so angry that he had tried to beat her (with a jump rope) and would have succeeded if her mother hadn't come after him with the broken handle of a chicken-feather broom.

Sometimes she got so involved in remembering what had happened that she forgot about the reader on the other end, and so she was surprised when George wrote back to tell her that her story had made him cry. He could not remember crying since his hamster had died in the second grade, and he thought that it meant their connection was getting stronger. Amina wrote back immediately to apologize for making George cry and to explain that it was not a sad story but a funny one, about her parents and the silly fights they sometimes had. Even if she and George didn't always understand each other, she never felt shy about asking him questions. What level did the American second grade correspond to in the British system? What had he eaten for dinner as a child? And what, she was very curious to know, was a hamster?

It had felt wonderful to have someone to confide in, someone she could trust not to gossip. (With whom could George gossip about Amina, after all?) It was a pleasure to write about difficult times in the past, as long as things were better now. By the time she and George started writing to each other, Amina was supporting her parents with the money she made from her tutoring jobs through Top Talents; they were living in the apartment in Mohammadpur, and of course they had plenty to eat. She still thought the proudest moment of her life had come when she was seventeen and had returned home one day to surprise her parents with a television bought entirely out of her own earnings.

The other benefit of tutoring, one she hadn't considered when she started out, was the use of the computers that many of the wealthy families who hired her kept for their children's exclusive use. All of her students were female, and most of them were between eight and fourteen years old; as they got closer to the O- or A-level exams, their parents hired university students to prepare them. Many of these parents told Amina that they'd chosen her because they'd been impressed by her dedication in passing the O levels on her own, but of course Amina knew that Top Talents charged less for her than they did for an actual university student.

Amina had seen one of her students, a fourteen-year-old named Sharmila, three times a week; since her parents both had office jobs, they liked Amina to stay as long as she wanted so that their daughter wasn't just sitting around with the servants all afternoon. Her mother confided that she thought Amina would be a good influence on her daughter's *character*; Sharmila was very intelligent, but easily distracted, and was not serious enough about saying her prayers. *She has been raised with everything*, her mother said, her arm taking in the marble floors of the living room and the heavy brocade curtains on the six picture windows overlooking the black surface of Gulshan Lake, which was revealed, even at this height, to be clogged with garbage, water lilies, and the shanties of migrant families. *She doesn't even know how lucky she is.* Amina nodded politely, but the way that Sharmila's mother complained was a performance. She would put on the same show when her daughter's marriage was being negotiated, exaggerating Sharmila's incompetence with a simple dal or kitchuri, so that the groom's family would understand what a little princess they were about to receive.

Amina had sworn Sharmila to secrecy on the subject of AsianEuro .com, and then they'd had a lot of fun, looking through the photos in the "male gallery" after the lessons were finished. Sharmila always chose the youngest and best-looking men; she would squeal and gasp when they came across one who was very old or very fat. More often than not, Amina had the same impulses, but she reminded herself that she was not a little girl playing a game. She was a twenty-four-year-old woman whose family's future depended on this decision.

According to her mother, the man could not have been divorced and he certainly couldn't have any children. He had to have a bachelor's degree and a dependable job, and he could not drink alcohol. He could not be younger than thirty or older than forty-five, and he must be willing to convert to Islam. Her mother had also insisted that Amina take off her glasses and wear a red sari she had inherited from her cousin Ghaniyah in the photograph, but once it had been taken and scanned into the computer (a great inconvenience) at the Internet café near Aunty #2's apartment in Savar, her mother would not allow her to post it online. "Why would you want a man who was only interested in your photograph?" she demanded, and nothing Amina could say about the way the site worked would change her mind.

"The men will think you're ugly!" Sharmila exclaimed when she heard about Amina's mother's stipulations. They were sitting on the rug in Sharmila's bedroom at the time, with Sharmila's *Basic English Grammar* open between them. Her student was wearing the kameez of her school uniform with a pair of pajama trousers decorated with kittens. She looked Amina up and down critically.

"Your hair is coarse, and you have an apple nose, but you aren't *ugly*," she concluded. "Now no one is going to write to you." And although Amina had the very same fears, she had decided to pretend to agree with her mother, for the sake of Sharmila's character.

As it happened, George did not post his picture online either. They sent each other the photographs only after they had exchanged several messages. George told her that her picture was "very beautiful," in a formal way that pleased her: it was almost as if he were a Bengali bridegroom surrounded by his relatives, approving of their choice without wanting to display too much enthusiasm, for fear of being teased. Months later, once they had decided to become exclusive and take their profiles down from the site, George told her it was the day he saw her photograph that he'd become convinced she was the right person for him—not because of how pretty she was but because she hadn't used her "superficial charms" to advertise herself, the way certain American women did.

Their correspondence hadn't been without its challenges. Normally she would go to the British Council in the mornings before her tutoring responsibilities began; since George often wrote to her at night before he went to bed, there was almost always a message waiting for her. But one afternoon a message had come when she'd happened to be at the library. It was 4:22 a.m. in Rochester (unlike most people's, George's e-mails always displayed the correct time), and she had been tempted to IM and say that she was online right at that moment. But when she'd read the message, she had been relieved she'd waited. She thought it was doubly disappointing to have gotten a message at a surprising time and then to have it turn out to be the message it was, startling in its curt brevity: George had been assigned a big project at work, he said, and wasn't sure when he would be able to resume their correspondence. He hoped she understood and that she and her family continued to be well.

She had received similar messages before, and it had always meant that the man had found someone else. She remembered the way that this particular message, more than any of the others, had closed down the day—so it seemed as if there would never be anything to look forward to again. She felt as if she had failed, and when she'd arrived home and reported what had happened, her mother's obvious disappointment had made her own even more difficult to bear. Even her father had held his tongue and kept himself from gloating about the unreliability of computerized matchmaking, and so she'd known he had been hoping this time, too.

It had been ten weeks before George had written to her again. Much later she'd wondered whether it was this hiatus that had made her fall in love with him. The message had come at the usual time, but it was even more unexpected than the last one, since she'd assumed he would never write again:

Dear Amina,

First, I should apologize for not writing for so long. I wouldn't blame you if you'd found someone else, or were even engaged by now. (I wouldn't blame you, but I would be very disappointed.) I promised myself I would write to you tonight and explain, but I've been sitting here a long time. I keep writing things and then deleting them.

It wasn't only the work, as you probably guessed. I do have a big project (I'll tell you about it if you're still interested), but believe me when I say I was still thinking about you. My friends have asked how I could be serious about someone I've never even met, but I think in some ways we know each other better than we would if we just went on dates. Do you know what I mean? I think I've been worried about getting serious because I thought you might just disappear or stop writing. I know doing the same thing to you was really stupid, and I'm sorry about that. I guess what I was thinking before I stopped writing is that I'm falling in love with you. There—that's something I wouldn't have said if we'd been face-to-face.

Well, Amina, I'm not sure you can forgive me, but I feel better having written it. How is your grandmother's health? Is your father working these days? And what have you been doing for the last two months? If the answer includes writing to someone else . . . that's what I get, I guess. I know I don't exactly deserve it, but please let me down easy.

Sincerely,
George

She had wondered if she ought to wait a day or so to write back, and then she had chastised herself for thinking about strategy. George had said that he liked her because she didn't play games; she wouldn't be like the women he remembered from college. If he liked her, she wanted it to be for the way she really was, and so she wrote back and told him that she hadn't been corresponding with anyone else. She didn't say anything about the disappointment (her own, or certainly her parents') but simply filled him in on the events of the last few weeks: her father's temporary employment at a shipping office and the pain in her grandmother's knees. Then she had printed out his note and brought it home like a gift to surprise her parents.

3 She hadn't believed there was a man on earth—much less on AsianEuro.com—who would satisfy all of her mother's requirements, but George came very close. He was thirty-four years old, and he had never been married. He had not only a bachelor's but a master's degree from SUNY Buffalo and had worked as an electrical engineer at a company called TCE for the past nine years. He liked to have a Heineken beer while he was watching the football game—his team was the Dallas Cowboys—but he rarely had more than two, and he

would think of converting to Islam if that was what it would take to marry Amina.

In his next e-mail, George told her about his "big project": he had been busy buying a house. He hadn't wanted to tell her about it until he was sure they were serious, because he was afraid it was "too soon" and she might think he was "moving too fast." When Amina read that she almost laughed out loud. Why would any man hesitate to tell a woman he was courting that he had just acquired a three-bedroom house with two bathrooms, a garage, and a backyard with plenty of space for a vegetable garden? He e-mailed her a photograph, which looked to her like something from a magazine: a yellow house with a gray roof and white shutters, taller on one side than the other. (This design was called split-level, and it was one of several similar houses on the tract, a group of homes that had been built by a developer in the 1970s.) George also mentioned that the tract was a family-oriented community, and that the schools nearby were excellent.

"My mother says he's probably divorced," Ghaniyah said when Amina showed her the picture of the house one day on her cousin's home computer. "She says there are a lot of bad people online, and she's worried about you."

"Please tell her not to worry."

"Otherwise, why is he unmarried?"

"Because he hasn't met the right person," Amina snapped. "It's not like here—where your parents have a heart attack if you're not engaged at twenty-five."

Ghaniyah held up her hands in a defensive gesture. "It's my mother who was asking. Personally I think you're really brave."

Amina's mother said she shouldn't have told Ghaniyah anything about George, but by that time Amina knew that he was coming to Desh to meet her, and what if he mentioned AsianEuro or Heineken beer himself? Her aunts were crafty, none more so than Ghaniyah's mother, her Devil Aunty. (Her mother used to reprimand her for calling Aunty #2 by that name, but when she laughed afterward Amina knew it was okay.) Her Devil Aunt was also the only one of her mother's three sisters who spoke any English, and she had a special way of asking one question in order to get the answer to another. Even before she met him in person, Amina knew that George wouldn't be prepared for that kind of Deshi trick.

She had expected disapproval from Ghaniyah and her aunt, but it surprised her when her cousin Nasir started visiting her. Nasir wasn't actually related to her; her father called him nephew because Nasir's father had been his closest friend. When his parents had died less than a year apart, Nasir was only eleven years old. Her father had treated him like a son, monitoring his progress in school, buying him presents (even when they couldn't afford it), and taking him to Friday prayers at the Sat Gumbad Mosque. When Nasir started college in Rajshahi, her father had arranged a place for him to stay near the university, with one of her mother's cousins and his family. (George asked her to use the word "relative" when she was describing her cousins in English; he said it made his head hurt, trying to understand who was who.)

When she was a teenager, she had been in love with Nasir, who was six years older than she was. He had been studying computer science, but he was like her father in that he loved to read poetry, especially poetry about the liberation of Bangladesh. When Nasir returned from college on visits to see his sisters, he would ride his motor scooter over to have dinner with Amina and her parents, and often he would recite his own poems after they finished eating. Her aunts and her cousins had teased her about Nasir, who was unusually tall and hand-some but very dark skinned. He allowed his thick, black hair to grow long and then cut it very short in order to save money at the barber-shop. He always spoke English with Amina, and when she responded, even if it was only in a whisper, he would tell her mother how clever she was. A few years after he'd finished university, Nasir got his visa and left to work in his cousin's restaurant in London. According to her mother, Amina had sulked for two months.

She knew that there had been some discussion about the possibility of her and Nasir marrying, once she reached the right age, and also that those discussions had gradually stopped. The rumors were that Nasir had antagonized his cousin, the owner of the London restaurant, and that he was unlikely to move to any more promising employment there. His elder sister Sakina, still unmarried at thirty-six, was encour-

aging him to return to the small apartment building in Mohammadpur that their parents had left them. Sakina was a formidable woman,
more than 1.7 meters tall, with a streak of white in her inky hair.
Most of their acquaintances had expressed reservations before Amina
left for America, but Sakina was the only one who had come to her
mother directly, demanding to know how she could take such a risk
with her only child. They thought of you for Nasir, her mother had
said at the time—that's why they're so offended. Whomever Nasir
married would be in thrall to Sakina, who was certain to act more
like a mother-in-law than a dependent spinster. Amina didn't think
her parents' feelings about Nasir had changed, but simply that they
hoped for a better life for her. She hoped for it herself.

She hadn't thought of Nasir in months when he showed up at their
door one afternoon with a book for her. She had been at Sharmila's,
staying late in order to e-mail George, and by the time she returned
home, Nasir was gone. He had stayed for two hours, her mother said,
and drunk six cups of tea; even more surprising, while he was in London Nasir had grown a full beard and started wearing a prayer cap.

"I expected a Londoni, and instead I found a mullah at the door,"
her mother joked. Her father, who had come in at the same time, took
Nasir's book eagerly from her mother and read the title aloud: *The
Lawful and Prohibited in Islam*. Amina could tell he'd been hoping for
poetry and was disappointed.

"He left this for Munni?"

"And this." She handed Amina a sheet of lined blue paper from a
schoolchild's copybook, folded three times. When she opened it, she
found an Internet address for something called the Islamic Center of
Rochester.

"A mosque in Rochester, isn't it?" her mother asked Amina
excitedly.

"Islamic Center," her father corrected. "Not mosque."

"A place to meet other Muslim women, then."

Her father took the piece of paper away from Amina. "Your husband will find a real mosque for you."

Amina wanted to keep the address anyway, but her father took it
and stuck it in Nasir's book. He flipped through the pages, stopping
here and there. Then he asked her mother whether you had to be a

guest to get a cup of tea in this house. Her father drank his tea and read the book until it was time to eat, and then when they were finished, he picked it up again. When Amina went to bed, he was still reading.

In the morning Amina was studying at the table when she noticed that something was different. It took her a minute to figure out that she didn't have to put any weight on the Southern Hemisphere in order to read; even when her mother set down her omelet and Horlicks (right in the middle of the Arabian Sea) the table didn't wobble.

"See what Nasir has done for us," her father said, turning from the sink with his face half shaved. "A perfect fit."

Amina looked down and saw that Nasir's book was neatly wedged underneath the left side of the table's round base.

"That book is about Islam," her mother said.

But her father spoke English, as if her mother weren't even there. "Something happened to Nasir's brain in London," he said. "Maybe he is leaving it over there. That is why I am glad my daughter will be going to U.S.A."

4 When Amina had arrived in March, she'd met the majority of George's very small family right away. They had dinner with George's mother, Eileen, every Sunday night, and often Eileen's sister, Aunt Cathy, would show up to join them. One of the first things Amina noticed about Cathy was the way she kept glancing at the diamond engagement ring on Amina's left hand. The ring was a family heirloom—it had belonged to Eileen and Cathy's mother—and so of course she could see how Cathy resented it going to Amina.

"That looks so lovely on your hand," Eileen had said, perhaps because she'd noticed Cathy staring, too. She turned to her sister: "George had to take it down two sizes, and I always thought Mother's fingers were thin."

"Eileen and I always said it would go to George when he married," Cathy informed Amina. "He was the boy. Even if Kim were going to marry"—she gave a short, barking laugh—"and I've given up hope, *she* wouldn't wear something like that. A blood diamond, she called it."

"It's an antique," George said. "You can't put it back in the ground."

"Exactly," Cathy had said, smiling tightly. "That's what I would've told her."

Aunt Cathy and her husband, an alcoholic and a "deadbeat dad," had divorced soon after they'd adopted Kim, and so Cathy had raised her daughter almost entirely on her own. Because she couldn't rely on Kim's adoptive father for money, she'd started her own business washing other people's dogs. That had seemed to Amina like a poor, almost Deshi sort of enterprise—something you invented with your own hands because you didn't have any other capital. But George said that Cathy didn't wash the dogs herself: she had three trucks and six Cuban employees who traveled around Rochester from house to house.

Amina had been extremely eager to meet Kim, not only to thank her for prompting George to look online for a mate, but simply because George's cousin sounded so interesting. She'd been disappointed to learn that Kim was away when she arrived and wouldn't be back until just before the wedding. Aunt Cathy and George had both apologized profusely for Kim's absence, though in different ways.

"You don't know where she's going to be on any given day," Aunt Cathy had said, during one of the dinners at Eileen's beautifully appointed table. Since there were only four of them, they ate in the breakfast nook, which was wallpapered in a pattern of red and blue sprigs that also matched Eileen's china cups and dishes. George's mother was a good cook and always remembered to make something separate for Amina, if there was pork in any of the dishes.

"Are you allergic?" Aunt Cathy had asked the first time this had happened, and George had explained that Muslims, like Jews, didn't eat pork.

"Oh, I can see how it would be dirty over there. You wouldn't want to eat any meat, would you? But our pork is very clean. As clean as chicken—next time, you'll tell Eileen she doesn't have to bother."

George's mother said then that it was no trouble to take a piece of chicken out of the freezer for Amina, but Amina's dietary restrictions had already gotten Cathy started on the subject of her own daughter.

"You can hardly cook a meal for her anymore," Cathy complained.

"No meat at all, no fish. She doesn't even eat eggs. And the last time I saw her, no onions. Can you believe that? *Onions?*"

"Why doesn't Kim eat onions?" Amina asked.

"Something to do with yoga," George said.

"When I think about what she was like as a little girl—that white-blond hair, big green eyes, the longest lashes you've ever seen. And so well behaved! People used to stop us on the street, ask if I wanted her to be in commercials. I'll tell you—that's hardly what you'd get if you tried to adopt today. Little Chinese girls everywhere, and now people are even taking them from Africa."

"When did you see Kim last?" Eileen asked.

"I can hardly remember! These places she goes—you don't even know what country she's in, one day to the next." Cathy turned to Amina. "That's the definition of torture for a mother. I hope you never experience it."

"Kim's at a yoga-training course in Costa Rica," George told Amina. "She's getting some kind of advanced certification." She had noticed a particular way George had of translating for her when they were with his mother and his aunt. Even if the thing that had been said had been said clearly in English she could understand—and she had quickly gotten to the point that she thought she could understand nearly everything—George might reprise it for her and then add some extra information he thought might interest her. After a certain number of Sunday dinners at his mother's house, Amina realized that having her there precluded George from joining in the conversation the way he might have had to in the past. He was always too busy making sure she understood.

"Kim'll make more money," he told her now. "And the certification will allow her to teach all over the world—not only in Rochester."

"That's exactly what I mean," Aunt Cathy had said. "Torture."

5   Amina had thought she would finally meet Kim at her bridal shower, which George's cousin Jessica had thrown for her at Great Northern Pizza Kitchen. But it turned out that Kim wasn't able to attend any of the wedding events, since she and her mother weren't speaking to each other.

Amina had been sorry not to have a woman her age to advise her, but Eileen and Jessica had both been very kind. Jessica was George's only cousin on his father's side, just as Kim was his only maternal cousin; she was two years older than George, with a similar build but darker coloring. She and Eileen had taken Amina to the beauty parlor on the morning of the shower, to have a "trial run" before the wedding, and they had stayed with her the whole time in case she had trouble telling the stylist what she wanted. When Amina had pointed out her bitten nails, George's mother had promised the manicure would fix it; when she'd asked about eye makeup, his cousin had said her lashes were so long that she didn't need it. Through all of this, the girl working on Amina's hair had simply smiled and nodded, as if she didn't care about getting extra work but simply wanted Amina to be happy with how she looked.

Amina tried to explain how this manner of working differed from what she would have encountered at home—where extra goods and services would have been pressed on the family of the bride from the moment they walked in the door of the shop—but Eileen and Jessica hadn't really heard what she was saying, because they'd been so surprised to hear that there were beauty shops in Bangladesh at all.

"Oh yes," Amina said. "They are very popular."

"But not near your village," said Jessica, with so much certainty that Amina hesitated a moment before correcting her. She explained that there were three beauty shops in the bazaar in Satkhira alone and hundreds more in the capital.

"But what about the women who cover their hair?" Eileen had asked, and Amina said she guessed that even those women enjoyed looking nice underneath the chador.

She had told George that she didn't need a wedding dress, that she was happy to get married in the clothes she already owned. She had ordered three new dresses before she came to Rochester, because tailoring was so much less expensive back at home.

"That's why I love you!" George slapped his hand on the kitchen table, as if he'd won some kind of wager. "You're so much more *sensible* than other women." Amina thought it was settled, but later that night George talked to Ed from his office, who reminded him that they would eventually have to show their wedding photographs to Immigration and Customs Enforcement.

"Ed says a white dress is better for the green card," George said. "My cousin Jess'll take you. Go get something you like."

The wedding dress Jessica chose for her was sleeveless white organdy, with white satin flowers appliquéd on the neck and the bust. George's cousin was protective of Amina, telling the saleswoman firmly that they were not interested in a strapless dress and that they were looking for something economical. Jessica agreed that she might eliminate the veil—Amina had never covered her hair and didn't intend to start on her wedding day in America. But even without it the dress had cost more than five hundred dollars, not including alterations. Amina stood on a wooden box with a clamp like a giant paper clip at her waist and tried not to cry.

"Smile!" the saleswoman said. "A lot of girls would kill for a figure like yours."

"No kidding," Jessica said. "I wasn't that skinny when I was four-teen years old."

"Don't you like it?"

"She's dumbstruck. Wait until George sees you in *that*."

Jessica chatted happily with the saleswoman as they paid for the dress with George's card, but once they were in the car she asked Amina whether everything was okay.

"Everything is fine," Amina said. "Only it was so expensive."

"George doesn't mind," Jessica said. "Trust me, I could tell. Are you sure there's nothing else?"

Ordinarily when she felt homesickness coming on, she was able to distract herself with some kind of housework. Vacuuming, in particular, was helpful. Now, sitting in the car next to George's cousin, she was unprepared for the sudden stiffness in her chest, and the screen that dropped over everything, making Rochester's clean air, tidy green lawns, and even the inside of Jessica's very large, brand-new car look dull and shabby. George's cousin was so friendly, and there was still no way she could explain to her what was really wrong. When they stopped at a red light, Jessica turned to Amina and put a hand on her arm.

"Because if something were wrong between you and George, I want you to know that you could tell me. I'm a good listener."

"Oh no," Amina said, "George is no problem," and Jessica had laughed, although Amina wasn't trying to be funny. She could tell that Jessica wasn't going to allow her to be silent, and so she searched for a question.

"What is the meaning of 'dumbstruck'?" she asked, feeling slightly dishonest. She had encountered that word for the first time in a conversational primer from the British Council, in a dialogue between a Miss Mulligan and Mr. Fredericks. *Your manners leave me dumbstruck, Mr. Fredericks," Miss Mulligan exclaimed,* and for some reason that sentence had lodged itself in Amina's head. Often, when someone had spit on the street in front of her, when a woman had elbowed her out of the way at the market, or when she'd run into one of her old classmates at Rifles Square, and the girl had inquired sweetly as to whether her father had finally found a job, she would think of Miss Mulligan and how dumbstruck she might have been had she ever found herself in Bangladesh.

"Oh, um—surprised. It just means surprised. I bet you wondered what I was talking about!"

But it didn't only mean surprised. It meant so surprised that you could not speak.

"I was just saying anything to keep that saleswoman quiet. She was skinny, but old-lady skinny, if you know what I mean. Saggy. I don't want to look like that, but I would like to lose fifteen pounds." As Jessica continued to talk about the foods she ate, didn't eat, and intended to eat, Amina concentrated on nodding and making noises to show that she understood. It was possible to be struck dumb by all sorts of emotions, not only surprise, and as they drove back toward Pittsford, Amina thought that there ought to be a whole set of words to encompass all those different varieties of silence.

6 Her mother wanted her to get married in a sari, although Amina argued that that kind of wedding, with the gold jewelry, the red-tinseled orna, and the hennaed hands, was really more Hindu

than Deshi, and as long as she was going to wear foreign clothes, they might as well be American ones.

"No need for a red sari," her mother conceded. "How about blue? Or green?"

"It has to be white," Amina said. "It has to be a real American wedding."

"Even a white sari," her mother said. "Some of the girls are doing it. I saw it in the 'Trenz' column." Since she left, her mother had been spending hours every day at the Easynet Cyber Café in Mohammadpur. It was amazing to Amina that her mother could navigate even English sites like the *Daily Star*, where she knew how to get to the Life Style page, with its features on "hot new restaurants" and "splashy summer sandals," its recipes for French toast and beef bourguignonne, and its decorating tips ("How about painting one wall of your living room a vibrant spring color?").

"A dress," Amina said firmly. "That's what ICE wants."

Of course her mother didn't really care about the dress, just as she would never consider visiting a restaurant (where who knew how dirty the kitchen might be) or painting one wall of her "living room" (the room where she brushed her teeth, chopped vegetables, and ironed her clothing) a vibrant spring color. The white dress was a way for her mother to talk about a worry she had had ever since the beginning—a worry that had been amplified by her cousin Nasir's visit—that Amina and George were not going to be properly married.

It was strange that her mother should be the one to have reservations now. Both of her parents had hoped that she might someday go abroad, but it was her mother who had worked tirelessly with Amina at every step of the long journey that had finally led her to Rochester. Her mother had always hoped to make her a famous singer, and when they had discovered that Amina hadn't inherited her mother's beautiful voice, they had tried ballet, the Bengali wooden flute, and even "Ventriloquism: History and Techniques," illustrated in a manual they checked out from the British Council.

Their first really serious idea was that Amina might study for the O levels on her own. They had gone to the British Council once a week, following her cousin's syllabi from Maple Leaf. In the mornings, when she would have been in school, Amina and her mother would sit at the table with *Functional English* or *New English First* and always the *Cambridge English Dictionary*. When there was a word in a book Amina didn't know, her mother would underline it very faintly in pencil so that it would be easier to review later, and if there were unfamiliar words in the definition, her mother would mark those as well. After she'd passed her O levels (much to the surprise of her Devil Aunt, who'd said there was no way Amina could succeed without formal preparation), she'd checked out one of those books again, and she and her mother had laughed at the number of words they'd underlined.

When she'd passed, they had been determined to apply to American universities. Amina had written letters of inquiry to ten colleges, six of which had responded. The University of Pittsburgh had encouraged her to apply for financial assistance, but even if the tuition had been entirely free, there would have been the cost of living in America to consider. Her parents had read the letter from Pittsburgh over and over again, as if some new information were likely to appear (Amina could bear to read it only once), and shown it to all of the Dhaka relatives, speculating about a potential "American scholarship." The whole family had then of course begun to gossip about the grandiose dreams Amina's parents entertained for her—their only child, and a girl.

A few weeks after the letter had come, Amina had been listening to the Voice of America. She and her mother had been following the broadcasts in Special English for years, and even after those became too simple for Amina, they had continued to turn on "This Is America" every day at 10:00 a.m. One morning after the broadcast, there was a program about different types of student and work visas, and the SAT, GMAT, and TOEFL tests foreign students might use to qualify for them. Amina had been half listening (these were strategies she had already considered, and all of them cost money) when the announcer said something that made her look up from her book. Her mother was ironing her father's best shirt and trousers, arranged on the ceramic tile as if there were already a man inside them.

"Of course, the easiest way to come to America is to find an American and get married!"

It wasn't as if she hadn't thought of it; ever since she was a little girl, she had loved everything foreign. When other girls had traded their dresses for shalwar kameez, Amina was still wearing hers: she had to put on the uniform white-and-gray shalwar kameez in order to go to Maple Leaf, but when she got home from school she would change back into a dress or a skirt. She didn't mind covering up: when she and her mother went out to the market, she would wear trousers under the dress and a sweater instead of a shawl and even tie a scarf over her hair. Her mother said she looked crazy, especially in hot weather, but her father had laughed and called her his little memsahib. Whenever he had money, he would buy her a Fanta and a Cadbury chocolate bar.

Most of all, she had always loved fair skin. Her father was brown, and before she was born he had worried that his child would be dark as well. But her mother was *ujjal shamla*, and luckily Amina had come out golden, too. Once, when she was about eight or nine, she had said how much she loved fair skin in front of her father's friend Rasul, who was as black as the fisherman who worked on the boats near her grandmother's house. Rasul Uncle had only laughed, but his wife had told Amina seriously that she had once felt the same way, and look whom she had ended up marrying. If you wanted one thing too much, she had said, God sometimes found a way to show you your mistake.

Amina had never forgotten that advice. It was a species of Deshi wisdom that she knew from the village, where her Parveen Aunty—the eldest and most traditional of her mother's sisters—often told her just this sort of truth about human fate. Parveen's husband had left her soon after Micki was born, running off with a distant cousin who was little more than a servant in their house. Two years before, Parveen had taken in the girl, whose potential was evident in her intelligent, tawny eyes and beautiful figure. She had fed her, imparted various lessons in household management, and even taught her to read, so that the girl might one day make a better marriage than she had any right to expect. The day after she had eloped with Parveen's husband, her impoverished mother had come to beg forgiveness, asking to be beaten herself for her daughter's error. Amina hadn't been there to witness this scene, but everyone had repeated what her aunt had said:

The more laughter, the more weeping.

And then:

Someone who is closer than a mother is called a witch.

Parveen's type of village wisdom was powerful, as long as you stayed in the village. But the farther away you got, Amina believed, the less it held. It was possible to change your own destiny, but you had to be vigilant and you could never look back. That was why, when she heard the announcer's joke on the VOA, the first thing Amina had thought of was the Internet.

7 The thing that had impressed her about AsianEuro.com was the volume of both men and women looking for mates. When Amina joined, there were six hundred and forty-two men with profiles posted on the site, and even without including a photograph, Amina's profile got several responses right away. As it turned out, the problem was not with making contact but with staying in touch. Sometimes (as with Mike G. and Victor S.) a man would correspond for months before he suddenly stopped writing with no explanation. Other times she would be the one to stop, because of something in the e-mail—in the case of Mike R., a request for a photo of Amina in a bathing suit, or "John H.," the admission, in a message sent at 3:43 a.m., that he was actually a Bengali Muslim living in Calcutta.

Her father had used these examples as ballast for his argument—the people who used those sites could not be trusted—but her mother had weathered each disappointment along with Amina, and her resolve on her daughter's behalf had seemed to grow stronger as the years passed and her husband's situation failed to change. They had never been like an ordinary mother and daughter, partly because Amina was an only child, and partly because they'd spent so much time together after she had to leave school. When she and George had begun writing to each other, she had translated his e-mails for her mother, and they had analyzed them with the same care they had once devoted to those textbooks. She hadn't hidden anything from her mother (even the Heinekens), and eventually they had both become convinced of George's goodness. They had been a team, discussing every new development, and so it was strange, once things were finally settled, to realize that her mother would not be coming with her.

She had been e-mailing with George for eleven months when he came to Desh to meet her and her family. Their courtship had more in common with her grandparents'—which had been arranged through a professional matchmaker in their village—than it did with her parents', who'd had a love marriage and run away to Khulna when her mother was twenty-two years old. Her grandparents hadn't seen each other until their wedding day, but they had examined each other's photos. She had thought of her grandmother the day that she had finally received George's photo as an e-mail attachment. She knew the photo hadn't been what she was expecting, but as soon as she saw it, she couldn't remember the face she *had* imagined. That face had been erased by the real George, who was not bad looking, with a strong brow, nose, and chin. He had admitted in an e-mail that he was trying to lose some weight, but that extra bulk wasn't evident in his face, which was flawed rather by a certain compression of features, leaving large, uncolonized expanses of cheek and chin. His hair was a faded straw color, and his skin was so light that even Amina had to admit that it was possible to be too fair.

She had put her hand over half the photo, so that only the eyes and forehead were visible. Could I love just those eyes, she asked herself, apart from anything else, and after a certain number of minutes spent getting used to the milky-blue color, she decided that she could. She covered the eyes and asked the same question of the nose (more challenging because of the particular way it protruded, different from any Bengali nose). She hadn't written back right away, but the following day at the British Council (an agony, to wait until the computer was free) she'd been pleased to discover that the photograph was better than she remembered. By the end of the day, she thought she could love even the nose.

Her father went to meet George at the airport, and her mother had come to her room to tell her he had arrived—although of course she had been watching from the balcony. The taxi could come only as far as the beginning of the lane, since their lane had never been paved. Her mother had worried about George walking down the dirt road to their apartment complex (what if it rained?), and they had even discussed hiring a rickshaw. But it would've had to be two rickshaws, with George's bags, and hiring two rickshaws to take two grown men fewer than two hundred meters would've made more of a spectacle than it was worth. Even from her hiding place on the balcony, behind her mother's hanging laundry, she could hear the landlady's sons Hamid and Hassan on the roof, practically falling over the edge to get a glimpse of Amina's suitor.

"What is he like?" she had asked, and her mother had reassured her: "He's just like his picture. Nothing is wrong."

George had stayed for ten days, and on the ninth day they had become engaged. Then he had returned to his work in Rochester, and Amina had begun the tedious quest for the fiancée visa. That had been November, and although they'd e-mailed almost every day, she hadn't seen George again until he had picked her up at Dulles International Airport in March of the following year.

8 Her visa had required her to get married within ninety days of her arrival in the United States. George had wanted to allow her to get settled, and his mother had needed time to organize the wedding party, and so they had waited more than two months. Her mother understood that it wasn't practical for George to pay for another place for Amina to live during that time, and she certainly didn't want Amina living alone in a foreign city. She'd agreed that Amina might stay in George's house until they were married, but she'd made Amina promise that she and George would wait to do *that* until after they'd had the ceremony at whichever Rochester mosque seemed most suitable. She had talked about the one thing Amina could lose that she would never be able to get back.

In Dhaka, Amina had meant to keep her promise, although she hadn't entirely agreed with her mother. Especially after she got to America and had time to think about it, it seemed to her that there were a lot of other things that could be lost in an equally permanent way. Her parents had lost their land in the village, selling it piece by piece as her father invested in a series of unproductive business ventures. (Now the same land was worth more than three hundred times what her father had sold it for.) After that they had lost their furniture and then their apartments in Mirpur, Mohammedpur, and Tejgaon, and only Ghaniyah's father's intervention—securing another apartment in Mohammadpur at a special price, through a business associate—had kept them from becoming homeless altogether. This way of living had taken its toll on her mother, who was skinny and prone to ulcers; Amina thought her mother was still beautiful, with her wide-apart eyes, and her thin, straight nose, but her mother claimed that she had lost her looks for good. Worst of all, her grandmother had lost Emdad and Khokon, and nothing she could do would ever bring them back.

Compared with those losses, whatever it was that Amina had lost on the third night she spent in George's house was nothing. George had agreed to her mother's conditions and had even purchased a single bed, which had been waiting for her in one of the bedrooms across the hall; on the first night, they'd brushed their teeth together like a married couple, and then George had kissed her forehead before disappearing into his own room. There were no curtains on the window of the room where Amina slept, and the tree outside made an unfamiliar, angled shadow on the floor. Everything was perfectly quiet. At home there had always been noise from the street—horns, crying babies, and the barking of dogs—not to mention the considerable sound of her father snoring. Even when they'd had more than one room at home, she'd always shared a bed: first with her grandmother and her aunt, and then with her parents. When she turned twelve, her father had suggested that she move to a cot, but Amina and her mother found that neither one of them could sleep without the other, and so her father had finally moved onto the cot himself.

On the first night George had sheepishly presented her with an enormous stuffed panda, almost as big as she was—a gift from his mother, who'd thought she might be homesick and in need of comfort. It would have looked absurd and childish to sleep with a thing like that, and so Amina had thanked George and set the panda on a wooden rocking chair in the corner of the room. She fell asleep right away and then started awake in the dark. She looked toward the window, trying to ascertain what time it was, and saw that someone was watching her.

Her scream was loud enough to wake George.

"Amina?"

Of course it was only the stuffed bear. She got up and opened the door to the hall. "I'm sorry," she said, but it took her a moment to locate the word: "A nightmare." She saw the strip of light under his door and hoped they might soon get up and begin the day.

"Okay," he'd said, from behind the door. "Good night." He'd turned off the light, and then she'd tiptoed down to hall to check the time. It was only eleven o'clock: seven more hours until she could plausibly dress and go downstairs.

At home she had worn a long T-shirt and pajama bottoms to bed, but on the third night she'd experimented by going into the bathroom in only a kameez. You look cute, George had said, and that had emboldened her; when he bent down to kiss her forehead, as usual, she looked up, so that they wound up kissing for real on the mouth. (This was something that had happened downstairs on the couch during the day, but never before at night.) When she pressed her body against her fiancé's, a strange sound escaped from George. It was as if there were a tiny person inside him who'd never spoken until now. That small, new voice—and the fact that she had been the cause of it—was what made her take George's hand and follow him into his own bedroom, which had belonged to the two of them ever since.

She was disappointed to learn how unpleasant it was, how unlike that kiss in the bathroom, which had given her the same feeling between her legs that she sometimes got watching actors kiss on television. It didn't hurt as much as her cousin Micki had said it would, but it was hot with George on top of her, and she didn't like the way he looked when he closed his eyes—as if he were in pain somewhere very far away. On the other hand, it was sweet the way he worried afterward, confirming anxiously that it was what she wanted. He asked her whether she minded breaking her promise to her mother, and the next morning, waking up for the first time next to someone who was not a member of her family, she had been surprised to find that she had no regrets at all.

9 Amina had been eager, as soon as they got settled, to invite Ed and Min to dinner. The four of them had so much in common, and you could even say that Ed was responsible for their marriage, since George had heard about AsianEuro from him. She'd suggested

it after the bridal shower, where she'd regretted not being able to talk to Min for more than a moment, but George had said that Ed and Min were very religious and socialized almost exclusively through their church. Amina decided that this was a kind way of saying that Ed and Min didn't want to be friendly with a Muslim; she suspected that if George's bride had been from some Christian country, she and George would've been invited immediately. Of course she might have simply dismissed them; she'd never been interested in becoming friends with extremists, of her own or any other faith. It was only that here she had so few opportunities for making friends.

It was about six weeks after she'd arrived, one warm May Saturday, when she ran into Min on a trip to Bed Bath & Beyond. She and George had split up to shop, and she'd spotted Min in the kitchen section, examining a set of bright-colored cookware. Amina hesitated for only a moment before approaching her.

"Hello—Min? I am Amina, George Stillman's fiancée?"

"Oh, hello," said Min. Her voice was reassuringly warm and enviably free of an accent. "I love this store, don't you?"

Amina agreed, although she found the size of Bed Bath & Beyond overwhelming and was having trouble finding the things on her list.

"They really do have everything. What are you here for?"

"A mat for the shower."

"I know where that is," Min said. "Let me show you."

This friendliness emboldened Amina, and as she followed the other woman through the store, she was determined to extend an invitation. One thing she had found about George was that he wasn't a social creature. It was possible that the idea of a dinner party simply didn't appeal to him, no matter how well he liked the potential guests.

"I am embarrassed not to have telephoned you before," Amina said. "Of course I—George and I—we would like to invite you to eat at our house. We owe you so much."

Min laughed, the high, clattery sound of tin plates under a tap. She was smaller than Amina, and she wore her long hair in a bun: Amina could see that there was a great deal of it, straight and lustrous black—hair like her mother's once was, let loose only at night.

"What could you owe us?"

"Because of the website," Amina said. "AsianEuro.com."

"Pardon?" Min said, sounding for the first time like a nonnative speaker.

"George wouldn't have known about it without Ed."

Min didn't stop walking, but her expression became suddenly wary and defensive. She looked as if she'd received some insult.

"I don't know what that is," Min said. "But if Ed knew about it, it was before my time."

"AsianEuro," Amina repeated, suspecting a misunderstanding. "The website where you met—and then we met. George first heard about it from Ed."

Min stopped in front of a pyramid of blue-and-white humidifiers that stretched almost to the double-height ceiling. "Ed and I didn't use a website. I barely knew how to use e-mail when I met him."

"But then how did you meet?"

"In church." Min spoke so naturally that Amina was forced almost immediately to give up the hope that she might be lying. "Ed came to Cebu with his church group on a Friendship Mission, and I was part of the welcome delegation. We fell in love at first sight."

"In the Philippines?"

Min nodded. "We wrote letters—I mean, paper letters—back and forth for a year, and then I came to Rochester to get married. We were already sister congregations, so even though my family wasn't here, it felt like getting married in my own church."

"That's wonderful," Amina said. Min was looking at her strangely, and so she told the other woman that she'd been confused and that it must've been another of George's friends who'd met his wife through AsianEuro. Then she assured Min that she could find the mat on her own and took a roundabout route to the travel cosmetics section, near the exit, which she and George had fixed as a place to meet.

She had debated, but she'd never mentioned meeting Min to George. If he had lied, it must've been out of embarrassment; maybe he thought it sounded better to have heard about the website from a friend rather than admit he was browsing dating sites on the computer. Amina had been conscious when she signed up that she was one of the only South Asian women on the site and that perhaps the men who were looking there were more interested in women who looked like Min—women from the Philippines, Vietnam, Thailand,

Malaysia, or even China. What made you choose Bangladesh, she had asked, since the only picture on her original profile was of her country's red-and-green flag, and George had said that he'd been curious about her because she was different.

10 Although she kept it to herself, the meeting had renewed Amina's anxiety about the Muslim ceremony, without which they wouldn't really be married. She wished now that she hadn't promised her mother they would have that wedding first. Her mother had been afraid that once they were legally married, George might change his mind about becoming a Muslim. George had promised to become a Muslim in the same way that he was a Christian: he believed in God, he told Amina, but he didn't think God cared very much whether people prayed or went to church. Amina repeated the first part of that formulation to her mother and then promised her that George wouldn't change his mind. In the eighteen months she'd known him, George had never changed his mind about anything.

The problem was that all of the mosques in Rochester seemed to be closed. They had tried the Rochester Masjid of Al-Islam, which had hours posted on its website but was nevertheless tightly shuttered when they arrived. When she looked up the Sabiqun Islamic Center, she got several articles about vandalism; according to the articles, someone had written "racial slurs" across the face of the mosque for the third time. (This was something she didn't mention to George, since it was sure to get him started on the subject of thugs.) In desperation one Saturday they'd driven out past the airport to visit the Turkish Society of Rochester.

George had wanted to spend Saturday morning at Home Depot, and the afternoon reinstalling the knobs on the kitchen cabinets, which had a habit of coming off in your hand. Amina had promised that they were going to have time to do that errand when they got home, but by the time they reached the Turkish Society, after several wrong turns, it was already two o'clock. They left the car on the street, in front of a pizzeria with the metal grate pulled over its face. Far down the block there were some teenage boys sitting on a porch smoking, but apart from them the street was deserted.

"I don't like the look of those kids," George said.

"I can go. You stay with the car." Amina was glad to go on her own. She was afraid that an imam might object to performing the marriage so hastily or impose some sort of time-consuming preparations, and if she had to argue, she would prefer to do it without George there. She believed that she could persuade a Turkish imam to do the ceremony, if she could only meet him face-to-face.

But George wouldn't let her go alone. When they reached the mosque, once again the gate was locked.

"Goddamn it," George said, and kicked the gate; the chain and padlock rattled loudly, and across the street two black women in fancy dresses and hats turned to look at her husband.

"It says open from noon to three," Amina said, pointing to the sign. She called out in English, "Anybody there?" and then more softly, "*Assalamu alaikum,*" but the courtyard remained empty. There were two small plastic bins affixed to the gate, with the printed instruction TAKE ONE; the first bin was empty, but the second still held several xeroxed yellow fliers. George took one automatically, and Amina was startled to see a printed banner advertising the same Islamic Center of Rochester that Nasir had found for her, almost two years ago now.

"I know that place."

George was reading the flyer. "It's right on Westfall Road—why didn't we go there first?"

Amina didn't want to explain about Nasir or her reluctance to take his suggestion. He had come back for his book one afternoon, only a few minutes after her father left on a long errand to a photo shop in Kaptan Bazar, on the other side of town, where a friend had promised he could get his old camera repaired cheaply. Amina had told him it was a waste of money, but her father said that he wanted to be able to take pictures at the airport.

Nasir came at such a perfect time that it was hard to believe he hadn't been watching the house. Until that moment, Amina had forgotten about the book under the table leg; she kept her eyes on her cousin's face, praying that he wouldn't look down.

"Please have something to eat," her mother said. "I'm just making Munni some Bombay toast." Nasir protested weakly, once, but her mother was already in the kitchen.

"My mother says you've left England for good."

"I was successful there in earnings, but not in life. I've come home to be successful in both."

Why, Amina often wondered, did Bengali men feel the need to brag about everything, especially when they were talking to a woman? From the moment she'd met George, he'd told her that his job was nothing special and that it was too boring to talk about with her, even though he was an engineer with a master's degree.

"What sort of business will you have here?" Amina asked, and she was pleased when Nasir colored and said that he'd only just returned and was still settling in.

"Munni, get your cousin's book," her mother called from the kitchen, and for a moment Amina panicked. Had her mother forgotten? She could hardly look down, for fear that Nasir's gaze would follow her own and find *The Lawful and Prohibited in Islam* pinned under the foot of the table.

"On the shelf in the bedroom," her mother added casually, and then Amina did look down: somehow, in between the time her father had left and Nasir had arrived, the book had migrated from the floor to her parents' room.

"Have you read it?" Nasir asked.

"Only parts of it," Amina said. "My father read it. I don't think he liked it as much as he liked the books you used to bring him." She smiled, but Nasir remained serious. He didn't seem to care what her father thought.

"Which parts?"

She thought about fibbing, but she had a feeling that he would only direct her to the correct chapters, and perhaps even sit in the chair in front of her, eating her mother's Bombay toast while he waited to get her reaction.

"'Marriage to the Women of the People of the Book.' And 'The Prohibition of a Muslim Woman's Marrying a Non-Muslim Man.'"

"What did you think?"

"Very interesting," Amina said. The book had been interesting. According to the author, there were two reasons a Muslim woman couldn't marry a non-Muslim. The first was the obvious one: the fact that a child would likely be brought up in the religion of its father.

The second reason was one she hadn't anticipated, but couldn't help appreciating for the elegance of its logic. Since a Muslim respected all of the prophets—not only Mohammed, but Abraham, Moses, and Jesus as well—a Muslim man could respect the beliefs of his Christian wife. But since Christians believed in only one prophet, Jesus Christ, a Christian husband would have to disdain his wife's prophet as a false one. And since each man was the head of his own household, it would be intolerable for a Muslim woman to live in the household of a Christian man.

"But it didn't change your mind."

"Why should it change my mind? My fiancé, George, plans to convert."

Nasir looked surprised, but only for a moment. "He says that today."

"He has said it all along."

"I know Englishmen."

"George is an American."

Nasir shrugged off the difference. "And what about your children?"

"They will be Muslim, of course."

"But will they pray? Will they fast?"

Amina regretted the joking tone she'd used earlier. She was insulted by the familiarity that Nasir assumed, whether because he had known her as a child or because they'd once been thought of as a match. She was a woman now, engaged to be married to someone else. Her mother should not even leave them alone together in the same room.

"My father will be here soon. You should go."

She still remembered the nights he would visit her father. Afterward she would have to ask forgiveness, but when he was in the room all of her resolve disappeared, and the only prayers she'd been able to offer were that he would stay for dinner and, after dinner, that he would sit up with her father talking, so that she could lie on the bed in the dark listening to his voice. When Nasir had called her a clever girl, the English words she knew had fled to some inaccessible place; when he'd touched her hair, it was as if all of the water in her body (the body, they had learned in Mr. Haq's science class, was 61.8 percent water) had turned to soda.

"Good-bye, Amina," Nasir said, though he had always called her Munni. "God protect you."

"Allah hafez," Amina said. "Good luck with your new business." Just out of curiosity, she looked straight into her cousin's heavily lashed eyes, but that Nasir was gone and it was an angry stranger who looked back at her.

Ordinarily she took her mother's side, but on the subject of Nasir she agreed with her father. How dare he tell her where to worship in America, as if he were her father or her brother? He had never even *been* to America. Standing on the pavement in front of the Turkish Society of Rochester, Amina saw the possibility for a compromise.

"I misunderstood," she told George. "I thought the ICR was farther away."

George sighed. "The wedding is next weekend. When are we going to go to Brighton?"

This, Amina thought, was the difference between an American and a Bengali husband. George might shake his head and look put-upon, but if she told him she had to be married by an imam, he wouldn't try to change her mind. She knew that if she asked him, he would take a day off of work next week just to go to the Islamic Center.

"Who knows if they could even do it next week."

George looked at her hopefully.

"Also, what are its qualifications? How do we know it is reputable?"

George nodded. He did not point out that Amina hadn't had any such reservations about the Masjid of Al-Islam, the Sabiqun Islamic Center, or the even Turkish Society of Rochester.

"It doesn't matter when we do it," Amina said, testing the idea by saying it out loud. "As long as we do it at some time."

"I want to do it," George said eagerly. "We'll do it in a couple of weeks, as soon as the wedding's over."

"The other wedding."

"That's what I meant," George said.

11 At the bridal shower, Jessica had wanted to know her favorite flower and had listened politely as Amina explained about the *krishnachura* and the romantic origins of its name. She'd felt silly when

Jessica had shown up at town hall on the morning of the wedding, carrying a bouquet of lilacs and apologizing because there were no *krishnachura* to be had in Rochester. Amina had assured her that lilacs were her favorite American flower. Then George's mother had arrived with her own wedding veil, which she shyly offered to Amina for the ceremony.

"She didn't want a veil," George said, annoyed with his mother, but Amina took her mother-in-law's side, just as a bride would have done at home. Jessica gathered up a few of the ringlets the stylist had created and pinned the veil so that Amina could wear it hanging down her back. Then the small party—Jessica; her husband, Harold; George's mother, Eileen; Aunt Cathy; Ed (without Min, who had excused herself on grounds of an unseasonable flu); and George's college friends from Buffalo, Bill and Katie—followed them into the office where they completed the paperwork for the marriage certificate. Amina misunderstood and thought that this was the wedding itself, so she was confused when the clerk ushered them into a small, carpeted antechamber with a bench and a framed poster of sunflowers and asked them to wait.

"Is there some problem?" she asked George, but George's cell phone was ringing. He frowned and went back into the office to take the call.

"Is something wrong?"

"Sit down," said Eileen, but Aunt Cathy grabbed her arm and wrenched her upright.

"Careful!"

"What is it?" Amina said, trying to keep the panic from her voice. For weeks she'd been convinced that something would get in the way of the ceremony; this morning she had prayed—not that nothing would go wrong, but that she would be prepared enough to see it coming and resourceful enough to find a way around it.

"If you sit, your dress will be ruined," Aunt Cathy said.

Amina was about to ask where George was when her husband-to-be came back into the room.

"What?" Amina said again, but Ed was telling everyone that George couldn't even forget TCE for as long as it took to get married.

"It wasn't TCE," George said.

"Was that my daughter?" Cathy said. "You shouldn't have even answered it. Thinking she can make up for it with one phone call. Her own cousin's wedding."

George turned to Amina, lowering his voice. "Kim wanted to apologize for not being here. She thinks she made a mistake—and she's dying to meet you."

But Aunt Cathy was listening. "It's a fifteen-minute drive—if she were 'dying,' she probably could've made it. It's not like she has any other responsibilities."

"She wants to have us over next week," George said.

"Come on," said Eileen, putting her hand on Amina's back. "It's your turn," and Amina was relieved to see that a door had opened on the opposite side of the room, and a short, bald man in a suit, a man who looked as if nothing on earth had ever disturbed his composure, was gesturing for them to enter. She understood that the wedding was continuing as planned, and she looked carefully around the room because she knew her mother would need to hear exactly what it looked like. There were two potted trees with braided trunks and three rows of white plastic folding chairs, half filled by George's family and friends. The deputy city clerk stood behind a wooden lectern underneath two certificates framed in gold. With the light from the window on his glasses, Amina couldn't see his eyes.

She hadn't expected to be nervous, and at first she wasn't. George had told her what her cue would be, and Amina allowed her mind to wander while she waited for it. When she'd left Desh, there was still the possibility that her parents would be able to come to Rochester for the wedding. Ninety days had seemed like enough time to plan, but when George went online to reserve airline tickets, they were almost fifteen hundred dollars each, even if her parents made stops in Dubai and Hamburg, Germany. George was willing to help pay for the tickets, but she could tell he wasn't happy about it, and so Amina had called her parents on a phone card and given them her opinion: it was a waste of money. She and George were getting married at the county clerk's office, and afterward there would be a dinner at Giorgio's Trattoria in Brighton. The whole thing would take maybe four hours (including driving time), and Amina and her father agreed that to fly twenty hours in order to do something that took four hours didn't make a lot of sense.

"What about the Muslim wedding?" her father had said. "When will that take place?"

"It will take place at the Islamic Center of Rochester," Amina said. "It will also be very short."

"Nasir's place?" She could hear the scorn in her father's voice, but the main thing was to please her mother. Neither ceremony was important to her father, who cared much more that Amina be legally married. Only once she was married could she get the green card, and only once she had the green card could she apply for her citizenship. As a citizen, her father knew, she could sponsor her parents, and in his mind the sponsorship was the only thing keeping him and her mother from making the journey to America.

"The ICR is a good place," she reassured him, and then, searching for additional details to impart, added: "Even the other mosques in Rochester encourage you to go there."

In the end, as she'd expected, the problem was not her father but her mother. Her mother had agreed at first, and they'd even made another plan: as soon as Amina and George could come back to Dhaka, they would go to a studio and take wedding photographs. They would buy wedding clothes, and Amina would go to the beauty salon; they would have more money to spend on the clothes and the photographs, since her father wouldn't be paying for a wedding. Once they had the photographs, her mother could look at them all the time; it would be no different than if they'd all celebrated a wedding together for real.

She had thought her mother was satisfied, and then a few nights later, Amina got a call after they had gone to bed. There weren't many minutes left on her father's phone (it was morning in Dhaka, and the Flexiload place in Kaderabad Bazar wasn't open yet), and so Amina had to use another card to call them back. Her mother was crying, and it was hard to understand her. Her father told her not to worry, but when she asked why her mother was crying, he said:

"She's crying because she's going to miss your wedding. She's going to miss it because I can't afford the ticket."

"No!" Amina said. "We decided—it didn't make sense. Twenty

hours for four hours. Three thousand dollars for one party!" She could hear hammering in the background: a new building was going up across the street. Her parents complained that the new apartments would be much better than theirs, but Amina was disposed to look on the bright side. The neighborhood was improving.

"Tell her it will be only a small party," she told her father.

"Your wedding party. What kind of terrible parents don't come to their own daughter's wedding?"

She started to argue, but her father wasn't listening. Her mother was saying something in the background.

"What does she say?"

Her father paused so long that she would have thought the call had been dropped, except that she could still hear the sound of hammering on the other end. It was morning in Mohammadpur: the sun behind the haze, the kids walking to school in twos and threes, the crows on the telephone wires, and the call of the vendors—Chilis! Eggs! Excellent Quality Feather Brooms!—or her favorite, the man who took your plastic jugs and gave sweet potatoes in exchange. Once again she had the disorienting feeling that her past was still happening, unfolding in a parallel stream right alongside her present. Only on the telephone did the streams ever cross. At the other end of the line, another Amina was hiding her head under the covers, stealing just a few more minutes before the cacophony outside forced her to put two feet on the cold, tiled floor.

"Tell me, Abba."

Her father's voice when it came was stoppered, strange, as if he'd swallowed something whole. "She says it would've been better if you'd never been born."

George shifted sleepily in the bed. "Tell them you'll call them back tomorrow."

Amina gripped the head of the bedpost. From their room she could see the house behind them, windows blazing in the dark.

"Tell her the food is going to be terrible," she whispered to her father. "Tell her there is a popular dish called 'pigs in blankets.'"

But George was awake. "Are you talking about food *now*?"

"It doesn't matter about the food," her father said. "The point is that you are her only child."

"Do you, Amina Mazid, take this man, George Stillman, to be your lawfully wedded husband?"

"I do."

The corresponding question was asked of George, and then the city clerk declared: "I now pronounce you husband and wife."

George leaned toward her, and Amina leaped back. From the chairs behind them, Cathy made a hiccupping sound. George's face tightened in a familiar way, like the mouth of a drawstring bag, and when Amina glanced behind her, she saw an identical contraction on the face of her new mother-in-law. She hurriedly stepped toward George, smiling to let him know that it was only that she was surprised, not that she didn't want to kiss him in front of his family and friends.

Many hours later, after cocktails at Aunt Cathy's, the reception dinner at Giorgio's, and then cake, coffee, and the opening of gifts at George's mother's house (Eileen had insisted that Amina call her Mom from now on), when they were home in bed together so much later than usual, George had asked why she hadn't wanted to kiss him.

"You didn't tell me," she explained.

"You didn't know there was kissing at a wedding?"

Amina had to think about that for a minute, because of course she had known. She had known since she was nine years old and her Devil Aunt had bought a television. She had seen it on *Dallas*, and *L.A. Law*, and *The Fall Guy*, and so there was no way to explain her ignorance to George.

"I did know. I guess I just didn't believe it would happen to me."

"You've kissed me a hundred times," George said, in a voice that suggested to Amina they might be about to have their first fight. She wanted to avoid that, especially tonight, because if there was anything she believed about marriage, it was that arguing the way her parents did was a waste of time.

"Not only kissing. The marriage in total."

"You didn't believe we were getting married? What did you think we were doing?"

It had started to rain, and that comforting sound lent the contents of the room a sudden, momentary familiarity, almost as if she'd seen them once long ago.

"In Desh, you can make your plans, but they usually do not succeed. But in America you make your plans and then they happen."

To her relief, George finally smiled. "So you planned to kiss me, but you were surprised when it actually happened."

"Yes," Amina said. "I was dumbstruck."

12 Kim had invited them in June, but soon after the wedding she suddenly went abroad again, this time to teach at a yoga retreat in France. It wasn't until September that they finally made a date to meet her for a cup of tea, in her apartment on Edgerton Street downtown. George had said that the houses in this area were cheaply built, and that the style of Kim's building—pale stucco ornamented with dark wooden beams—was a reference to a type of architecture popular in England hundreds of years ago. He said it looked pretentious on these modern Rochester apartments. But Amina liked the street where they'd parked their car. They walked past a women's clothing boutique where everything in the window was black and white, a bookshop, and a café with tables outside, where college students read and talked in intimate groups. The air smelled of burning leaves, a scent somehow sharper and more distilled than it was in their yard in Pittsford.

Kim lived on the fourth floor, and they were both breathing heavily by the time they got to the door. George had said that his cousin was twenty-seven, two years older than Amina, and so he could remember when his aunt Cathy and her husband, Todd, had adopted her. He had been seven when they brought her home—a nine-month-old baby girl—a year before Todd had gone off to Florida with another woman, abandoning his wife and child. George had said that Kim looked nothing like her mother, that she was tall and thin and dressed in an eccentric way, but when Amina pressed him for more details, he had become impatient and said that she was going to meet his cousin and could form an opinion herself.

George rang the bell, but Kim must've heard them coming up the stairs, because she opened the door almost immediately. She was certainly tall, almost as tall as George, but unlike most of the women Amina had met so far in Rochester, she was very thin, with a flat chest and narrow hips. George and his adopted cousin had similarly sandy blond hair, and light-colored eyes (though hers were more green than blue)—but no one would have mistaken them for biological relatives. Kim was unmistakably pretty, with regular features, a smooth, high forehead, and a perfect, bow-shaped mouth. Her hair was wavy and hung nearly to her waist, and her skin was fair, with undertones of pink and gold. Most extraordinary, she was wearing a long Indian shirt, a kind of kurta with a red and purple pattern, over a pair of black leggings. Her feet were bare, and her toenails were painted a brilliant royal blue.

"I can't believe you're finally here," she said. Then she stepped forward and wrapped her arms around Amina—not the kind of hug George's mother often gave her, which involved the arms and a glancing touch of the cheeks, but a true embrace, laying her head for a moment on Amina's shoulder, as if for comfort, before she stepped away.

"I have all different kinds of tea—jasmine, green, tulsi. I know you prefer coffee," she said to George, "but I don't have any."

Amina thought she'd misheard. "You have tea made from tulsi leaves?" Her mother was a particular believer in the beneficial properties of the tulsi leaf for ailments ranging from eye strain to stomach cramps and rashes and took it regularly, in both tea and tincture form.

"That's what I'm having—let me make you some." Kim disappeared into a galley kitchen, almost as small as the one in Mohammadpur, and George led Amina through an archway into the apartment's single room. The room was dominated by a futon bed made up to look like a couch and a fireplace, which Kim had filled with houseplants. Amina recognized spider plants, aspidistra, and aloe, but there was one very beautiful species that she didn't know, with a single, red waxy bloom. The apartment seemed bigger than it was because of three large windows, which Kim had outlined with strings of tiny white Christmas lights; beneath the windows was a long, low wooden table, with potted plants and a collection of jewelry and figurines, artfully arranged as if in a case at a museum. Among the miniatures Amina recognized the Buddha and several Hindu deities, their fierce expressions and odd many-armed postures crafted from silver, bronze, and jade. On the wall above the bed Kim had thumbtacked a Tibetan painting on silk, with an inscription below in that forbidding alphabet, the letters like tiny knives. Because there were no proper chairs (and George would have been uncomfortable on one of the colored cushions scattered over the rug), the two of them sat on the bed.

Amina knew of course that George's cousin had lived in India, but somehow she hadn't imagined that so much of that place would've made its way into Kim's daily life. Her own idea of India encompassed the Taj Mahal, the great saint's tomb at Ajmer (where her father had always dreamed of making a pilgrimage), and her youngest aunt, Sufia—who had won a vocal scholarship to a music school in Calcutta, married a Hindu, and was now the mother of twins. The rest of the country was simply colored shapes on a map, and she had only the vaguest notion of yoga as a Hindu religious ritual.

"You've been here before?" she asked her husband.

"I helped her move in," George said matter-of-factly. "When she got back from India."

"When was that?"

George thought for a moment. "She was back in the U.S. in 2001, but she didn't come home to Rochester until '03—about a year before I met you."

"Is she a Hindu?"

"Who knows." George was looking glumly at the rug, which was dotted with tufts of red and orange wool that was coming off on their socks. She could've guessed that this apartment wouldn't be to his taste. Her husband was casual, even sloppy, about the state of the house, but he had a bias against the curios and mementos that had decorated his childhood home: he had taught her the word "knick-knack," a pejorative. He believed that if you hung something on your wall, it should be there for a reason, and so their walls were sparsely decorated: his own diplomas, a map of the world oriented to Asia (which he'd bought when she arrived), a photograph from his parents' wedding, and one from their own. He preferred that everything be framed, in spite of the expense.

The exception to George's general rule about souvenirs was the refrigerator, which was covered with magnets from each state he had visited. Although he'd had the opportunity for international travel only once before coming to meet her in Bangladesh, he had visited forty-five of the fifty states, and he hoped one day to see Alaska, Hawaii, Alabama, North Dakota, and Nebraska, too. His first trip out of the country had been to Mexico, where he had gone with other college students to build houses for poor people.

When Kim returned with the tea, Amina couldn't help herself. "Excuse me, but do you practice some religion?" She had been afraid of offending George's cousin, but Kim smiled as if this were a question she was eager to answer.

"I don't, but I've always felt the lack of it. My mom is pretty Christian—you've probably noticed already—and she still gets on me about going to church. Somehow it never made sense to me."

"These are souvenirs then?" She was pleased she'd remembered the word and hadn't had to resort to "knickknacks."

Kim nodded. "That's exactly right."

"And what is that plant, please?" She pointed to the pot with the red flower, but Kim shook her head.

"I just went to the nursery and picked out whatever I thought was pretty. I don't know anything about plants."

"Amina's been doing a lot of gardening," George said. "Our grocery store isn't up to her standards."

Amina knew he was teasing her, but she flushed anyway. "The grocery store is the most wonderful I have ever seen, only the large-sized vegetables are not as tasty as homegrown."

"Oh, I agree," Kim said. "I wish I had a garden—I'd love to see yours."

"I will be happy to show you. Only it's not very beautiful right now." Amina sipped her tea, which was both familiar and not—the bitterness of the herb masked by licorice and honey. She wished Kim had returned from France last month, when her dinner-plate dahlias were in bloom. George had said they were so beautiful that they didn't look real. "But please come," she said hurriedly. "Right now I have no job, so I'm free all the time."

"Amina's going to look for work as soon as her green card comes," George said.

Kim looked very serious. "What do you want to do?"

"Any job," Amina said. "I am not particular."

"She was first in her class in Bangladesh," George said. "She worked as a tutor for the college entrance exams."

Kim looked impressed—the first person in Rochester who had, when George insisted on mentioning it. "I have a friend who teaches in the Monroe County system," she said. "I can ask her if you want."

"She has to get her degree first," George said. "She passed her O levels—that's the British system—just studying on her own." George suddenly sounded as if he were back at the green card interview, reciting her credentials to the ICE officer. "But then she didn't have the opportunity to go to college."

"I dropped out," Kim said. "I don't know if George told you—pretty much the stupidest thing I've ever done. Everyone warned me, George included, but I didn't listen."

"You convinced yourself you couldn't do it," George said.

"He used to help me with math when I was a kid," she said. "But then he went off to Buffalo for college, and I think I just kind of gave up."

"You didn't need help with the writing," George said. "I remember Aunt Cathy bragging about it—you always got As in English."

"I liked to read," Kim said. "But I was terrible in math."

"I'm the opposite," Amina said.

Kim nodded. "Well, but I'm sure you'll keep going with school. I get distracted—I've always been that way. I wanted to go to India, which turned out to be the best thing I ever did. Have you ever noticed that—the way the best and the worst things in your life can be all twisted up, so you couldn't have done one without the other?"

It wasn't that she didn't understand Kim's idea, but that she knew this kind of abstract talking made George uncomfortable. He didn't mind discussing his feelings, or even her own, but he liked them to be presented in a rational way that emphasized cause and effect. She might say, "I feel down today because I miss my parents," and that was fine, but he didn't want to hear, for example, about her mother's peculiar moods, which had started even before she left home and had no one discernible trigger. As she often did with her mother, she tried to bring Kim back around to the concrete.

"When did you go to India?"

"In '99," Kim said. "Just backpacking around with a girlfriend. We'd been cocktail waitressing together in Manhattan for a while—she'd heard you could live there on five dollars a day. We budgeted ten and figured we could stay six months at least. She went home after three, but I decided to go down to the yoga place in Mysore—we'd met this couple in Varanasi who told us about it. I got completely hooked, obviously. When my course was done I didn't want to come back to New York, and someone said foreigners could get work as film extras in Bombay. And so I went up there." Kim cradled her teacup in her hands and looked at the rug. "And that's where I met Ashok."

Amina was fascinated. She thought about the dinners with Eileen and Aunt Cathy: in spite of their friendliness, and the satisfaction she herself took in executing such a normal American responsibility, there were always moments of strained silence in which she could tell everyone was trying hard to think of something to say. In all of those dinners, she wondered that no one had ever brought up Kim's history in India, or the man named Ashok she now mentioned as if Amina already knew who he was.

Because George was obviously not going to do it, Amina asked, "Who is Ashok?"

Kim looked up at George, almost as if he had betrayed her.

"Why would I go around talking about you? I don't do that."

Kim turned to Amina. "Your husband is very moral. But this is important. And I want you to know, because I hope we're going to be really good friends."

"Kim," George said, a kind of warning.

Kim closed her eyes and took a deep breath—her inhalation and exhalation took so long that there seemed to be something indecent about watching it—and then opened her eyes and fixed them on Amina. "I met Ashok at the Mehboob Studio in Bombay. People had told me you could get a job easily, and they were right. The minute I showed up, they cast me in something that would start filming the next day. There were about twenty of us—long-term backpackers, mostly, and also a couple of yogis—and we were supposed to be lying around this hotel pool in our bathing suits, drinking cocktails. Of course the cocktails were colored water, and they were disappointed that more of us didn't have two-piece bathing suits, but we were all there for long stays, trying to be really respectful of local culture—we were proud we'd left our bikinis at home. Anyway, we were supposed to be lying there when the hero came running through, chasing the bad guy, and then they were going to fall in the pool. Two of the girls had to be swimming in the pool and look all scared and surprised—but they didn't pick me for that, thank God." Kim looked down at her chest and smiled. "They picked the busty ones, and I'm like, a double-A."

Amina looked at George, who had taken out his Palm Pilot and was scrolling through his messages. For once she didn't mind his inattention—she was embarrassed herself by the mention of bikinis and bra sizes. Still, she was eager to hear the details of Kim's story, which she was already imagining relating to her mother tonight in the remaining forty-seven minutes on her Hello Asia phone card.

"I remember I was disappointed when I saw the hero. He was kind of short, and he had this weird facial hair—I thought all those Bollywood stars were supposed to be really cute."

Amina had to keep reminding herself that Kim was two years older than she was. A certain openness in her expression, compounded by an especially earnest way of speaking, made Amina feel like an older married woman listening to the adventures of a girl.

"And then I saw these two guys standing over in the corner. One of them was sort of thin and awkward, with a mustache, talking to the other one like he was trying to impress him, and the other one—of course the other one was Ashok." Kim gave Amina a small, sad smile. "He was much better looking than the star—the most handsome man I'd ever seen. I'd sort of made friends with the girls lying on the chairs next to me, and they were making fun of me because I couldn't stop staring at him. I'm not usually like that"—Kim looked at George, as if daring him to contradict her—"in spite of what my mother might tell you. But I felt like I had to find out who he was. There was a servant, a kid, really, who ran over and brought them sodas—we were all hungry and thirsty, but all we got was that colored water—and when he came back over to our side, the other girls waved him over and asked him. It turned out Ashok was the director's son."

Amina had finished her tea but didn't know where to put her cup.

George had set his carefully on the floor, undrunk, on top of a book with a red cover: *Into the Heart of Truth*. While Kim was talking it had gotten dark outside, in the uncannily sudden way of Rochester evenings.

"We should get going," George said. "We're going to hit the traffic."

"On Saturday?"

"There's always traffic down here." George glanced at Kim. "I don't know how you stand it."

"I mostly walk or bike," Kim said, getting up easily from her cross-legged position. "Everything I need is right here, even my studio." She looked at Amina shyly, as if she were a celebrity Kim had been longing to meet. "I was thinking—tell me if this is too boring for you—but we're looking for a new receptionist at Yoga Shanti. It's probably not much more than minimum wage, but there would be perks—free classes and stuff. My guru is amazing, and I know he would love you."

"Thank you," Amina said. She imagined telling her mother that she was working in a yoga studio: it would be like saying she'd come to America and apprenticed herself to a Hindu priest. Although there was something very appealing about a job in this neighborhood, with someone she already knew, she was grateful to George for his habitual caution about jumping into things.

"Let's wait and see once she has her green card. Convenience is going to be most important, since I'll have to drive her."

"I really wish you lived down here," Kim said quietly, while George was using the bathroom. "Then we could meet all the time."

Amina was touched by Kim's overtures. After her failure with Min, the only women she'd met were Annie Snyder and Jessica. Annie was busy with her children, and according to George, Jessica had a very stressful administrative job at Strong Memorial Hospital. "Neither one of them is going to have a lot of time," he'd told her. "Don't take it personally." She hadn't taken it personally, but she had been disappointed, and she'd resigned herself to the fact that she would have no hope of meeting anyone before she got a job. She was almost glad for that disappointment now, since it made Kim's enthusiasm even more thrilling: the most interesting person she had met in Rochester was also the one who wanted to be her friend.

When they got in the car, George was quiet, but he didn't seem sorry to be leaving. They had been planning to go to a restaurant for dinner, but once they got back on Monroe Avenue, George asked whether she would mind just picking up a pizza on their way home. Amina said she wouldn't mind.

"Kim is wonderful," she said. "Thank you for taking me to meet her." Sometimes George said nothing, and in order to continue the conversation, she had to play both parts, at least until something she said elicited a response. She thought that was better than having a husband who couldn't keep his mouth shut, the kind of boasting, posturing husband she might have found in Desh.

"And she's very beautiful."

"Do you think so?"

"Of course—don't you?"

"She's my cousin." George sounded slightly offended. "I don't know what it's like over there, but we don't think of cousins that way."

"We don't think of cousins that way either," she said quickly. "At least modern city people don't." Amina thought of Nasir. "But Kim isn't your real cousin—you said she was adopted."

"That's where all her problems come from."

"Does she have many problems?"

George gave an expressive snort. "She means well, but she's too forward. You've heard this expression, 'dirty laundry'? She'll tell you all her business the first time she meets you." He turned up the heat, and a blast of hot air shot out around Amina's legs. She put her hands up to the vents greedily, and for once George didn't say anything about "allowing the mechanism to do its job." The car heater was one of the small Rochester pleasures that she couldn't have imagined before she left Bangladesh; she loved the feeling of being sealed into the cocoon of the Honda, looking out at the lights of the city, which were sharp and distinct in the cold, so different from the hot, hazy nights at home. She found that George was most relaxed when he was driving, and there was no better time to ask delicate questions than when he was keeping his eyes on the road.

"How come you didn't tell me about Ashok?"

"Is it important?"

"It's interesting," Amina said. "That is why I'm surprised you didn't tell me."

"I've known Kim since she was a kid. All that drama doesn't seem so interesting to me anymore."

"Oh but it is," Amina said. "Did he become her boyfriend, do you know?"

"I think they were married," George said.

"Married!"

"Briefly. But in some kind of ceremony over there, so I don't know if it was really legal once they got back here."

Amina was startled. "They came here together?"

"They came back so that he could do a business degree—at NYU—that's New York University, in Manhattan."

"I know that."

"They were living together there—Kim had a bunch of temp jobs. Please don't ever mention this in front of Cathy, though."

"Her mother didn't know?"

"Oh, she knew. But she was furious, and so they weren't talking. And then after he went back to India, Kim didn't want to admit it to her mom. She stayed in Manhattan for a little while—she was a mess—and then she finally decided to move back here. But even after she got to Rochester, she didn't get in touch with her mother. It took her four months to call Cathy."

"But she talked to you."

George nodded and adjusted the vents now that the car had warmed up: he didn't like the heat as much as she did. "It was awkward—I was caught in the middle." He sounded aggrieved and slightly resentful, as if it were Amina who had put him in that situation.

"But why didn't she go back with him? I mean, if they were married?"

"Who knows? Why do women do anything they do? Except for you," George amended, as he always did. "You're logical."

"Thank you. I had to be practical because of our circumstances in Desh," Amina said. "That is how I learned it." She waited another moment, but when George didn't say anything, she ventured another question.

"Is it very common, not talking with your parents?"

"Common enough."

"I can't imagine not talking to my parents."

"Mm," said George, who was probably calculating the expense of a lifetime of phone cards.

"Sometimes I'm afraid about raising children in America." She looked at George, whose face was defined by the dashboard lights. She thought he looked suddenly and surprisingly handsome, as well as more uncertain than she'd ever seen him.

"You're right to worry. The schools are terrible, and the values they're getting at home are probably even worse." George's voice became more confident. "All the TV and video games, hardly a book in the house. Did you know that forty-four percent of American children watch television right before bed?"

"I was thinking of myself more. Maybe that our child would wish he had two American parents. Perhaps he would be angry at me, the way Kim is angry at Aunt Cathy."

But George didn't seem to be listening. "There should be a test for people before they become parents."

"Do you think we would pass the test?"

George looked at her quickly, and then away. "Of course. You want children, right?"

Amina felt her face getting hot in the dark, as if she and George hadn't already spent seven months sleeping in the same bed. "Yes."

"We should wait until you're settled. Until we know about your classes, what the requirements are."

She thought of her mother, without whom she'd couldn't imagine having a baby. It would be three years before Amina could get her citizenship, in 2008; only then could her parents apply for the immigrant visas they would need to become permanent residents in the United States.

"I would like to work for some time first, to save money," she said.

"Don't worry about the money," George said. But he didn't push her. "We have a few years, anyway. I want you to feel ready."

A moment later he reached over and patted her knee, before returning his hand to the wheel.

13 The green card came the last Monday of September. In the evenings George drove Amina around to different stores and restaurants, and in each place she filled out an application. Then she began to wait. The housework took perhaps an hour and a half of her time, if she stretched it out, and then there were eight more hours until George got home from work. She watched more television than she liked to admit, especially movies, which George thought were good for "cultural acclimatization." Amina liked romantic comedies, and after she had seen one or two a day for three weeks—her favorites were *Sleepless in Seattle, Mystic Pizza,* and *Pretty Woman*—she began to consider what it was she found so appealing about them. It wasn't the expensive trappings of these onscreen courtships, she decided, but the foreign idea of a decisive moment—some gesture meaningful only to the couple involved—so that even if they were in a crowd of people the proposal was personal and unique.

Of course it was always different in real life. Only a few days into his visit to Bangladesh, she and George had begun to talk about things that it would be necessary to do "if" Amina were to come to America; after several of those conversations, the "if" had become "when," and then two days before he was supposed to leave, George had produced a gray felt pouch from the money belt he wore around his chest. The ring was a family heirloom, and that was why he didn't want her to wear it until they got home to Rochester.

George had unsnapped the pouch and shook its contents into his palm. The ring was a large, round diamond, flanked by two bright, triangular baguettes. The band was platinum, which was part of what made it look so foreign: she'd never pictured a wedding ring as anything but gold.

"Do you like it?"

"It's beautiful." She could tell that the diamond was large and expensive, and so she was surprised by the plainness of the design. She knew her mother and her aunts would be impressed by its value rather than its beauty, although her cousin Ghaniyah might find it attractively "international." Amina touched the stone with one finger, discovering that she was both eager to wear it and relieved that she wouldn't have to wear it here at home.

Her parents had gone to visit an elderly relation of her mother's in Lalmatia, leaving Amina and George alone together for the first time.

"Try it on," he encouraged her, and so she'd put the ring on her finger. It was certainly striking, but it was much too big for her, and its effect was to make her finger look small and dry, like a child who'd been playing in the dust.

"We'll have to have it adjusted." George hesitated a moment. "You don't want me to get down on one knee or anything?"

"We don't really do that here," Amina said.

George nodded, relieved. Then he leaned over and kissed her on the mouth, so quickly that she hardly had time to register that it had happened. Her new fiancé's face flushed in a surprisingly dramatic way.

"I won't say 'I love you' now."

Amina nodded. She'd never heard anyone say "I love you" to a romantic partner, except on television. Certainly her parents never did. Occasionally a girl at Maple Leaf had said "I love him" of a pop singer or movie actor while her friends rolled their eyes and shook their heads.

"I think people say it too much these days, until it doesn't mean anything. I think it should just come out naturally, when you really feel it."

"That makes sense," Amina said, because some response seemed to be required.

George smiled. "I'm glad we agree about this stuff," he said, and then he leaned forward to kiss her more deeply, putting one hand on her waist and the other on the back of her neck. The kiss lasted a long time, and George's tongue was very much involved in it, and because the thought of her parents coming home and seeing this happening was so unimaginable, she felt as if a small part of her were already somewhere else.

When she got to Rochester, he had shown her the safe he'd installed on the floor of the closet, where he kept the title to their house as well as the appraisal papers for the ring. She was shocked when she saw that the ring was worth nearly ten thousand dollars and suggested to George that they keep it in the safe along with the papers.

George had laughed. "That's actually a good idea," he said, "except my mother and everyone will want to see you wearing it." He smiled. "Me, too."

She checked her e-mail constantly, but for the first two weeks she heard nothing from the stores where she had applied. She knew she would have to take anything that was conveniently located, since George would have to drop her off on the way to work. But when she thought about telling her parents about a job, Amina said a silent, extra prayer: *Please,* she asked God in the empty hours of the morning as she dusted the picture frames and pulled every blade of grass from the flower beds around the house, *please let this job be something respectable and clean—selling housewares, for example, or gardening supplies—rather than anything to do with animals or serving food.*

Here was something she had noticed about God. He often granted one prayer when you were making another or gave you something you'd asked for in the past, long after you had stopped wanting it. When she opened her e-mail on Friday morning, she found four new messages: three that were probably junk, and one from Nuddin786 @yahoo.com. She clicked on the message almost without thinking and was startled to see her nickname. These days, it was only in phone calls with her parents that anyone used it.

Dear Munni,

Assalamu alaikum! I bet you are surprised to hear from me. Well, after our last meeting I was afraid you are angry. So I have waited some time to mail you. But yesterday I went to visit your parents and they welcomed me very nicely. We sat for two hours talking about you and your success in America. I am glad to hear of it! And I pray for your green card and work permit to arrive soon.

Here the days are cloudy, but no rain. I am working now, at Golden Horn Internet, Inc. Our boss is a Turkish man, very good. There is also a small mosque in the basement of our building. Three of our office mates pray there with me, but five others are not regular. Your parents tell me it is difficult for you to observe the correct prayer timings, so am sending you this link (www.qibla.org) where you can find the timings for Rochester. Please look at it straightaway!

Do you read the Daily Star? Myself, I still follow BBC Online. (You know I do not love England, but I have some love for BBC.) You will laugh to hear that I even enjoy the music from their television broadcasts! That was my favorite time of day over there—me and my flatmates eating together in front of the television, watching BBC for news and the cricket. Every time I hear the music, I am thinking, "Well, I have survived another day." Munni, I wonder if you ever have these thoughts?

Just this week on BBC I am reading that the U.S. Senate voted for rights of prisoners in Guantanamo and Iraq. But U.S. president Bush still opposes that! They say the U.S. people are starting to know of the crimes their government is committing, and the president is growing unpopular. I wonder, how could they not know of them when they have seen reports and pictures? I am curious to hear what you think.

Your mother and father have told me that you were married in a mosque. Tell me, was it the same ICR I wrote for you on a paper, the last night I visited in Mohammadpur? Walking down the lane to your parents' home, I was thinking of past-Munni and present-Munni, trying to make a bridge between the two. It is difficult!

Please write soon. Allah Hafez,
Nasir

She read the message three times, and then she went into the kitchen to clean the dishes. She didn't like the dirty dishes to sit in the dishwasher, especially since it took the two of them so long to fill it up, and ordinarily she just washed them by hand. Today she found herself wedging the plates between the plastic prongs, sometimes knocking one carelessly against its neighbor. Had Nasir omitted the final part of his mail, she could have simply dismissed him. What country on earth didn't have terrible secrets? Certainly their own was no exception. It was the people you had to judge when you were talking about a country, and someone like Nasir—who had gone to England, but only lived in an apartment with other Deshis, working at a Deshi business and eating curry at home with his Deshi flatmates—would never understand the place where he had lived. It was no wonder he'd run back home at the first opportunity.

She would tell him she didn't read any paper (except sometimes the headlines on MSN) and that she couldn't stand depressing news.

If he mentioned any of that business again, she would put his e-mail address on her blocked list, and that would be the end of their correspondence. But she wondered if she would have the strength to discard any message from home, when the time between George's departure for work and his return was so long. It was not a question of "surviving," because she was perfectly happy—or at least she would be once she found a job. As it was, she couldn't escape the fact that she needed something to fill up all of those hours.

Her teenage feelings for Nasir were deep in the past; still, she was shocked to read such a perfect expression of the way she thought about herself. She struggled to find some connection between the girl she so often imagined at home in her parents' apartment and this American wife, using the dishwasher and the washing machine, checking her e-mail on the living room computer. The task was made more difficult by the fact that there was no one in Rochester who'd known that past-Munni, and no one back at home who knew the present one. Sometimes she wondered whether the two girls would simply grow farther and farther apart, until one day they didn't even recognize each other.

14 For a week there were "no new messages from your contacts," and then they all came at once: some information from MCC, responding to her e-mail about their teaching certification program; a message from her cousin Ghaniyah, who announced that she was engaged to be married; and, most important, an e-mail from the Human Resources Department of MediaWorks, giving her a number to call at their Henrietta location. Amina called right away and spoke to a man named Carl, who confirmed the amazing news. She, Amina Mazid Stillman, had an American job: she was a sales associate at MediaWorks in the South Town Plaza.

She knew George was glad that she wanted to work: he told everybody how he couldn't manage to keep her at home. He also said that he hoped their schedule wouldn't change after she started her job. George was the manager of his team at work, and he liked to arrive a little early. He liked to get organized, check his e-mail, and drink his coffee before anyone else arrived. He explained to Amina that managing people was about gaining their trust, and that his team members respected him for being punctual. Once you gained your team's respect, managing them was easy; but if you ever lost it, you could never get it back.

George was happiest if he could leave the house by six thirty, which meant that their alarm went off at five thirty. He got up and took a shower: he was a morning person, unlike Amina, and he never hit the snooze button.

"What's the snooze button?" she had asked when she'd first arrived, and George couldn't believe that she'd never had an alarm before. She'd had her mother, who woke up with the *azaan*. Amina could sleep through even the most insistent call to prayer, and her mother always came into her room after her own prayers were finished. Then Amina would wash and pray while her mother made her an omelet. It was only after she had the thin, slightly sugared "mumlet," fried in ghee—which she couldn't reproduce in Rochester even with the same ingredients—that she was really awake.

She loved the idea of the snooze button, temptingly larger than all the others, but she could never use it. Now she got up and fixed George's Chex and banana (he did not like eggs so early in the morning) and poured his Tropicana orange juice. George had his breakfast in his bathrobe, and then he changed into his khakis and shirt: short-sleeved now that the weather was finally warm again. She was disappointed to find that he didn't need to wear a tie; she'd been under the impression that every American man wore a tie to work, unless his job was in a restaurant or a shop.

She felt lucky to have gotten a job that had nothing to do with food. She'd called her parents as soon as she heard:

"A bookstore," she told her father. "Books and CDs and all types of media."

"She's in charge of selling books," she heard her father say, and then her mother grabbed the phone and wanted to know her salary.

"Seven dollars and fifteen cents per hour," she said, and even her parents knew that wasn't much, but they converted it—521 taka per hour—almost twice what she'd been making as an English tutor at home. Amina knew that as soon as her mother hung up the phone, she would call her sister, Amina's Devil Aunt, to tell her about the bookstore. The conversations were shorter when Amina called home because phone cards were so much more expensive in Rochester.

"Good luck," George said as he dropped her off in front of the shopping mall on the first day. She was wearing the black trousers she'd had tailored at home, along with a gray cardigan sweater Jessica had given her (because it made Jessica's hips look "a mile wide"). Amina knew she was pretty: she'd never liked her nose, but since arriving in America she'd begun to appreciate her eyes, large and heavily lashed, and the fullness of her lips. When her curls were kept under control, people here admired them. Her skin was clear, and she'd never felt the need for makeup. Even her Devil Aunt had often praised Amina's figure, slightly disparaging her own daughter Ghaniyah, who had smaller breasts and a thicker waist. This morning she had looked in the mirror and found herself somber and unfeminine, but at breakfast her husband had smiled and said that she looked great—that she was turning into a real Rochesterian.

George had given her his watch so that she could be sure of the time, but even with the strap as short as they could make it, the watch was as loose as a bangle. It was good to arrive five minutes early, but twenty minutes made you seem desperate. Amina knew the way her English could sabotage her when she was intimidated, and so she walked slowly past the shops—Linens 'n Things, OfficeMax, Bare Necessities—as if she were interested in their contents, practicing an introduction in her head. *Hi* (not "hello") *I'm* (not "I am") *Amina. I'm a new sales associate. I'm starting today. Is Carl in, please?*

She was standing in front of Old Navy when she realized it was 7:54. Where was MediaWorks? She'd been so focused on using up the time that she'd forgotten to locate her destination. She looked up into the cavern of stores, but there were so many of them. Why had she assumed she would just come upon it?

She approached one of the janitors outside a restaurant. "MediaWorks?"

The janitor looked at her blankly and shook his head. "No English." He pointed to the sign next to the escalator, and Amina went to stand in front of it, but with little hope. She was good with maps, but these color-coded, floating rectangles were foreign to her, tiny black numbers running like spiders around their edges. She could find Old Navy, number 12, but what was 12 doing next to number 3? Where was Jo-Ann Fabrics, which was just on the other side of the escalators, but represented by no rectangle she could see?

It was like a nightmare. She had a physical sensation of panic; if she'd had to describe it, she would've said it was in her stomach—although it was more like a lightness in her sexual organ, a feeling that sometimes came upon her at surprising moments (unfortunately not when she was doing that with George). She could hear her mother's voice, *Inshallah*, but it wasn't God's presence she felt. It was her mother's, hovering beside her just as she had every day Amina visited the British Council, traveling all the way there and back with her by rickshaw so that Amina wouldn't have to go alone.

Amma, she thought, where are you?

A girl stepped onto the escalator. She was about Amina's age, skinny, with very white skin and straight black hair. She was wearing heavy black eye makeup and drinking from an enormous fast-food cup of soda. Black rubber bracelets snaked around one arm, and as the girl rose in Amina's direction, she could make out an elaborate bit of Chinese writing peeking out of the collar of the girl's red polo shirt. She did not look friendly, but it was 7:58 (by George's watch), and Amina had already resolved to ask for help. The girl saw her looking and frowned; she was stepping off the escalator before Amina recognized the miracle. She had doubted, and God had sent this girl—across whose right breast, in bright yellow letters, was spelled the name MEDIAWORKS.

"Excuse me! MediaWorks?"

"Doesn't open till nine." She was wearing a name tag that said, LISA, GREECE. Amina had never met a Greek person before, but the badge gave her confidence. Lisa was an immigrant, but she was white; therefore the job was a good one. She hoped that a similar badge had already been prepared for her: AMINA, BANGLADESH.

"Hello," Amina said. "I am new sales associate. Carl—"

"Oh, Carl," the girl said. Her voice was pleasant and ordinary, and immediately Amina hoped that she might make a friend. She imagined George's surprise, to see her hopping out of the car in the morning, waving to a girl with a Chinese letter tattooed on her neck.

"I'm Lisa. You can come with me."

"Thank you so much!" Lisa looked at her strangely, and Amina struggled to calm herself. She was not going to be late after all. "Have you been working at MediaWorks very long?"

"My whole freakin' life. It feels that way, anyway. Don't worry—it's all inventory at the beginning, but after a while they put you on the floor. I'm not sure which is worse, though—the customers are so stupid. It's like, they want to exchange movies they've already *watched*."

They were approaching MediaWorks, which was right across the atrium, one floor above where she'd been standing. Amina couldn't believe she'd missed it. Her heartbeat was doing its trick again, traveling all over her body as if it were on vacation. *Slow down,* she instructed it. You only got one chance to begin your first American job, and Amina wanted to be proud of the way she had behaved.

"How many shifts did they give you?"

"Three," Amina said.

Lisa shook her head. "You'll get more. They're just testing you. Even Ethan gets more than that, and he's a disaster. Personally I think they hired you so they could fire him, as soon as they're sure you'll work out. Last week he asked me to cover the beginning of his shift so he could go out and buy Plan B for his girlfriend. I mean, seriously? That's totally TMI."

Amina smiled and nodded at Lisa, but her ignorance was clear.

"Hey, where are you from, anyway?"

"Dhaka, Bangladesh," Amina said, and when Lisa looked blank: "It's near India—and China. Excuse me, but what does that say?"

Lisa touched her neck. "This?"

A man's voice called out from inside the store. "Lisa—get in here!"

"It was supposed to be 'fire,' but the guy fucked it up and did the one next to it in the book. So now it's 'love,' and I can't afford a freakin' do-over."

"Lisa! Do you get paid to hang out with your friends?"

"The wonderful Carl," Lisa said. "Come on, I'll introduce you."

" 'Love' is nice," Amina said, as she followed Lisa into the store.

15 She and George had practiced taking the bus from the South Town Plaza, and in the afternoons, it stopped near enough to

Skytop Lane that she could walk home on her own. It was a cloudy but temperate autumn day, nearly fifteen degrees—no matter how long Amina lived here, she thought her brain would never recalibrate to Fahrenheit—and she lingered on the way home, taking pleasure in having completed her first day without any obvious errors and examining the unfamiliar plantings in other people's front yards. When she came through the back door, her father was shouting into the answering machine. He spoke English in his messages, with great effort:

How is day one! Your amma is fine! I am fine! How is George? Please you are calling us soon, using the card!

Amina dropped her bag and got to the phone just in time. "Abba, Abba—I'm here."

"She's there!" her father shouted, and then her mother grabbed the phone and started asking questions. Amina explained about Lisa and the Chinese tattoo and Carl, whom Lisa hated but who wasn't actually that bad. She explained about inventory, which she had done for seven hours, earning $50.05 (minus $13.95 for her MediaWorks polo shirt). She told her mother how Lisa loved Diet Pepsi, and how she'd bought two more large cups of it during the day, along with chow mein from the food court. Amina had brought leftover prawn curry in a Tupperware and so she'd had to explain about Tupperware, and promise to bring some for her mother the first time she went home to visit. Her mother repeated to her father the prices of the polo shirt and Lisa's lunch, and then her father took back his phone.

"Your amma doesn't want to tell you," he said, and Amina could hear her mother arguing in the background. "We went to the doctor, and she is fine." Her father switched to English: "Only it is hard for her to keep the weight on, no matter how much shondesh she eats." This was a joke, because her mother loved that particular sweet, especially the very soft, pure white Satkhira shondesh with its crunchy grains of sugar that they stopped to buy every time they visited her grandmother. "I try to make her eat bananas, but she only likes the village type. And now she has seen fitness exercises on television, and is practicing them every day."

"The clean air in Rochester will improve her appetite," Amina promised, without much conviction. It was a discouraging time to talk about their plan. Of course the plan was for the future, and her parents had always understood that it depended upon George. Before she'd left home, Amina had e-mailed George to ask about old people in America. A lot of the things she'd heard about America had turned out not to be true: teenagers did not have sex in public; the majority of black people were not criminals (George had several black colleagues at TCE); and although most American women had jobs, there were also some like Annie Snyder who stayed at home with their children. Amina had wondered if the perversely named old-age "homes" would turn out to be a similar sort of myth, but George had confirmed their existence. If an old person stayed in his own home, sometimes a person would be hired by the family members to care for him.

"A servant, you mean."

"We say nurse. Or 'caretaker.' But most people can't afford that. Most old people wind up in homes." George had agreed with her that it was very sad, the way that Americans shut up their parents and grandparents even when there was nothing wrong with them, and Amina had reported that attitude back to her parents.

Amina's mother had been excited when they read on the Internet about the cost of babysitting in America: think of the money Amina and George would save if she looked after her grandchildren for free. Her father could take care of the yard, and if her mother did the cooking and the shopping, Amina would have time to work more hours. It all made perfect sense in Desh, especially when George told Amina that there were three bedrooms in his house.

What she hadn't understood until George had explained it was that Americans didn't *like* to live with anybody besides their spouses and their children. George's own mother, Eileen, was sixty-six years old, perfectly healthy, and soon after the wedding had startled Amina by acquiring a boyfriend named Bob. If she eventually couldn't manage to live in her house in Brighton, George had promised to help her find an apartment somewhere in Pittsford. He and Amina would help her, he said, but Amina shouldn't worry that his mother would ever want to move in with them—even though they had those two extra bedrooms upstairs. "She's too independent for that," he had told her, as if this unnatural refusal made him proud. They had still never discussed her own parents directly, and she cherished the hope that George might feel differently about a pair of older people who had no interest in being "independent" but just wanted to be near their only child. She and George didn't disagree very often, but when they did it was always because of "cultural differences"—a phrase so useful in forestalling arguments that she felt sorry for those couples who couldn't employ it.

"Don't worry," her father said. "The cool weather is coming. I'm going to take her to the village and fatten her up. Shondesh and bananas, shondesh and bananas, morning, noon, and night."

"I miss you so much," she told her mother, when she got on the phone to say good-bye. "I missed you at my job today."

"English, English!" her mother insisted. "I am practicing."

And so Amina had to keep it simple. "Four bananas per day," she instructed her mother. "Four bananas and five plates of shondesh."

16 She showed George her badge as soon as he came in the door. "It says 'Pittsford'—as if they think I was born here." Carl knew where she was born—she'd had to give him a photocopy of her green card—but she thought someone else was probably in charge of making the badges. It was possible that this person couldn't spell "Bangladesh" or, like Lisa, had never even heard of it.

"It doesn't make a difference where you were born," George said. "It's where you live now that counts."

She was making a chicken pulao, even though there was leftover curry in the refrigerator. She wanted to show George that things wouldn't change now that she was working, and so she had decided to make something fresh. The curry would last for days in their enormous GE refrigerator, and you never had to worry about the current going out.

"Lisa is my colleague, and her badge says 'Greece.' But I think she's been living in Rochester for some time."

George laughed out loud—a rare thing. "Do you know where Greece is?"

Amina was offended, and she added too much paprika to the rice. "Of course. Underneath Italy, in the Aegean Sea." By the time Amina was seven, she could find every country on the tablecloth. (The cloth didn't have every country in the world, because it had been made from outdated maps; for example, Bangladesh was missing, still one wing of bright green Pakistan.) One day she'd come home from school to find that her father had covered all of the country names with thin, white tape; after that, she'd had to do it from memory.

"Nope," George said. "Let me show you." He went out to the garage to get the Rand McNally *StreetFinder*, and put it down in the least convenient place, right where she was slicing the vegetables. She was still irritated as he flipped through the pages, but it turned out he was right: in the top, left-hand corner of the map, bisected by highway 390, was a town called Greece.

"You'd probably meet some Bengali people if we lived there."

"There are Bengalis in Lisa's neighborhood?" She had seen a lot of Indians at Wegmans, and once on the sidewalk near Home Depot she had passed an old woman in a sari and sweater, speaking Bangla into a cell phone, but she'd never actually been introduced to anyone who wasn't white.

"There are more immigrants there than in Pittsford."

"How much does an apartment cost there?"

"Depends. You know that."

"An apartment for your mother, when she gets old."

"She'd want to be here, or in Brighton."

"But if she wanted to live in Greece."

George shook his head and tugged playfully at her braid. She plaited her hair at home now because he'd said he liked it, although she hadn't worn it that way for years. "Little Miss Curious. Maybe eight hundred dollars a month, if it was just one bedroom. My mother might want two."

As George revealed these facts, Amina stored them up, so that she wouldn't have to ask again. She knew that together they would pay 25 percent of their income in taxes each year, and that some of this money was deducted from her paychecks in advance. The rest was called her take-home pay. If she continued sending half of this to Bangladesh (my "send-home pay," she joked to George), it would take years to save enough so that her parents could rent their own apartment in Rochester. If she had to pay their rent, she would never be able to contribute anything toward the cost of college, nor would she be able to cut down her hours once they had a child without relying heavily on George for her parents' maintenance.

They had been eating in silence for several minutes when Amina remembered the other question she'd wanted to ask.

"It's an expression," George said. "You can figure it out—it just means a second plan you come up with in case the first one doesn't work out."

"Is there any other kind of Plan B? A kind you can buy at a store?"

George looked up from his plate. "Oh my God, Amina. Are you—?" Her husband didn't finish his sentence, and she didn't know how to do it for him. Something she'd said had drained what little color there was from his skin.

"You *are*?"

"I am—what?"

"Pregnant?" It came out as a whisper. "But why would you want to—"

"Want to?"

"Use Plan B!" George exclaimed. "I thought we said we wanted a child."

"We do," Amina said.

"But when did you miss your period?"

"I had it three weeks ago."

"So why do you think you're pregnant? Did you take a test?"

"I don't think I am."

George managed to look both relieved and exasperated at once. "Then why are you asking about Plan B?"

"Lisa mentioned about it. She says another colleague bought it for his girlfriend."

" 'Mentioned it,' " George said. "No 'about.' God, don't scare me like that."

"But what is it?"

"It's an abortion pill. You use it after you have sex, if you think you've had . . . an accident." He set down his fork and put one of his hands on top of Amina's. "I'm sorry, but you really threw me. I thought you were saying you wanted an abortion. I didn't think your religion even allowed that."

She always felt slightly offended when George referred to Islam as "her religion," failing to acknowledge that it would eventually belong to both of them. He hadn't gone back on his promise to convert, but he still often spoke of Islam with the same kind of timidity his mother and his aunt employed, as if her faith were a wild animal whose behavior couldn't be reliably predicted.

"In Islam you may use contraception for good reason," she said. "Financial hardship or the mother's health. Most people I knew at home used it. But abortion is very bad."

"I don't believe in it either," George said firmly. "It's all right for other people—I'm not a maniac like Cathy—but not in my family."

"Aunt Cathy does not believe in abortion?"

"No way—she's a crusader. She marches and everything." George adjusted his glasses the way he always did when he was getting ready to explain something. "The issue's been blown out of proportion in this country, because it's simple enough for everyone to understand. It's just a way to choose sides. I understand that people make mistakes, and I respect their choices. But that kind of thing won't happen to you and me."

She didn't tell George that she had been an accident—a happy one, her parents always said, but nevertheless an accident that had almost killed her mother. The birth, which had happened in the village in the traditional manner, without her father present, had been so difficult that they had feared for her mother's life. She had presented in the breech position, and after nearly two days of labor, the midwife had suggested that the baby be dismembered, sacrificed so that her mother might live. No one had said "live to bear sons," but at that point it was already clear that the baby was a girl. Her mother had been beyond speech, and if not for her brother Emdad, the midwife might have been allowed to make the decision. Emdad had suggested that they wait another hour, and ten minutes later Amina had been born, not only alive but screaming.

Her mother often said that she had been a miracle, and it wasn't fair to expect God to provide them another in their lifetime. They had made their plans themselves, exhausting A, B, C, and D before they had finally hit on one that worked. And now here she was in America, serving her husband a second helping of chicken pulao. In another three years her parents might be here, too, with a baby asleep in a solid American cradle upstairs. It was not impossible, she thought, as George complimented her on the meal. There were several paths to everything, and some of them were hidden when you started out. Her mother would say that God created those paths, but to Amina it seemed as if the paths were there; it was only that you needed God to help you find them.

17   Once she started working they got into a pattern, having sex twice a week: once over the weekend, and once during the week. It wasn't always on the same days, but the intervals were similar. If it happened on a Sunday, it would often happen again on Thursday; if it were Friday, the next time would be a Monday or Tuesday. Normally it began with George suggesting they go to bed earlier than usual. Once they were there, in their pajamas with their teeth brushed, he would turn to her and ask if she was tired. If she didn't want to, she could simply say that she was, and he would accept it without protest. Normally, though, she didn't refuse. It didn't hurt the way it once had, nor did it give her any kind of physical pleasure. Her satisfaction came instead from the knowledge that she'd mastered a previously intimidating facet of adult life.

They had done it on Sunday night, and so she was surprised when he turned to her on Monday, later than usual.

"Are you tired?"

"A little," she said, not looking at him. Did he really mean to do it again tonight? Mondays were always the hardest for her; she was shyest with Lisa and Carl, as if there was a part of her that started a new job all over again at the beginning of each week. She made a point of preparing food in advance on Sunday afternoons, so that she wouldn't have to cook when she got home the next day. She had a book open on her lap, *The Secret Life of Bees*, which George's mother had recommended, but she hadn't really been reading; she was just waiting for him to finish with his own book and turn out the light.

George put his hand on hers so that she had to meet his eyes. "You don't like it."

"I have always enjoyed reading novels," she said. "It's only that Mondays are tiring for me."

"Not the book," he said impatiently. "I mean, you know, us—together—having sex." She could see that he was embarrassed because the lines on his forehead deepened and joined in the middle. "I'm doing something wrong."

This idea was so surprising that Amina failed to say anything.

"I don't have a lot of experience either," he said. "I've never told that to anyone, but I guess I should now. There were only three girls before you."

"What is the normal amount?" She didn't mean to tease him, but George looked stung.

"It depends. One of those girls had been with ten people before me—and she was only twenty-five."

"And is she married now?"

"Oh yeah," George said. "She got married way before I did. And moved away."

"Who was she?" Amina asked eagerly. She had always been curious about George's sexual life before he met her; it was something her mother had wanted her to ascertain in advance, but Amina had drawn the line at that kind of question.

"It doesn't matter anymore," George said. "I just wish I knew how to make you—you know, when we're doing that."

"I am doing something wrong?"

George shook his head. "Make it good for you. I wish I'd asked someone—I mean, before. But American girls expect you to be experienced. And I hate talking about it."

"Me, too," Amina said. "I didn't even like when my girlfriends talked about it at home."

"That's how I feel—it's private." They had turned off the overhead light, and only the reading lamps were lit. "I like your shoulders," he said suddenly.

"My shoulders?"

"They're so small and perfect. And then—" He touched her shoulder, and ran two fingers down over her collarbone, very gently along the side of her left breast. She needed a small in everything in Rochester, but she'd observed that American women her size didn't have breasts like hers; they pressed against the thin cotton in a way she knew excited him.

"That shape. Don't worry—I know we did it last night. I'm just saying—you're really beautiful."

"We can," she said, and was rewarded by his expression.

"But I want to do something for you—I mean, I want to make you come."

"Come where?"

George looked at her. "Are you kidding?"

She thought he was about to laugh at her and she resented it. "No."

"You know—what happens to me."

"What?"

"I mean, at the end."

"How could I do *that*?"

He did laugh. "It's different. Look." He pulled her down on the bed so they were lying next to each other. Then he put his hand inside her underpants.

"Could we turn out the light?"

"Could we leave it on?" he said. "You're so pretty. You can close your eyes if you don't want to look at *me*."

"I didn't mean—" she began, and then she closed them. What George was doing didn't feel bad, although she wished he weren't watching her. She tried to think of something else, and what appeared was a picture that had come to her sometimes at home, when she was in the apartment alone, studying. She had imagined a man coming toward her through the lush green fields of a tea plantation—she thought she must have gotten it from an old movie. The man didn't have any recognizable features; she was rather seeing herself through his eyes, as they sank down to the ground and caressed each other. First the man would unbutton her jeans (in this fantasy, she had always been wearing the jeans she did not yet own), sliding his hand between the denim and her panties. She tried to concentrate on George here in her bedroom in Rochester, but the stranger returned; somehow the fact that she was picturing the wrong man, in the wrong place, increased her excitement, and she moaned audibly.

"Oh my God," he said. "You're going to come."

But she did not. When he was finished she could tell he was disappointed he hadn't managed to do what he'd intended, and she put her head in the hollow just below his shoulder, so that they might lie together without having to look at each other. He took her hand and wrapped it across his chest, so that they were even more closely intertwined.

"It's also called 'climax,'" he said, resuming a lecturing tone that was comforting in its familiarity. "I'm doing something wrong. But if we keep practicing I'm sure we'll get it."

It was 11:30, and she knew she would be exhausted at work in the morning, but strangely she didn't mind.

"Just not on Mondays," she said. "I'm so tired."

"Mondays will be abstinence day," George said. "Abstinence makes the heart grow fonder—that's something they used to tell us in sex ed. That's sex education—we used to have to go every week."

Amina lifted her head to look at him. "In *school*?"

"But they didn't teach us the stuff you really need to know." George stroked her arm slowly, from shoulder to wrist, and suddenly she thought of how different it would be if her parents were in the bedroom next door. They would have to whisper and keep the lights off the whole time.

"I love you," George said, and Amina didn't hesitate:

"I love you, too."

18 Her parents might have met each other earlier, if not for the war. In March of 1971, when it began, her father was a twenty-year-old engineering student at Rajshahi University. Abdul Mazid and Nasir's father, Noresh, had been two of the first to put down their names when the university had issued the call for volunteers. As college students with engineering training, they'd been sent to Dehradun, the famous Indian military academy in Uttar Pradesh, for guerrilla training. They learned to operate the Indian self-loading rifles, as well as light and submachine guns, and drilled with explosives and grenades. Noresh was bored by the strategy sessions with the Indian officers, but Abdul Mazid had a knack for thinking several steps ahead; he always seemed to have the answer their instructor was

looking for. He befriended the Deshi commander of his own district as well, and when the commander returned to Khulna, both Abdul Mazid and Noresh went with him. Amina's father, her mother often told her, had been the bravest man in his company, once begging the commander to be allowed to mount a dawn raid on a fortified Pakistani forest camp. Her father had fought so fiercely, and inspired his men so successfully, that they'd routed the Pakistani unit with only twelve men, taking four POWs, a cache of G3 "tak-doom" rifles, and a carton of King Stork cigarettes. No less than Lieutenant General Sagat Singh, the Indian IV Corps Commander, had sent congratulations to her father from the front.

Abdul Mazid and Noresh fought for six months together, during which time Amina's father assumed command of the unit. When he was wounded during a guerrilla operation, blowing up electrical pylons behind Pakistani lines, it was Noresh who brought him first to a makeshift field hospital in Satkhira and then home to Kajalnagar. By the time Noresh reported back to the commander at Shyamnagar, Lieutenant General Niazi had surrendered to the joint command of Indian and Bangladeshi forces at the Race Course Maidan, and Bangladesh was free.

Her parents saw each other for the first time at her aunt Moni and uncle Omar's wedding, in the spring of 1978. Her father had immediately made inquiries, but her mother's father had politely let her father's family know they weren't interested. In spite of Abdul Mazid's impressive military service, and the college degree that he'd gone back to finish after the war, his family had a reputation in Kajalnagar as people whom bad luck followed.

Abdul Mazid's grandfather had been an estate manager for the local *zamindar* and had been clever enough to lease a great deal of that man's land before Partition; in 1950, when the *zamindari* system was formally abolished, Amina's great-grandfather had become the owner of more than two hundred acres of land. That land had been divided between two sons, Amina's grandfather and his brother, neither of whom had managed it well. When his brother died in his early forties, his three sons were left with thirty of the least desirable acres, small parcels that they had sold as soon as they were old enough to do so. Amina's grandfather had done only slightly better, holding on to forty acres. But as land prices began their dramatic ascent all over the country, his brother's widow had become obsessed with the idea that her three sons had been cheated, inheriting the poorest of the family land. Her sons grew up believing that Abdul Mazid would inherit land that should rightly have belonged to them.

Amina had never known her paternal grandmother, who had died along with a stillborn baby before her father was two years old. He'd been raised by the wife of a poor tenant farmer on his father's land, a woman with five children, who looked after her father in exchange for payments of rice and grain. Amina couldn't imagine what it would be like not to remember your own mother; there had been no one to tell him, through looks and touch and angry scoldings, that he was the most precious person in the world to her. Her father had once joked that his own father hadn't noticed he existed until he came back from the war. She'd never spoken about it with her mother, but she sometimes thought this tragedy had defined her father's personality—the reckless disregard for his own safety that had made him such a success as a soldier but a failure as a provider ever since.

To her mother, her father at twenty-seven was a hero of the war; more than that, he was soft-spoken, educated, and, she had once told Amina, the first person she'd ever met who singled her out from her three sisters as worthy of attention and interest. The two of them exchanged six letters and met twice in secret; a month after her elder sister's wedding, Fatima Areebah defied her parents for the first and only time and took a bus to Khulna with Abdul Mazid. They were married and spent the night in a hotel. The next day they returned to Kajalnagar, where they lived with Dadu for more than a year. During this time, Omar and Moni resettled in Dhaka, where Omar's family owned an apartment building. Omar was a natural businessman, acquiring more real estate and eventually forming his own development company, and Abdul Mazid and his new bride soon followed them to the capital, where Omar put Amina's father to work as a construction supervisor. Her father was grateful for the job, which would sustain him while he looked out for a way to make his fortune.

Her mother returned to her own village for Amina's birth, in 1980, and her father took a leave from his job with Omar. He went to see his new daughter and then visited his father in Kajalnagar, where he ran into a childhood friend with a business idea too tempting to resist: Baag Import-Export was going to bring in powdered milk from Australia and send back jute fiber to be used for the backing of carpets. Abdul Mazid quit his job with Omar and sold the first quarter of his land to invest in the scheme. When it failed, a year later, her parents decided that they should return to Dhaka while Amina stayed in Haibatpur with her grandmother until their luck improved.

Amina had joined her parents permanently in Dhaka when she was six years old, but their troubles had continued. There was no shortage of promising opportunities: normally her father had been the one optimistically waiting for news of success, while her mother had always remained cautiously fearful. As a child she had shared her father's enthusiasms, but by the time she was twelve years old, she had begun to shift to her mother's point of view. They had stopped hoping for miracles and only prayed that whatever new endeavor her father had become involved in wouldn't leave them worse off than they already were.

The year she was twelve had been the worst, because they'd fallen seven months behind on the rent. Her mother had sold what little jewelry she had to pay Amina's school fees; there was enough for another year, if they were careful, and then her father had heard about his cousins' fishing project. These were the same cousins who had disputed her father's ownership of his land; the fish farm they had recently started was enjoying unprecedented success, and they were planning to expand into shrimp.

Amina could never remember the proper names of her father's eldest cousins, who were called Bhulu and Laltu within the family, but her parents always referred to the youngest by his more formal name: Salim. She clearly remembered seeing Salim in Kajalnagar as a child, because of his physical defect and the story that was attached to it. Salim was tall, well built and fair skinned; if it weren't for his left eye, permanently stuck in an unnatural, upward-looking position, he would've been more handsome than his older brothers. His deformity was common enough, less damaging in a man than in a woman, and he should have married easily in spite of it. When he turned nineteen, his parents made an offer to a poor family with an especially pretty daughter in a nearby village. The family declined, and Salim's parents took the answer as a serious insult. They mocked the other family's pretensions all over the village, but of course the reason for the girl's parents' demurral was clear to everyone. Amina's father said that Salim had always been sensitive about his eye and that, after two weeks in which his rejection was the subject of discussion all over the village, he couldn't stand it. One night he had gone to the girl's house in the village with a plastic cup of battery acid and thrown it through the open window where the girl was sleeping next to her five-year-old brother. Neither had been killed, but both children were badly burned, and the girl's beautiful face was permanently disfigured. The message was clear: if she wasn't going to marry Salim, she wasn't going to marry anyone at all.

That had happened just after the war, and Salim's family had bribed an officer at the *thana* headquarters, who delayed filing the charges from the girl's family until Salim had left the country. He spent ten years in India and then returned unexpectedly—not destitute, but without fortune or family—for his father's funeral. He had moved in with his eldest brother Bhulu's family, and his reputation for strangeness intensified. Although it was widely believed in the village that Bhulu and Laltu brought him into the fish farm out of charity, it was Salim who had contacted her father to ask if he wanted to go in on it. Salim told her father that if he could raise the capital, the three cousins would agree to give him an equal share of the profits, as a kind of reconciliatory gesture for the years of enmity between the two branches of the family.

At the time they were living in Mohammadpur with the kindest of all their Dhaka landlords—a man that she and her mother called Long Nose, but only behind his back. Long Nose was a widower who lived in the ground-floor flat with his eldest son's large and noisy family. He clearly admired Amina's mother, but he was always proper about it, coming up to the fifth floor to sit and chat with them only when her father was at home. At that time their complementary needs—his loneliness, their poverty—had provided the equilibrium on which a true friendship had rested. It hadn't occurred to Amina at the time, but she thought now that her mother, frustrated by her inability to change their situation, would have been flattered by Long Nose's attention, and the idea that his leniency with regard to the rent was in some way her doing.

Her father had never liked the idea of a quarrel and was inclined to believe the best of people. He had accepted his cousins' proposition and, instead of paying the back rent to Long Nose, used the last of her mother's jewelry money for the fishing project. He had made the trip back to Kajalnagar alone, staying in the village for several weeks and calling with enthusiastic reports about their prospects. Soon, however, Moni had heard rumors from one of her sisters-in-law in Kajalnagar, who said that Amina's father was being deceived. His cousins had doctored their books and even stocked their ponds with borrowed perch in honor of his visit. They were only waiting for him to return to Dhaka, after which they would dismantle the beds they'd constructed and begin spending the money he'd given them. In fact, her father's cousins were already bragging that they'd outsmarted Abdul Mazid, whose land ought to have belonged to them anyway.

Amina's mother had been skeptical of the fish farm from the beginning, and now she was mortified—not only by her husband's failure, but by the way the story was circulating in both Kajalnagar and Haibatpur. Nanu had never warmed to her third daughter's husband; after the elopement, she had tolerated Abdul Mazid's presence in the village when they visited but never spoke to him directly, and insulted him by handing her daughter money right in front of him. That made it all the more surprising when Nanu decided to intervene after the fish farm scam, contacting the district commissioner of police, who had been a close friend of her late husband. The commissioner succeeded in getting some of Amina's father's money back on grounds of fraud, but his cousins were furious; because of Salim's reputation for violence, Nanu had invited her son-in-law to come from his home village and spend the night with her in Haibatpur.

This reconciliation between mother and son-in-law had gone some way toward consoling Amina's parents for their humiliation. Her father had called them in Dhaka to say he'd be home the following day, and Amina remembered that her mother had gone to sleep that night cheered by the knowledge that her husband was being treated with respect in her childhood home for the first time. Very early the next morning, she and her mother had woken to a scratching at the front door. They had both leaped out of bed, but her mother had been the one to grab the biggest knife from the kitchen and stand in front of Amina just inside the door. They'd heard a metallic clanking, followed by the sound of footsteps running down the stairs.

"Salim," her mother hissed—an intuition later confirmed by several sources in the village. She thought he'd been trying to rob them and had lost his nerve; it was only once they tried the knob that they discovered they'd been locked in. They could hear the padlock rattling in the old slide-bolt latch on the other side of the door. There was no way to get out.

Her mother had screamed for Long Nose, even though it wasn't yet five in the morning, and their landlord had come upstairs and reassured them through the door. He called the blacksmith and waited there three hours for the man to arrive. By that time most of the other tenants had squeezed with Long Nose onto the small fifth-floor landing—a collection of curious faces—to inquire about the drama that was playing out in their building. When the door opened, Amina and her mother were bombarded with questions: *Who was the culprit? Where was her father? Would the person who had done this menace the building again?* The amazing thing had been how Long Nose herded everyone away, only making sure himself that she and her mother were safe before acting as if everything were normal, so they wouldn't be any more embarrassed than they already were.

Both Long Nose and her parents believed Salim had intended to set the building on fire—trapping Amina and her mother inside while the other tenants ran to the street for safety—and they thanked God that something had scared him off. Sometimes now, when Amina suffered a particularly discouraging day—when a customer yelled at her, or she was forced to wait an extra half hour in the unheated bus shelter outside the mall—she would remind herself of that dreadful morning in the apartment in Dhaka and try to imagine her parents' faces if they could have glimpsed then the privileged circumstances of their daughter's life right now.

19 Amina had been at MediaWorks for only six weeks when Carl doubled her shifts, just as Lisa had said he would. Now she worked every day but Wednesday and Sunday and took home two hundred and eighty-six dollars each week after taxes. She waited until George had gotten used to her new schedule before she brought up the question of her parents again, one night after dinner. They were sitting in the den, watching the Cowboys game on television.

"Look at that," George said. "Right through. I told you they don't have the defense this year."

"The bachelor's degree and then the master's in education are going to take at least eight freakin' years."

George looked up at her, smiling with his mouth but letting his forehead frown. " 'Freakin'?' "

Amina hurried on before he could laugh at her. "I mean, if I go part-time."

"You can give up MediaWorks when you start school," George said absently. "You won't have time for both once we have a baby."

"I have to save some money," Amina said.

"I'm going to pay for those classes. You don't need to worry about that."

"In case I lose my job."

"If you lose your job, I'll give you the money to send home."

"I won't lose it. I'm a hard worker, Carl said. And Lisa says that MediaWorks is being bought by an international consumerate."

" 'Conglomerate,' " George corrected. "If it's being bought by a conglomerate, why do you need to save your money?" He was talking to her, but his eyes were on the screen. Now he put one hand on his forehead. "Oh no—I can't watch."

Amina was holding the remote, and so she turned off the set. George took his hand away and looked at her. "What are you doing?"

"You said—"

George looked irritated. "I was just—okay, here." Once he'd taken the remote and found his channel, however, he put his arm around Amina. "What are you worried about? I said you can do the program. It doesn't matter about the money. Do you want to wait to have the baby until you're finished with school?"

Amina shook her head. "That's too long."

George looked relieved. "I agree—so what's the problem?"

Amina could hear her mother's voice in her head again, and so she took off her glasses (even though George said he didn't mind them). She stayed close to him on the couch and twisted her engagement ring on her finger. She was still unable to look at it without thinking of the sum it represented.

"I want to save money for a rental apartment."

George had been watching the commercials, but now he muted the sound. "An apartment! What would we do with an apartment?"

"You said an apartment in Greece could be eight hundred dollars per month."

George didn't move away, but he dropped his arm from her back. "This is about your parents again."

When he was upset, his shoulders moved closer to his ears. It was 100 percent different from the way her father got when he was angry, yelling at her mother and sometimes even leaving the house. Her mother would yell back, call him Madcap or Monkey's Son, and then when he'd left she and Amina would laugh. She was able to mock him, but she also obeyed the traditional proscriptions, never using either of her husband's names. She referred to him as "my husband" or "Amina's father," and if she needed to get his attention in public, she would ask Amina to call him. When he returned home after one of their arguments (pretending nothing had happened), she teased him and called him Thunder, because those bursts of temper were both loud and brief.

George, on the other hand, never got angry, something her mother said she ought to be grateful for. She said Amina was lucky to have a husband like that, but her mother didn't see George when he looked the way he did now, staring willfully at the players on the screen, as if they had the power to take this conversation away. If she hadn't known him better, she would have thought he was praying.

"So my parents won't have to live upstairs," she said. "They could still help with the baby. But they would not be here in this house."

George picked up a small, decorative pillow embroidered with a blue star and put it in his lap. She knew that this was something his mother had made for his father early in their marriage, but what this gift might signify in an American courtship of the early 1960s, or at what point in a relationship it might be appropriate to present such a token, was beyond her. Other than this pillow, there was nothing

Amina knew about George's father, except that he had grown up in Texas and then moved to Rochester for a job with the Xerox Corporation. No matter how many questions she asked, there was a great deal of George's life before he met her that she knew she would never be able to imagine, and of course the same thing was even more true of him with regard to her.

"It doesn't make sense," he said finally. "They don't know how to drive—even if they could help with a baby, how would they get to us? You know what bus service is like. How would they do their shopping?"

"I could shop for all of us at once."

George shook his head. "You won't have time. And they'd be miserable—trapped in the house all day."

"Maybe if the apartment building had a little yard. They enjoy gardening," she said, although she was afraid George was right. The only way her parents would really be happy in America was right here in the house with them.

"Not to mention the winter. I'm worried about you when it gets to be February—but two old people?" George looked at her, and she was afraid he could see that she was starting to cry. "I'm sorry I can't ask them to live here. Even if it were the right thing for them—and I don't think it is—I couldn't do it. We'd never have any privacy again."

Amina could feel her face flushing: she thought she'd camouflaged her hopes about her parents' emigration, but now it seemed as if George had known what she wanted all along. He replaced his father's pillow firmly in its customary position on the couch, and at once she understood that their previous discussions on the subject had been his way to prepare her. She wondered if a part of her had known he would say no, and if that was why she'd waited so long to talk to him directly. All of George's arguments about her parents' happiness made sense, and at the same time they were completely beside the point. She was here, and so this was where they had to be. The three of them would never have begun talking about Amina marrying abroad if it were going to be a question of permanent separation. Could she now begin getting used to the idea that she would live apart from her parents forever? The finality of it made her stomach drop, and it was even worse to think of how they would feel.

"You like being alone together, too—don't you?"

Amina nodded, but it seemed to her that "alone together" was something to strive for if you lived in a bustling house full of children, grandparents, aunts, and uncles. Here they were now, alone together, and with the TV on mute, the only sound was the indistinguishable electric purr of all their appliances working in conjunction.

George looked at her for a long moment, until she had to look away. "It's late," he said finally. "Let's go to bed now," and his voice made it sound as if Amina were the one who had swept away years of careful planning with only a few words, instead of the other way around.

She followed her husband up the stairs and into the bathroom, where he was looking at himself in the mirror, holding his toothbrush but not brushing.

"I'm getting old." George traced the lines at the corners of his eyes. "Look."

But Amina couldn't stand to look. It wasn't that George was old but that he felt sorry for himself that drove her crazy. If her father was Thunder, then George was Smoke—and how could you argue with someone who began to disappear as soon as you opened your mouth?

20 Ghaniyah was married just after Eid, and by the end of November her brother Rashid had designed a website and posted 1,678 photographs. Amina had already heard the details about the food, her cousin's various saris, and the yellow-and-gold bedroom set her aunt and uncle had gifted to the new couple. Nevertheless, she was eager to skim through the thumbnails: Ghaniyah having her hands decorated at the *gaye holud*; Ghaniyah posing in front of the mirror with an artificially apprehensive expression; Ghaniyah laughing as she danced with the youngest girl cousins. In one photograph Amina came upon her own mother unexpectedly, in an unfamiliar royal-blue-and-silver sari, her face barely visible in profile as she fed her niece a perfectly round and golden bundi laddoo by hand.

Amina skipped the pictures of the groom's family, but she was able to examine Ghaniyah's new husband, Malik, in the 214 pictures of the couple on the red-and-gold dais in the wedding hall, as well as those taken in the restaurant and in the parking lot in front of the hotel. Her cousin's husband was stout and prosperous looking, with a wide, confident face and short, gelled hair. He looked more comfortable in the suit he wore for the ceremony than he did in the orange silk kurta he put on for the reception, but by that point in the festivities both bride and groom had the dazed and patient look of people who'd been greeting, kissing, and bantering with their relations and friends for several days already. She stared hard at the pictures of her cousin, wondering how she could be both so familiar and so unlike herself. It wasn't only the embroidered crimson sari, the makeup, and the jewels, but the studied poses and generic backdrops: Amina had turned her back for a moment, and Ghaniyah had been transformed into a bride just like the ones the two of them had been admiring in photographs since they were little girls.

This was the beginning of her first December in America, but the snow hadn't come yet; Amina watched the sky every day. Already on the tract people had begun to string up lights in the trees in their front yards and along the gutters of their houses. Her favorite house was number 59, where a family of wrought-iron deer—a buck, a doe, and two fauns—were illuminated from within by pure white flame-shaped lights.

They were planning a small Christmas dinner with George's mother and Cathy—Kim was teaching a New Year's meditation retreat in Belize—and the prospect of that unfamiliar celebration had made her regret that she hadn't insisted on taking George to the Eid potluck at the ICR. He had offered to leave work early that day, but she could tell it was inconvenient for him. Before she'd started working, she was dying to meet other Muslim women in Rochester, but once she had her job, that eagerness abated a little. It had occurred to her that they would certainly meet the imam at the potluck, and he would ask where they'd been married. Amina would have had to say that they had only done the civil ceremony, and therefore in God's eyes, they weren't married at all.

It was also possible that the imam might have asked whether she'd been fasting, and she would have had to say no. She certainly wasn't going to fast at her new job. She would've had to explain it to Lisa, and Carl might have wondered if she seemed to be weak or sick. She would never lie about being a Muslim, but there were no opportunities for falsehood because Carl and Lisa didn't ask. They certainly weren't the kind of Americans who lumped all Muslims in with Osama bin Laden and his followers—in fact, she'd never heard either one of them refer to any piece of news that had occurred outside of Rochester—and she hadn't seen the need to bring up her religion at all. She had felt a pang at missing Eid altogether, but when she thought of meeting dozens of new people, of telling her story again and again (answering the inevitable questions about their unusual courtship and marriage), she was convinced she'd made the right decision. And so she'd told George that there would be many other years when they could go.

The snow came overnight, and in the morning it was still falling outside the kitchen window. It was surprising to see it coming down, not straight and light the way it did on calendars and in the Switzerland of Indian movies, but in wild switchbacks, swirls, and eddies, more like a river than like snow. You could see it best against the three black spruces that divided their lawn from the street, and Amina was staring at those trees when George came downstairs.

"Look," she said, and George did not make fun of her or mute her pleasure in any way. He came up behind her and just stood without touching her, watching over her shoulder as if this were the first time he had seen it, too.

"It's better than I thought," Amina said. "It's not like in pictures."

"Like rickshaws," George said, which was a joke only the two of them could understand. She had e-mailed about rickshaws to George—who said they sounded dangerous and inhumane—but when he'd arrived he'd said the Deshi rickshaws weren't like the old-fashioned Chinese ones he'd seen in a book. He'd liked the way each one was individually painted, with mosques and pairs of lovebirds, and was good-humored about the drivers, who'd joked about his size and vied with each other in anticipation of the profits associated with driving a foreigner.

"It isn't sticking," her husband said, going to get his own coffee while Amina watched for another minute, the white flakes falling on the yellowish lawn. It was rare for him to take any extra time in the morning, and it made the day feel like a holiday. "That's because of global warming. Did you know that the last two decades were the hottest in four hundred years? It's happening so fast, there's nothing they can do to stop it."

"Do you think there will be more snow?"

"It'd be nice to have something that stuck." He glanced out the window, calculating the odds.

"White Christmas," Amina said hopefully, and when she looked back at George he was smiling.

"You never know."

21 The snow came for real in January, and by the middle of February, Amina felt as if they were being slowly buried. Her parents checked the New York weather on the BBC and called to ask how she was managing. Her American self clenched her teeth to keep them from chattering, wore pantyhose under her jeans and turtlenecks under her sweaters, but her Bengali self complained to her parents about the kind of cold that got in through your mouth and your ears and froze your insides, so that you kept shivering even once you were inside a sturdy, centrally heated Rochester house. "Three more months," George told her, but the notion that the snow would disappear by May was incredible—where could it all go?

One night she half woke to the sound of sirens. George had raised himself onto one elbow and was looking toward the windowless wall that insulated their bedroom from the street.

"Finally," he said. "Teach them a lesson this time." Then his head dropped back to the pillow. Amina almost got up—she wanted to see the blue police lights spinning the way they did on television—but the thought of getting out from underneath the down comforter was too daunting.

When she woke up in the morning it was hard to believe the sirens hadn't been a dream, until George went out to check the mailbox. He came back inside to say it was untouched—the cops had gotten to the thugs before they could do any damage—and to marvel at the fact that kids would bother joyriding in weather like this. Amina fixed his Chex and a protein shake she could drink slowly; it was her day off and she was looking forward to getting things done around the house.

After he left, she put on her red parka and went into the yard. The sky hung in soft, gray drapes over the roofs of the houses. George always said he'd do the shoveling once he got home, but he'd been so grateful the first time she'd surprised him that she'd gotten in the habit of doing it herself. She liked the quiet while she worked, interrupted only by the clang and scrape of the shovel on the asphalt and the way the chemicals in the Rid-Ice seemed to melt the snow by magic. It was best when Annie Snyder or another of their neighbors was outside; she liked to wave casually as she accomplished this very local chore. No one was in evidence this morning, and she was about to go inside when she saw a silver car speeding up Skytop Lane. A gloved hand waved from the driver's side, and then Amina recognized Kim.

She leaned the shovel against the side of the house and brushed the snow off her trousers—an old pair of George's that she'd hemmed to wear in the garden over the summer. George said that she looked like a circus clown, with a belt gathering the pants at the waist, but Amina couldn't see the point in dirtying one of her own pairs when her husband had so many old ones he never used. She had wondered if Kim wore Indian clothes all the time, and she was relieved when George's cousin got out of the car to see that today she had put on ordinary dark blue jeans and a plaid jacket, too light for the weather but not exotic in any recognizable way. She was carrying a bouquet of flowers without much color to them, some wildflower or herb with a few tightly closed white buds, and a small package wrapped in cellophane. It occurred to Amina that they'd brought nothing when they'd visited her.

"These aren't for you," Kim said, as if she could read Amina's mind. "I brought bath salts instead, but now I'm thinking—you don't take baths, do you?"

"Not often," Amina admitted. The idea of sitting in her own dirty water disgusted her.

Kim was nodding already. "That's an American thing—boiling ourselves for no reason in tons of hot, potable water. Oh well, you can regift these," she said, putting the pretty blue package in Amina's hand. "I'm sorry I didn't call first—is this a bad time?"

"It's a wonderful time," Amina said. "Please come in."

But Kim hesitated in the driveway. "George should do this for you."

"He would," Amina assured her. "Only it's so hard and icy when he gets home—even if he's home at four thirty."

"Rochester," Kim said, shaking her head. "I bet this isn't what you pictured." She didn't wait for an answer but glanced across the street. "They're still at the hospital, I guess?"

"Who's at the hospital?"

"Oh," Kim said. "I thought you knew. It's Dan Snyder. He's only forty-five, but he's had this heart problem ever since he was born. Last night he had a seizure and they took him in to Strong Memorial."

"I didn't know you know the Snyders."

"Annie and I went to high school together. We were the same year, but we weren't friends then—I wasn't part of her crowd." She smiled gently. "Hers was the right crowd, and mine was the wrong one."

"Which one was George a part of?" Amina asked, although she thought she already knew the answer.

"We were never there at the same time, of course, so I don't really know. I hung out with stupid kids—really self-destructive. But George had the confidence not to make that mistake." She smiled at Amina. "I bet he was just sort of an individual."

Amina looked across the street at her neighbors' house. Annie had left the garage door open, an empty black mouth.

"Do you think there was a siren?"

"You mean, on the ambulance? Sometimes they turn them off at night, if it isn't an emergency. But I would think so, for a heart."

Amina nodded. "George doesn't know. He thinks it is thugs."

Kim looked confused.

"Who have been destroying mailboxes."

Kim looked at the heavy-duty rural mailbox, which was exactly as it had been the first day Amina had taken it out of the box. "Mail-boxing, you mean? But no one's hit yours, it looks like. Anyway, he knows now. He's the one who e-mailed me—that's why I brought the flowers. She might not have been friendly to me in high school, but she was really nice after I got back from India. I thought I'd just leave these on the doorstep."

"If you want to bring them inside, I can put them in a vase," Amina suggested. "Then when the Snyders get home, I can take them. Otherwise they might freeze."

"I didn't even know that could happen to flowers," Kim said. "It's not too much trouble?"

"Yes," Amina said. "I mean, no. Please come this way."

"Do you use the front door? I think that's nice. George always goes in through the garage."

Ordinarily they didn't use the front door at all, but Amina had felt that they ought to go in the more formal entrance, since Kim was a guest. Now she realized that because Kim was family, the garage might have been more appropriate after all. They went into the kitchen, where Kim put the flowers in the sink. They had only one vase, but George's cousin found it on the first try, in the cabinet next to the refrigerator.

Amina was relieved to remember the lemon squares she'd made three weeks ago, freezing the uneaten portion. Now she put them on a plate to defrost in the microwave and set water on the stove for tea.

"Please don't go to any trouble," Kim said. "I really just came to see you. I mean, I know you said I could, but I felt like I needed an excuse. Honestly—I might not have bothered with flowers for the Snyders otherwise. I was thinking that while I was driving over from the studio this morning—not very nice, but true. That's something about yoga: it sort of brings things up about yourself. Good and bad things."

Amina tried to follow this while keeping an eye on the lemon squares rotating in the microwave. One of the things that had always encouraged her about her future with George was the fact that he'd bought this house after he'd met her. You did not buy a three-bedroom house with a washer/dryer and a microwave if you didn't in your heart one day expect to have a big family. If George's definition of family was more limited than her own, that was simply the result of cultural differences; she cherished the idea that he might eventually relent and see the beauty of having three generations under one roof.

"I stopped practicing yoga when I was with Ashok. His family thought it was silly, something for foreigners, and somehow I didn't need it then. But when I got back to Rochester, it saved my life. That and George."

"George said you and Ashok got married?" She had been unsure of whether or not to bring it up directly, but Kim nodded eagerly.

"A Hindu ceremony, but very plain and small. No white horse or red sari or anything. I wore a dress from home with a scarf and a little mehndi on my hands. We had a pundit do it in a small temple near Malabar Hill—have you been to Bombay?"

Amina shook her head.

Kim smiled. "That's funny. I know you're from Bangladesh, but maybe because you sound Indian—talking to you makes me feel like I'm back there."

"I've never been to India, but I also dreamed of marrying in a foreign country. My relatives in Dhaka used to say we were 'sleeping under a torn quilt and dreaming of gold.'"

"That's beautiful."

"It's a beautiful way of saying a nasty thing. My mother wanted me to wear a sari, but I chose a white dress."

"Actually I wanted to wear a sari. I wanted to have a big wedding and invite my mother and George and his mom and everyone. Of course my mother never would've come—we weren't even speaking to each other then. And his parents wouldn't have allowed us to have that kind of wedding anyway."

"Weddings are expensive," Amina suggested.

Kim shook her head. "They're rich," she said. "And he's their first son. They did everything for him. He went to Cathedral—that's the fanciest high school in Bombay—and then to Cambridge. I didn't even know what Cambridge was then, if you can believe that."

"But they didn't want him to have a big wedding?"

"Oh, they did," Kim said. "Just not a big wedding with me."

"But he insisted."

Kim seemed to have stopped talking and was pulling at a thread that had come loose from one of her plaid cuffs. She hadn't touched her lemon square or her tea.

"I don't have the right kind of tea," Amina apologized.

"It's not that," Kim said, and when she looked up Amina noticed again her remarkable eyes, a dark pond-water green. Now they had a glassy sheen. "George would think badly of me if he knew. He wouldn't be wrong either—I don't know why I think I can tell you."

"George knows you were married," Amina said. "He doesn't think badly of you."

Kim shook her head. "I haven't told anyone here, but I was pregnant. It was an accident, and we'd already decided to get married before we found out. I kept asking him to tell his parents we were engaged, but he put it off, and then of course it looked bad when we finally told them. They thought I'd tricked him. And then my mother-in-law wanted me to end it. There was an abortion clinic not far from where they lived—they didn't call it that, of course. We went by there a few days later, just me and her—supposedly we were going to visit a Parsi friend of hers on Hughes Road. But once we'd parked she called the house and told me the woman wasn't feeling well. She suggested we take a walk—which was totally weird, because she never walked anywhere—she said she wanted to point out some sights: the Gandhi Museum and the Towers of Silence." Kim gave Amina a bitter smile. "Anyway, we went back to the car after about ten minutes—she had her arm locked through mine, the way women do there, you know—and it turned out the driver was waiting for us right in front of it: Billimoria Hospital for Woman Care. 'If you ever have a female problem'—that's what she said—'this is where you'll come. You can walk right in anytime. Give them my name and they'll take you.'"

"You weren't married yet?"

Kim shook her head. "They said they thought we were too young, and they wanted him to go to graduate school first. Ashok stood up to them about the marriage, but I think neither of us was really prepared for a baby. And so I thought it would be okay—I was so happy we were going to be together forever. I figured we'd have kids later."

"So you went to—the hospital?"

Kim nodded. "And then two weeks later, we got married. That's when I knew they'd lied. It didn't have anything to do with our ages—a lot of Ashok's friends had kids already. But his parents hardly invited anyone to the wedding. I could see they hoped it wouldn't work out. And they knew if we had a kid . . ."

Amina thought she'd never seen anyone cry quite as beautifully as Kim did. She made very little effort to wipe the tears away, but they didn't seem to interfere with the rest of her face, which retained its delicate coloring.

"It's different after you do it. I could picture what our baby would look like: Ashok's beautiful skin, his features, my eyes. It was tiny—ten weeks—but I realized I was in love with it already. It would've come in November, and I know this sounds silly—but I knew it was a boy. I wanted to call him Hari."

Kim calmed herself. "I thought we'd have our own apartment, not too close to his parents. I'd read this article about attachment parenting—you know, breastfeeding and cosleeping and everything. I knew I wanted to do most of it myself."

"What is cosleeping?"

"Oh—it's when you sleep with the baby, instead of putting it in a crib."

"That's the way we do it at home."

"Exactly," Kim said. "*You* know. I wanted to do everything naturally—no formula or anything like that. Homemade food. Just the opposite of the way I was raised. I thought I'd tell my mom that if she wanted to see him, she could come and visit us. I never wanted to bring him back here."

Amina expected some qualification or excuse: after all, she'd just moved halfway across the world to spend the rest of her life in Rochester. But Kim didn't seem to recognize that particular awkwardness.

"You'd think that would be the way they'd do things in the cities there, too—but it's almost worse than here. Nannies living in the house with you; bottles of formula; rich people are even using those awful disposable diapers now, when it used to be kids just running around bare-bottomed. I wanted to do it the village way, basically."

"In the village you live with your family, though," Amina said. "You don't have your own apartment." There were a lot of other things about village life she thought might surprise her new friend, but she didn't want to undermine Kim's admiration for her culture, which she thought was genuine if not especially well informed.

"Well, except for that," Kim said. "That wouldn't have worked, in our case."

"But your mother didn't know about—the baby?"

"God, no. She would say it served me right, doing something like that. She's very pro-life. And I mean, they encouraged me, but I'm the one who decided. I knew I'd made a mistake from the moment the sedative wore off—the worst mistake I've ever made. It was awful because I'd always known my mother was wrong and that abortion was a lifesaver for women. I hadn't had any problem going into it. And then after it happened, all I could think of was that I wished she'd somehow stopped me. How it was final, and it was my fault."

"Oh," Amina said. "I don't—"

"I know it's a lot to ask—but if you could please not mention anything about this to George?"

Amina hesitated only a second. "I won't say anything." She was still struggling with the idea that Kim was confessing something of this magnitude—something she hadn't even told George. She'd lived in Rochester nearly a year, but this was the first time anyone had told her a secret.

"I thought Ashok and I could start over in New York. Leave it all behind. But I didn't realize how hard it is to make it work, after something like that."

"How long were you in New York?"

"Only about four months. That was five years ago—the baby would be six now." Kim smiled sadly. "I had an ultrasound the week before we decided to do it. I still have those pictures."

The phone rang, and Amina started. "Excuse me," she said. "I'm sorry. My parents call sometimes during the day."

But it wasn't her parents; it was George.

"Hi, honey," he said. "How's it going?"

"Fine."

"Good—listen, will you do me a big favor? If I tell you exactly how to do it, can you go across the street and check if the Snyders' porch lights are still on? If they are you're going to have to get the key—it's underneath that planter that looks like an animal, a badger or a beaver or something—and unlock the front door. There's been an emergency with Dan, and Annie's been at the hospital all day with both kids. She says she thinks she left the alarm off and the lights on."

"Kim is here."

"What do you mean?"

"I mean, she's visiting. She came to bring flowers for the Snyders."

George sounded irritated. "She didn't need to do that."

"We were just having tea."

"Well, if she's just sitting there, she can go and do it. It'll be easier—let me talk to her."

Amina handed the phone to Kim, who assumed a patient expression, as if George were an older brother who habitually talked down to her. At one point she rolled her eyes at Amina and smiled.

"Yeah," she said. "Yeah, yeah—I know. I can do it on my way out." She paused for a second while George asked a question.

"India," she said. "Comparing notes."

She hung up the phone, and then put her hand over her mouth. "Sorry, Amina—that was dumb. Did you guys want to talk again?"

"It's okay," Amina said. "I'll see him tonight." She had about a thousand questions for Kim about Ashok and her mother-in-law and the apartment building in Bombay, but Kim was already slipping into the leather clogs that she'd left at the door without having to be asked.

"I should go," Kim said. "You were getting a lot done before I interrupted you. I can take the flowers myself, as long as I'm going over there."

"Please come anytime," Amina said, walking Kim to the back door this time. "Thank you for the bath salts. I'll try them."

Kim gave a little laugh and then turned away quickly, as if she were suddenly ashamed. Amina watched her hurry out through the garage and down the driveway and then, hardly looking, cross the street with the bouquet clutched in one hand.

She went back into the kitchen and began clearing away the tea and the uneaten lemon squares. But she could feel her heart beating fast. It was the kind of story she could remember the girls at Maple Leaf whispering to one another: a clandestine affair followed predictably by tragedy. Now here was an American tragedy, and as sorry as she felt for Kim, who had lost both a husband and a child, there was a part of her that was secretly thrilled. Of all the people Kim might have told, she had chosen Amina.

22 That evening George got home at five, later than usual. He told her at length about a colleague who might possibly be fired while she finished preparing dinner. She waited to bring up the subject of Kim until they were sitting at the table.

"Did you ever meet Ashok?"

George was looking at his new BlackBerry in his lap and didn't look up. "Who?"

"Kim's husband—Ashok. Did you meet him?"

"No," George said. "He answered the phone once, when I called her after 9/11. She started a job in Manhattan three days before it happened—did she tell you that? I think that was part of what made Ashok want to leave, after a while. She told me every time he took a backpack on the subway, people would stare at him."

"That doesn't happen to me," Amina said.

"We don't live in Manhattan," George said. "Plus, you don't exactly look like a terrorist."

"Well, did Ashok look like one? Kim says he was from a wealthy family."

"Who knows? People were panicking. Look—I'm glad you and Kim are becoming friends. That's what she hoped would happen."

"You didn't hope?"

"I want you to be friends with whomever you want. I don't want to pick them for you. Kim doesn't always make the best choices, but she's generous—you have to give her that."

"Give her what?"

"She's generous," George said. "That's all I mean. She rushed right over after I e-mailed."

"Why did you e-mail her?"

"Because that's what you do."

"But you didn't e-mail me."

George had the same exasperated look he got when there was water on the basement floor or one of the kitchen drawer pulls came off in his hand. "You hardly know them. Did Kim tell you how serious it is? He may have to have a pig heart."

"A pig heart!"

"Well, maybe not the whole heart. I think it's just the valve."

"What is the valve?"

"Like on a faucet," George explained. "The part that allows the blood to circulate."

"They're going to put the valve of a pig into Dan Snyder?"

"It's amazing what they can do now. Strong is a great hospital—he's lucky he lives in Rochester."

Amina thought of what her cousin Nasir would say about that. There was a section in *The Lawful and Prohibited in Islam* entitled "Medical Necessity," but she doubted anyone who'd contributed to that book had thought of the possibility of an actual piece of pig being put inside a human body.

"He's lucky he's not a Muslim," Amina said, but George had taken his plate into the kitchen.

"Make sure to wear your boots tomorrow," he said when he returned. "It's supposed to be the storm of the season."

She was disappointed when she arrived at MediaWorks the next morning to find only Carl in the stockroom. Lisa had been sick all the previous week, and Amina had taken over some of her shifts; she had made more money than she had any other week of her life ($343.20), but she'd missed Lisa, whose aggressive banter with Carl at least broke up the long stretches of the day without customers.

Ordinarily when Carl was in the stockroom, he was either looking for something in particular (which Lisa had invariably misplaced) or straightening the shelves; Amina was surprised to find him sitting on an unopened UPS shipment box, drinking his coffee.

"Lisa is sick again?"

Carl looked at Amina as if he didn't recognize her, and then nodded.

"Will you be needing me to work her shifts?" She would have to call George in that case, since the bus didn't run on their route after five; he would have to pick her up when he was finished for the day.

"No. You can go home at the regular time."

"But who will—?"

"I can close up. It'll be slow tonight, because of the snow."

It occurred to Amina that this scenario—herself and Carl, an unmarried man less than ten years older than she was, alone together in the stockroom—would be unthinkable to her parents, her aunts, and even her cousin Ghaniyah. She'd had the same realization in other situations: when she had skipped her *dhuhr* because there was nowhere private to pray at MediaWorks, and she felt too strange putting down a mat in the stockroom. Or when she'd drunk half a tall glass of Aunt Cathy's sangria, before she had understood that it was made from wine. Because those things were unthinkable, there was a way in which they hadn't happened: they had happened only to her American self, a person about whom her Bangladeshi self was blissfully unaware. She asked forgiveness for these errors in her prayers, but if she failed to mention them to her parents, she didn't feel she was committing further sins.

"Is Lisa very ill?"

"No." Carl focused on Amina, as if he'd only just now noticed she was there. "I'm sorry I didn't tell you before, but Lisa isn't coming back."

Amina stared at Carl. "Lisa is fired?"

"Laid off."

"But Lisa is good," Amina said. "She says funny things sometimes, but she's the one who taught me to do my job. I couldn't have learned it without her." She wondered if this sounded insubordinate, but Carl didn't seem to notice.

"You're much better than Lisa. But unfortunately I have to give you notice, too. I'm sorry about this. We'll stay open another two months—wishful thinking, in my opinion—and then I'll need you for a few days of packing up after that."

"But what about the new owner? The international—" She paused, afraid to mangle the word.

"No dice," Carl said. "They dropped MediaWorks a couple of weeks ago. The owners were banking on that deal, and now they're sunk."

Amina didn't understand, but she didn't want to ask Carl to explain. She thanked God for providing her with such a sympathetic husband; she almost looked forward to telling George, since the loss of her job at least confirmed her prescience in opening the savings account. Of course George would say that he could send money to her parents until she found another job, and as much as Amina wouldn't want to, of course she would agree. She couldn't bear the idea of withdrawing her small savings ($2,147.53 to date) when that was the only tangible proof of her progress toward the apartment.

More than anything she dreaded telling her mother about Media-Works, which was unfortunately not one of those things she could avoid mentioning without feeling she was lying. The loss of a job was an all-too-familiar event, and her mother would be sure to see in it signs of future trouble. At least with her father, there was always optimism, even if it was groundless. If one thing went wrong, her mother had a maddening tendency to feel that everything else would follow it. That was a characteristic of her grandmother's, too—one that her mother had always mocked and then suddenly folded into her own personality without even noticing.

George had been right about the weather. When Amina left Media-Works, the snow was coming down fast; a powdery layer the thickness of three fingers coated the frozen gray mounds on the sidewalk around the bus stop. The only other person in the shelter was an old black woman, sitting right in the center of the bench with all her things around her so that there was no room for anyone else. She was wearing a clear plastic scarf over her hair, printed with flowers; her nanu and her aunts would love something like that, and Amina had almost gotten up her courage to ask where it came from when the woman startled her by speaking.

"Coming *down*." She shook her head, as if the weather were a permanent condition, a new burden for the two of them to bear. "And not stopping anytime soon."

"Do you think so?"

The woman raised her eyebrows at Amina. "Don't take it from me. Take it from Glenn Johnson at 13WHAM."

Amina nodded, although she'd never heard of Glenn Johnson. Apart from MediaWorks customers, this was her first real conversation with a black person. "Excuse me," she said. "Where did you get your scarf?"

"This?" The old woman touched her head, laughing. "You want one?"

"For my grandmother," Amina explained. She wondered if it was possible the bus wouldn't come on a day like this and was glad she wasn't the only one waiting. During the hours she'd been at work, snow had fallen on the trees, building to an unlikely height on even the thinnest branches. It was indisputably beautiful, and it made her think of her first drive in from the airport with George. He had been in a keyed-up mood—the same way she'd been at the airport in Dhaka seventeen hours earlier. But by that point in her journey she felt as if she'd been woken in the middle of the night and forced to perform a role in a bad movie: the set was cold and harshly lit; she was seated next to a stranger; and she couldn't believe any of it was really happening.

"You've never seen roads like this, I bet," George had said. "See how everyone stays in their own lane." But she hadn't been watching the road. She'd been looking at the bare trees along the side of the highway, thinking she'd never seen anything uglier in her life. She had thought of what cunning it must've taken for America to have kept this unflattering season a secret from the rest of the world.

She was relieved now to see the headlights of the bus coming down West Henrietta, at exactly 4:35. The snow made it seem later than it was.

"Your grandma can get this cheap at Kmart—doesn't she know that?"

"No," Amina said, and when the woman looked surprised, she added, "She can't go out on her own. She stays alone with a caretaker."

"What's the matter with her?"

"Nothing. Only that she is old. And she gets sad sometimes."

The woman made a sympathetic sound. "Don't I know."

Amina stepped aside while the woman greeted the driver by name and waited for him to lower the slow, automatic stair (so different from boarding any kind of bus in Desh). As she put her pass over the electronic sensor, she half turned back to Amina, as if to reassure her.

"But your grandmom is lucky," she said. "She has you."

ESL

1 She started college in the summer term, a year after she'd arrived. She would turn twenty-six in July, and she was still two years away from becoming a citizen. According to Ghaniyah's *Femina* magazine, she was no longer a newlywed, but the goals that she'd set for her first three years in Rochester seemed very distant. Even if everything went as she hoped, she wouldn't have an American passport until July of 2008. As soon as she received it, her parents would expect to begin the visa application process. But now that she'd lost her job, the questions of where they would live and how she would pay their rent were more insoluble than ever.

The first night she came home from ESL, she told George that it was like having the whole world in one room: she had never imagined that there were so many different kinds of foreigners in Rochester. George had thought she might place out of the ESL requirement altogether, but he'd forgotten how much better her speaking was than her writing. Her score put her at the intermediate level, and so she signed up for ESL 125 and Calculus I. In ESL she sat next to a Lithuanian girl, Daina, who chattered constantly with another girl Amina had assumed to be Russian. Only later did she discover that Laila was actually Turkish but had been raised in Moscow. There were two Afghans who sat at the back of the room and spoke only to each other, and a Turkish boy, Abu, who could not refrain from giggling every time he tried to say something in English. Jamila was a Somali woman who wore a head scarf—her family was also Sunni, she told Amina after class one day—and Pico was from the Congo (only now you weren't supposed to say the "the"). Pico's British-inflected English was the best in the class, and he was never afraid to raise his hand.

Their teacher, Jill, had asked to be called by her first name. Amina guessed her to be in her late forties, but it was hard to be sure. She had short, bobbed hair, dyed black, and the kind of childlike features that made her look younger than she was; it was only when you got up close that you could see the lines at the corners of her eyes and mouth. Jill told them that she'd been teaching at MCC for seven years and that she lived in Brighton with a cat and two parakeets. She said that she'd begun her career teaching English in Thailand, where she'd gone when her marriage hadn't worked out.

"A lifetime ago—big mistake," she said, smiling at them. Abu laughed, as did Daina, putting her hand over her mouth, but Pico frowned, as if he disapproved of such a confidence from a teacher. The rest of the class only smiled uncertainly with Amina. Jill told them she'd spent five years in Bangkok and then returned to Rochester and gone to SUNY Brockport for her teaching certificate, taking poetry classes at the same time. She had even published a book of poems, called *The Floating Market*. "It was a big seller, I can tell you. My mom and dad have ten copies." Jill smiled. "But I love poetry and I'm going to inflict it on you guys." One of their first assignments had been a three-paragraph response paper on the poem "Crusoe in England," by Elizabeth Bishop. Amina had received a check, which meant that her work was acceptable if not distinguished, but when she looked over at the paper on Pico's desk, she'd seen a bright red check plus plus.

On her way home from school that day she'd run into Pico on the bus; she'd gotten on after him, and there were no seats, but her classmate had insisted on standing up and giving her his. Amina had wished he hadn't, partly because Pico's skin was so dark—almost purple—that people on the bus turned to stare at him, and partly because it meant they had to manage a conversation. Pico had stood over her, holding on to a pole, and she'd said the first thing that came into her head:

"My husband ordered the movie *Congo* from Netflix." Amina didn't think she'd ever seen Pico smile, and so it surprised her when he laughed out loud.

"Did you enjoy it?"

"We didn't watch it yet."

"Well, if you do, remember that they made all that up," Pico said. "That's not what my country is like."

Amina thought about talking to Jill, as she might have to a teacher at home, to ask whether there was anything extra she could do to improve her grade on the response paper. But when she imagined approaching the teacher in this politely humble posture—not fake, but not entirely genuine either—the words she thought of were in Bangla rather than English. And so she threw the assignment away and resolved to do better the next time.

Amina knew she was a different person in Bangla than she was English; she noticed the change every time she switched languages on the phone. She was older in English, and also less fastidious; she was the parent to her parents. In Bangla, of course, they were still the parents, and she let them fuss over her, asking whether she was maintaining her weight, and if she'd been able to find her Horlicks in America.

Was there a person who existed beneath languages? That was the question. As a teenager, Amina had thought there was. She had believed that she'd been born with a soul whose thoughts were in no particular dialect, and she'd imagined that, when she married, her husband would be able to recognize this deep part of herself. She thought that this recognition was how she would recognize *him*. Of course she hadn't counted on her husband being a foreigner, a person who called her honey rather than Munni. In a way, George had created her American self, and so it made sense that it was the only one he would see.

2

Munni,

Assalamu alaikum. It is after midnight now, and I am sitting at the computer at home. Probably everyone in the building is sleeping except for my Sakina Apu, who stays up late watching television. It is raining, but they say the floods will not be so bad this year, inshallah. The window is open and so I am getting the smell of the "belly" flower from the veranda.

I was sorry to hear from your parents that you did not observe our holy festival last year. What happened? I am sure there must be some sort of celebration at the ICR I mentioned about—or at least you might fast at home? Both years I was in UK I enjoyed breaking the fast at the restaurant with the other Deshis there—that was the only time our boss (my cousin) was generous with us. Walking around the streets on those days when I was fasting, doing my errands, I used to feel something special—it's hard to explain. But it was like I had a secret from everyone around me.

I think of you often, but try to keep from writing—I know you are busy with work and your life in America. Your parents give me all your good news, and I truly admire everything you are doing for them, Munni. They are wonderful people, and I will miss seeing them.

Now I will confide in you my own news. Last week, Sakina Apu sent a letter to the parents of a girl. She and Shilpa said the girl is good in all senses, but—my bad luck—she won't even agree to meet me. The reason: because I am not an MS holder. (She herself does not have a master's degree, but never mind.) My sisters became furious, saying that it is an excuse—that this family cares only for taka, and now we know. Perhaps, but I cannot be angry. Maybe it is my temperament that keeps me from finding a life partner. I cannot care about all the things that other people care for—Allah knows what will happen to me.

I have begun printing stories from the BBC. At first I am pinning these stories up around my desk, so that I would be sure to remember them, but my boss has asked me to take them down. He said my other colleagues think I am showing off my knowledge of English! I think you will also laugh at this notion. I took down my papers, but they are there on the BBC for anyone to read. I do not advise you to read them, because I do not want you to be shocked by the abuses they describe. (Though I am sure you have seen the terrible pictures from the Abu Ghraib prison.) You say that President George Bush is no worse than our two "Begums," and perhaps you are right. But is the crime not more severe, the bigger the man who commits it?

I am glad that you have found a good George ;-) in America, and I am sorry to bother you. You are right that I have an obsession with "depressing news." At night as I am trying to fall asleep, I think of those prisoners still in their cells, crying out to our God. And so it is perhaps a good thing that my sisters have failed again, and that it is only myself and the tiktiki who are disturbed by my tossing and turning.

Allah hafez.
Your friend,
Nasir

She reported to her parents that her classes had begun, but it took her a month to tell them that she'd lost her job. Her mother had started to cry, of course: she said she had a feeling they would never see each other again. When Amina told her that was ridiculous, her mother simply sobbed harder and handed the phone to her father, who asked whether her Chinese friend could help convince the boss to take her back.

"She isn't Chinese," Amina said patiently. "She has a Chinese tattoo. And anyway, she was also laid off."

Her parents couldn't understand the difference between "laid off" and being fired, even when she explained it to them exactly as George had explained it to her.

"And I don't know why you need to gossip to everyone about my job right away."

"We are not gossiping!" her father exclaimed. "Who told you that?"

"I have been receiving e-mails from Nasir."

"Nasir!"

"Why has he been visiting you so often?"

"Not so often." The connection was weak, and her father struggled to make himself heard. "He came one time. Your mother insisted on cooking for him." She could hear her mother arguing stridently in the background; she couldn't make out the words, but of course her mother was saying that it was Nasir, and he'd shown up at their door. How could she not invite him in for something to eat?

"If you'd only waited to tell everyone," Amina said. "I could've gotten another job and no one would've known."

"Yes!" her father shouted. "Please tell us as soon as you get another job! We'll let everyone know!"

Amina was so exasperated that she almost hoped that the call would be dropped. Instead the connection got stronger again.

"Have you told Nasir not to visit again?"

"How could we tell him that?"

"He said that he was going to miss you, so I thought you must have told him not to come again."

"Ah." Her father coughed unnaturally.

"Is he going somewhere?"

"He has a good job at Golden Internet. Where would he be going?"

"Golden Horn," Amina corrected. "But he knows you're not going to America yet, so why does he say he'll miss you?"

"Oh yes," her father said, as if it had suddenly occurred to him. "Your mother gave notice to Mrs. Khan last week. We are moving home to the village until you come for us. You'll need to send much less money, only half. And you can save for the future."

"Tell Mrs. Khan you changed your mind!" Amina exclaimed. "How could you go back there now?"

"It's only another two years," her father said. "Your nanu has room for us. Why should we spend so much money here in Dhaka when we are only waiting to come to America?"

"How could you give up your apartment?" The apartment in Mohammedpur was a good one, and the rent was fair. It had been a comfort to know they had it, as she struggled to imagine how she would save enough for an apartment and even sometimes wondered whether Rochester was the right place for them. Now everything was different. Her nanu would have them in the village, but not forever—and so if they were going there she had no choice but to somehow find a way to bring them here.

"It's more than two years—twenty-six months, at the earliest! Who knows how long it'll take?"

"That's true," her father said cheerfully. "Or perhaps it will be even less time!"

3 When she'd first arrived, there had been some talk about Amina working for Cathy at Shampooch, and as soon as she lost her job, those conversations began again. Amina smiled and nodded politely whenever Cathy brought it up, but she told George privately that it was impossible. When she imagined telling her mother that she'd got-

ten a job washing dogs—and then imagined her mother telling her Devil Aunt—she thought she would do absolutely anything to avoid taking Cathy up on her offer.

"Amina doesn't like animals," George had said at dinner last Sunday night, but the look on his aunt's face was so shocked and hurt that Amina had tried to mend things.

"That's not true," she said. "I like dogs and cats very much in America. Dogs in Bangladesh are not very nice, because the climate is too hot for them. They go crazy and their fur falls off."

"Oh, that's so sad," Eileen put in.

"Amina wants a job where she can stay clean," George insisted. "She wouldn't like washing dogs."

Cathy looked surprised. "Well it's not like I can't easily find a couple of Cuban girls to do it. They're illegal, and so they don't have a lot of options. Of course they're going to have babies, and so we'll be paying for the bilingual programs—as if Rochester schools don't have enough problems."

"You employ illegals," George said. "Where would Shampooch be without them?"

"I wouldn't employ them if they weren't *here*. I voted W. twice, but I can tell you, I wouldn't do it again. They can call it a guest worker program if they want, but everyone knows it's amnesty, pure and simple."

Later in the car Amina asked whether Aunt Cathy had been offended by her hesitation about the job at Shampooch.

"She'll get over it," George said. "I was more worried about you."

George had cracked the window, and the humid summer air reminded her of home. "Does Cathy dislike me?"

"No," George said quickly. "No—she's just bitter about her own life. And she's competitive with my mom. She'd like Kim to settle down with someone, have kids—all that stuff."

"I can understand Cathy," Amina said. "My mother's sisters are also competitive that way."

George nodded. "That whole thing with the Indian guy almost killed her."

"Ashok."

"Do you want to stop at Cold Stone for ice cream?"

Amina agreed because she knew it was George's favorite. "That would be nice," she continued, "if we were all having dinner together at your mom's one day. You and me and Kim and another husband."

"Mm," George said. "Let's take it one step at a time, okay?"

George took her job-hunting for the second time, at the Pittsford Wegmans, Radio Shack, and the Gap. Amina filled out applications everywhere, but George said it was a bad time to look, since high school and college kids who were already working part-time would increase their hours as soon as summer started. He thought that Amina should wait until everyone went back to school in September.

"Take it easy," George said. "Do your homework and spend time in the garden. You'll get a job in the fall, and then you'll wish for days like these."

She didn't feel she could mention her parents again, after their last conversation, and so she simply told George that she liked to be busy. "When there's nothing to do, I get jumpy."

"We don't want that," George said tolerantly, but she knew there was another reason he wanted her to relax. They'd been talking in bed the other night when George had asked suddenly whether she was ready to start trying to have a baby. She didn't feel any less frightened of having a child without her mother to help her, but it was at least two years until her parents would be able to apply for citizenship—even if the problem of where they would live could be solved.

"Okay," she had told him, and George had smiled and made a little production of getting up and going to the medicine cabinet, throwing away the blue package of Trojans that always sat in the upper-right-hand corner.

"Is there anything I'm supposed to do?" she asked him, thinking of how strange it was to be asking this question of her husband. Of course she might have asked her mother on the phone, but she knew that as soon as she mentioned it, her mother wouldn't be able to talk about anything else. Amina thought longingly of Micki, a year older than she was and already a mother of three. Of all her cousins, she'd always felt closest to Micki. When they were little girls living with Nanu and Parveen, they'd been like sisters, but Micki had stayed in the village after Amina left. When she was sixteen, she'd taken over the village baby school from Shoma Aunty, who had taught the two of them when they were small. Micki showed such patience with even the most disobedient child, was so pretty, with such skills in the kitchen and the house, that in spite of the scandal with her parents' marriage, everyone said that Parveen would have many choices once her daughter came of age.

Amina still thought she knew her cousin better than anyone: even as a teenager she could see that Micki was obedient not out of a desire to please but because she'd already concluded that it was the only road to happiness—at least if you were a girl. Micki might have had the opportunity to leave the village as Ghaniyah and Amina had, especially if her father had stayed at home, but she would never have talked the way they did, mocking its backwardness in order to distance herself from her own place and people. Surely God loved someone like that better than he loved a person like Amina, who spent so much energy trying to escape the very spot where he had seen fit to bring her into the world.

Micki would have been able to tell her in the plain village way how to go about getting pregnant, without any of the silliness and affected embarrassment of her Dhaka friends. But Micki didn't use e-mail, and they hadn't been in touch since Amina had left the country. She knew her cousin had married a man from their own village called Badal, who worked as an auto mechanic in Satkhira, but even if she were able to get his cell phone number from her grandmother, Amina would be shy about calling out of the blue. She certainly wouldn't be able to mention family matters under those circumstances. She thought for a moment of Kim, whom she hadn't seen since that afternoon in the garden. Her confidence that day suggested that she might want to become Amina's intimate friend, but you could hardly discuss starting a pregnancy with someone who was still grieving over the loss of one.

"I think there are kits and things," George said, flushing. "To tell you when your best time is."

"My mother got pregnant very easily," Amina said quickly. "Too easily. She always says they should've waited."

"Do you want to wait?" George asked. Amina thought of what her mother had said, about how George would see the logic of having them live in the house once a child was born. She was starting to wonder if that was true, and even whether it was what she wanted—now that she could actually imagine having her parents in the room next door. Looking at her husband, waiting for her answer, she realized that apart from everything else, she wanted to please him.

"No," she said. "I'll be twenty-six in July. We should start now."

George smiled. "Crazy to think it could be next spring," he said. "I mean if it happened right away."

"Would you like to have a boy?" Amina asked, to distract herself from the possibility of next spring.

"A boy would be nice," George said. "But I was thinking one of each."

4 Amina didn't stop calling the places she'd left her applications, but the summer sped by without a job materializing. One night at the beginning of August, George suggested that they pick up chicken from the Boston Market restaurant for dinner. While he was choosing from the drive-through menu, Amina noticed a sign—WE ARE HIRING—pasted to the inside of the glass. Instead of driving to the pickup window, George parked the car, and they sat and ate their dinner inside so that Amina could fill out an application. There was an elderly couple eating by the window, but the only other person in the restaurant was the middle-aged woman standing behind the cash register, her lips moving slightly as she counted coins from a paper-wrapped roll.

"Will you give it to her?" Amina asked George when she was finished, but George shook his head.

"They have to see that you have initiative," he said. "Take your time. I'll swing around and get you."

Amina approached the woman, who was wearing a great deal of face powder, perhaps because she suffered from spots. (She could not have been trying to lighten her skin, since she was as white as George.) You could look past the registers and see into the kitchen, and what was visible was surprisingly clean. Rather than the bones and peels you would expect—she and George had eaten chicken, potatoes, and salad—the counter was stacked with paper and foil-wrapped packages, as if it were not a restaurant but a pharmacy.

"Excuse me," she began, but the woman had obviously already noticed Amina. She smiled and took the application before Amina could say anything else.

"I saw you filling it out," she said cheerfully. "Do you have experience?"

"I was working at MediaWorks," she said, hoping the woman wouldn't ask how long it had been since she'd had that job.

The woman frowned. "No casual dining experience?"

"I've never worked in a restaurant." Amina tried not to sound as if she were proud of that fact, but she couldn't help remembering Nasir's e-mail. She had chastised her father, but that was because she had lost her job. If she'd been able to keep it, a part of her would have been thrilled that everyone knew how successful she'd been so far in America. She thought of Ghaniyah and what she would say when she heard that Amina was working in a kitchen, where her clothes would be dirty at the end of the day and her hair would smell like grease.

On the other hand, Amina reminded herself, she wasn't Ghaniyah. Her parents couldn't afford a spectacular Deshi wedding with seven hundred guests, or expensive jewelry that would be worn only one time. Considering where she had started, it was incredible that she was where she was right now: standing in a Boston Market restaurant in Rochester, New York, at seven o'clock in the evening while people at home were yawning and drinking their first cups of tea.

"I'm a fast learner," she told the woman behind the counter. "My boss at MediaWorks said I was the best employee he had ever had."

The woman nodded. "Normally, we wouldn't consider someone who'd just done sales—this really is a different kettle of fish. But Tanya left on Friday without a word to anyone—not that I expected much more from her—and we've got to have someone on Tuesday. Could you start on Tuesday?"

"I can start at any time."

"I'm Nancy, by the way. I saw you sitting over there and I thought, She looks responsible. I have that sense—I can always tell about people."

"Thank you," Amina said.

"If we hire you, you'll have to be here before eight in the morning. Are you a late sleeper?"

"We are up at five," Amina said.

"See?" Nancy beamed. "I can tell. So what are you, anyway?"

"Pardon?" Amina said, although George had told her a thousand times that Americans never used that word.

Nancy repeated her question more slowly, raising her voice so even the old people in the back turned around to look.

"I was an English tutor," Amina said, and then because she did know what Nancy meant, she added: "That was in my country—in Bangladesh."

"*Bang*ladesh." Nancy hesitated. "That isn't the Mideast, is it? I'm sorry to ask, it's just that my husband's a protective—that's a volunteer for our fire department—and our daughter lives in Jersey. So it hit us pretty hard, everything that happened down there . . . you know, on 9/11."

She hadn't yet encountered anyone who blamed her for the September 11 attacks because she was a Muslim or because she came from a country that had once been part of Pakistan, but this was a misperception she'd anticipated and been prepared to correct. She had known that Americans wouldn't be familiar with her country's history, and she'd been ready to explain about the Liberation War, and to tell people that her father still had a scar on his leg from his service as a Freedom Fighter against the Pakistanis. It was the Pakistanis who'd let in Al Qaeda and the Taliban, she had planned to clarify.

The explanation had been unnecessary up until now, and some part of Amina had been disappointed. Because no one asked, she couldn't be sure that they understood, and although most of George's friends and relatives were BAs (or even MAs) in something, many of them had politely inquired where Bangladesh was located. (Kim, who had dropped out of college, was in fact the only person who'd known exactly where it was.) In any case, it was a relief to finally be asked, especially since the question had been put so simply that Amina had no difficulty answering in English.

"Bangladesh is not the Middle East," she said. "It is in South Asia."

Nancy smiled and nodded. "I thought so. There's another girl here from Vietnam—a real sweetheart. Well, I'm acting as if you've got the job already. I have to check your references, but you can expect to hear from me on Monday. Bright and early!"

"How'd it go?" George asked when she got back in the car.

"Good," Amina said. "She said she would call me Monday."

"I bet you'll get it," he said. "You make a good first impression." He grinned at her, but she wasn't in the right mood. She turned back as they left the parking lot: she couldn't see Nancy through the windows, but the empty tables looked bleak under the fluorescent lights. She was good at doing math in her head, and she'd immediately calculated that if she worked as many hours as she had at MediaWorks, and kept this job for the two years that remained before she could apply for her citizenship, she would've saved only enough for fifteen months of rent by the time her parents arrived.

George was driving in a relaxed way, one hand at the bottom of the wheel.

"What about the job with Kim?" she asked.

He looked over at her, startled, and then back at the road. Rush hour was over, and she noticed they were speeding slightly in the dark.

"That was months ago," he said after a moment. "And I thought you said your parents would disapprove?"

"I could tell her it's a place for fitness exercises," Amina said. "My mother is mad for calisthenics."

George braked suddenly for the turn onto South Main, forgetting to signal.

"Maybe Kim could ask the boss for an early shift for me . . . so it would be convenient for you to drop me off."

"I doubt it's still available." He sounded disappointed in her, although she'd never thought he had anything against yoga. "But go ahead and ask—if that's what you want."

5

Dear Nasir,

Did my parents tell you I'm learning to drive? Perhaps they have also shown you the photograph of our house in Rochester. The yellow and red flowers by the front door are called "mums," and I'm the one who planted them.

Thank you for your good wishes about my job, but I'm actually not working at MediaWorks anymore. Now I have a better job that pays more. And it's easy! I work at the desk of an exercise studio, where people come to take fitness classes. My hours are good, so I'm saving well for when my parents arrive.

As for our holiday, I will celebrate Eid in my own way this year. Maybe it's different for me, having married a U.S. citizen, but I don't need to have secrets from the people around me. I never fasted back in Desh, and my parents never bothered me about it. I wonder—if I had married a Deshi Muslim, would you be asking me these questions?

Well, Cousin, I'm sorry to hear about the girl your Sakina Apu contacted. But it's for the best. I'm sure you will find your Other Half. Look at George and me. We found each other from 8,000 miles, and we are so happy.

I agree with your boss that you should take down those newspaper articles. George and I have one disagreement on the subject of depressing news and pictures. He likes to get all the facts, even when there is nothing he can do. If I can't do anything, I don't like to think of these things. Who knows? Perhaps if you are more cheerful, Allah will send the right girl.

Please send my best regards to your sisters.

Sincerely,
Amina

The desk where Amina sat, underneath a framed poster of the Buddha, was in a room with burnt-orange walls, dimly lit and scattered with votive candles that burned throughout the day. The smell of the yoga studio was familiar in its elements, but combined to make something overpowering and foreign—a heady mixture of sandalwood soap, patchouli oil, and cardamom from the pot labeled CHAI, simmering on the hot plate in the kitchen. It was Amina's job to make the tea when she arrived early in the morning, after which she turned on the computer and selected one of a stack of CDs, contemplative flute and sitar music, which she set on shuffle for the rest of the day. She watered four large ficus trees, as well as a thriving collection of spider plants and aspidistra hanging from the ceiling in cradles of woven hemp, and then sat down at the desk, waiting for the phone to ring and consciously keeping her eyes from straying to the three recessed niches in the walls, where smoke-stained Hindu idols sat among candles, garlands, and offerings of oil.

She had come for her interview on the first of August, and Kim had called her the night before to help her prepare. She had reassured her that the guru was a kind and open-minded person, but had suggested that Amina might want to wear her own clothes to the interview. For a mortified second she thought Kim was referring to the gardening trousers Amina had been wearing when they last met: Did her new friend think she made a habit of going around in her husband's old clothes? But it soon became apparent that Kim thought the guru would like Amina better if she dressed the way she had in Desh.

"I don't want you to pretend to be someone you're not," Kim said. "It's just that you don't have a ton of experience, and I was thinking that the way you look might help. That's how I got my first waitressing job."

"You wore Indian clothes?"

Kim laughed. "No—much worse. The interview basically consisted of standing up and turning around, so that the manager could look me up and down."

"Would I have to wear shalwar kameez every day?" Amina had asked. "I mean, if I get the job?" She thought her mother might be able to find a way to send more, but that it would be hard to explain why she needed them.

"Oh no," Kim had said. "The last girl always wore jeans. It would just be for the interview."

Kim's guru was older than she'd expected, but handsome, with a face that looked as if someone had cut it from stone. There were lines across his forehead and around his eyes in the way of white people who were not vigilant about sun protection, but his sleeveless black Yoga Shanti T-shirt revealed his tanned and muscular arms and shoulders. Lucas's salt-and-pepper hair was pulled back in a short ponytail, and he wore a single gold earring in the shape of ankh. He spoke with an accent Amina couldn't identify, pausing for an unnerving amount of time between thoughts and looking at Amina in a way that reminded her more of a doctor than a boss. They had sat with Kim on cushions like the ones in her apartment, drinking tea, and the guru had observed that Amina's hips weren't open, and that that was why she was uncomfortable sitting cross-legged. They would have to get her into a class or two, he had told Kim, who nodded solemnly and then smiled at Amina as if to reassure her that the yoga classes were optional.

Amina had told Lucas an abbreviated version of how she'd come to Rochester, and about her job at MediaWorks and her classes at MCC, but Lucas had been most interested in hearing about her early life in the village.

"I was there in '71," Lucas said, startling Amina, until she realized he was talking about the Concert for Bangladesh rather than the country itself. "Forty thousand people in Madison Square Garden."

"I—" Amina began, but stopped herself; telling Lucas she'd been born nine years after the war had ended might rudely emphasize her relative youth. "I love Paul McCartney," she said instead.

She wasn't sure whether it was her clothing or Kim's influence, but Lucas offered her the job as soon as they finished talking. She could work a morning shift, which would allow George to drop her off on his way to work. Her classes at MCC were in the evenings at the Brighton campus, and so she would have the afternoons free for her schoolwork.

"It doesn't make sense for you to go all the way back to Pittsford on the days you have class," Kim said. "Why don't you just use my apartment? I'm mostly in and out. And it's easier to get to Brighton by bus from here anyway."

"Thank you," Amina said. "But I would be in the way."

"I could take you to Namaste," Kim said, as if she hadn't heard. "That's the Indian market in Henrietta. You could teach me some Bengali cooking."

"You'll sure be spending a lot of time with Kim," George had observed, but at first that wasn't the case. When Amina arrived in the morning, Kim was already teaching the Mysore students, who did their yoga—Amina learned to say "practiced"—in a warm, silent room at the back of the studio. The Mysore room was open from 6:00 a.m. until noon every day except "moon days," when no one practiced because the full moon affected their balance. The students, who were mostly thin and solemn young women, came in and out according to their schedules, and so Amina didn't see Kim until it finished. At that time she would often go out with the other teachers for chai tea lattes from Starbucks—her weakness, she told Amina—and once she got back it was almost time for her to teach the Basics class, attended by a different population of plump and talkative Rochester ladies.

Kim had shown her where she kept the spare key, in a shoe outside the door, and eventually Amina became convinced that her friend genuinely liked having her there. They went to the Indian market, where Amina was thrilled to find red, yellow, and green lentils sold in bulk, ground coriander, dried mango, and even frozen kajoli fish. Namaste had all the Maggi hot sauces as well as jarred lemon, garlic, and mango pickle; in the fresh produce section she found karela, mukhi, and her beloved kolmi, so much more delicate than the American spinach she'd tried from Wegmans. Some of the vegetables were organic, which meant that they hadn't been sprayed with pesticide—so it was almost as if you'd grown them in a garden at home. Kim was knowledgeable about different types of chemicals and their harmful effects; she was especially concerned about parabens in cosmetics and BPA in plastic bottles.

"People are starting to be aware of it here," she said. "But what about in a place like India?"

They were standing in front of an alphabetized wall of Hindi movies. Amina recognized some that had been popular the year before she left—*Main Hoon Na, Masti, Murder*—but George's interest in her part of the world didn't extend to its cinema, and so she resisted the temptation.

Kim was still talking about plastic bottles. "They think they might be causing birth defects—or even infertility in high-enough concentrations."

"I've been trying to get pregnant." She'd spoken without thinking, but when she saw Kim's face she wished she'd kept this piece of information to herself. Had she been insensitive? She'd been offering up a personal failure, the way you did when you wanted to advance a friendship between women, but now she considered that her casual introduction of the subject might seem callous.

Kim smiled faintly at Amina, then looked back toward the vegetables. "I'm sure it'll happen soon."

"I don't know," Amina said. "Maybe there's some problem. For my mother it happened so quickly."

"You really want a baby now?" Kim asked. "Or is it George?"

"I want one," Amina said. "As long as my parents can come to help us take care of it. Only I didn't know Americans don't like to live with parents."

"George doesn't want them to come?"

Amina hesitated, feeling disloyal. To say anything would be to air the kind of "dirty laundry" George believed in keeping to themselves.

"Do you want me to talk to him for you?"

"Oh—no," Amina said. "Please."

"Maybe he'll change his mind when the baby comes," Kim said. "There are these herbs you can take—they're supposed to taste awful, but I know someone who did it and had twins."

"I don't want twins," Amina said quickly.

"Well, let me know if you want me to say something to him," Kim said, putting her string bags down on the counter. "He listens to me. And there are some things about your culture George just isn't going to understand."

6 Although ESL was listed only by its number in the catalog, Jill renamed it; *Migrations and Transformations,* she wrote on the white board on the first day of the fall quarter, saying that the class was not only a way to improve their English, but to "consider putting into narrative the journeys that led us all here." In the margin of her first paper, about her online courtship with George, her teacher wrote *Great ideas, more organization!* and the following week, when she described her early childhood in the village: *Amina—this is fascinating stuff. But where's your thesis statement?*

Amina often wrote the papers in Kim's apartment after work while she waited for George to pick her up. Sometimes the apartment was so untidy that she would start by doing a little bit of housework—washing the dishes in the sink or watering the plants. When Kim noticed, she would be effusive in her thanks, insisting that it wasn't necessary, but it seemed to Amina the least she could do in exchange for Kim's generosity. If she was working on a problem set for calculus, she appreciated the quiet of the apartment, but on the days when it was English, she always hoped Kim would come home early. She would read it through and help Amina put things in the right places; if there was no thesis statement, her friend could always come up with one. Then she would make tea, and they would talk until Amina had to leave for the bus, or they heard George honking the horn outside.

Kim loved Amina's stories about Desh and was often able to determine which of them would please her teacher best. For example, Amina had suggested writing about the triumphant day she'd bought the TV to surprise her parents—from a neighbor who worked for LG in the electronics department of the export fair at Sher-e-Bangla Nagar. Kim, however, argued in favor of the story about the time Amina's grandmother had seen the white legs of a ghost dangling from the tree outside her house. This had happened on an evening when Amina and Micki had been in their playhouse, involved in some complicated domestic fantasy; by the time they'd come home, the whole village was talking about what Nanu had seen. A Hindu herbalist with a stall in Satkhira had come to investigate the site and recommended that

Nanu put an offering of fruit out each evening for a week on the steps of the pond. The ghost was never seen again, but every morning the fruit was gone—messy scraps of flesh, pit, and rind littering the steps and the ground underneath the mango tree. Kim had suggested that she also describe the house where she and Micki had played: the clay cups that had furnished their kitchen and the banana leaves that had served as plates. She told Amina to be sure to include the fact that the house had belonged to a Hindu, who had fled to India during the purges that accompanied the war—it was that history that gave the story depth and meaning.

Amina understood that she was supposed to write about her own experiences, but if she'd had a choice she thought she might have preferred describing Kim's. Often when they were finished with Amina's homework, she would ask Kim about India. After their conversation at Namaste, she was careful to stay away from the subject of pregnancy. Instead they talked about Kim's life in Bombay before her marriage—a topic her friend never tired of discussing—and, when that was exhausted, the months Kim and Ashok had spent living together in Manhattan.

Once they started dating officially, Ashok had taken Kim to the horse races, to the tennis club, and to the fabulous wedding celebration of an Australian businessman and a Bollywood actress on an island in the Arabian Sea. They dined habitually at expensive restaurants, where the maître d's greeted Ashok by name and referred to Kim as "madam." In his parents' second home outside the city, an open farmhouse on a hill surrounded by villages, Ashok rowed Kim out into the middle of a still, sparkling lake. All around them were low hills and fat clouds; insects skimmed the surface of the water, and Kim couldn't believe the uncanny softness of the air. Of course the peaceful landscape wasn't as empty as it looked, and the tiny, rounded huts that Kim admired from a distance each contained a family. They kissed in the middle of the lake, his hand in her sun-bleached hair, and Kim, at least, was startled when they returned to shore to find a crowd of gawking villagers.

To Amina these experiences were wonderful, but Kim described them as painful and full of errors. She remembered once having a bad cold; after a day of watching her hack and snort into tissues, Ashok had observed casually that "Indian women don't really do that." And as soon as he said it, she had begun to look around and notice that while a lady might hold a tissue over her nose at a particularly noxious intersection, wipe the seat of a taxi or the rim of a glass, she certainly didn't expel her own body fluids in public.

For as long as she could remember, Kim said, she had looked at her mother and been privately grateful to her unknown biological parents for her height and slender build. She had felt glamorous going into a small boutique on Malabar Hill to buy an outfit for the wedding they were attending; Ashok had told her to put her purchases on their account at the store, which was owned by a friend of his mother's. As a teenager she'd never had enough money for what she wanted—and, she admitted to Amina, there were a few times when she'd shoplifted clothing just for the pleasure of getting away with it—but she'd always been conscious that she knew how to choose things that would look good on her. In India Kim was thrilled by the variety of garments and fabrics, and she'd fallen in love with a pale green-and-gold lengha, which she knew Ashok would admire. But when she'd gone behind the curtain with a shopgirl to help her get dressed, Kim had discovered that the blouse was made for a woman with a narrower frame. The girl went to retrieve what they had in larger sizes (none of them as pretty as the first), but these were designed for older, heavier women with larger breasts. The saris themselves could be wrapped to suit the figure, but the girl wasn't used to doing it for someone so tall, and a good portion of Kim's ankles showed beneath the heavily decorated hem. She had been embarrassed, returning home empty-handed, to find both Ashok and his mother waiting to see what she'd selected.

"But you always wear Indian clothes," Amina said.

Kim laughed. "I wear my own version. This kind of thing." She indicated the bulky sweater she was wearing over an unseasonable cotton dress and a pair of black tights. "But trust me—I look stupid in a sari."

"I can't wear a sari either," Amina said. "I trip."

"But you have the right figure for it," Kim said. "You need curves. And Ashok always said he hated shalwar kameez—that it was a Muslim thing, designed to hide a woman's body." She smiled at Amina. "He was totally ignorant about your religion, obviously."

"That might be true about shalwar kameez," Amina said. "I prefer Western clothes, but a shalwar kameez is comfortable for women."

But Kim had moved on to Ashok's character, her favorite subject. One of the things she liked about him was his definite opinions about India, both positive and negative. After spending several months at the yoga retreat in Mysore, with people whose knowledge was as sketchy as their enthusiasm was absolute, it was appealing to be with someone confident enough to deplore some of what he saw around him. But even when he was critical, Ashok was never ashamed; he was *of* the place he was from more solidly than anyone she'd ever met.

The thing she didn't like was the way he looked at other women.

"He always used to say he *appreciated* women, and why was I so threatened by that? Part of growing up around movie stars, I guess. I felt like it was a test—like, was I cool enough to handle it? And so I pretended that I was, and then it got worse."

"That's different from Desh," Amina said. "Well-educated men don't do that."

"And I felt so pale and gawky all the time," Kim continued. "Everyone looked like you."

Amina flushed, because of course Kim was flattering her. She hadn't gotten fat in America—as her relatives had joked she would—but she thought her looks had nevertheless declined. It had something to do with her clothes: jeans or casual trousers never fit her correctly, and she couldn't bring herself to wear the kind of fitted tops that emphasized a figure like hers. At home she'd been a respectable 1.6 meters, but once that was translated to an American five foot two inches, she'd suddenly become short. She pinned her hair back and wore her glasses all the time, and she'd grown accustomed to the dowdy, serious person who greeted her in the bathroom mirror before work each day.

"But I look wrong here," she told Kim. Around the women who frequented the yoga studio she felt perpetually diminutive, and that physical feeling augmented the psychological sense of her own childishness that she felt in America. As soon as she had mastered one set of references, she was thrust into a situation that required another. The yoga students were kind and seemed to appreciate her, in the same way they appreciated the smell of the incense and the Sanskrit letters stenciled in purple on the orange wall. Whether those words meant something to Lucas, something related to the astonishing contortions she observed through the plate glass, pushing a basket of clean towels from the laundry to the changing rooms, or were simply decoration, Amina didn't know. She wasn't any more familiar with boutique shopping in Bombay or the challenges of dating someone in the movie industry, but she knew what it was to feel that you would never become fully adult in the country where you lived, would never understand the jokes or master the graces that came so naturally to everyone around you.

7 Kim had been thrilled by the apartment Ashok rented in New York City: a loft on the twenty-first floor of a building just north of Madison Square Park, with views of the Empire State Building. She had never bought new furniture before, and she loved going into Crate and Barrel with Ashok, standing next to him as he selected a bed, a living room set, and a glass-and-steel dining table. He paid no attention to the prices and wanted everything to be as modern and clean as possible. (Kim told Amina that she wished her mother could be there for five minutes and then disappear, just to see where her daughter now lived.) He asked her where they ought to go to find household help, and she laughed at him: she said it would be ridiculous to hire someone to clean what was after all a relatively small space and that, since she wasn't working, she would have plenty of time to do the housework and the shopping herself.

The apartment was only a short subway ride from NYU, but Ashok was displeased with it almost immediately. He thought the small bedroom was claustrophobic and the air-conditioning too strong; he was constantly walking around in a wool sweater. Bathrooms, he thought, ought not to be next to kitchens, and he often used the half bath near the entrance. The apartment was one floor below the penthouse, and Ashok found the sound of the wind oppressive.

He had told her long ago that he was a Brahmin, laughing off this antiquated distinction as if it were an affectation of his grandparents' generation, but Kim couldn't help wondering if this was somehow connected to his obsession with hygiene once they arrived in New

York. The enemy, as it turned out, was not only dirt but clutter: if Kim left a magazine in the bathroom, or papers from work out on the table that served as desk and dining table, Ashok would frown with irritation upon arriving home. She learned to put things away immediately after using them and to wash pots as she cooked, since it was hard for her husband to enjoy a meal if he could see the dirty pots sitting out in the open kitchen. They kept their shoes on a rack just inside the door, and Ashok always went straight to the bathroom, where he took off his socks and stepped into the bathtub, squeezing a drop of antibacterial soap onto each foot and then expertly washing one with the other, using a frantic scrubbing motion. He had taught her to wash her feet that way in India, since they were always wearing sandals, but she noticed that he performed the ritual even more thoroughly in New York, where they both wore shoes and socks.

At first Kim hadn't known what to do with herself during the day, apart from taking care of the house, cooking, and shopping. As a child she had been fascinated by cooking shows, which seemed to depict a realm of luxury and style wholly absent from her mother's worldview. In her first Manhattan apartment—a place on Avenue C shared among four girls—Kim had been the only one of the roommates who cooked, in exchange for a smaller share of the grocery bill. Those girls had been hugely grateful for the casseroles, pastas, and roasts (she was not yet a vegetarian) that Kim would prepare every other day and leave in the refrigerator for whoever got home at whatever time, and she had come to think of herself as a good cook. But of course she'd never learned to make the dishes Ashok missed once they got to New York.

One night her husband told her they were going out on a date, and took her to a formal Indian restaurant on Forty-fourth Street. They had champagne to begin and then a bottle of wine with dinner, and Ashok ordered the dishes as if they were back in Bombay, and might as well have a taste of everything. The waiter was deferential in a way also familiar from Bombay, and she could see Ashok relax into the person he'd been when she'd first fallen in love with him, confident and at ease with his position in the world. At the end of the evening he asked her what was customary to tip in restaurants, and thinking of her own waitressing days, Kim had said 20 percent; it was only when she paid the credit card bill that month (she paid all the bills with Ashok's checkbook) that she saw they'd spent two hundred twenty-five dollars on a single meal.

Although the allowance his parents had given them seemed princely to Kim, once she started managing their finances she immediately saw that Ashok had spent an unreasonable percentage of it on furniture and rent. He talked casually about asking his father for more, but Kim was afraid that would reflect badly on her; she could hear his mother talking about how she was living off of Ashok. She'd always thought that the one useful thing Cathy had taught her was economy: for as long as she could remember, she'd been aware of what everything cost and took almost as much pleasure as her mother in a bargain. She took the train to the old C-Town she remembered from her East Village days, sometimes stopping at the farmers' market in Tompkins Square Park for produce. She found a discount store that catered to students furnishing dorm rooms, where she outfitted their kitchen and discovered certain "storage solutions" that made it easier to keep the apartment the way Ashok liked it. The standard of care her husband required allowed little time for thinking about either the past or the future, and Kim said she felt a satisfaction she'd never before experienced when she heard his key in the lock and knew that everything in the apartment was as he would want it. Occasionally she even thought of Ashok's mother, and wondered if she'd known things about her son that Kim hadn't when she'd given her blessing to their move to New York.

"I'm making him sound like a real pain," Kim said. "But if you met him, you'd understand. It was like, I felt so special when I was with him. Like a princess—like you imagine when you're a kid. It was just a totally different world. I can't believe I've never shown you a picture. Do you want to see one now?"

Amina nodded. Kim had shown her a photo album from her first backpacking trip to India, in which the pictures had been mostly documentary: a naked child selling bananas on the ground in a marketplace; a procession of pilgrims in black loincloths outside an ornamented temple; a mahout on an elephant threading his way through a street dense with rickshaws and the same brightly painted Tata trucks that she knew from home. Now Kim left the album on the shelf and went to her desk, where she started going through a drawer. "I try not to look at this too much," she said. "I get miserable. But showing you is a good excuse."

Amina had hoped for a family picture, one that included Ashok's parents, but Kim had pulled out a single snapshot of the two of them. They were at a sort of public promenade, in front of a grand archway, and you could just see a harbor beyond it. A crowd of Indians stood behind them: tourists, vendors, and the sort of idle, staring young men that Amina was familiar with from home. Ashok had black sunglasses pushed up on his head and was wearing a collarless gray linen jacket. His hair flopped in his face, and he was indeed handsome enough to be a movie actor, with sharp cheekbones and large, liquid black eyes. He and Kim were just about the same height. Kim was wearing a short-sleeved blue dress with a belt and small buttons down the front, unlike any of the clothes Amina had seen in Rochester, as well as a fair amount of lipstick, eyeliner, and mascara—cosmetics that she normally went without. She was smiling at the camera and holding a heart-shaped balloon.

"This was before—"

"Before we got married," Kim said. "It was my birthday that day, and we made love—I thought that was a stupid euphemism before I met him—and then we were just wandering around. We ended up at the Gateway of India, and I wanted to take a picture with one of those tourist photo guys. He usually hated that kind of stuff, but that day he said okay. I was twenty-three."

"And you're still in love with him?"

It was the second time she'd seen Kim cry, but this was less graceful than before. Deep pink blotches came out on her pale skin, and she wiped her nose on her sleeve. "Completely."

"He's very handsome," Amina said diplomatically, although nothing she'd heard about Ashok so far seemed to justify Kim's devotion.

"It was also the sex," Kim said. "To be honest. He was just the only guy who could make me, you know, like every time. This doesn't make you uncomfortable to talk about, does it?"

"No," Amina said, although it was one of those times she would've liked to dismiss her Deshi self entirely, ask it to wait in the hall.

"I mean, I feel like I can tell you this—I've been with a lot of people.

I sometimes wish I hadn't, but it's destructive, hanging on to the past like that. Instead I'd rather think that all those guys were the path I had to take to get to Ashok. And then with him it felt like we were just this deep physical match. Like my body recognized him that day on the film set, before I even turned around to look at him."

Amina was standing by the window, looking down at the few human shapes hurrying past on the sidewalk outside. It was November, and the season had officially changed; according to 13WHAM this morning, the temperature would drop below freezing overnight. When she saw George's car pull up at the curb, she actually blushed, imagining what he would think if he'd been able to hear the conversation they were having.

"He's here," she said.

"Oh my gosh, you think I'm disgusting," Kim said. "I shouldn't have told you all that stuff."

"Not at all," Amina said. "Please don't worry."

"But you do—I can tell."

"I'm happy to have someone to talk with about—family matters," Amina said. Kim looked startled for a moment, and then she burst out laughing. Before Amina could stop her, she was hugging her again.

"I'm so glad we're friends, Amina," she said.

8 Kim had begun her temp job on September 8, 2001. They could use the money, she argued to Ashok, and it would take her mind off everything that had happened in Bombay. It was a small advertising firm on Thirty-first Street, and her responsibilities had mostly to do with documents, which needed to be photocopied and distributed around the office each morning. She was already standing at the copy machine on her third day of work when the first plane hit the tower. There was only one other person in the office, a young account executive named Charlie, whose mother calling from Pittsburgh was the first one to tell him what had happened three miles downtown. Charlie and Kim were looking at the computer, discussing where they might go to see a television, when the boss came in and told them about the second plane. Kim remembered Charlie saying, "That can't be an accident," and Kim asked what it could mean.

"I'll tell you what it doesn't mean," the boss said. "It doesn't mean we're not still getting fucked over on the Patterson account. So let's focus, people."

In fact, Patterson had closed their offices for a week; three days later, when the bridges finally opened, Kim and Charlie's boss had done the same, driving straight out of the city to his brother's house in Englewood, New Jersey.

"Were you scared?" Amina asked. They were in the empty studio after class, cleaning up the towels, water bottles, and stray pieces of clothing the students had left behind. Kim took a soft cloth from a drawer and began polishing two brass incense burners that hung on chains from the ceiling, framing a portrait of the elephant god, Ganesh.

"No," she said. "Not really, to be honest. It sounds awful to say, but it was actually kind of exciting. I don't know how to explain—it didn't feel like something that had happened to me. You know that thing people said, *We are all New Yorkers*? I didn't feel like a New Yorker. Not that I felt Indian or anything, but all the missing persons signs—they didn't seem real to me. I think Ashok was more upset about it than I was. He sealed all our windows with that blue tape—you know, like electricians use—because of the smell. His parents called us every day, and he kept telling me to call my mom. But I figured she thought I was in India, and she wouldn't worry. I mean—I hadn't even called her when we got married."

Two months after the attacks, when she finally did get up the nerve to call, Cathy had collapsed in tears on the phone. She'd said that when she didn't get a call after the first attack on American soil since Pearl Harbor, she'd assumed her daughter was dead.

"I know we haven't been on the best terms," her mother had told her. "But I said to Eileen, 'If she's alive she would call. There's nowhere on earth she could be where she wouldn't hear about this.'"

"But I was the one in Manhattan," Kim told Amina. "Why would I have been worried about her in Rochester? I said that, and then it was just the same old conversation—about how she'd done her best, but it wasn't enough for me." Kim stopped her polishing and stood with the cloth in her hand. Her clothes—a pair of lime-green shorts and a magenta T-shirt with the Devanagari om—were at odds with her somber expression. "Years had passed, but we were still arguing about the same stuff. These patterns repeat themselves, with parents and children—that's another reason I went to India. If I was going to have a family, I wanted it to be totally different from the one I'd had." She lifted her left foot and rested it against the inside of the opposite thigh, standing comfortably on one leg. Behind her Amina could see a heavy, cold rain falling outside two narrow windows to the street.

"It's funny to think I didn't know you then," Amina said. "Or George."

It had been dinnertime in the old Mohammadpur apartment, and the television had been on; they'd learned about it first from the BBC, even before their friends and relatives began to call. Her mother had watched for five minutes and then declared that it was the end of student visas.

"My mother said we might as well stop thinking about the U.S.," she told Kim. "As soon as we heard it on the news. She said my only hope was Europe."

"What about your father?" Kim asked.

"He said that America was going to need Bangladesh for an ally against the terrorists. He was really excited. He said that now the U.S. would finally give up on Pakistan."

"They were both wrong," Kim said.

"Actually my mother was right about the visas—there were fewer of those. The fiancée visas changed right after I got here. It got much harder to come, especially from a Muslim country."

"Has George ever been to the mosque with you?"

"We looked around. There is one place—my cousin at home recommended it. But we've been so busy—we haven't gone." Amina had looked online again this year and seen that the Eid potluck was the night before her calculus final. She knew there would always be an excuse and that it was important just to take the first step, but it was the kind of thing that got harder the longer she waited to do it. She imagined the people she would meet at the ICR—perhaps even other Bengalis—who had joined as soon as they arrived in Rochester and were now part of a genuine Muslim community. What would they say when they heard it had taken her almost two years to visit for the first time?

"You haven't gone at all?"

Amina had the peculiar urge to defend herself, almost as if she were talking to another Muslim—Nasir, for example. "At home women usually aren't permitted in the mosque," she told Kim. "So this isn't different for me."

"But you *can* go here," Kim said. "Don't you want to? I'd love to go with you—I mean, if that's allowed."

"Anyone is welcome," Amina said, because of course it would be wrong to discourage anyone who showed an interest in her faith. "It would be nice if you could be a witness at our wedding—I mean, our Muslim wedding ceremony. We've always meant to do that."

"Oh, Amina!" Kim lifted up on her toes several times, as if her excitement required some corresponding action. "I'd love to! But shouldn't we wait until your parents get here? So they can be part of it?"

Amina stared at Kim. For the first time someone other than herself and her parents had expressed faith in their plan—had, in fact, spoken of it in English as if it were a certainty. She nodded, concealing her emotion because she thought Kim might try to hug her again, and she was never going to get used to the casual frequency of American hugging. She took a paper towel and began wiping the top of the radiator, trying to avoid looking up into Ganesh's oddly human eyes. She couldn't help noticing that the Hindu god was seated on a large gray rat.

9   In March of 2007, Amina passed her driver's test. George took her out to Giorgio's to celebrate the license, as well as the second anniversary of her arrival in America. They were one month shy of another anniversary as well: they didn't talk about it, but this month marked the eleventh since they'd begun trying to have a baby. She would sometimes catch him looking at her with an injured expression, as if he suspected she were preventing a pregnancy on purpose.

She'd gone so far as taking her temperature in the mornings and allowed herself to buy a package of ovulation predictor kits each month. They had become an expensive habit, but George never said anything about them; now, instead of having sex at regular intervals, they obeyed the smiley faces on the plastic sticks. For the first three months, she'd been relieved to get her period, but once it had been half a year her innate urge to succeed took over. George brought up the question of a doctor first, asking if she wanted him to go and be tested. She had the feeling that this was his way of asking her to go, but the thought of an American doctor putting something inside her and looking around was too strange. She couldn't help seeing in their failure to conceive a kind of sign about the other impasse in the marriage: it was now only a little more than a year before she would be allowed to apply for citizenship and sponsor her parents' applications, but she and George were no closer to an agreement on that subject.

"Maybe we should try a little longer," she had told him, and she'd been relieved when he didn't force it.

"It could be stress," he said. "Did you know it takes the average person ten years to adjust to a new country?"

"I don't think adjustment is the problem."

"The first two years are the hardest—according to this website I found. After that it gets much easier."

Whether or not it was a sign she was adjusting, the spring and summer did seem to move faster than previous ones. She learned online that the first stirrings of conception could feel like menstrual pain and that there could even be spotting, and so she refused to believe that she had failed each month until she had soaked through a pair of underpants. She had never particularly noticed pregnant women, in part because they were not so visible in Desh: women tended to stay closer to home, and when they ventured out, their condition was more easily concealed underneath their looser clothing. Here in Rochester they seemed to be everywhere—circling the tract in their jogging clothes, obstructing the aisles of the supermarkets, and arriving in droves for the new prenatal class that an instructor named Stacey was offering on Monday and Wednesday mornings.

It was difficult not to mention this preoccupation to her mother, with whom she talked nearly every day. Her mother was in the habit of calling early in the mornings, before Amina left for Yoga Shanti, to give her a report on whatever had happened in the village the previous day. She had begun visiting a *pir*, a celebrated healer who lived two hours from her nanu's by bus; it was this man, revered as a saint by some of the local people, who had prescribed the tulsi drops her mother believed had finally cured her ulcers. It didn't matter to Amina whether it was the drops themselves that had been effective or her mother's faith in them. The important thing was that her mother was eating and gaining weight.

"You need to continue them regularly, to be sure," Amina had said the last time her mother called. "You'll go for your medical exam before you apply. The doctors are very strict."

"I am cured," her mother said, "one hundred percent. The only problem is my sleeping."

"You still aren't sleeping well?" Her parents had been living in the village more than a year now, and her mother's insomnia had begun soon after they'd arrived. She was afraid, she told Amina, especially at night. She couldn't sleep because she felt that "something was coming." Her mother had always seen things that other people couldn't; she was especially susceptible to ghosts and jinnis, who had appeared to her ever since she was a child. Once, when her mother was only fourteen or fifteen, she had been sitting in her parents' courtyard chopping vegetables when she looked up to see two soldiers standing at the gate in ragged clothes. This was during the war, less than a month after her brother Khokon had been killed, and Nanu hadn't left her bed since she'd heard. Amina's mother didn't scream right away, because she recognized the boys as her distant cousins, childhood playmates of her dead brother. She ran into the house to tell her parents—who were napping under the mosquito net—describing how the elder had been supporting the younger, who wore a bloodstained bandage on the left side of his chest. Her father ran out into the yard, but Nanu knew her daughter had been seeing ghosts: she gave her a hard slap across the face to bring her back to her senses.

When Nanu told the story, she always pointed out that it was a blessing the boys' mother, who had been visiting just two days earlier, hadn't been there: how terrible for her to hear that her sons were standing in the road and then to run out and find only a pair of small black pigs, snuffling in the pile of coconut shells by the gate. Only a week after Amina's mother's vision, the mother of those two boys heard the news that her younger son had died near the Indian border, from a bullet wound just below his heart.

10 George got the news about Cyclone Sidr early, through his Google filter. Reading VOA online sent Amina into a panic—they were comparing it to Bhola, when half a million people had been killed. But when she reached her parents, they assuaged her anxiety. Everyone in Nanu's house was safe, although no one had been able to contact her dadu, her father's father, who was more than eighty years old now and lived alone in Kajalnagar. As soon as it was possible to leave the village, her parents went to find him, traveling sometimes by rickshaw and sometimes on foot. The eleven-kilometer journey took them an entire day: a day in which they saw pots and pans, bedsteads, clothing, and children's toys floating free across the fields. They saw dead bodies, human and animal, beginning to decay in the sun, as well as those animals that had survived by taking shelter on the roofs of partially submerged houses, crying pitifully for food and water. Her mother even reported that they'd spotted delicious shrimp and lobster swimming freely right next to the road, escapees from local fish farms flooded by the storm. She had pointed out that someone's bad luck was another person's dinner.

Her mother's account of the storm left Amina guiltily relieved. She believed that Cyclone Sidr was the "something" that her mother had been predicting, and now that it had passed—sparing her parents, her nanu, and even her dadu—she thought that her mother would start to sleep. Instead she had become even more apprehensive, calling Amina almost every day and insisting on whispering in case there was someone listening, a habit that compounded the unreliability of her parents' cell phone and made her mother almost impossible to hear.

But it wasn't the intermittent reception or even the whispering that exasperated Amina so much as a familiar trick of her mother's: to bring up a subject in such a roundabout way that Amina had to pry it out of her, as if she were the one who'd wanted to discuss it in the first place. It was one thing when she'd lived at home in Desh and had hours to chat with her mother; it was another early in the morning in Rochester, when there were breakfast dishes in the sink, a bus to catch, and eight hours of work and classes ahead of her.

"Never mind," her mother had said yesterday morning. "You're too busy to talk."

"I'm not too busy," Amina said, moving to the counter and keeping the faucet on a trickle, the way the water always came at home, so that her mother wouldn't know she was doing dishes.

"This village is more dangerous than it was when you were here," her mother said. "Plus, everyone knows we're going to America next summer."

The certainty her mother gave the words—"next summer"—was startling. As the months before the citizenship application dwindled, the problem of her parents' emigration took on a sickening urgency. Tell her, Amina thought suddenly: tell her now.

"They know you and George are coming to get us," her mother said.

George doesn't want you to come and live with us.

"They think we're rich."

I can't get pregnant.

"I'm afraid to sleep near the windows. Even your father's worried."

She couldn't say anything, and her cowardice made her sharper with her mother than she would otherwise have been. "Are you talking about thieves?" she demanded.

"Not common thieves—they wouldn't dare come to your nanu's house."

Her mother's evasions made Amina conclude that her father had gotten into trouble again. It seemed implausible that he would risk another business scheme in the year before they planned to apply for their visas, but she knew him well enough not to rule it out. "Something about Abba?"

"No! Your father is not to blame. He's given up all of his projects— he's exhausting himself trying to find the birth and marriage certificates. It's very difficult to get these things here," her mother reminded her, as if Amina were an inexperienced foreigner rather than a person who'd scrambled to collect all of her own visa paperwork only three years earlier.

"I don't want you to worry," her mother continued, before she could say anything. "Especially now."

"Why now?"

"You need to stay calm. Drink plenty of water and don't make the food too spicy. Try not to stand in the doorways—that can cause a difficult labor. And check eggs before you eat them—never eat an egg with a double yolk. That's why your India Aunt had the twins."

Her mother kept talking about the imminent pregnancy and their arrival in America, and Amina let the phone drift slightly below her ear, so she could hear her mother's voice without understanding the words. She turned off the water, and for a moment she was a newcomer again, alone in the house after George had gone to work. The stillness had been so complete that some days she'd wondered whether she could make a noise if she wanted. She'd felt not only invisible but incorporeal and doubted as she made her way from room to room that her feet impressed upon the carpets. She had glanced at herself in mirrors as she passed and was sometimes startled by the familiar image—a skinny girl in a homemade blouse—as if she'd expected the house itself to be blind to her.

She heard her mother pause for an answer. "What?"

"Which way does your bed face?" her mother repeated. "You know your head shouldn't be pointing toward the door."

"I'm not pregnant," Amina said quietly.

"Just in case," her mother said. "You never know!"

That night Amina had thanked God more fervently than usual for her job, which had allowed her to end this conversation on the grounds that she had to shower and dress. If someone had told her in those first lonely days that there would come a time when she wouldn't look forward to phone calls from home, and would even sometimes dread them, she wouldn't have been able to believe it.

11 Just after Thanksgiving, George told her that Annie Snyder was pregnant for the third time. Dan left for work later than George did; she often saw him from the kitchen window on those cold mornings, moving quickly from his house to his car, looking no different now that a pig's heart was beating in his chest. (*Valve,* George corrected her—it's only the valve.) Sometimes she would see Annie waiting on the edge of the lawn with her older boy for the school bus, balancing the younger one on the lump of belly that was already protruding underneath her long down coat.

Amina rode to work with George every day but Thursday, when she took the bus because her shift didn't start until noon. It was on one of those December Thursdays, going for the mail in her own parka and boots, that Amina noticed Annie waving to her. She waved back, and when the school bus pulled away, her neighbor crossed the street to speak to her. The temperature was near freezing under a sharp blue sky, and the old snow was encased in a treacherous layer of ice. Over the last year, Amina had developed superstitions about both cold and physical activity, and in the second half of each month she tried to expend as little energy as possible, staying indoors and letting some of the housework slide. It was ridiculous to think that standing in the cold could prevent a person from becoming pregnant, but she longed for the couch and the warm house, a cup of the FertiliTea Kim had bought her from Lori's Natural Foods Center, which out of embarrassment she'd hidden from George under the sink behind the detergent.

"This is awful, isn't it?" Annie said. "And we still have practically the whole winter to go."

"It was winter when I came," Amina said. "I remember I'd never seen trees without their leaves."

Annie smiled uncertainly. "That's funny—I guess you wouldn't have. Listen—I just wanted to say thank you for what you did when Dan was sick last year. Last night I was lying awake, and I realized we never did. Looking in on the house and everything."

"It was nothing."

"And the flowers and the muffins. George took care of the house, but I know those came from you."

"George took care of it afterward. But the first day it was Kim."

Annie gave her a quizzical look. "Kim Neeland?"

"The flowers were also from her. George thought she would understand the alarm better, so she was the one who went to your house. I didn't do anything except muffins—that was no trouble."

"But the card said from you and George," Annie insisted.

"Did it?" Amina said. "It was so long ago."

She thought the child must be getting cold. Her face was bright pink in the opening of a pink hood, but she looked otherwise unperturbed, already accustomed to weather that Amina would continue to find unnatural for the rest of her life. If she and George ever managed to conceive, would her own child develop the same defenses, or would she shiver and suffer, longing for a climate she had never experienced?

"You're working with Kim at that yoga place, aren't you?"

"Only administration," Amina said quickly. "I don't do any yoga myself."

"Oh, I love yoga. I did it when I was pregnant with the first two, but I'm getting lazy this time around." Annie hesitated for just a second. "But Kim always looks great."

"She's very healthy."

"But she's still not dating anyone?" The child began to fuss, and Annie talked to it in a silly way, kissing its face and shifting it to the other hip. "Do she and George still get along?"

"Yes," Amina said, and because the question seemed to demand some further response: "She's his cousin."

"Well, but she was adopted," Annie said. "Right? I didn't know her well in school, and then she was living here only a couple of months before she moved downtown."

"Here in Rochester?"

Annie looked at her curiously. "I mean when she was living here"—she indicated the house—"with George, before she moved downtown. I remember her trying to plant something one day— delphinium, I think. But she didn't bother to clear the beds the way you did, and you saw they didn't come back. Of course he'd only just bought it in March, so she didn't have time to do much."

"In May," Amina corrected automatically. George had bought the house in May of 2004, four months after they'd met. Kim had once taken refuge with George—long ago, after her breakup with Ashok, when she'd returned from New York City "a mess"—but that was at his old apartment in Brighton. She had never lived in this house, and she certainly couldn't have been living there in the winter and early spring of 2004, when Amina and George had been exchanging their first messages.

Her neighbor was nodding slowly, her arms clasped around the child at her hip. "Well, you know best. But I could've sworn it was March because I was just pregnant with Kyla and I felt awful. Lawson was a terrible two, and I was stuck inside with him, bored out of my mind. I remember when they took the sign down—all of that snow." Now Annie was looking at her with barely concealed eagerness, trying to divine what she knew. "Kim was sweet with Lawson, always spoiling him with toys and stuff. We were worried George would be lonely when she moved out—but then of course he found you."

Some old instinct kicked in, and Amina adjusted her expression. She was grateful suddenly for her skin, which didn't flush in an obvious way. "George is so generous," Amina began, and she was startled to hear her accent returning, as strong as it had been a year ago. Suddenly she sounded like a well-to-do Deshi lady, imperious and blunt—in fact more like her aunt than her mother. "And Kim has such troubles."

"I think you're both very generous," Annie said, glancing again at the house. "I should take this one inside before she freezes." She turned to the child. "Is da little nosy frozen?" The little girl laughed, revealing a set of miniature teeth.

"Please say hello to Dan for us," Amina said, and because she needed Annie to believe that nothing she'd revealed was a surprise, that Amina had been perfectly aware that Kim had been living in this house—*their* house, that George had bought "too soon" in their courtship—she added: "George and I would like to invite you for dinner."

"Oh—we'd love that. It's just a question of sitting. If you know anyone?" Annie added, but Amina shook her head.

"I'm afraid I don't know any babysitters."

12 She took the bus to East Avenue, and then walked to Edgerton Street. She entered the apartment building and climbed the four flights to the door, waiting a moment before she tried the key in the lock. Kim wasn't home. Amina was struck as usual by the blithe disarray of the apartment: the futon bed unmade, strewn with clothes; a dirty mug and plate on the floor; a towel hanging over the

back of a wooden chair. Amina instinctively reached to pick it up, and then stopped. She had often wondered that Kim wasn't more embarrassed about the state of her apartment, given that Amina was a guest: she apologized for it (her "reaction" to years with Ashok) but in an effusive, theatrically self-deprecating way that had never convinced Amina, even when she had found it charming. Now this disregard for propriety struck her as characteristic in a more threatening way.

She knew Kim didn't teach until the afternoon, and so she was probably out shopping. Amina had already decided that she wasn't going in to work—at some point Kim would come back and find her here—if necessary, she could wait all day. Apart from tidying or watering the plants, she had always been careful not to disturb the things in Kim's apartment more than necessary. She was pretty sure Kim wouldn't have noticed, but she had certainly never opened a closet or a drawer. She'd been conscious that Americans protected their privacy more closely than anyone she'd known at home, and that fact had kept her from exploring the apartment as thoroughly as she would have liked.

Now she began with the desk. The picture in the drawer was still there: when she glanced at it, Ashok's expression seemed to have changed. Now there was a slight smirk at the corner of his mouth, as if in wonder at her ignorance. Amina moved into the bathroom, where even the medicine chest became interesting when she pictured its contents scrambled with George's things at home. Apart from a great number of all-natural creams, scrubs and exfoliants, and a sleep aid made from valerian root, there was nothing much to discover, and so Amina moved into the main room. She leafed through a book called *The Yoga of the Yogi* that was sitting out on Kim's desk, and then a date book: either Kim didn't have many engagements, or she was the kind of person who bought a calendar but couldn't remember to write things down. The closet door was open and Amina stepped inside. It wasn't any of the hanging things that caught her attention but a pair of flip-flops—real plastic Bata chappals, the pattern on the sole worn smooth. The shoes were sitting on the highest shelf; if she hadn't noticed them, she might also have missed the brown paper envelope, wedged underneath a pile of sweaters. She had to stretch to reach the envelope, but she didn't hesitate. She felt as if she'd been absolved of any trespass by everything she'd learned in the last twenty-four hours.

Letters were what she'd expected, and so at first she was disappointed. The photographs were printed as a horizontal strip—there were four of them—each inside a black-and-white arc, like the space opened up by the single wiper on the rear window of a car. Each image was dark and grainy, indecipherable, a black oval with a milky center, and it took several moments for Amina to understand that she was looking at a human fetus. The quality of the paper, and of the envelope itself, was much finer than you would find at home; Amina thought the clinic where Kim's mother-in-law had sent her must have been a place exclusively for rich people. She was replacing the pictures carefully in the envelope—calculating that they must now be eight years old—when she noticed the information printed in a minuscule font along the margin:

NEELAND, KIM 26   RAB4-8-D/OB   MI 1.2   FETAL DX CENTER OF ROCHESTER
GA=8W6D   8.9CM/1.4/25HZ   TLS 0.1   04/17/2004 11:45:12 AM

Amina stared at the date, wondering if she were making some kind of obvious mistake. But the facts were printed clearly on the page. If these numbers were correct, Kim had gotten pregnant in February of 2004—right here in Rochester. A month later, George had decided to buy a three-bedroom house in a genteel suburb known for its excellent school district. He had moved in immediately, bringing along his pretty, eccentric cousin, who had planted delphinium in the overgrown beds around the house, and then perplexed the neighbors by leaving before summer had even started.

If Kim had been eight weeks pregnant in April, she might have discovered the pregnancy at the beginning of March—right around the time that George stopped writing to Amina. It crossed her mind that Kim might have gotten pregnant with someone else's child, and even that George might have taken her in under those circumstances. But the fact of the house made that easy explanation impossible to believe. She remembered the way Annie had looked at her in the driveway, and the way she'd spoken of George and Kim as if they'd been a couple. During that ten-week break, when Amina was working up the courage to go back on AsianEuro, they had been setting up a life together.

And then something had happened. It was hard to believe Kim would've had another abortion, if she were telling the truth about the way she'd felt the first time. Had she miscarried? And if so, how could George have resumed writing to Amina immediately afterward? Why would he have gone on AsianEuro in the first place, if he were already involved with his cousin?

It had been more than two years since she'd sat in Kim's apartment for the first time. Her memories shuffled and reordered themselves like the numbers on her parents' old flip clock, baldly revealing their humble mechanics. From that first visit, George and Kim had been acting out a drama for her benefit, and now she saw that the pretense stretched even further back. Who knew? she wondered. Had Annie guessed what had happened, or had she simply thought George and Kim had a romance that didn't work out? Did George's mother know, and did Cathy? There was more to Cathy's antagonism than simple bigotry, if she'd really hoped to settle her flighty daughter with someone as solid and dependable as George. More disturbing, Amina could now explain how warmly Eileen had welcomed her, a stranger about whom she knew nothing—if she'd thought any alternative was better than the one at hand.

She was sitting on the futon with the envelope of pictures in her lap when she heard the key in the lock. She nearly cried out, but controlled herself; instead it was Kim who started and gasped.

"Amina—you scared me! I mean, you're welcome anytime—it's just, Lucas said you were sick. I'm glad to see you, actually—I was just at the market and they had all this great—"

But she had seen the envelope. She set two cloth grocery bags carefully on the kitchen linoleum and her keys on the counter. Then she turned back to Amina and smiled.

"Can I make you a cup of tea?" Kim was wearing kneesocks with imitation fur boots that laced up her calves and a long, white sweater with wooden buttons. In place of a knit scarf, she wore a brightly colored embroidered shawl, knotted so many times that her hair stood out wildly around her shoulders.

"No, thank you."

Kim glanced at the envelope, and back at Amina. "It wasn't serious. I mean, in spite of what you're holding. I always knew he didn't really want to marry me—if it came down to it." Her voice had a strained quality that Amina had never heard before.

"But he asked you." Amina kept her eyes on her plain brown socks, wishing suddenly she hadn't removed her shoes.

"He's a gentleman," Kim said. "I was so screwed up, you know, after I got back. It happened the first time right after I got to Rochester, when I was staying with him in Brighton. And then, you know, every once in a while after that—the way it is with those things."

A flush was creeping from Kim's neck to her ears. If George had made Kim pregnant without even trying, the failure to conceive was certainly Amina's fault. The worst thing was that Kim knew it, too.

She looked down at her engagement ring—to which Cathy had reacted so pointedly. She tried to keep her voice neutral, but it came out a strained whisper:

"Did he offer you this ring?"

"Oh, God—no," Kim said. "Of course he knew I wouldn't have worn it. And really, we were just getting something out of our systems. I'd never gotten over Ashok, and George knew that. But he was thinking of marrying and having a family. It all started as a game— I used to tease him. I said we should find him a real wife. We looked at Match and eHarmony, but you know, you have to register and everything. We picked AsianEuro because you don't have to log in—and you can look at all the girls for free."

George had pointed out the computer to Amina as soon as she'd arrived, the desk where he'd sat to e-mail her, and it had been thrilling to see for the first time the place she had hazily pictured in her mind for all of those months. Now she amended the picture to include Kim standing just over his shoulder, her unbound hair brushing his wrist, her skin smelling of scented oil. Had she been the one to click the mouse on the attachment Amina had been so embarrassed and so excited to send: the picture of herself in red lipstick, modeling Ghaniyah's red silk sari? If it had been a game, then hadn't it also been a kind of foreplay between them—looking at the desperate girls from halfway around the world together?

"A *game*."

"Well, but not afterward," Kim hurried on, "I mean, I didn't even know he'd continued it, after I moved out. I didn't know until my mom told me George was going to Bangladesh to meet a girl."

She remembered the note that touched her so deeply—about his own hesitancy—and how their correspondence had intensified suddenly after that. It wasn't hard to imagine George seeing one avenue closing and moving unsentimentally to pursue another. After having written those e-mails, and received a favorable response, he must have reasoned that it made sense to seek a return on his initial investment, rather than beginning again with someone new. He'd needed to justify his period of silence (and his house), and so he'd come up with an explanation. He might have been so eager to forget the recent past that he'd even convinced himself.

"You wanted to have the child with George?"

"I thought about it," Kim said. "At first." She shifted from one foot to the other, looking around the apartment as if its condition were a misfortune that had befallen her, over which she had little control. "You know, they were always disappointed in me—my mom and Aunt Eileen and everyone. Eileen used to say I had potential, if I would just apply myself to something. But after a while even she stopped expecting anything from me—I guess I stopped myself. George was the only one who thought I could do anything, stick with anything. He kept telling me what a great mother I was going to be."

Amina stared straight ahead. If there was one thing she was not going to do, it was feel sorry for Kim.

"But it started to drive me crazy. When it first happened, I said I was going to take something. The morning-after pill, we call it."

"Plan B."

Kim looked surprised. "That's right. Anyway, George was completely against it. He's more conservative than he lets on, you know. He'd already been looking to move, and then he found the house—and a month later we were moving in there. All I could think about was this *thing* inside me, getting bigger every day. After a couple of weeks I wouldn't get out of bed, and he told me I had to go to the doctor. He literally dragged me to the car and sat there in the waiting room, like he thought I was going to run away or something. It wasn't until I got in the office that I realized I could make the decision on my own. I signed the papers, and then there was nothing he could do."

"You had another abortion?"

Kim was still standing by the counter where she'd put the bags, as if it were Amina's apartment and she were waiting for an invitation to sit down. She didn't answer the question.

A part of Amina wanted simply to walk out, but there was another, stronger part of her that needed to understand.

"I found these," she said. "I was looking at them—I thought they were from India."

Kim was already shaking her head. "Oh—I don't have those."

"You told me you kept them."

"I don't have them here. And I mean, no offense, but if I'd wanted you to see them, I would've shown them to you. Or left them out on the table. What were you doing—going through my closet?"

Amina was prepared to defend herself, but she'd gotten better at determining what was sincere and what was a performance, and she thought the irritation in the other woman's voice sounded false. Kim had hidden her face behind a curtain of blond hair, bending to remove first her boots and then the long wool socks.

"You felt sorry about Ashok's child—but not George's? You didn't care about getting rid of that one?"

Kim stood up, biting her lip in a childish way. Her expression was the same one Amina remembered from the day they'd gone shopping at the health food store: a defensive wariness at odds with the way she ordinarily presented herself.

"I only did it once. And who are you to judge?"

"What about India?"

Kim's eyes got wide. "I wasn't pregnant in India—okay? I made that up."

"You—*what*?"

Kim took one of her yogic deep breaths, adopting an expression of patient forbearance, and came out of the doorway into the room. She dropped cross-legged onto a bright cushion, wrapped her arms around her legs, and put her chin on her knees.

"I used to imagine what it would be like to have a baby there, but

Ashok wasn't ready yet. I thought they all might get to like me more, once we had a child."

Amina was still struggling to reconcile the truth with what she'd believed for almost two years. "But you never got pregnant."

"I used to slip up a little, but he was insanely careful. There would've been no way."

"George wasn't careful?"

Kim shrugged. "George wants a family."

Amina's lungs closed up, and it was hard to breathe. She felt as if someone were walking on her chest in heavy boots.

Kim stretched her legs out in front of her, pushing her hair back from her face with one hand. "And honestly? I guess there was a part of me that wanted to tell you. George was completely against it, of course, and his mom didn't even want me to meet you—that's why I didn't come to any of the wedding stuff. She and my mom didn't know about the pregnancy, but they knew we'd moved in together." Kim looked at her earnestly, as if everything that had come before might soon be forgotten. "But I thought if there had been a way just to tell you straight out, you'd understand."

Amina thought she recognized what Kim was doing. She'd noticed it ever since she'd arrived in America, not only in life but on television. You might cheat, steal, lie, but if you confessed, you could be instantly forgiven—as if the bravery it took to admit it made the thing itself all right.

Kim glanced absently at the table and picked up a wooden necklace with a saffron silk tassel. She fiddled with the beads, threading them through her fingers, keeping her eyes on the ground. Suddenly Amina hated her.

"You thought I'd understand."

Kim smiled in a relieved way. "Yeah. I mean—I always knew you and I would understand each other."

"You thought I'd understand about you and George—living together and getting pregnant and everything."

Kim's expression changed, and she looked like she was about to speak. But Amina had dropped the photos on the futon and was moving blindly toward the door.

"Amina!" Kim called after her, but she picked up her shoes and hurried down the steps, grabbing the railing to keep from slipping in her stocking feet, so that at least Kim wouldn't see the expression on her face.

13 She didn't remember until she was on the bus going home that George was supposed to pick her up at Kim's that afternoon. She called as soon as she knew he'd gone into his afternoon meeting and left a message saying that she'd come home early from Yoga Shanti, since she wasn't feeling well. When he got home that evening, she was waiting for him in the kitchen.

"You're feeling better?" He removed his parka, looking at her with more than the usual amount of concern.

"Not really."

"Is it your stomach?"

"Yes," Amina said.

"Nausea?"

Suddenly she understood him. "Since about ten this morning. But I'm not pregnant."

"Are you sure?"

"*Yes.*"

George stepped back. "I'm sorry," he said. "I thought . . ."

She had been practicing what she would say all afternoon, but now that the time had come, she couldn't begin.

"Look," he said gently. "I know you don't like doctors. But it could be something very simple. They have things they can do to help us—I'll go, too. It could be me, now that I'm getting older."

"You were fine four years ago."

"What?" He was looking in the cabinet for the tortilla chips, which he'd finished yesterday. It occurred to her that this wasn't a conversation she could've had in English a year ago.

"Otherwise why did you buy this big house?"

George turned slowly to face her. His left hand, with the gold ring, gripped the countertop. "Because I hoped to meet you."

"But you bought the house in March."

"I told you when I bought the house."

"You told me May."

"I told you as soon as I knew we were serious. I always wanted a family."

"Did you want a family with Kim?"

"*What?* Jesus—who've you been talking to?"

"I've been talking to Annie," Amina said.

"Annie," George repeated. "But Annie—"

"She didn't know about Kim's pregnancy. I found that out on my own."

George frowned at his shoes, which he'd neglected to take off at the door for the thousandth time. They were brown loafers, narrower at the toe, with worn places where you could see his broad feet deforming the leather. She turned away, taking a package of chicken parts from the refrigerator.

"Do you have to cook tonight?"

"It's already defrosted. I have to make it now."

George waited, sitting on the couch without turning on the television. He'd switched his beer for a caffeine-free Coke. When dinner was almost ready, he got up without her asking and put the Brita water pitcher on the table.

"I wanted to tell you," he said when they sat down. "At the very beginning I wanted to tell you. But I was afraid you'd stop writing to me."

"When you stopped writing to me."

"What would you have wanted me to do when she got pregnant?" George's voice rose in frustration. "I thought I'd better try to make it work. You didn't just talk to Annie, did you—it was Kim. What did she tell you? Did she say I was in love with her?"

"She said you were getting it out of your system."

For a second George looked relieved.

Amina's face got hot. "And that you and she were playing a game."

"I didn't say I'd never been involved with anyone else," George said. She looked at him.

"But I misled you about Kim. I'm sorry about that."

"Not misled—you *lied* to me. You stopped writing, and I knew you had someone else. I wasn't stupid—but then you said it wasn't that. You said it was because you were buying this house—for us!"

They were still standing over the table, as if the meal had been prepared only for show. The dishes steamed convincingly.

"How long did she live in the house, George?" His name sounded strange in her mouth. In almost thirty years of marriage, her mother had never said her father's name.

"Only two months. Until she—until she had the abortion. Otherwise it would've taken even less time. We used to fight about everything—nothing like you and me."

"And so—in this game you played together—she helped you pick me."

George jerked his face away, shutting his eyes for a second. She could see the faint, boyish freckles at his temples. "It wasn't like that."

"Not for me."

"Not for me either—I started thinking about you all the time, especially after you sent the picture. I felt guilty about it."

"Guilty for what?"

George didn't say anything.

"Your game was my whole life."

He shook his head. "She's a witch—that woman. She likes to cause trouble." His expression was frightened, pleading. "My mother told me not to mention Kim to you at all, but—"

"My mother said not to tell things, too. But I did tell you everything."

George took off his glasses, brushed one hand over his face, and replaced them without wiping the lenses. He looked at her. "I was going to tell you the rest after you got here. But then Kim and I patched things up—we talked after I came back from Bangladesh. I told her I'd asked you to marry me, and she was really happy for us. She said not to say anything—I guess she was afraid you might not come." George hesitated. "I was afraid."

She looked at her husband and understood that he was the kind of person for whom a lie only counted if it was said out loud. At the same time she could sit in the places of her relatives, who would point to all the concrete evidence that she'd been duped. She even could see the situation from Kim's perspective, believing that once she and Amina got to be friends, they could all coexist peacefully in Rochester. The only people she couldn't bear to imagine were her parents. When she thought about going home, disgraced, it wasn't her own shame but the thought of their despair that paralyzed her—knowing they'd let her go for nothing.

When they went upstairs, George asked whether she wanted him to sleep in the other room.

"I will," she said, and she could see immediately that he'd thought she would say no. He was genuinely frightened now that she would leave him, and she wondered whether he thought she would really consider going home. He touched her awkwardly on the shoulder and disappeared into their bedroom.

She went into the room across the hall and lay down on her back on the blue quilted bedspread, remembering how she'd admired it when she first arrived. The stuffed panda George's mother had brought her still sat on top of the dresser, its fur stiff with dust. Now she got up and retrieved it; she had the urge to embrace something inanimate. She wondered what had really been going through her mother-in-law's mind when she'd left it here for Amina. Even if Eileen hadn't known about Kim's pregnancy, what had she thought about a foreign fiancée moving in less than a year after her niece moved out? How had she and Cathy felt when they discovered that their children—the stolid introvert and the wayward gypsy—were living together? Amina thought that Cathy would've been secretly pleased, and pretended the opposite, whereas Eileen would've done everything in her power to point out the perils of such a relationship to George.

She held the bear as the light under the door went dark: George had turned off his lamp. After a while she found that it wasn't Kim and George she was thinking about so much as Ashok. In particular there was something Kim had told her one windy January day, when Amina hadn't been able to face the wait in the freezing bus shelter. Kim had taken her back to the apartment, where she had been in the midst of organizing her closet, weeding out things she no longer wore. Occasionally she would offer something to Amina, but they were such different sizes that almost nothing fit.

"After he left I tried to figure out what had done it. I mean, I knew he was unhappy—but I figured there had to be something specific."

"The straw that broke the camel's back," Amina had said, pleased to supply the idiom.

At that time in Manhattan, Kim told Amina, there were all kinds of people too frightened to take the trains. The fact that the attacks hadn't happened on the subway, but in an entirely unpredictable location 110 stories in the air, didn't matter; even Kim, relatively untouched by the disaster, found that her heartbeat sped up and that she exchanged glances or even a nervous joke with the other passengers when the train stopped in the tunnel. Ashok was of the opinion that the subways were actually safer now than they'd ever been, and so Kim was surprised one morning to see him setting off in running shoes to walk to school. He had a thing about sneakers—what he called trainers—he didn't believe they should be worn at any time other than during sporting activities. He had a very clean white pair that he used to wear in India when they went to the Willingdon Club for tennis; at first he had attempted to give her lessons, but Kim had shown no aptitude and had preferred to sit on the sidelines watching him play with friends. Finally he had told her that it looked strange, her sitting on the court like that, and that she ought to go and have a lemonade with some of his friends, young people who could always be found in the club's bar or café, involved in serious conversations the import of which Kim invariably failed to grasp.

When she asked him about the sneakers, he told her he was no longer taking the subway but wouldn't say why. She had pressed him, and he said it wasn't what she thought; he wasn't scared. He had said that she had no idea what it was like for him to live in this city. But because her idea of their relative positions was so firmly fixed—Ashok with his family and his houses and his Cambridge education, and herself, perpetually struggling to keep up, with no advantage other than the way she looked—she found it hard to credit this idea of her husband as a second-class citizen.

"Okay," she said finally, in the midst of another argument. "Give me an example. Has anyone said anything directly to you, or is it just the way you think people are looking at you? Because everyone's looking at everyone these days—we can't help it. You've said it yourself—Americans are such babies. It's been so long since anything happened to us."

And that was when he'd told her about the Bangladeshi. Ashok had been waiting for the subway a few weeks earlier, when a young South Asian man in an ill-fitting suit and a bright purple tie had approached him on the platform. The man had begun in Hindi and, when Ashok had stopped him to say he didn't speak the language well, had tried Bangla before switching uncertainly to English. (Ashok had assumed the man was a Bengali from India, and it was only later that he had the leisure to discover his true origins.) The man asked Ashok his shoe size and whether by any chance he knew the corresponding European size. Ashok knew his European size, but the pair he was wearing was one Kim had bought for him after their arrival in New York; he politely told the man that he had no idea about American shoe sizes.

This politeness, Kim said, was not quite authentic, but you would have had to know Ashok to hear the condescension in his voice. Kim had begun to explain what the man had wanted, but Amina had known already. This was a man exactly like her father, only much more successful—a man who had come close to realizing her father's lifelong import-export dream. He had made it to America with suitcases full of Bangladeshi shoes and needed the correct sizing information before he tried to interest local retailers. Perhaps the size conversion was only a pretext to start a conversation; if he talked to as many prosperous South Asians as he could find, he might eventually discover a fellow Bengali with the connections to help realize the entrepreneurial fantasies that had brought him here. No doubt he had a family sequestered in some familiar part of Dhaka, waiting for the great and only miracle of their lives: for those suitcases full of shoes to be transformed into American dollars.

"Could you look?" the man had asked. He would have asked quietly, in the baldly plaintive tones of the desperate, easily casting off his own dignity in front of a man he'd never see again.

Amina pictured the handsome young man in the photograph and could see the expression of concealed distaste, the moment of hesitation, when he was faced with the Deshi salesman. At the same time she knew what must have happened next even before Kim told her: a person brought up as Ashok had been was of course unable to refuse a request from a stranger. He bent down and removed one shoe, lifting the foot in its clean sock just slightly so as not to touch the subway floor. At that moment (and here was where Amina's imagination failed her) three New York City police officers had arrived, sprinting across the platform, shouting warnings and frisking the men as a curious crowd looked on. Both Ashok and the Bengali were instructed to remove their shoes and walk the rest of the way through the station in their socks; it was a day that had alternated between rain and sleet, turning the cement platform into a kind of slop sink for the collected filth of downtown sidewalks. By the time they reached the street, where they were shoved into a waiting car, this cold and greasy mixture had seeped between Ashok's toes and ruined the cuffs of his trousers. He had waited six hours to be questioned by two detectives for twenty minutes and released at 4:30 p.m. with an apology for "any inconvenience" and a joking reminder to keep his clothes on in the subway. He had not learned the fate of the salesman.

When Kim got back to the apartment that evening, Ashok was already there, freshly showered and dressed, calm and unusually solicitous of her. He hadn't told her about the incident immediately, and she'd enjoyed his mood that night without questioning it. Many weeks later, when she had come home to find a note in an envelope centered on the bedside table between the telephone and the lamp, she thought it must have been that November afternoon that he'd decided.

Ashok left just before Christmas, and the holidays passed for Kim in a daze of grief. She continued to go to work, but spent the rest of her waking hours in bed or on the couch; Ashok had left enough rent money for December and January, and although she knew she should get out by the thirty-first and save the twenty-six hundred dollars, she was incapable of taking the steps necessary to accomplish it. Something had happened to her stomach after he left, and unless she ate the blandest foods, she suffered diarrhea and vomiting; she figured she was saving some money by existing on a diet of Top Ramen and ginger ale. The sickness was helpful, she'd told Amina, because it was often the only thing that got her up from the couch.

They hadn't socialized in New York, and outside of work she'd known only one person—the woman who'd traveled with her to India the first time. Waking up from a nap late one Saturday afternoon, something had possessed her, and she called information; miraculously her friend had been listed and had answered the phone on the second ring. She'd been thrilled to hear from Kim and had immediately invited her to a club in the East Village the following night. The next morning Kim had showered—taking perverse pleasure in the state of the bathtub, which had not been cleaned since Ashok had left—and gone to Cheap Jack's, picking out a white-and-gold vintage dress, a cream-colored wool jacket with a fur collar, and a pair of gold stiletto sandals. She had gone for a manicure and spent almost three hours dressing and making herself up. She was aware that the look, a kind of 1940s Hollywood glamour, was one that would have particularly appealed to Ashok; it was cheering to pretend that she was dressing up for him.

She didn't have the money for it, especially after the morning's expenditures, but she took a cab; when she arrived, she saw her old acquaintance standing in line outside with a group of young people, all of them dressed in dark jackets and distressed jeans. She told the driver to let her out on the next block, where she walked until she found a bar. She stayed for three hours and was approached again and again; even through the haze of alcohol, she could see how remote these male creatures were from Ashok. She managed to walk to Union Square when her money was finished and take the 6 train to the apartment, where she collapsed just inside the door. Once in the night she woke up to vomit, not quite making it to the bathroom, and then dragged herself to the couch.

It was the following day, a cold January morning at around eight o'clock, that her cousin George—an early riser who would already have been up for several hours—called to check in, as if he somehow knew it was time for her to come home.

14 In the morning George went to the basement to use the neglected Bowflex, and then Amina heard the noise of the shower. She went to the kitchen in her robe and fixed coffee and

breakfast. When he came down, dressed for work in a green-and-white-striped shirt and belted khaki trousers, she put the bowls on the table and went back to the sink to clean up.

"I was thinking," George said.

Amina prepared herself for another apology. She wished he would simply be quiet and go to work.

"I mean, I've been thinking for a while—I don't see why your parents shouldn't stay here."

Amina was standing over the sink. She was wearing her old white bathrobe, which she had brought from home, and which was too light for this time of year. She could feel gooseflesh on her arms.

"They could stay in the bigger room, but they could use the bathroom downstairs. I mean, so they could have their own."

"You're only saying that because of all of this," she told George, resuming the washing up in the sink.

George turned around in his chair. "Will you leave that, for God's sake!" He knew the way she felt about swearing. "I mean, will you come here please, so that we can talk?"

She left the kitchen and sat down at the place opposite. George's pallor and the puffiness of his eyes didn't evoke any feelings of compassion, nor did she take pleasure in his obvious distress. He looked to her like a stranger, and she marveled at the fact that they had spent nearly three years living together as husband and wife.

"It doesn't have to do with any of this. It's because we slept in two rooms last night." George was looking at her earnestly, both hands on the table moving slowly closer to her own. "You were right. We have the space. It's more practical."

His face, newly shaved, looked young and uncharacteristically hesitant. What a strange thing, she thought, to find out one day that you had built your whole life on a mistake, and the next to discover that this fact would allow you to have your dearest wish. She wondered if this was a unique predicament, something related to the unusual circumstances of her life, or a more general human condition.

These were the places her mind went, but Amina wasn't debating. If George was offering, there was no question that she had to accept.

"If I tell them, you can't change your mind."

Cold squares of watery light crept across the table, picking out the worn places in her bathrobe, the reddish gold hairs on George's arm.

"I won't change my mind."

"They'll come as soon as I get my citizenship," she said. "They won't have to wait."

George nodded, almost eagerly.

"I still want a baby," she told her husband, who was gripping his coffee mug as if to keep his hands steady.

"So do I. Of course I do."

"And I want to get married again. I want to have the Muslim ceremony. I feel sorry that we didn't do it. Also for what I promised my mother."

"About our . . . about not sleeping together before the wedding, you mean?"

Amina wished she weren't wearing her bathrobe. Her hair was frizzy from sleep, and she hadn't yet changed her underwear; she felt she was at a disadvantage, sitting across from George in his pressed shirt and trousers.

"My mother wanted us to wait for both ceremonies, and we didn't even wait for one."

George looked as if he were trying to keep from smiling.

"What's so funny?"

"Nothing." He reached across the table and took her hands. Then he stood up, raising her out of her seat so that he could hug her. "It's just that I'm so glad you're not angry. Do you want to go to the ICR this weekend? We can talk to the imam and fix a date."

Amina allowed herself to be hugged. She waited for George to sit down again.

"No," she said. "I don't want to do it until my parents come. I want them to see it."

"Whatever you want," George said.

"You can still sleep in our room."

George looked puzzled. "Where else would I sleep?"

"I mean before the wedding. Except I want to use the other one."

George sat back down. "You don't want to sleep together anymore?"

"Right," Amina said. "Not until we're really married."

"How can we have a baby, if we don't—?"

"I don't want to have a baby until my parents are here to help me."

George was quiet for a long time. He played with the salt and pepper shakers his mother had given them, made to look like tree stumps.

"It's December," he said finally. "It'll be eight months before they could get here—at the earliest."

"Yes."

"My God, Amina! We're *married*."

"Your God," Amina said. "Not mine."

Citizens

1 In February Kosovo declared its independence from Serbia; the U.S. government projected a $410 billion deficit for 2008; and the French president married a supermodel. There was a rash of violent burglaries in neighboring Penfield, and the New York Giants won the Super Bowl. And then, one Friday late in the month, when a thin sheet of ice covered the thermometer outside the kitchen window so it was impossible to read, her husband came home to tell her he'd lost his job.

Amina didn't have class on Fridays. It was the middle of the morning, and she was sitting at the computer working on an essay when she heard the kitchen door open. She called out in fear, thinking of the Penfield burglaries; but as soon as she saw his face, she knew. It was as if she'd suddenly turned a corner at an ordinary Rochester intersection and, instead of another street of neat lawns and houses, had discovered an unpaved lane criss-crossed with electrical wires, a dog nosing in the dust, a clutch of little boys playing *dung guli* at the edge of an open sewer.

George got three weeks of severance pay, and then he registered for unemployment. He would get four hundred and five dollars a week, just for filling out a form online. He told her that when his father had lost his job at Kodak in 1974, he had had to go down to the office on Union Street, where occasionally an acquaintance would walk by and spot him standing in line on the sidewalk. He said that he was grateful for the privacy of the modern system; a check was deposited in their account every week, and no one but Amina saw him sitting and filling out the form.

Amina was working again: she'd been hired by the Monroe Avenue

Starbucks a few days after Christmas. She got fewer hours than she had at Yoga Shanti and made slightly less money, but when classes began after the break she was able to walk between work and school. Her manager was a friendly young man named Keith, with bright blue eyes, a shaved head, and a gold tooth that glinted in the back of his mouth when he spoke, who remembered all the customers' names and the way they liked their drinks prepared. Amina had never gone back to Yoga Shanti, but had left a voice mail for Lucas explaining that her husband's schedule had changed and that it was no longer convenient for him to drop her at the studio. Lucas had called back to say he was sorry she was leaving, and even offered that she might come back if George's schedule should change again. She wondered if Kim had given him a fuller explanation, but the calm and even way that Lucas spoke made it impossible to know.

For months she'd been afraid of running into Kim in the drugstore or the supermarket or the mall, but gradually it became obvious that in Rochester such an unexpected meeting was unlikely. They did their marketing in Pittsford, and the Starbucks where Amina worked was in Brighton; especially once George lost his job, there was no reason for them to go downtown at all. In Desh you would be almost certain eventually to meet a relative or neighbor with whom you had a feud; spaces were smaller, services more limited, and everyone was in one another's business. Quarrels at home were explosive, public, and necessarily brief. In Rochester, Amina thought it might be possible to stay angry for a lifetime.

When she moved into the spare bedroom, she had suggested that she pay George rent out of her salary. George had angrily rejected that idea, and so she'd liquidated her old bank account. There was no need for it now that her parents were coming to live with them. She continued to send them half of each paycheck but deposited the rest, with the result that when George was laid off, their balance was higher than it had ever been.

"We can manage for ten months on our savings," he told her. "Especially if we're careful. After that we'll have to think about selling the house."

She had scanned and sent her parents a copy of her Coffee Passport: a green paper booklet strikingly similar to her old Deshi passport, with a circular insignia bearing the legend "Starbucks Coffee" in place of the "Government of the People's Republic of Bangladesh." She included a printout of *Fortune*'s "100 Best Companies to Work For," with Starbucks at number 29, but she couldn't take pleasure in it herself. What did it matter that she had gotten a better job when George was no longer being paid?

George said that there was no point in quitting MCC now, since they had already paid for the spring and summer quarters. She was taking English 101 and statistics, and both classes would continue through the summer; she planned to study for her citizenship exam at the same time. She would get her American passport in July, and her parents would apply for their immigrant visas. If all went well, she could travel to Bangladesh as soon as her classes were finished in August to bring them back.

Of course all of that had been decided when George still had a job. She went through the blue folder of forms that she'd printed out months ago and then back to the USCIS website to look at the federal poverty guidelines, a form she hadn't bothered even to open the first time. Because Amina made too little to convince USCIS that her parents wouldn't require federal assistance, George had been prepared to file something called an affidavit of support. George's former salary had been more than three times the amount required for a sponsor.

Now she saw that a household of two was required to make 125 percent of the federal poverty guidelines, which worked out to $18,212. Had George lost his job in the second half of the year, the forms would've been filed, and no one at USCIS would've had to know about it. As it was, form I-864A, the Contract Between Sponsor and Household Member, required that he list his current annual salary. Amina immediately calculated that unless George found a job in the next few months, their estimated household income for 2008 was likely to be close to the minimum.

"You don't want them to question it," George said, when she showed him the form.

"I could quit MCC and try to get more hours at Starbucks," Amina said, but George thought that was impractical.

"It's bureaucracy," he said. "Pure and simple. Anyone who met us would realize that your parents won't be on welfare."

"They live very simply," Amina said. "You won't be able to believe it. And if my mother does the cooking, we'll spend less."

George waved this away with an irritated swipe of his hand. He was sitting on the couch, where he'd been reading the *Democrat and Chronicle*, and Amina marveled at the change in him. He'd been using the Bowflex regularly since he'd lost his job—he told her offhandedly one day that he'd lost fifteen pounds—but she didn't think it had improved his appearance. His waistline was trimmer, certainly, but his face looked almost too thin, and there were purple smudges underneath each eye.

"I could ask Jess I guess."

She knew that George's cousin had a good job as an administrator at Strong Memorial, where her husband, Harold, was a pediatric surgeon. George and Jessica got along well, and although he'd told Amina on several occasions that he couldn't stand Harold, it seemed like a perfect solution.

"*She'd* do it in a heartbeat."

"He won't?"

"He will—and he'll never let us forget it."

Amina was enormously relieved. She thought she never would forget it, whether or not Harold took pains to remind her.

"I'll have to find a way to thank them," she said. "Maybe we could invite them to dinner?"

George didn't say anything.

"I could make something special—tandoori prawns or that lamb pizza you liked?"

George made a disgusted sound. "I don't want to have Harold to dinner."

"Or maybe your mother would invite all of us?"

"Wonderful," George said.

Sarcasm had been the hardest thing to get in English; it had taken her at least a year to catch that tone in George's voice that meant he was saying the opposite of what his words suggested. She hardly ever had to ask him to repeat himself now, and she no longer made the kind of mistake that had amused him in the past. Communication was supposed to be the secret to a successful marriage, but she sometimes thought things had been better between them when they'd understood each other less.

"It would be better than having it here, wouldn't it?"

"Better and better," George said. He got up from the couch and went down to the basement, where he was replacing some mildewed insulation. It was a job he would once have hired someone else to do. As she listened to the sounds he made in the basement—the clanking of tools being removed from their box, then a pause, and then the weary resumption of hammering—she thought of what it must've been like for him, moving into this house. He would have been so excited, thinking of the tiny baby growing inside of Kim—8.9 centimeters, according to the ultrasound—and all he would've been able to do was to get out his toolbox. He would've fixed everything that needed fixing, and many things that didn't. He might've even had projects he hadn't shared with Kim, sketches on scrap paper: a swing, a doll's house. She thought of the moment in the doctor's office, when Kim had told him, and then the trip to the clinic—how he would have sat there staring at his own idle hands, wondering at the turn things had taken, utterly powerless to change her mind.

She looked back at the USCIS website's list of "family-based forms": the I-134, which Jessica would be required to fill out if she agreed to be her parents' financial sponsor, was free, but the two I-130 forms Amina had to file separately for her parents each came with a $355 processing fee. Now that he had lost his job, George was the only person who wouldn't have to sign a single form—although he was the person who would actually support Amina's parents once they arrived. None of it made any sense, which George would say was typical of any kind of bureaucracy. But Amina had expected better of America.

One afternoon, when George's mother called to see how they were doing, Amina decided to explain her predicament.

"That's criminal," Eileen said. "You and George, of all people. Of course Jess will do it. And I've been wanting to talk to you about a get-together anyway. I thought we could do it in July, as soon as you get your citizenship. The only problem is my kitchen."

George's mother had been planning to renovate her kitchen since the fall, but the work was perpetually delayed. She was having vari-ous travails with tiles and appliances, which she sometimes discussed with Amina when she called and George wasn't at home. Eileen "thanked her lucky stars" that she had Bob, who was a retired con-tractor and would be able to intervene if something went wrong.

"What if we did it at Cathy's house?" Eileen proposed. "I'd do the cooking, so you won't have to worry about bacon bits in the salad or anything."

Amina was quiet. At Christmas they had excused themselves from Cathy's church-group potluck, saying they'd never hosted Eileen and Bob for the holiday at their house, and Amina had hoped that would become a pattern—until they could stop seeing Cathy altogether. Whether George had told his mother what Amina had discovered, or Eileen had simply guessed, Amina didn't know. George's mother had in any case stopped inviting Cathy to dinner on Sundays. The dinners themselves had become more infrequent because Eileen said she knew Amina was busy with work and school. But she guessed that George's mother also might have been ashamed of what she had concealed from Amina.

"Of course it would be only us," Eileen said quickly. "And Jess and Harold. Just the six of us and Bob, if that's all right?"

"Of course," Amina said. One dinner was a small price to pay for what Jessica had agreed to do, even if it had to be at Cathy's house.

"Wonderful," Eileen said (but not in the way George had said it). "It's been way too long."

Amina had always prayed when she was at home at the right times, but now she began making up prayers she'd missed, and adding some-thing extra at the end of the *namaz*. Most often she asked God for two things: to help George find a new job and to allow her parents' paperwork to proceed without incident. As the weeks passed and the first of these requests remained unfulfilled, Amina felt a nagging guilt about her own laxity. There was nowhere to pray at Starbucks, and she'd only once visited the "Interfaith Chapel" at MCC—really a class-room the college had dedicated to prayer at the request of its Christian students. The problem was that the *maghrib* usually fell in the middle of her math class, and if Amina had gone out to pray at that time, she would've missed nearly half the lesson.

Of course, her schedule was no excuse. At home she had never believed in a God who was strict about prayer times or fasting; she believed, as her father had always instructed her, that God forgave everything as long as you devoted yourself to him alone. She wondered if it was simply that she couldn't face God after what had happened, as she knew she must—to ask him to cure her of her pride and to help her forgive her husband and his family for what they'd done. But the less she prayed, the more she missed God. She told herself that that was a ridiculous feeling since God was everywhere. And so she thought it must be that she missed only the ceremonies of God: the early morning *azaan* or the sight of the men in her neighborhood streaming toward the mosque on Fridays or even the familiar presence of her parents' prayer rugs, rolled up next to each other like another married couple, in the space between the television and the door.

2 Soon after George lost his job, the cardinal had appeared in their yard. Amina had noticed the noise first: a peculiar thwanging sound, soft but solid. It wasn't until she was working outside one day that she'd seen the bird himself, pitching his body repeatedly against the window screen. She thought he might eventually break it, but if he did any damage, it was only to himself. After each sally, he repaired to his habitual perch in the oak tree, ruffling his plumage and calling imperiously to others of his kind.

George said that the bird must've gone mad from eating the poison people put in their yards for the moles and suggested that they get a bird feeder. The feeder attracted jays, wrens, and a large population of sparrows, but the cardinal ignored that commonplace sustenance in favor of the paradise he imagined to be just out of reach. Amina found that her temper was shorter these days. She went into the yard and yelled at the bird; she waved a stick the way she might have at a dog at home. But the bird continued to throw himself against the house, a half an hour at a time, several times each day, paying no attention to Amina's threats or the fact that the house was already inhabited. He had set his sights on it and wouldn't be deterred.

Jessica filled out the I-134 and sent it in, and then it was just a question of waiting. Amina thought often of the green card application, and how she and George had struggled to prove the validity of something that was absolutely real. She had felt indignant along with her husband as he berated the people who used marriage as a path to legal residency. Look how hard they make it for the rest of us, he had said. It occurred to Amina, now that ICE was no longer interested in their personal life, that they were living in much the same way as those opportunists they had once deplored.

They hadn't slept together for three months. She assumed abstinence was more difficult for George than it was for her, though he never mentioned it. If he had complained, it might have hardened her resolve. But his silence had begun to make Amina doubt the wisdom of her decision: she knew there were instructions in the Qur'an about the duties of marriage, and she thought that she might in fact be committing one sin in an attempt to do penance for another.

She couldn't help being impressed by the fact that George got up at the same time he always had; he did his workout in the basement, had breakfast, and then sat down at the computer to look at Monster and engineerjobs.com. Although he sent his résumé somewhere every few days, most of the companies didn't call him back, and the ones that did had already hired someone or needed someone "with a different skill set." Once he even found a listing from his former employer.

"They're advertising for jobs," he said, pointing to the screen. "Look at this. They want young guys who'll work part-time, no benefits. They'll replace me with two kids and still save money."

At night he watched television until late, which made it easy for Amina to get ready for bed by herself, since she needed to get up for school and work in the morning. Once she was in bed, however, it was often difficult to fall asleep, and there were many nights when she would still be lying awake when George came up to his room at eleven thirty or midnight. She turned off her light when she heard him on the stairs and resisted the urge she sometimes had to call his name. If George had any of the same feelings, he also kept them to himself.

George had said that her own salary was so negligible that it wouldn't make a difference to their situation, and so she continued sending the monthly allowance to her parents. Her father spent it on buses, taxis, and rickshaws, as he traveled within the district and then back and forth from Satkhira to Dhaka, trying to obtain the documents the American consulate required for the visa. It was strange—having won this concession from George at such cost—not to be able to deliver the good news to her parents, who had always believed they were coming. Amina had concealed the real hurdle, and now her mother busied herself inventing imaginary ones.

"The problem is not once we arrive in Rochester," her mother said. "If we arrive safely, then there are no problems."

"Why wouldn't you arrive safely?"

"Your father is disputing with his relatives again."

"What kind of dispute?" Amina wondered if the old antagonisms with her father's cousins could have been stirred up when her parents had gone to check on her dadu after the storm. But those men had been interested only in her father's land; now that there was no more of it to sell, she couldn't imagine what further motive they might have for harassing her parents.

"They're envious," her mother said. "They want a share of whatever profits we make in America."

"What profits?"

Her mother hesitated. "I mean, if we set up a business. Import-export, maybe, all types of jute handicraft. Or a catering business—we could call it Indian food, since no one there knows Bangladesh." Amina had to control her temper. It wasn't the first time her mother had mentioned opportunities for making money in America, allowing herself to become infected by her father's credulity. Each time Amina had explained the practicalities of the situation, and each time her mother had quickly pretended to understand, in a way that made her doubt she was paying attention at all.

"You can't set up a business in Rochester. You don't know anything about the laws here. They're strict about everything—all kinds of paperwork. You wouldn't be able to get a work visa, even if you wanted one. You can tell Abba's people that."

Her mother hesitated for a long moment, and then she lowered her voice so that it was almost impossible for Amina to hear her.

"They think we stole from them."

"You mean the land Abba inherited?"

"Your grandmother's coming in—I can't say anything. If she thought your father's people were after us, she wouldn't want us to stay. They might come here, and who knows what they would do?"

"To Nanu's place?"

"How are your classes?" her mother said loudly. "Are you still getting one hundred percent in math?"

"I don't think Nanu would ever make you leave."

"Keep studying just as hard," her mother continued, in the same bright tone. "Don't get lazy, even though you're at the top. Life is so unpredictable, Munni—you never know what might happen."

3 Amina did have to study harder than she'd expected for her statistics midterm, and she didn't speak to her parents for five days while she prepared. She had heard about Cyclone Nargis, but expected her parents wouldn't be any more worried than they had been about Sidr last year. And so she was surprised when she called to check up on them the day after the exam.

"*Alhamdulillah,*" her mother said when she answered. "The storm is moving toward Burma. It isn't going to hit us after all."

"Thank God," Amina said. "And everyone's fine otherwise?"

"We're fine," her mother said. "The connection is clear—can you hear it? Where do you think we are?"

The line was indeed clearer than usual, and she wondered if Moni and Omar could have invited them for a visit. She knew that living with her nanu drove her father crazy and that both her parents might be grateful for a holiday in the city.

"You're at my aunty's place in Dhaka?"

"We are in Dhaka, you're right!" her mother said. "But not at my sister's. Here—your father wants to say hello. He'll tell you."

And then her father got on the phone and explained how they had come to Dhaka to stay with Nasir.

"Your cousin called to ask if we were going to be all right. We told him everything was fine, but he insisted. He's always thinking of us."

"I'm always thinking of you, too," Amina reminded him. "I had an important test in school today, but I was distracted."

Suddenly her father's voice was full of concern. "You didn't do well? Will it affect your grade?"

"Let me talk to Nasir, Abba," Amina said firmly, and she was surprised when her father didn't protest. He put him on immediately, as if he'd been standing right there listening. She hadn't written to Nasir for more than a year, not since she'd argued with him about her failure to fast. Now she was ashamed of the e-mail she'd sent and the secret pleasure she'd taken in his inability to find a bride. She hadn't even thought to ask him for help, but he was the one who was looking after her parents in her place.

"I want to thank you," she said formally. "You've been very kind to my parents."

"Why should you thank me?" Nasir responded in English. "You are becoming a *bideshi* over there—'thank you' this and 'thank you' that. Of course I will invite my aunty and uncle if I am afraid for their safety. And I am enjoying having them. I learn all sorts of things about you—stories from when you were a little girl, all your nicknames."

Amina felt defensive. "My parents weren't worried. My mother believes she can see the future."

"And you see, she is right—the storm didn't come. But she wanted to come here anyway. She is worrying about other things."

"I know," Amina said. "But what? She won't tell me."

Nasir put his mouth away from the phone to cough. "Some problem after the visit to your dadu. Your father says these are family matters. To do with his family only."

She could hear her father saying something in the background, and she wondered whether he could follow Nasir's half of the conversation. It occurred to her that Nasir had chosen to speak English not to show off, but in order to talk to her privately.

"You can tell me," she encouraged him. "If you say it fast, my father won't understand."

"Something to do with jewelry," Nasir murmured.

"E-mail me," Amina said. "Can you send a message today?"

Nasir hesitated, but when he spoke his voice was resolute. "You should talk to your parents yourself, Munni. You'll be here soon enough."

She would've asked him to put her father back on, but she had less than three minutes left on the card.

"How long will they be staying with you?"

"They can stay as long as they like. Your father has some business here, with the visa paperwork. It is more convenient to be near your uncle's office."

"Tell them I need to talk to them tomorrow. Tell them to call at seven a.m. here in Rochester." Nasir didn't say anything, and so she repeated the instructions, trying to keep the irritation from her voice. It wasn't his fault that her parents were being difficult, inventing reasons to move from one place to the other.

"Yes, okay, Munni," Nasir said. "I am praying for you."

"Thank you again," Amina said, without thinking.

Nasir laughed. "Okay, little memsahib. So long."

4 George didn't get so much as an interview in May or June. He filled out his unemployment forms every Sunday night and periodically went downtown to check the bulletin board at the Rochester Works! Career Center. When she heard the car pulling back into the garage after one of those visits, she couldn't help imagining that he might come hurrying through the door to tell her about a job that was perfect for him, that he could interview for right away. She'd once done the same with her father. But in spite of his optimism, her father was never surprised when one of his schemes failed to deliver; nothing in his past had led him to expect a steady income. George had grown up with the idea that such a job was his right, and so he was both shocked and angry when it was taken away.

She didn't tell her parents about the disaster that had befallen them; they were consumed by their own worries, and she hoped that in the three months before their arrival, George would find another job. Her father told her that her mother had been acting strangely ever since they'd returned from Nasir's to the village. She talked more and more about her sister Moni and how she secretly envied their emigration plans, and she often turned down food, saying she was afraid to eat. Once, her father had woken up because he was being bitten by mosquitoes and discovered that her mother wasn't in their bed: she'd neglected to close the mosquito net, and her father's arms and legs were swollen with bites. He'd gotten up and gone out into Nanu's courtyard, where, after a few moments, he heard splashing from the pond. He said that he knew it was her mother even before he saw her, her head going under again and again, as if she were looking for something on the bottom. When he tried to bring her out, she'd resisted, and only the threat of all of her relatives waking and finding her bathing in the middle of the night was enough to make her climb the stone steps, wrap herself in a shawl, and allow her husband to lead her back to bed. Amina's mother wouldn't speak at all that night, but in the morning she had told her father that she'd heard Kwaz, the water saint, calling her from the bottom of the pond.

"I want you to come now," her mother pleaded on the phone, and Amina had to explain again that her citizenship interview was in two weeks. Every night after dinner, while George was watching television, she studied the hundred questions, memorizing the branches of government and the names of U.S. territories. Some questions were easy ("Why does the American flag have thirteen stripes?" "Who was the first president of the United States?"), but some tripped her up every time ("What stops one branch of the government from becoming too powerful?" "Name one American Indian tribe.") She invented mnemonics, especially for the questions involving numbers: twenty-seven was the number of constitutional amendments and also the age she was last year. Her nanu was one of nine children, enough to fill every seat on the U.S. Supreme Court. The last three digits of her father's phone number were 435, which was also the number of voting members in the House of Representatives.

Words were more difficult. She had the same trouble with the strange-sounding Native American tribes that she often did with the Italianesque names of the drinks at Starbucks: her head was so full of English that there was no room for another language. Once she had even failed to remember a word in Bangla. She had been at school, walking past the dry fountain where students gathered to study and eat their lunch, and for a few seconds, no matter how hard she searched, she couldn't bring those two syllables—*jharna*—to mind.

"That makes sense," George said. "One language pushes the other out." He didn't offer any solution in the moment, but a few days later their Netflix came in the mail, and she saw that he'd ordered *The Last of the Mohicans*.

"I didn't think you could forget if you watched a whole movie about them," he told her, and so she'd taken a night off from studying to sit on the couch and watch it with him. She had just finished her shower and had plaited her hair; she was wearing sweatpants and a tank top, but she hadn't put on a bra. She allowed herself to think of what could happen, but she didn't change into anything more modest. She didn't know if she wanted to have sex with her husband, but she knew she wanted the comfort of sitting on the couch with him without the pressure of speaking or even really of thinking, of allowing herself two hours to change her own situation for the fantasy on the screen.

About three-quarters of the way through the movie, for an experiment, she allowed herself to lean against George the way she once had: he adjusted his position to accommodate her head on his shoulder. The British woman was trapped behind the waterfall with the adopted white son of the Indian chief, kissing in the dark.

"Like Niagara."

"Except about one-twentieth the size."

"I'd like to go someday."

"It's not expensive," George said. "When I'm working again. We could take your parents."

This generous suggestion moved Amina, as did the scene in front of them. Now Hawkeye vowed to leap into the river to conceal himself so that the French soldiers would have mercy on Cora and her party. Even in the face of peril, however, Cora didn't want him to go. It was in such situations that the strength of love revealed itself; although their own situation was less picturesque, Amina doubted it was any less dramatic. Their backgrounds were as different as Hawkeye's and Cora's—perhaps more so, since the onscreen hero and heroine had at least their native race in common. She had escaped a broken country, and George a broken heart; they had chosen each other in spite of warnings from both sides, and she thought those naysayers had made them both more determined that their union would succeed. He'd written to her for all the wrong reasons—deceptively at first, and then in desperation over another woman. But hadn't she been desperate, too? Even if neither of their motives had been pure, wasn't it possible that something pure had come of them now?

It gave her pleasure to imagine George's surprise and his eagerness, when he found out he wouldn't have to wait any longer. Between the movie and her own emotions, she felt ready, almost eager for something that had once been a duty. The scene onscreen had devolved into fighting, and she had trouble following the plot.

"Do they get married?" she asked George.

"Does who?"

"Hawkeye and Cora."

"I'm not going to spoil it for you."

"I haven't been paying enough attention."

"Do you want to go upstairs? You won't forget the Mohicans, will you?"

"I'll remember the Hurons now, too."

George got up and switched off the television, and they climbed the stairs together for the first time in several months. He turned for a moment on the landing, as if he were going to say something, and then hurried into the bathroom and closed the door. Instead of going to her own room, she went into the one they used to share and sat down on the bed. Was it possible she was more nervous than she had been the first time? She could feel her pulse in her ears, and when George turned the handle on the bathroom door, something made her jump to her feet.

"What are you looking for?" he asked, not looking at her. "Your phone is downstairs on the table."

"I was thinking we could . . ."

He looked up. "Really?"

She nodded.

"Oh, Amina." He sat down on the bed, but carefully, as if she were something that might break.

"I want the light to be out."

He switched off the lamp with its pleated shade, and their skin was suddenly the same dark blue in the dim room. Then he smoothed her hair in a way she liked and kissed her, hesitantly at first, on the mouth. But when he touched her breasts he groaned. "I missed this so much."

She had always found it disconcerting when he talked during sex, as if the language was a bridge between this act and the rest of their lives. She thought it ought to be separate, undiscussed. They undressed themselves, as they always had, and she lay down beside him.

"I want you to come this time." He was on top of her, trying to be inside her, but he could feel she wasn't wet enough. "Let me try this," he said, and suddenly he was moving down her body, kissing her there. She knew what he was doing: she'd heard about it from the girls at Maple Leaf and knew that some people believed it was haram, while others said that because it wasn't expressly prohibited, it was all right between husband and wife.

But we are not husband and wife, she thought—not really. What George was doing felt so strange that she couldn't imagine taking pleasure in it, and she was relieved when he returned to his normal position on top of her. And yet once he was inside her, she found that it was altogether different, as if he'd unloosed something with his mouth. She wondered if this was what Ashok had done to Kim, and then she thought that the worst thing to do right now would be to think about Kim. She concentrated on pushing back against her husband, and she was surprised by how fast and hard he came.

George rolled off of her and lay down on his back. "You didn't?"

"I don't know."

"You would know." He was disappointed, and she thought she ought to have lied. She wondered why it mattered so much to him.

"Can I ask you something?"

She nodded, and then remembered he couldn't see her in the dark.

"Was this because you feel sorry for me?"

"No."

"You wanted to?"

"I missed it, too." Her guilt about lying compounded the guilt she felt about violating her own conditions; she had thought that this hiatus in their sexual life might make it possible to begin the marriage again on firmer ground. Now she saw that the interval had actually made things more difficult.

George rolled over and looked at her. "I feel like I never know what you're thinking anymore. Or whether you're still angry at me."

"I'm not angry right now."

"I'm going to get another job."

Did he think she was upset only about his job? Or did he simply not want to talk about the other, harder problems?

"I know."

"You don't believe me, but you'll see," George said, as if she hadn't spoken.

"I'm not sure we should do that again."

George was quiet for a moment. "Really?"

She had been feeling since they'd finished as if she might cry, and now she allowed it to happen, her shoulders shaking in the dark. George sighed and patted her back.

"It's okay," he said. "It's going to be okay," and in that way she was absolved from answering him. After several minutes he removed his hand from her back and turned over, but it was a long time before she was sure he was asleep.

She hadn't thought of Micki in months, but now she remembered when her cousin first told her about what happened between men and women. They had been sitting in that abandoned hut, and Micki had been insisting Amina acknowledge what she was telling her: that all married people did it and that Amina would have to do it one day, too. She remembered it had seemed enviable at the time that Micki's parents were divorced. That meant that her mother, Parveen, slept in the familiar way: in some combination with Nanu and the two of them, while Amina had to imagine her own parents alone in an apartment in Dhaka, engaged in that unsettling act. She had known that men forced themselves on women, but Micki said that there were women who allowed it even before marriage. Neither one of them could understand why any woman would do something like that before she absolutely had to, especially when it was likely to ruin her life.

She thought it might be awkward to wake up next to George, and so she got up quietly and went into the other room. She wondered if Micki also remembered that conversation in the playhouse—if she'd thought of it since her own marriage. Tonight had made her understand how it might be pleasurable for a woman, even if she couldn't imagine risking her life for it. She allowed herself to believe that something had changed between them and that whatever obstacle had been keeping them from conceiving a child might have been removed by this unexpected tenderness. It wasn't impossible, given where she was in her cycle; if it had happened tonight, she might fly home in three months, pregnant with her first child. She might enter the village triumphantly, with a baby in her belly and her American husband at her side. The timing would have worked out so perfectly that the credit could go only to God.

5 They had been talking about buying a new bed for the master bedroom and putting the old one in the room where Amina was sleeping now, which would eventually belong to her parents. One weekend at the end of June, George suggested that they go to the mall to look for one. They hadn't spent an afternoon at the mall since he'd lost his job, and Amina packed a lunch as soon as they got up on Saturday morning.

"What are you doing?" George asked. "We can't take that into the mall."

"We can eat in the car, then," Amina said. "We'll save at least fifteen dollars."

George shook his head at her neat Tupperware containers. "Let's just enjoy ourselves. Okay?"

The Marketplace Mall was decorated for the upcoming Fourth of July holiday. A summertime display had replaced the electric trains they'd had at Christmas. It was set up on a low platform to accommodate children and enclosed by a Plexiglas barrier. Where there had been Ivory Snow on tiny evergreens and a papier-mâché mountain—with plastic skiers going up the lift and down the slope in two continuous loops—there was now a parade route lined with tiny spectators, holding tiny gold paper sparklers. A float actually moved along the route: Uncle Sam raised an American flag while a white-gowned beauty queen waved amid confetti sequins. Beyond the parade, a team of children played baseball while others swung on mechanical swings over patches of cloth flowers, painstakingly applied with glue. A modest cardboard sign stated that the expense and labor for the project had been shouldered by the Ladies' Improvement Society of Downtown Rochester.

"My mother would love that," Amina said as they made their way toward Sears at one end of the mall.

"The one at Christmas is better," George said. "She'll be here in time to see it."

As soon as they found the appropriate department, a young salesman approached them and introduced himself.

"Let me guess," Craig said. "You folks have been sleeping on the same mattress for seven-plus years, and all of a sudden someone's having back pain." He turned to George. "There's nothing worse than tossing and turning in the middle of the night—is there? Waking up your wife because you can't find a comfortable position."

"We need a new bed because my parents are coming to live with us," Amina said. "Our old one is fine."

She'd only said it to change the subject, to keep the salesman from talking so casually about the two of them in bed together, but she could see from George's face that he wished she hadn't mentioned her parents.

But Craig only nodded in an enthusiastic way. "These days a lot of people are going for the foam mattresses. They don't sound comfortable, but you've got to try one. They actually developed this stuff for NASA—there's a whole scientific explanation I could give you, but most people just like to lie down and judge for themselves. There's one right over here."

Amina thought of saying that George was an engineer, and might like to hear the scientific explanation, but she was afraid the salesman might ask where her husband worked. Instead she followed George to a king-size bed with a polished wooden headboard and a price tag encased in plastic: $2,499.00.

"We're looking for a queen," George said. "Just the box spring and the mattress."

"This is the RhapsodyBed, top of the line," the salesman said. "Try it out. No charge for a nap."

George lay down on the bed, but Amina only sat carefully on the edge.

"Do you see what I mean?" Craig said. "She could be jumping up and down over there, and you wouldn't feel a thing." He turned to Amina. "Don't be shy."

Amina lay down on her back, as far from George as possible. They were facing the store's front window, and shoppers with bags eyed them as they passed.

"I'll give you a minute," Craig said, "and you can come back and take a look at the box springs. We have plenty of nice ones, although they're not going to feel like the Rhapsody."

When he was gone, Amina sat up quickly and lowered her voice. "Who pays twenty-five hundred dollars for a bed?"

"No one," George said flatly. "They just do it so you feel like you're getting a bargain later. It's comfortable though."

"Sit up," Amina whispered. "People are looking." But George remained on his back.

"So what."

"They think about *that*."

"I think about it, too," George said in his normal voice. "But we don't do it."

Amina looked at her husband, who was staring at a ceiling fan rotating above their heads, the dark brown wooden blades of which were tipped with brass. She was startled to see the expression on his face, somewhere between laughter and fury.

"We did it the other night."

"Will that happen again?" His eyes remained on the fan.

"When we're married—after my parents get here."

George exhaled sharply. "How exciting."

"You're the one—"

"I *know*. It's my fault—I screwed up." He looked at her. "Hey, do you even know that word? 'Screw'?"

Amina started to get up, but he grabbed her shoulder. She thought of shaking it off, running out of the store—and then where? Even if she managed to locate the car in the lot and calm down enough to drive it, it wasn't as if she had anywhere to go.

"Look—don't," he whispered. "Please. I'm sorry—I shouldn't've said that. You just—you have all these plans. Do you ever just, you know—"

"I thought that's what you liked about me—how I'm so practical."

George dropped his hand. "I did—do. I just sometimes feel like it's about your plans more than me."

She looked at him as if she didn't understand—an old habit. But of course she knew what he meant.

"Like, I'm just a piece of the puzzle."

"At first we were puzzle pieces. Now we're the puzzle." She hadn't meant to be funny, but George looked at her and laughed for real.

"I think everybody is, when they get married," she continued. "Even if you live together and all of that."

George lay down again. "You might be right."

"You're just guessing about the other person until then."

He smiled.

"What?"

"Let's get it," he said.

"What?"

"The bed—the Rhapsody. Why not?"

"Are you crazy?" She saw Craig watching them from across the room, noticing her husband's sudden good humor. If he approached them now, she was afraid George would hand over the credit card.

"We wouldn't do that even if you were working. You're not thinking."

"No—I'm not."

She did the percentage instantly. "That's an eighth of our savings."

George put his arms behind his head, as if he owned the bed already. "More or less."

"It's the price of two airline tickets."

George's expression changed suddenly. He gave her a look that made her wish they could start the whole day again from the beginning.

"Yeah," he said. "When you put it like that."

A family of four had stopped outside the plate-glass window and was having a conversation, gesturing toward George and Amina on the luxurious bed.

He had turned his head away, and so Amina touched his shoulder. "Please sit up."

He glanced at the family but refused to meet her eyes. "You only care how things look."

Amina stared at her husband, prone on the bed. She didn't know how you could live with a person for three years and still have such a wrongheaded idea about her personality. What George was describing was everyone she knew at home, her extended family and all of her girlfriends from school. Amina was the one who'd done everything her own way, ignoring their endless whispering. How could he fail to see how hard she had worked to escape it?

She was thinking of how she might explain this to him when the salesman returned.

"It's hard to get up, isn't it? You know, the foam mattress can be used on a more economical bed frame. If you like—"

But George had gotten up and, without a word, was already walking out of the store.

"Thank you," Amina began. "We need to—"

"Think it over," Craig finished for her. He reached out to shake her hand, and the touch of a strange male palm, which had become so routine that she hardly thought about it, suddenly felt as embarrassing as it had the first time she'd been expected to do it.

Craig handed her a card, which she realized she was still holding fifteen minutes later, when she and George were seated at Friendly's with thirteen dollars' worth of chicken sandwiches, fries, and soda, not speaking or even looking at each other. She put the card in her purse, thinking of the thousands of similar cards her father had hoarded over the years. If she were at home she might give it to him: *Here's the card of the man who sold us our mattress,* and her father would be impressed by the raised red lettering, would save it in one of the neat stacks in his bureau drawer, organized according to his own invented system. When she was little she used to like to watch him sort through them, laying them out on the bed in her parents' room, frowning and speaking very softly to himself, as if they were a divining tool only he could read.

6 The interviewer, a friendly young woman with red hair and beautiful teeth, began by asking Amina the number of stripes on the flag. Amina started to explain the significance of the thirteen stripes, but the interviewer laughed and said that was extra credit.

The questions that followed were also among the easiest on the list: *Who is the vice president of the United States? When do we celebrate Independence Day?* There was no mention of Native Americans or checks and balances. When George picked her up afterward, Amina was able to tell him she'd been awarded a "seven out of six."

A few days after the exam, her parents received their medical clearance from a doctor near the embassy in Baridhara. Now that the only hurdle was the visas, Amina began preparations for their arrival in earnest. When George had first lost his job, the only benefit either one of them could see was that he would be able to come along and help to bring her parents back to America. It would certainly be much easier to manage their anxiety and make all of the arrangements if he were with her. In the past he had always been a calm and efficient presence, unlikely to be fazed by the kind of setbacks they were sure to encounter once they got to Desh. By the time she arrived, she would be a U.S. citizen, complete with a blue passport, but Amina didn't have any illusions. If there were a problem at the embassy, God forbid, it would be an enormous help to have her white, native-born American husband standing next to her in line.

She had instructed both her mother and father to use "Mazid" as a surname on the forms, although it was properly her father's nickname and not a last name at all. She preferred the sound of it to "Gazi," her father's family name, and had already used it on all of her own documents. In addition to talking them through each piece of paperwork on the phone, Amina spent a portion of every day packing gifts for her relatives. The gifts were things she'd been accumulating during the three years she'd been in America, and so she didn't have to feel guilty about buying a lot of presents now that George was unemployed. She had been storing them in the large, purple suitcase in the room where she now slept, and the suitcase was already three-quarters full.

There was the Anaïs Anaïs eau de toilette that she'd bought from overstockperfume.com, along with six Dole pineapple juice boxes, two canisters of Wegmans protein powder, and a single box of Ziploc bags (just so that her mother could see what they were). For her father there was a digital wristwatch made by Sony and three bulk packages of 100 percent cotton Fruit of the Loom underwear and socks. Of course her parents were almost definitely coming right back with her, and all of the things she was bringing were available here in Rochester. Still, she reminded George, it was impossible to know how long it would take to get her parents' visas. She thought it was better to bring everything with her; that way she could have the pleasure of giving them unfamiliar things.

She had bought colored soap shaped like seashells for her nanu and all her aunts, pens that wrote in six different colors, and plastic head scarves for the rain. There were travel alarm clocks, green-apple candies, and "handmade in Rochester" lavender sachets. (The last was something Eileen had suggested, and although she'd accepted them politely, she was sure no one at home was going to be very excited about some sweet-smelling seeds in a handmade muslin bag.) Her nanu was also getting a bottle of Active Senior multivitamins, the label of which showed a white-haired grandmother in a red tracksuit playing tennis; even if her grandmother distrusted the foreign vitamins, Amina figured that the label as an artifact would be worth the weight of the bottle. There were NY Giants T-shirts for her male cousins, and neon rubber bangles for the girls, and there was her own favorite purchase: a box of twenty pressed-tin Christmas ornaments painted to resemble common American birds, which she had bought on sale last December 26 with the thought that they could be individually presented to anyone she might have forgotten.

The suitcase had already been packed and repacked several times when her parents finally received their visa interview date: August 17. Amina and George immediately went online to look for tickets, but they were even more expensive than they'd been three years ago, the routes byzantine in their complexity.

"We better be sure the dates are right," George said. "If we have to change them, there's a two-hundred-fifty-dollar fee per ticket." His voice was resigned to the potential expense in a way that was worse than if he'd complained.

"It will be the first time they've ever flown," Amina apologized. Recently her parents had offered to come to America on their own, a disingenuous move that she wished she'd never mentioned to George. She could see he hadn't let go of the idea, as he trolled through flights with two and three stops, and she was afraid he didn't understand why it was impossible. Her mother was unpredictable; she'd passed her medical exam, but who was to say she wouldn't have one of her outbursts during the interview? They were supposed to get their visas immediately afterward, but if there was a problem, her parents could be kept waiting indefinitely. Even if everything went perfectly, she couldn't imagine what they would do in the massive Dubai airport for six hours, or how they would find the connecting flight to New York once they left the Bangla-speaking attendants from the first flight.

"I'm worried about them in the airport for all that time."

"We're not going to be able to sit together," George said.

If she were pregnant, she thought, he wouldn't argue. He would assume she needed him with her. Her period hadn't come since the night they'd shared a bed, and although she tried not to think about it, she hadn't given up hope.

"These prices are without the tax," George said.

Her own first flight, from Dhaka to Dubai, had been crowded with rude young men going to the Gulf to work, fingering cheap local phones that would soon be useless, desperately trying to prove their own worldliness to one another. One of these had been seated next to her, and so Amina had been forced to pull out her copy of *Jane Eyre* (the only book from her O-level preparations with which she hadn't been able to part) and turn the pages regularly during the entire three hours to be sure he wouldn't speak to her.

That experience had made her doubly pleased when her seat-mate for the longer flight had turned out to be a completely different type of Deshi: a middle-aged woman, beautifully dressed in a hand-embroidered top and slacks, with a great deal of gold jewelry. At home Amina had been satisfied with her outfit—a blouse with a collar, jeans, and the University of Rochester sweatshirt George had brought her—but now she suddenly felt sloppy. Her neighbor carried a soft black leather handbag, from which she pulled various amenities: a tube of hand cream, individually wrapped antibacterial towelettes, chewing gum, and bottled water. Her food she carried separately in an insulated bag with a zipper: some sort of dry vegetable, mung dal, rice, bananas, and a paper-wrapped package of homemade pakan pitha. She refused everything the flight attendant offered, except more water, and did not offer Amina anything to eat, even though she obviously had more than she needed. Her mother would have been appalled by this display of bad manners, but it made Amina smile. Clearly this woman had become an American already, and if she could do it, why couldn't Amina?

She pulled out *Jane Eyre* again, as a conversation starter rather than a deterrent, but the woman reclined her seat and put a mask over her eyes. Amina wasn't sleepy, and she had found a song she loved: "Original Sin," by INXS (which she'd referred to as "Inks" soon after she'd arrived, making George laugh). As she listened, she wished for George's grandmother's diamond ring, which might have made her seatmate remove her mask and reveal herself more open to conversation.

Now George sat at the computer, his finger joylessly poised over the ergonomic mouse, in the same spot where he had once sat down (alone) and written to ask her if she was "still interested." Amina remembered her naïve reply: once she had even believed their courtship similar to that of her grandparents. Now she knew the difference. How the old matchmaker who had arranged that marriage would have laughed if she could have seen the way Amina and George had come together! She wouldn't have been able to comprehend the distance or speed with which their original communication had traveled, but she would have been shocked by the primitive nature of the information itself. *Name, age, languages spoken, physical appearance, hobbies, and interests.* This was a woman who had known every young person in Haibatpur and the surrounding villages—who not only knew them, but had watched them grow up. She knew their families, the way they practiced their religion, their worldly successes and failures, habits, favorite dishes, their peculiarities, illnesses, private and public griefs. She would have thought of the matches long before she was hired to arrange them and augured auspicious days in advance. By contrast George and Amina had trusted their introduction to a machine, something made of metal and plastic, blind and dumb, which approximated human knowledge with an electrical alphabet only two characters long. Was it any wonder they struggled to understand each other now?

She turned to her husband and made a decision.

"I'll go myself."

George looked up hopefully.

Amina rehearsed the reasons aloud. "It's the end of the rainy season—the roads may still be flooded. You won't be able to stand the food, and what if you get sick this time? We won't need an extra hotel room in Dhaka—if I go alone, I can stay with my parents. And we can save the twelve hundred dollars on your ticket."

When George protested, it was only in the routine way of someone who knew things had been decided in his favor. "What if there's a problem at the consulate?"

"I'll have all my forms, our marriage license, and everything. If the Americans there need to talk to you, they can call your cell phone."

George was already nodding. "That makes much more sense," he said. She heated leftover egg-and-potato curry for dinner and then watched half of *The Bourne Identity* with George. When she went upstairs to get ready for bed, she saw that her period had come as usual.

7   She was going to miss the last three weeks of the term, but both
    Jill and her statistics teacher had promised to help her finish on time. She'd worried more about Starbucks, but Keith had agreed to hold her job for her, on the condition that she wouldn't be away more than fourteen days. He reminded Amina and Kendra, who usually worked her shifts with her and was also an MCC student, that the entries for the "Reach for the Stars" contest were due by the end of the month. Kendra asked for the details about the contest, but there were two posters in the store and Amina had already read every word of them. All you had to do was write five hundred words about your life and how you would use the ten thousand dollars in tuition money; as hard as it was for her to resist a contest, Amina knew she wouldn't have time to write another essay before she left. She reminded herself that the other entrants would be native English speakers and that she would never have won anyway. Even that much tuition money wouldn't have solved their financial problems. It was the thought of winning, of being selected from a crowd of others and chosen for some unusual fate, that intoxicated her.

When she had been in class 7, there had been a contest in math. You could prepare, but no one knew exactly what sort of problems would appear on the exam. Each class had its own test, with its appropriate level of difficulty, but the competition was school-wide. There was no money being awarded, of course, but the students with the highest percentages of correct answers would be given gold, silver, and bronze medals, just like in the Olympics, which were happening that year in Seoul. (The Games were being hosted in Asia for only the second time in their history, and six athletes from Bangladesh had qualified.) Amina was fixated on the gold medal: all she needed was a perfect score. She often got 100 percent in math, nearly always coming in first in her class. It was assumed that she would be one of the gold medal winners, and she came home and told her parents that a bet had been organized, that even Ghaniyah put the odds on Amina coming in first. There was another girl, Zainab, who habitually raised her hand with Amina, but she was less consistent and prone to freezing at important moments.

Her mother said that wagers were un-Islamic, but her father thought that was only if money was changing hands. In fact Amina hadn't bet because it would look conceited (and, more important, tempt fate) to predict your own success. But she was sure she was going to win. On the morning of the exam, she and her mother arrived by rickshaw together as usual, and Amina had pointed out that several girls had new red hair ribbons in honor of the contest.

"Hair ribbons don't get you a gold medal," her mother said, and that was how Amina knew that she was excited, too. When the test was put down in front of her an hour later, she raced through it. If Zainab also scored a hundred, she wanted everyone to see that she was the one who'd turned in her paper first. It had taken a week for the teachers to tabulate the scores, and on the morning of the announcement, without saying anything, her mother had presented Amina with a set of new red hair ribbons. She had touched them surreptitiously on the way into the classroom, making sure they were still in place, but as it turned out, the only medal winner from class 7 was Zainab, who had shared the silver with a little girl from class 4. When the gold was announced, not only Ghaniyah but several of the other girls glared at Amina for acting so confident and then letting them down. When their teacher returned the exams, she saw that she had made four simple computation errors—nothing to do with algebra but the kind of thing she might have caught easily, if she'd bothered to look over her work.

It was almost a relief to confess on the way home; her mother hadn't said anything, but had directed the rickshaw-wallah to the barbershop, where at first Amina thought they were going to meet her father. Instead her mother instructed her to get into the chair herself and then told her father's barber to chop off her hair at the ears. The hair was putting too much weight on Amina's brain, her mother said, and God had punished both of them for their vanity. The next day in school Ghaniyah had laughed behind her hand, shaking her head.

"I'm sorry, Munni—but you look exactly like the little boy who brings the eggs."

8 Eileen's dinner party took place on a warm, wet night in early July, when their car unexpectedly failed to start. It was raining heavily, and George had to knock on the Snyders' door to ask Dan to pull their station wagon into the driveway, so that he could connect the jumper cables. When they finally arrived at Aunt Cathy's, they could see from the cars in the driveway that they were the last ones.

Amina made George take off his muddy shoes before stepping into Cathy's kitchen, but everyone inside the house had kept theirs on. Jessica and Harold were standing in the living room, drinking wine and talking to Bob, while Eileen and Cathy worked in the kitchen.

"Samosas!" Eileen said, taking the container from Amina. "These are my favorite."

"I brought a dish with cauliflower, too," Amina said. "I can't do it as well as my mother does."

"Wonderful!"

Cathy eyed Amina's Tupperware. "You're lucky your stomach doesn't give you the same trouble mine does," she told her sister.

Since Amina had seen her last, Cathy had dyed her hair an unnatural, bright auburn color. It was cut very short, a style that seemed to emphasize the smallness of her head. She had dressed up in a black velour pantsuit, but her face looked older; her cheeks sagged on either side of a tiny, bow-shaped mouth.

Everyone had moved into the kitchen, and Amina thought of how strange this type of socializing would seem to her parents, if they ever actually made it to Rochester. When her mother had guests, all of the dishes were prepared for them in advance; usually she didn't sit down at the table, but only moved around the apartment serving food. Certainly no guest had ever been in her kitchen, which was too small to admit more than one person anyway.

Amina asked Eileen for a task, and George's mother set her up with the vegetables for a salad, which she sliced on a cutting board next to the refrigerator. Aunt Cathy's refrigerator was covered with magnets, like their own, only hers were primarily instructional: there was one from the fire department and one from poison control, and the others were decorated with Christian pictures and sayings. WEEPING MAY ENDURE FOR A NIGHT, BUT JOY COMETH IN THE MORNING, and THERE ARE THREE THINGS THAT ENDURE FOREVER: FAITH, HOPE, AND LOVE. BUT THE GREATEST OF THEM IS LOVE. Eileen took a lasagna out of the oven and put it on a trivet on the table.

"This looks delicious," said Bob, whose red sweater and white beard made Amina think of Santa Claus.

Cathy waved her hands in front of her face. "Don't thank me— I didn't do a thing. I keep making mistakes, cooking for these two. Eileen did everything this time."

"Everyone sit, please," Eileen said loudly. "This isn't fancy, but I can't tell you what a pleasure it is to cook in an intact kitchen. Poor Bob—we've been eating at Friendly's and the Olive Garden for months."

"I like Friendly's," Bob said pleasantly, taking his seat in a chair next to the sideboard. Amina tried to help Eileen serve, but George's mother patted her shoulder and asked her to sit, and so she sat down between Jessica and George, directly across from Cathy. Eileen had put the samosas in the middle of the table with a Chinese sweet-and-sour sauce (Amina hadn't been able to find tamarind, now that she no longer went to Namaste); everyone helped themselves except Cathy and Harold.

"How's your new job?" Jess asked Amina brightly. She had obviously come straight from the hospital, and Amina was impressed by her navy-blue blazer and oversize pearls. "I keep meaning to come in to Brighton for my Frappuccino."

"I don't mind the register, but making the drinks is difficult—people are particular."

"What about you?" Harold turned to George. "Anything on the horizon?" Amina had met Jessica's husband only once, at the wedding, and she'd been uncomfortable enough then that she hadn't retained a strong impression of anyone. Harold was thinner and shorter than his wife; he had fine gray hair that stood out in a kind of cloud around his head, sparse but unruly. Amina had been surprised to see that he was dressed in jeans, a plaid shirt, and sneakers—less formal than she would've expected for a doctor. The only thing that made him look at all distinguished was a massive gold watch on his left wrist. In spite of his grumbling about the dinner, George had put on a collared shirt and slacks, as if he were going to TCE.

"I'm looking into a couple of things," George said.

"It's brutal out there," Harold said. "I know a guy down in New York City—a stockbroker—he says all this recession crap is just semantics. It's a depression, he says, pure and simple, and it'll be around a lot longer than people think. Credit card debt, bad mortgages—we're blaming the banks, but it's us. We've been living beyond our means for a long time."

"Oh my goodness," Eileen said. "We haven't even toasted our new citizen. Amina—congratulations. We're so proud of you." They all lifted their glasses: hers was the only one filled with water.

"Apparently ninety-seven percent of American high school students can't pass that test," Harold remarked. It was the kind of fact George ordinarily reveled in, but her husband had put down his glass and was eating silently, all his attention focused on his plate.

"I read that somewhere. Basic civics, and they have no idea—we're talking about sixteen-, seventeen-year-old kids. That should tell you everything you need to know about our schools."

"It's all right if you study," Amina said. "Only there are so many forms. It's been hard for my parents, too." She smiled at Jess, trying to think of how she might thank her and Harold for the sponsorship without emphasizing the reason they needed it.

Jessica glanced at George and then back to Amina. "When will they actually arrive—I'm forgetting?"

"It could be as early as August—depending on when my passport arrives."

"They'll be living in the house with you?" Harold asked.

"You knew that," Jessica said lightly. "I think I told you they were planning that."

Harold pursed his lips and exhaled sharply in George's direction. "Good luck, buddy. You're a better man than I am."

Amina suddenly hated Harold: his unkempt hair, expensive watch, and his too-casual clothes. There were a thousand things she'd like to say about the benefits of living together with your parents, especially once there were children. She'd often heard the story of how her mother and Moni had gone home to join Parveen in the village, helping her nanu while her nana was dying. Her youngest aunt, Bristi, had even come from Calcutta, bringing special ayurvedic medicines. They had washed the bed sores on his back and sometimes even cleaned up after the old man, when he lost control of his bowels. How could you force your parents to ask those things of strangers? How could you forget all they had once done for you? You left them helpless in a public place, which you insisted on calling a "home."

"I don't know," Cathy said. She had been so quiet that Amina had wondered if she were even listening. "I think about what's going to happen to me. With the diabetes and my heart. My friends without children are all scared of getting old—but I tell them my situation is hardly any different. Now I think there's a problem with the boiler—the shower's scalding one minute, ice cold the next—but who can I call? I can look in the phone book, but then who knows who'll show up. They come in here and see a woman on her own . . ."

"I can look at your boiler," Bob offered.

"Oh, Bob's wonderful with that kind of stuff," Eileen said. "Cathy, you should've asked before."

Cathy looked tearful. "What I mean is—it's wonderful to have a child who *wants* to look after you."

Amina had the strange feeling of being grateful to a person she had only a few moments ago wanted to strangle.

"This is normal in my country," Amina began, while George and

Bob accepted seconds of Eileen's lasagna. Suddenly there was an insistent electronic noise under the table. Harold jumped up, leaving most of his first helping untouched. He left the room and returned a moment later to say he was needed at the hospital.

"A ten-year-old with a pneumothorax. Life threatening, if we don't do it right away."

They all stood up as Harold made another phone call, and Jess collected his jacket from the closet, helping him into it while he talked. He covered the phone to thank Eileen for the dinner and then put a hand on George's arm. "Good luck, buddy," he said again, and even though she knew he was referring to George's job hunt, the phrase offended Amina. After Harold had shut the front door behind him, the six of them remained standing, as if a dignitary had left the room.

"Sometimes I miss him at night, but I'm so proud of him," Jess said, finally taking her seat again. "He's just a wonderful surgeon, everyone says so. He has this detachment—he can keep his head when other people would be falling apart. I mean, some of these cases just break your heart." Jess looked up at them. "But this isn't a subject to talk about in front of a young couple."

"I'm the same age you are," George reminded his cousin.

"*Your* age doesn't matter." Jess smiled at Amina. "I'm a Nosy Nancy, but I can't help asking—are you thinking of children yet?"

Amina looked at George for help, but he was noisily stacking the dishes.

"Leave it, leave it," Cathy said. "If I can't be trusted to cook, at least I can be useful cleaning up the mess."

"I always wanted our own kids, of course," Jess continued. "But it didn't happen for us. For a while we thought about adoption, but we were older by then, and they make it hard for you. And Harold didn't want to try other countries. He said you never know what you'll get." Jess paused, and her face and neck suddenly got very pink. She took a large swallow of wine and began complimenting Eileen again on the lasagna, which she said was delicious, but not too heavy.

"It's the pesto," Eileen said. "That's the secret." Jessica gave her aunt a grateful look.

"You don't know what you get at home either," Cathy remarked.

"You and I will clear, Catherine," Eileen said briskly. "You young people sit for a minute." But Jessica got up immediately and went to the living room to refill her wineglass, and George followed a moment later. She could see why Jessica had been embarrassed, but Amina hadn't been offended. People said things without thinking or didn't recognize the way something would sound until it was out of their mouths. Her mother had often criticized her for the same thing at home. George had been right about Harold, but as usual she'd charged ahead, practically insisting on this dinner. Now she wished they hadn't come.

"I'm going down to look at that boiler," Bob said. "Let's see if I can figure what's going wrong. It sounds like your mixer's shot."

Amina wondered if she should try to help Eileen and Cathy in the kitchen or go into the living room with George and Jess—to thank her personally now that Harold was gone. But both pairs were deep in quiet conversation, and she felt as if she would be intruding on either. She lingered in the open doorway, pretending to examine a framed needlepoint rendering of the Lord's Prayer. She'd heard of the Lord's Prayer, but never actually read it, and now she struggled to decipher the squared-off yarn letters: FORGIVE US OUR TRESPASSES, AS WE FORGIVE THOSE WHO TRESPASS AGAINST US. Her father would have been able to bring the corresponding Qur'anic verse to mind; all she could remember was *Behold, Allah is forgiving, merciful.* Nevertheless, the similarity was comforting. There was only one God, and so somewhere inside this piece of sewing was hidden the one she knew.

The doorbell rang, and George and Jessica looked up from their conversation.

"Oh God," Jessica said. "He must've forgotten something. The pager? Eileen, do you see it in the kitchen?" Jess hurried into the foyer to get the door: Harold had come to the front this time. "Oh, he's going to be so—" they heard her say, and stop.

"Hi," said a woman's voice, and Amina knew immediately. "I'm sorry to interrupt."

"Kim," Jessica said. "Did you—is that your bike?"

"I should have driven," Kim said. "I didn't know it was going to rain."

Eileen had come in from the kitchen, still holding a dish towel decorated with hens, and when Amina turned around she saw Cathy in the doorway, a look of anticipation around her neat, small mouth.

"Cathy," Eileen said quietly, and the other woman shrugged.

"Don't look at me. I never know when she'll show up."

Jess came into the dining room, followed by Kim. Kim looked around the room, her eyes holding Amina's a second too long. She was wearing a tan belted raincoat over a pair of purple yoga pants, and her hair and her clothes were soaking wet, dripping dark spots onto Cathy's pale green carpeting. Amina was struck by the way Kim's hair lost its color when wet, and also by the almost translucent whiteness of her skin. There were bluish smudges under her eyes, as if she hadn't been sleeping.

She turned to Cathy. "I was out biking—I thought I'd stop by. But then it started."

"It's been raining for hours," Cathy said.

Kim nodded. "I'm soaked."

It had been raining when she set out, but Kim had taken her bike anyway. Did she think she'd cut a more sympathetic figure this way? There was an intensity in her expression that Amina associated with alcohol, but she'd never known Kim to have a drink. It was the drama of the situation she'd engineered that excited her.

Amina looked at Jessica, to avoid making eye contact with Kim. George's cousins were standing next to each other—the one who resembled him and the beautiful foundling—and the contrast between them was stark. Jessica looked down and fingered her wedding band, and Amina thought she knew what she was thinking. Being married to Harold might not be easy, but it was better than the upheaval and uncertainty of Kim's life. She was thinking that Kim's looks, her worldliness, and style hadn't gotten her very far, while she, Jessica, had stayed in Rochester and made a life many people would envy. She was thanking her lucky stars.

"I needed to talk to you," Kim told her mother. "I didn't want to do it over the phone."

Amina glanced at George. Her husband had an ability to remove himself from an uncomfortable situation, to fix his mind on some useless piece of trivia—anything other than the problem at hand. She would have expected him to absent himself that way now, and so she was startled by his expression: a kind of fierce compassion, tender and undisguised. She saw that his hands were clenched at his sides, as if to keep them from reaching spontaneously for Kim.

She looked away, but there was nowhere safe to rest her eyes. George's mother and his aunt were watching her, as if she rather than Kim were the one creating the scene. Eileen clearly pitied her, while Cathy's curiosity was undisguised. Immediately three things became clear to Amina. Her husband was still in love with Kim. Kim had never loved him back. And everyone in this room had long been aware of those facts, except for Amina.

Kim crossed her arms in front of her chest. She was shivering. "I'm so sorry to interrupt the party. I'll get out of your hair now." But she remained standing where she was.

Cathy shook her head. "For months I don't hear from you. I don't know whether you're here or on the other side of the world. And then all of a sudden you just show up and—" She leaned on her sister's arm, then gasped and put one hand over her face, as if she were too upset to go on. For the first time Amina saw a similarity between mother and daughter, something learned rather than inherited.

"Why not call or send an e-mail first, Kimmie?" Eileen said quietly. "Wouldn't that have been better? Upsetting everyone, and getting all wet."

"Oh, she won't answer my e-mails," Kim said. "I have to barge in on her." She appeared to be talking about her mother, but Amina felt the sting of the words as though Kim had been addressing her directly.

"Well, we're about to go. Then you two can have a little chat." Eileen spoke in a light, reassuring way, as if it were an ordinary Sunday dinner, as if the evening had gone beautifully and was now regretfully drawing to a close. "Why don't you go upstairs and dry off a minute."

"Don't go because of me," Kim said. "I really just came to say good-byc."

"No, no," Eileen said. "Everyone was getting ready."

"I'm going back to Bombay," Kim told her mother. "I don't have the ticket yet, but I wanted to let you know."

Cathy exhaled sharply.

"She's trying to do better," Eileen reminded her sister.

"I've talked to Ashok, and we're going to try to make it work." The name, spoken out loud, seemed to send a current of electricity through the room; Amina thought she could feel it leaping from Cathy to Eileen to George. "He really can't be happy here. In the last generation everyone wanted to come here, but now, with the economy and everything—I mean, the opportunities are all over there." She continued addressing her mother, as if no one else in the room would be interested.

"I know I haven't always told you the truth—but I never lied about how it felt. Only what happened."

Cathy laughed shortly. "*Only* what happened! What else is there, Kimberly?"

"Never mind what happened," Eileen said. "We have to think about the present."

"You're like a yogi, Aunt Eileen. That's exactly what it's all about."

"All right, Kimmie," Eileen said. "Just go take your shower."

"I'd be careful in that shower," Cathy said.

"Sometimes I'm embarrassed by what really happened," Kim insisted. She turned to George: "Like when we were kids."

George made no acknowledgment of this but continued staring dumbly at his cousin, as he had since she'd mentioned Ashok.

"I remember people asking questions at school—who were my 'real parents' and all that. I was ashamed and so I'd make up a story. I guess I've always done it."

"We left our shoes outside," George said, finally looking away from Kim. "We have to go."

Eileen nodded, as if the second of these statements followed logically from the first. "I'm so glad you two could come."

But Kim wouldn't let them leave. She dropped the pretense and turned to speak directly to Amina.

"I think of you whenever I go into Starbucks. I thought you must've entered that contest they're having."

"Oh no," Amina said, but she wasn't surprised that Kim had noticed it, waiting in line for all her chai lattes. There was something in both their personalities that was attracted to an unlikely gamble. It was juvenile, Amina thought, one of the things she liked least about herself, and she tried to sound now as if a contest with a ten-thousand-dollar prize was of little consequence to her. "I have way too much to do before I leave."

"I wanted to tell you I went to the ICR—right after you left Yoga Shanti in December. I said I was just curious, and everyone was really nice. There were people from all over: Indonesia, the Middle East, and India. I even met a Bengali woman—I told her all about you." She seemed to expect some reaction, but when Amina didn't say anything, she continued, "The place is huge, with this beautiful stained glass. There wasn't even enough parking for everyone."

"What's this?" Cathy asked.

"International Center of Rochester," Kim said, without missing a beat, but she was still looking at Amina. "It's a place for immigrants, so they don't feel alone here. I thought Amina might like to go, to meet people."

"Thank you," Amina said, keeping her voice even. "But I'm so busy now with work and college."

"Maybe when your parents arrive." Kim gave her a significant look that infuriated Amina. How dare Kim make suggestions about how Amina ought to live her life, after everything she'd done? What qualified her to meddle in other people's affairs, after she'd made such a mess of her own?

"How wonderful that you'll be going back to India." Amina kept her voice even with effort. "Perhaps things will work out better for you this time."

Eileen looked at Amina in surprise, but Kim only shrugged slightly, hardly reacting to the provocation. Her hair was beginning to dry in blond tendrils around her face.

"We really have to go," George muttered. "Thanks for dinner, Mom."

Kim glanced back at Amina, as if the two of them were the ones who shared a secret, and then allowed Eileen to give her a gentle push toward the shower. As she walked upstairs, Eileen and Jessica exchanged a look of mutual gratitude that Amina suddenly envied. No matter how kind her mother-in-law was, the two of them would never enjoy that kind of silent understanding. How could she have thought it would be any other way?

"Will you take your cauliflower?"

"Oh no," Amina said. "We have more at home."

"It was so good," Eileen said, wrapping the plate with foil. "Don't let it go to waste."

9 The night before she left for Desh, Amina spoke to her mother on the phone six times. Her father had wanted to travel to Dhaka just to meet her at the airport, and only her most strident warnings about how angry she would be if she were to see him in the throng outside of Zia International Airport were enough to make him promise to stay in Shyamnagar. It was bad enough, Amina said, that she had to take a bus seven hours to the village and then return to Dhaka two days later. Since it was going to be the last time she would see her nanu, probably forever, there was no help for it, but for her father to make an additional journey was pointless.

She would arrive at night, and there wouldn't be a bus to Satkhira until the morning. She would stay with her aunt and uncle in Savar, and her uncle's driver, Fariq, would pick her up at the airport.

"If your aunt is unfriendly, don't mind her," Amina's mother said. "She's just envious that you're bringing us to America. She keeps asking why George isn't coming with you. And she wants to know why you haven't had a baby yet."

"It's only one night," Amina said. "They had Fariq buy me the bus ticket. I'll have to leave the house at seven in the morning."

"We'd still like to come and meet you," her mother said. "What if something happens to you at the airport? And I don't feel safe here, even another two nights."

"I have schoolwork to do," Amina said. "I don't have time to talk anymore tonight." She had to e-mail Jill her Amy Tan paper before she left, and she still didn't have a conclusion.

"Maybe a hotel is better," her mother said, as if she hadn't heard her. "Could you still reserve one?"

"George lost his job four months ago," Amina said. "We had to ask his cousin Jessica to sponsor you. She went to a lot of trouble, and who knows if we're even going to be able to keep this house."

Her mother was silent on the other end of the line, and even as she knew she'd done something drastic, there was some relief in confessing the bad news. It had been more than two weeks since the dinner party, but the shame of it wouldn't leave Amina. She didn't know whether Kim had actually left when she'd planned, and yet it would have been humiliating to ask George for information. She had a crazy urge to tell her mother about the look on her husband's face when Kim had appeared, soaking wet and begging forgiveness, but even if she'd had the nerve to do it, her mother never could have understood.

"You see how much stress we've been under," she said instead, sounding harsher than she'd intended. "What are you so frightened of? You've lived in that village almost half your life."

Still her mother was quiet, and she worried that she'd gone too far. Had her mother put the phone against her chest and gone in tears to find her father? She knew this was only her pride, but she hoped there was a way to keep her father from learning about George's failure.

"Amma," she said. "Are you there?"

She heard her mother breathing.

"Promise you won't tell Abba. Promise me."

"Engineering job?" her mother said in English.

She hadn't known her mother knew those words. From the easy way she pronounced them, Amina could tell that her mother had repeated that formulation again and again, to combat other people's skepticism and quiet her own doubts. George's "engineering job" had been like a piece of magic, powerful as anything her *pir* could give her, and the loss of it now was as wrenching as it had been to Amina.

Her impulse was less to comfort her mother than to be comforted by her. As a child on the long bus rides to Haibatpur, she would curl her body over her half of the seat and put her head in her mother's lap. Something about that position allowed her to sleep for hours, even through the madness of the horn, while her mother sat quietly, shifting every once in a while under her weight and running her fingers through Amina's hair.

"Is my father there?"

"No, no."

"Where is he?"

"He's gone to the pharmacy with your uncle Rana." Her tone made Amina think she was lying, but she didn't have time to draw it out.

"Your nanu and Parveen are in the kitchen. No one knows I'm calling you again."

"Never mind." Amina tried to make her voice soothing. "Hang up the phone and don't tell them anything I said. Don't even tell them you called me. Everything's going to be fine, I promise."

She expected her mother to argue: How could everything be fine if George didn't have a job? But it was almost worse to hear her meekly agree.

"I'll be on the plane in eleven hours," Amina said. "I'll see you in less than three days."

Her mother didn't warn her about being careful at the airport, or the danger of her bags being ransacked by thieves. She didn't ask whether the food on the plane would be such that Amina could eat it, or speculate about the best answers to the questions her aunt would surely ask. She said good night and quietly hung up, just as her daughter had instructed, and from this Amina understood that her mother no longer believed they were going to be reunited. She thought she was going to die in that village, pursued by whatever ghosts she was so frightened of, because her only daughter hadn't arrived in time.

A Proposal

1 The stale air of the terminal, heavy with mildew and insecticide, gave way to the more powerful organic rot of the August night. The humidity was almost twice what it had been when she got on the plane in Rochester, and she felt the weight of it on her skin. It had been raining, and there was the smell of things burning: garbage, diesel, refuse, and cooking oil. Amina had been in no hurry to return to it, but in dreams this odor was the one thing you couldn't reproduce, and so now it was the difference between thinking of home and being here.

A sea of disembodied arms reached through the iron bars of the barrier, grabbing the air. It was democratic at least: relatives and drivers jostled right up next to the taxi men, con artists, and thieves. The airport police held the crowd back with their sticks, but they didn't make eye contact with the passengers. Once you were outside the terminal, you were on your own. Amina was carrying four hundred American dollars and the credit card in a money belt against her stomach, a trick she'd learned from George when he'd come here to meet her. He'd had all sorts of ideas about securing his valuables on that trip, and she remembered at the time feeling privileged to hear about them, as if it were somehow flattering that he mistrusted every citizen of Bangladesh apart from her.

An hour before the flight landed, she had slipped into the toilet and changed into a shalwar kameez, the same one she'd worn for her interview at Yoga Shanti. Kim had admired it then, but perhaps there was something wrong with the way it hung on her body now, because all of a sudden she noticed that the men calling out to her had switched to English.

"Here, madam! Good clean car—"

"Your bags, madam. Allow me."

"My taxi, yes, okay miss, this way."

She scanned the crowd, but her parents weren't there. She realized suddenly that she'd expected them to disobey her instructions and appear. Good, she thought, *good*—but she couldn't conceal her disappointment even from herself. She'd been ready to be exasperated, to chastise them for making the long trip, and instead she felt loneliness bubbling up in her like water into a well. What was worse than going home to find no one you knew?

She finally saw her uncle's driver, Fariq, a few paces behind the barrier. As soon as he spotted her, he swept in and relieved her of the suitcases with a darting, practiced movement. There was nothing aggressive about it, and at the same time he made it clear that she was his. The taxi drivers—dark, bony men with reddish teeth, shirts hanging loose on their bodies—stepped back. She'd known Fariq for years, but she was struck now by how modern and prosperous he looked in a fashionably patterned shirt and black jeans, his mobile phone clipped to his belt.

"Your uncle has a new car," he said. "The black one over there—an Acura." His phone rang, and he answered it; she reached instinctively into her purse for her own to call her parents, before remembering it was useless here. She listened to Fariq instead, heard him telling her aunt that he'd found her without any problem.

"Two large ones," he said—of course her aunt was eager to know how much luggage she'd brought with her.

"Your uncle will have gone to bed, but your aunty is sitting up for you," Fariq said when he hung up.

Her whole body was tired, but her mind had the jangly, wakeful feeling that sometimes came over her when she was lying in bed at night in Rochester. As soon as they left the airport, the traffic was stop and go, and she thought of how exasperated George had been four years ago, describing his trip back to the airport. What could've been going on at that hour? he had wanted to know. She'd explained that it wasn't any particular thing, that the city simply hadn't been built for cars, or for the number of people who currently inhabited it. He had wanted to see the famous parliament buildings lit up at night, but his driver hadn't understood and had taken another road.

For a while they crept through the cantonment area past the high, white walls of the military buildings, some studded with broken glass. She would have liked to continue south on a tour of her childhood: Tejgaon, Motijheel, Mirpur, and Mohammadpur, where they'd lived for various lengths of time; the genteel neighborhoods where she'd taught her students; and the university district where she'd gone with her mother to visit the British Council. It felt wrong to be cutting across the city in her uncle's new car, heading west toward Savar.

She turned around when they reached the Mirpur Road, looking back toward Dhanmondi. Maple Leaf was all the way on the other side of the lake, but that was the way her mother had taken her by rickshaw to school each day. It seemed incredible that it could be the same road, the same asphalt, that they had traveled so many times together. You thought that you were the permanent part of your own experience, the net that held it all together—until you discovered that there were many selves, dissolving into one another so quickly over time that the buildings and the trees and even the pavement turned out to have more substance than you did.

She was still looking out the window when a motorcycle went by, and two young men ducked to look at her—to see what kind of woman was being chauffeured in the fancy new car—before cutting Fariq off and continuing to weave in and out of the creeping traffic. Instinctively Amina pulled the scarf over her head, and at once the urge to sleep became too powerful to resist. For the rest of the two-hour drive, the scenery went by without Amina to notice it.

2 It was nearly midnight when they arrived at her aunt and uncle's new apartment in Savar, but all the lights were burning. Her uncle wasn't sleeping after all, but sitting at a long wooden dining table drinking tea. Apart from the table, and twelve chairs with green satin cushions, there was no other furniture in the room. A telephone sat on the floor next to the jack, and through one door she could see a

massive canopied bed with a modern red-and-gold spread—her aunt and uncle's room.

She heard her aunt's voice in the kitchen: "Has she arrived? It took so long—all the dishes are cold. Munni, come here, let me look at you." But her aunt came to her, wiping her hands on a towel and embracing her, then stroking her hair, as if she were a little girl.

"All by yourself. So far. I can't believe it." Her aunt was shorter and smaller than she remembered; her hair was pulled back in a tight bun, and she was wearing an olive-green shalwar kameez, finer and more ornamented than Amina would've expected given that she was the only guest.

"We called your parents as soon as we heard from Fariq that you were safe. We knew it would be too late by the time you arrived here."

Amina nodded, but she hadn't thought there would be a "too late." Of course she talked to them all the time, but a phone call from inside the country was different. She'd expected to hear her mother's voice tonight, and all of a sudden she was afraid she might cry. She went to her suitcases quickly and spent a few minutes rummaging (although the appropriate gifts were at the very top, where she'd been sure to pack them): the perfume for her aunt, and the pocket-sized travel alarm clock for her uncle. She could feel her aunt looking from across the room, trying to get a glimpse of what else was inside. While they were opening their gifts, she found the box of Christmas ornaments and chose the robin for Ghaniyah: a bird that always seemed to Amina to be calling out for attention, hopping and stamping like a spoiled child.

"This is just a trinket for my cousin," she told her aunt. "The most famous American bird. Please tell her how sorry I am to have missed her."

Her aunt was still looking at the bags. "How did you manage all of this on your own?"

"Emirates is very comfortable. And I didn't want to ask George to come here again—he's so busy with work."

"Such a shame the two of you weren't able to come for their wedding. And now bad luck—the two of them off touring. They said they never had a honeymoon—*honeymoon! We* didn't need honeymoons when we were young, I told them—the wedding was enough for us.

But they just laugh at me. And India is so expensive these days." Her aunt looked at Amina pointedly. "You didn't take a honeymoon, I'm sure."

"I had just arrived in America. I didn't need to go anywhere."

"You're much more practical than my daughter. Now you'll eat. We've finished, but you must be starving."

Her aunt brought a knife and fork with the food, even though they'd always eaten with their fingers when she'd visited in the past. She wasn't hungry: the nap in the car seemed to have produced only a desire for more sleep, but her aunt was carrying dish after dish from the kitchen.

"My parents said the wedding was beautiful," Amina said. "They said the food was delicious."

Her aunt frowned. "The sweets weren't fresh enough. They should've been made just that afternoon. And the mutton was dry. I'm sure they said so."

Amina began the ritual denial, but her aunt cut her off: "Your mother looked so skinny. I gasped the last time I saw her."

"She's always been thin," Amina said. "She'll be very fashionable in America."

"That's what I tell everyone, when they ask." Her aunt tapped her forehead: "It's only up here that I worry."

"Sit, sit," her uncle said. "At least we have chairs."

"The furniture is coming," her aunt said crossly. "They made a mistake with our order. We're getting everything new—I don't know if your mother told you. All of the old things were shipped to Chittagong for Rashid. Your mother told you about his job at the new international university? And Marin is pregnant—they'll do the ultrasound in two weeks to determine the sex." Amina had always been a little frightened of Ghaniyah's older brother, who'd been a math prodigy as a child and gone to college to study computer science when he was only sixteen years old. She knew her aunt and uncle had counted on Rashid going into business and making a terrific fortune and were disappointed by this university job. But naturally her aunt didn't complain about the things that really bothered her.

"One son all the way in Chittigong, and my son-in-law is such a big, important man—he never has time for dinner with his in-laws. Why do we need this huge apartment? I asked your uncle. Who will ever come to see us? Except you," she added, looking Amina over. "And you look so tired. How many jobs do you have over there?"

"Only one," Amina said. "With Starbucks, the international coffee chain store. It's close to my college campus." She was about to say something about Starbucks's ranking in *Fortune*'s top 100, but she caught herself. It no longer mattered what her aunt or anyone thought. In nine days she and her parents would be at the airport, inshallah, out of the family's reach forever.

Her aunt was sweating in spite of the air-conditioning. There was moisture on her upper lip, darkening the mustache that she'd been struggling to eradicate for as long as Amina could remember. Moni and Amina's mother shared their nanu's elegant features, but her aunt was so much more substantially built that on her that kind of beauty looked almost masculine. Amina thought of her mother, who would be cold at this temperature, and experienced another wave of longing. Now that she was back, all of the bickering they'd done over the phone could be forgotten. That had been the stress of being separated; secretly she believed that her mother's anxiety was only because she missed her. In Rochester they called it empty-nest syndrome. Now that she had come for them, her mother would return to normal, and they would never be separated again. A night and day seemed too long to wait.

Her uncle yawned and folded his paper. "I'm ready for bed. I hope you ladies won't keep each other up too late gossiping."

"She comes here for one night only," her aunt complained. "Less than two weeks to spend at home. And I had to beg her mother to stay with us when they return to Dhaka."

When her uncle had gone to bed and she had finished eating, Amina suddenly felt better. It was midmorning in Rochester, and she had a surge of energy: her body must've gotten the idea that she'd just fed it breakfast. She could see that her aunt was exhausted but didn't want to go to bed yet. There was something in particular that she wanted to say to Amina.

"I hope the excitement of seeing you won't be too much for your mother. Parveen's been worried, too."

"She's been under a lot of pressure, waiting all this time," Amina said. She was aware that she was defending her mother for exactly the kind of behavior that had driven her crazy over the phone in Rochester; now that her aunt was needling her, however, it was impossible not to take her mother's side. "She'll be better once we get to Rochester."

"I only hope there are no problems," her aunt said darkly. "Of course they have to leave Shyamnagar as soon as possible. I was hoping you might come earlier."

"It had to do with the paperwork. It wasn't up to me when I came."

"I only wonder if you'll be safe there."

"Safe in the village?" She felt she was taking her aunt's bait, but there was no other way to find out what she meant.

"You know I respect your father." Her aunt pleated the hem of her orna, which she now wore even in the house. Her mother said that Moni was becoming more religious, that she'd started putting an abaya over her clothes when she went out shopping. But her father laughed and said his sister-in-law was only trying to hide the fat.

"But I can't help worrying when your mother calls me in such a state. This was right after they returned from your dadu's, after the storm. It's gotten much worse since then."

"*What's* gotten worse?" Amina demanded.

"If your father had taken something that wasn't his, no one could protect him. Especially if he'd taken it from his own people."

It took several moments for her brain to absorb the strangeness of what her aunt was saying. She was looking at Amina in a probing way that made it almost impossible to think, since she was concentrating on concealing her thoughts as much as she was on having them.

"My father is the most honest person I've ever met," she said finally. "Too honest—he's not crafty or clever, the way you have to be to succeed in business."

She wouldn't have said it if her uncle had been in the room; she liked her uncle Omar, who had always been kind to them. She thought he'd succeeded not out of any deviousness, but because he was the type of person whom God willed to be successful. Others were not meant to be so. It didn't mean that God loved them any less, but the world couldn't be full of only one type. The sooner you knew which type you were—and which were the people in your family—the sooner you could accept your lot and be happy.

"Of course you don't want to think about that," her aunt said. "You're his daughter, so it's natural."

"I don't like gossip," Amina said. "That's what I like about America. People say things straight out." She felt herself flushing as she said this; once, she had believed it.

Her aunt was looking at her carefully. "No one will believe that gold was stolen from them. Even if it is true."

Suddenly Amina remembered her last phone conversation with Nasir, coded because her parents were standing right there.

"Are you talking about jewelry?"

But now that her aunt had ascertained that she knew more than Amina, she was satisfied.

"I don't know your father's family. How should I know what they have?"

"But what gold do you mean? You know my mother sold the things Nanu gave her years ago. And she never had any wedding gold."

"Of course this wasn't your mother's. Why would your father have to steal that? But you'd better ask your parents—I don't want to repeat hearsay. Especially since you seem to dislike it so much." She gave Amina a tight-lipped smile. Her aunt's complexion was sallow in the overhead light, and Amina could see their two miniature figures reflected in the black window across the room. "You must be so tired, and you'll have to be up early to catch the bus."

Amina didn't say anything.

"You barely ate, Munni. Maybe our food isn't up to your standards anymore."

"The food was delicious, Aunt."

"Oh, I hardly cook anymore. It's Borsha—my new girl from the village. These girls are lazy, but at least they're good in the kitchen. They're too ignorant to take shortcuts."

Her aunt and uncle did have a second bed, a narrow twin with one of the plush blankets Amina remembered, printed with moons and stars. She had thought it would be difficult to sleep in Dhaka now that she was accustomed to Rochester's deep nighttime hush, but Savar was quieter than Mohammadpur, and her aunt and uncle's generator drowned out what noise there was. She couldn't blame her wakefulness on the city, and she hadn't brought a book to read, and so she lay in bed thinking of what she'd heard from Nasir and her aunt. Both stories had several pieces missing. It was impossible to think that her father could've stolen anything, much less gold jewelry, but she had an uncomfortable feeling that there might have been a misunderstanding. Her father had a tendency to leap several steps ahead in his own financial dealings, so that he often believed an agreement had been reached or a partnership struck before there was good reason to do so. The gold jewelry was the detail that bothered her, since it had appeared in both her aunt's and Nasir's accounts. Coming from two such disparate sources, it was hard to believe it was a fabrication. And if her father had come into possession of gold in some legitimate way, why hadn't she heard of it?

She was awake for nearly three hours and fell into a deep sleep only just before morning. She dreamed she was back in Rochester; it was raining hard, and the red geraniums she had planted in pots were getting crushed. As she began to bring in the geraniums, she noticed two small figures coming up the hill where Skytop curved and disappeared toward Wood Hill, fighting with an umbrella that was turning inside out in the wind.

Amina retrieved the big golf umbrella from the hall closet and started out into the storm to help her parents. Her mother was in only a thin shalwar kameez, without even a sweater over her shoulders. They were calling her—oddly they weren't using her nickname—and she yelled that she was coming. She had almost reached them when the wind lifted her parents several feet off the ground, where they hovered eerily. And it was only then that Amina realized, to her horror, that she was looking at a pair of jinnis, who had craftily adopted human forms in order to lure her out of her house.

The calling got louder and more insistent—*Amina, Amina*—until she finally managed to open her eyes and see a young girl, her aunt's new servant, Borsha, looking shyly at her own bare feet on the marble floor.

3 It was raining when she arrived at the bus depot with Fariq, who told her to wait in the car. He'd reserved her seat yesterday, and now he was negotiating with the driver, giving him a tip from her uncle to look after the showy foreign suitcases and make sure that her father received them safely on the other end. She used the few moments alone in the car to dial her father's number from the phone her uncle had lent her—a spare—and was startled when it went on ringing. Even when she called too late or too early from Rochester, he only very rarely missed it; sometimes there was a problem with the phone itself, but her parents were always available. She wondered if that was the trouble today, although her uncle had said he'd been able to reach them easily last night. Of all the mornings in the world, this was the one she expected they would keep the phone turned on. How could she be sure her father knew which bus she was on and that her parents would be waiting for her at half past three in Satkhira?

Fariq and the driver had agreed upon a price, although Amina didn't see the money change hands, and her uncle's driver returned to the car looking relaxed: he had fulfilled his duty for the morning. There was already a crowd around the Satkhira bus, and Amina found that the depot looked much worse to her than it had in the past. A mob of people clamored at the ticket counter, and there was a wide lake of black sewage between the station and the street, over which a mother and father were in the midst of passing three small girls in hair ribbons and stiff, garishly ornamented dresses. She wondered if her reaction to the scene was the effect of her time in America or simply of arriving in her uncle's air-conditioned car, which made the transition to the street much more dramatic than it was if you traveled by rickshaw.

"Please ask my aunt to try my father again later," she told him, when he got back in the car. "I might lose service on the way, and I want to make sure he knows I'm on this bus." Fariq took the phone without asking and redialed the number, as if her difficulty might be the result of general female incompetence. She reminded herself that this characteristic in Bengali men was one of the things she'd left the country to escape and was perversely pleased when Fariq had no better luck with the phone.

"No problem with the connection," he said anyway, as if he had settled things.

She had called George this morning, and her aunt had been unusually sensitive, going to take her bath while Amina was on the phone. George had been sitting at the computer, doing his e-mail and waiting for her call. He asked her if it was nice to be home.

"It's wonderful," she said. "My aunt cooked all my favorite things last night, and now I'm going to the village to see Nanu and my parents."

"Great," George said, and she could hear in his voice that he didn't feel threatened by her past or the pull it might exert on her now that she was back. What did he have to be jealous about, after all?

There was a long silence, in which she'd heard George typing.

"I'm calling from my uncle's old phone," Amina said. "You don't remember, but I called you from this phone the first time we ever talked, because we weren't getting a good signal from our house. That was before my aunt and uncle moved to Savar, but this phone is the same one. My mother was trying to distract my aunt, but she couldn't do it because she was so interested in hearing us herself."

"Do you know the population of Savar?" George asked.

"What?"

"It's three hundred seventy-eight thousand thirty-four, according to the 1991 census. That's the only number I could find, and it's almost twenty years old. Imagine what that number is now."

"I don't know," Amina said.

"But you remember the population of Rochester," George coaxed. "Two hundred nineteen thousand, give or take. And that's the third-biggest city in New York. Savar's only a suburb, and it probably has twice as many people!"

"I should go," Amina said. "My aunt's getting out of her bath."

"Okay," George said cheerfully. "Call me when you get to the village, if you can."

"Yes, okay," Amina said. "George?" But she didn't know what she wanted to say. She wanted him to say something about what had happened to them in between the time they'd made that first call and this one, but she knew he wasn't going to do that. "I was thinking about your trip here—about when we decided to get married."

"Yeah." George laughed. "I was so stressed out."

"Me, too," Amina said. "But I mean, did we ever really decide?"

George assumed a familiar, patient tone. "What do you mean?"

"I mean, did we ever say 'Let's get married' or anything?"

"Of course," George said. "We already knew we were getting married that day in your parents' apartment. Otherwise why would you have tried on the ring?"

But Amina couldn't recall a particular moment.

"Why are you worried about this now? Is everything okay over there?"

"Yes." Something clattered to the floor in the kitchen, and her aunt's voice floated, querulous, from the other end of the apartment.

"So I'll talk to you in a few days."

"Yes, okay."

After they had said good-bye and hung up, she sat on the cushionless window seat holding her uncle's phone, looking out the window at a brick interior courtyard that had flooded in the rain. Leaves and other detritus were floating in the water, which had already acquired a greenish-brown algal scum, and as she watched a newspaper drifted into view, opened neat and flat, as if there were some underwater reader turning the pages. Its front and back covers faced the sky, and of course you couldn't read the text from this distance.

She had breakfasted with her aunt, who was in a mild, generous mood, almost as if the conversation the night before hadn't happened. She'd given Amina three clean handkerchiefs, as well as several containers of food in a neat Jamdani Sarees bag. To Amina's surprise, she had also apologized for not offering her parents an alternative to the village when they'd decided to give up the apartment, and begged her to not to let her mother change her mind about staying in Savar when they returned.

"She says you might also stay with that relative of your father's—some Nabil or Nasim?"

"Nasir," Amina corrected. "Not a relative, just a friend."

"But he's a single man, no?" her aunt persisted. "His place couldn't be comfortable." She added that she was going to buy another bed just in case the furniture didn't come in the next few days. "Then you'll have to stay with us," she had said triumphantly, and Amina had promised that they would.

The bus hit a jam in Savar, and they were stuck for almost an hour. But once they left the suburbs behind, the traffic abated, and soon the bus was careening west toward the Padma, which they would cross by ferry. They passed the last factories, and then the red fields of the brickyards: HOME BRICKS in solid black letters across the kilns. Her seat was in the first row, but she didn't like to look straight in front of her; the driver played chicken with the oncoming traffic, swerving and laying on the horn at the last minute. Instead she looked out the side window as they rushed past field after field of jute and paddy. She had forgotten the saturated color of the rice shoots, bottle green, as if they had a light inside them.

After two hours they reached the river. She got off the bus with the other passengers and climbed a steep, rusted staircase to the top deck of the ferry for some air. She thought George would've liked to photograph the spindly bamboo fish traps that jutted out of the river like giant sprung bows and the fishermen, oblivious to the crowded car ferry, crouching on the rafts to check the nets. She had told her husband again and again that Bangladesh was beautiful once you got out of the city, but in the nine days he'd spent in her country they hadn't had the chance to go farther than the National Martyrs' Memorial in Savar. Now she wondered if he would agree with her. There was a thick haze, but you could just make out the vegetation on the bank opposite; clumps of water hyacinths floated like tiny islands in the ferry's path. If you stood very close to the rail and trained your eyes directly in front of you, it was possible to see a landscape with absolutely no people: just a large black cormorant, gliding low over the water, its improbable blurred shadow the only evidence of the hidden sun.

Amina tried her father's phone again, but now she got no signal. When she returned to the bus, she found she'd lingered too long on the deck: the only seat available was at the very back, next to an old woman eating pungent dried fish from a newspaper packet, making satisfied sounds with her lips. They eased off the ferry and onto the road, and Amina turned resolutely toward the window opposite, concentrating on the trees to avoid nausea. Could she still identify them? Guava, mango, and jackfruit were easy, date and coconut palm, but which were the betel palms? Could she spot a *krishnachura* without the telltale red blossoms it would have lost this late in the monsoon? She remembered how she'd dreaded this uncomfortable trip as a teenager, how she'd stayed up the night before so that she could pass most of it asleep. Now everything—the birds, the trees, the sight of a young man just standing by the road, watching the traffic as if it were his job—was a picture to take back with her and own forever. Compared with this, the junk she'd brought along in her suitcases was nothing.

The old woman finished chewing and began interrogating her. Where was she going? Was she married? How many children did she have? Why was she traveling alone? Amina told her that she'd been married only six weeks ago and was now going to visit her grandmother, who had been too sick to come to the wedding. Her husband had wanted to travel with her, she said, but he had taken so much time off from his work at the bank for the wedding that it had been impossible. Of course she would have preferred to travel with him, but she couldn't wait to taste her aunt's cooking, which was the best in the village. Even her own wedding food couldn't compare: the mutton had been overcooked, and the sweets had not been fresh enough.

The woman, who had seemed as if she might keep prodding Amina for information all the way to Satkhira, was satisfied with this topic. For the next hour she talked to Amina about the deficiencies of meat and produce in the capital compared with what you could find in the villages, particularly in the south. She had been in the city visiting the family of a girl, a possible match for her son. Her son was tall and fair and had inherited land near Satkhira from his grandfather, but this girl's family was haughty and demanding, even questioning the value of a degree from Khulna University.

"She is fair, but short—as short as I am," the old woman said. "Who are they to be so picky?"

Finally, after nearly an hour, the old woman fell silent; a few minutes later, she was asleep. It was getting toward the hottest part of the day, and the air in the bus was so wet and thick that any movement was uncomfortable. They passed a herd of small brown-and-white goats, and a man with a stick who stopped to stare at them, but the rest of the landscape was perfectly still. Everything was so green that you almost expected to look up and see a green sun in the sky, igniting sparks in the flat, glass paddy. At intervals you could see a woman with a basket at her feet, an orange, yellow, or turquoise figure crouched double, harvesting rice or dal or mustard. Amina had never been in danger of becoming one of those women; her nanu and even her dadu's status in their villages mitigated against that. But she'd been born in the same type of village: it was extraordinary to think of how different her life had become.

Amina looked at her watch—a stainless-steel Seiko that George had given her for her first Christmas in Rochester—and discovered that they were ahead of schedule. Not surprisingly, the driver had made up the time he'd lost at the beginning of the journey, and she wondered if her father would've thought to come early. She couldn't imagine standing in the road with the two large suitcases, but she knew everyone at home would berate her for acting like a fool if she tried to negotiate the fare alone.

They crossed the last small river, swollen at this time of year and smothered in a green profusion of water hyacinths. There was no indication of water at all; if not for an abandoned wooden skiff, half submerged, the river could be an overgrown path or even a flower bed. She thought of the yard in Rochester, and the way Kim had arrived that frigid February day—insinuating herself into Amina's life with a gift and a confidence. Kim would like that useless boat and the children crouched by the bank poking something in the water with a stick, who stopped to wave at the bus as it passed. Unlike George, photography wouldn't be her main motivation: she would want to get down and talk with those children, even if the only way they could communicate was with their hands, to admire and to be admired by them. She was a person, Amina thought, who couldn't resist putting herself into every vista she encountered.

Satkhira was as she remembered it. First came the furniture makers, carving chairs and bed frames in the shade of the cotton trees. There was a new Emma Motors showroom, with a sleek row of motorcycles behind glass, but otherwise the open shops were the same as they had always been—pharmacies, dry goods, sweets—overrun with flies, always with more proprietors than customers. She scanned the taxi rank for her father several times and felt the panic squeezing her chest: he wasn't there. The old woman next to her had woken up and was collecting her parcels; now that they were here, her interest in Amina had evaporated.

"Hurry," she hissed. "Push. There's my son—the handsome one right over there."

With a sick feeling, Amina got up and started making her way to the front: she was being jostled from every side, and it was a struggle just to keep her feet. She saw the bus driver standing outside, smoking a cigarette, and she knew she would have to approach him to get her suitcases; of course he would ask for more money. She was so focused on what she had to do that it wasn't until her feet were on the ground that she noticed the gaunt figure in pink standing by a cluster of rickshaws. As she watched, the woman took two hesitant steps forward, into the sun, and an anxious, hollow face peered out from under the orna.

"Amma!" she cried, but of course her mother had already seen her.

4 The drivers crowded around her when they saw her luggage, but her mother had already arranged their transportation. A man who'd been squatting in the tented shade of a mechanic's shop bounded forward to collect Amina's suitcases. He was small, almost black, with a threadbare lungi and hard, ropy muscles in his arms and legs, and he ignored the taunts of the drivers: *Bhai, bhai—where's your car? Are you going to carry those all the way to Shyamnagar?*

"Where's Abba?" Amina asked. "You didn't come alone?"

Her mother shook her head. "Wait just a minute, just wait. When we're on the bus." Her mother was clutching her arm, as she had since they'd found each other, allowing Amina to support her but also guiding her in the direction she wanted to go. The bus was already there waiting, a small blessing, and they boarded with the porter, who sat in the front with their suitcases. Amina and her mother took seats a few rows back.

"His van is at the market in Shyamnagar," her mother said. "It will be much cheaper." Amina regretted for the hundredth time in only a few days telling her mother about George's job. She had plenty of money, and she dreaded another hour on another bus, this time over the decaying local roads. But it didn't seem worth arguing with her mother, who was obviously concentrating fiercely, in the midst of executing a complicated plan.

"Where's Abba?" she demanded again. "Why isn't he with you?"

"Your uncle Ashraf accompanied me," her mother said. "But he has some business in Satkhira. He hired this van-wallah, and then he waited with me until it was time for his appointment."

"But how did you know I would be on that bus? Did my uncle Omar reach you?"

"We came early in the morning. We arrived before seven a.m."

Amina was incredulous. "You've been standing there for seven hours?"

"Standing and sitting," her mother said. "Ashraf bought me two cups of tea. And I went to the good shop to buy shondesh." Her mother produced a small white box from the plastic bag she was carrying. "Eat, eat. I bought three boxes."

It was all Amina could do not to shove her mother's hand away.

"Why didn't my father come to meet me?" Her voice was louder than she intended, and the other passengers on the bus—country people clutching all manner of bundles—turned to look at them.

"Hush," her mother said, as if she were still a child. "Your father is fine. He is in Dhaka now, but he'll call us on your nanu's phone tonight. After supper."

"In Dhaka?"

"We'll talk about it."

"Why wasn't he answering his phone? I called three times."

"You didn't want him to come to Dhaka. You told him you would be angry if you saw him at the airport." The bus dipped into a hole in the road; Amina wasn't paying attention, and she came down hard on the hard seat.

"Hold on to me," her mother said.

"But where is he staying?"

"With Nasir. He'll shift to Moni and Omar's when we arrive. I'd like to go tomorrow, but your nanu is already upset about your visit being so short."

"But why is he in Dhaka, if he wasn't going to meet me?"

"He was supposed to meet you—but he was worried it wouldn't be safe."

Amina heard her aunt's voice again in her head. She'd hoped there would be some easy explanation for Moni's warnings, and now her mother was reinforcing them, being equally cryptic. It wasn't that she thought anything her mother was saying was untrue, but only that she wished she wouldn't tell the story so dramatically.

"Safe from *what*?"

Her mother adjusted her orna. Then she wrapped her arm around Amina's waist, pulling her toward her and cushioning her from the jolt that came a moment later, as if she could somehow see the road ahead of them. She didn't let go after the bad patch was finished and spoke in her smallest voice, further muffled by the cloth across her face.

"Your father went to Dhaka three days ago. He wanted to be there when you arrived. I didn't mind—it was a good thing for him to do. It's not so bad living with your nanu when he's not around. I can manage her. But she drives him crazy, and then he drives me crazy about it. If I'm crazy, I'm always telling them, it's because of the two of you."

Amina laughed, but her mother was immediately serious again.

"He was planning to stay with Moni and Omar, of course—and then they called to warn us. Apparently they had a visit from Salim."

"My father's cousin?"

"Everyone in your father's village knew you were coming to take us to America. Of course Bhulu and Laltu must've assumed your husband was coming, too—we all did." Her mother gave her a pointed look, which Amina tried to ignore. "They thought we'd be staying with Moni and Omar, so they sent Salim to Savar the week before you arrived. He told your aunt and uncle lies—they didn't believe him, of course—making threats to your father. He said Abba wasn't safe if he stayed in Dhaka."

"What kind of lies?"

Her mother looked at her sharply. "Why would I repeat that non-sense? He's insane—everyone knows it. What *wouldn't* he say?"

Amina looked at her mother: she couldn't believe what three years had done. She was emaciated—her aunt hadn't been wrong about that—and the hair that Amina could see coming out from under the scarf, which had been mostly black when she left, was now almost entirely gray. The bright pink outfit had the effect of making her look smaller and much older than she was, as might happen if you tried to pack some treasures from this country into one of the brand-new purple suitcases from Kmart.

"But what does he want from my father?"

Her mother looked at her with a trace of exasperation. "Money, of course."

Amina was about to ask why anyone would come to her father for money, but her mother was already standing, pushing to get off the crowded bus. The van-wallah had gotten down and was loading her suitcases into his makeshift vehicle. Her mother chided him gently about the position of the suitcases, suggesting a different configuration to balance the weight. She nudged Amina into the back of the van, where she had to bend her neck slightly to accommodate the curve of the roof. The frame was covered on the inside with layers of newspaper and paste to make a smooth canopy, and the outside was protected with sheets of plastic, carefully stitched into a waterproof cover. As girls she and Micki had loved sitting at the very back, letting their legs dangle off the edge and making faces at other children they encountered on the road.

Her mother let her hand rest carefully on top of one of the purple suitcases. She looked as if she were going to speak, then stopped her-self. All around them were fields of paddy, wet and green after the rain. They passed a small, square fish pond enclosed by mango trees. A woman was squatting there, collecting water in a open-mouthed copper jug. The water was so still, you could see her reflection on the surface of the pond.

"That's the road to Babur Bari," her mother said, as if Amina might not remember it. "So much looting these days. This country is very bad."

"What are they looting?"

"Bricks. Women take bricks from the ruins, and then they sell them to the foremen at the construction sites."

"Amma, what do they want from us? Abba doesn't have any money."

"But they don't know that." Her mother spoke slowly, as if she were addressing a child. "They think your American husband can give them whatever they want."

Amina thought her father's cousins were a nuisance, nothing more, and that her mother was imagining the worst as usual. But she couldn't free herself from the idea that her father had unwittingly involved himself in something unscrupulous. She was afraid that if she cornered her mother and demanded to know about the gold jewelry, she might lie out of shame or embarrassment.

"Abba will be angry I told you about Salim. He wanted to spare you all this."

"Of course you needed to tell me." Amina tried to sound soothing. She thought the whole story would come out, if she could simply be patient with her mother.

"But your father always felt terrible about how frightened you were that time at Long Nose's. After he got home that afternoon, I remember he said he'd never seen you so scared."

"I don't like being shut in. I'm not afraid of *people*."

"That's when Long Nose gave you your nickname."

"I was Munni before Long Nose."

Her mother shook her head impatiently. "Not Munni—don't you remember? He used to call you Mynah."

They passed the turnoff to the rest house, with its artificial lake and miniature zoo: a failed tourism scheme by the local MP. Up ahead was the familiar silhouette of the primary school and then, before she expected it, her uncle Ashraf's new concrete house and the path into the village.

"'Little Mynah, you will fly away one day'—he would say that when we saw him in the corridor. You hated it, of course."

"I don't remember that."

"But he was right," her mother said.

5 Parveen was waiting when the van stopped outside her grand-mother's gate. As soon as Amina stepped down, her aunt began to cry. She clutched her niece and then pushed her away to examine her, holding her head between two hands so Amina could hardly hear.

"So skinny still," she said. "Don't they feed you over there?"

"That's the fashion," her mother put in. "They want to be that way."

"I'm not a good cook like you, Aunty."

Her aunt beamed. "Wait until you see what I've made."

Her mother handed the package of shondesh to her aunt, who confirmed the shop it had come from, nodding her approval. Then she turned back to Amina.

"We thought you might not arrive."

"I told you I was coming," Amina said. "Where's Nanu?"

"She was napping," Parveen said, "*Ai*, Amma! Come and see. Your granddaughter is back from America."

"Don't wake her," Amina protested, but her grandmother was already coming around the corner of the house. The house had been painted recently, mustard with dark green shutters, and the new palm fence extended around the pond and garden. It was the time of day when the light turned orange, dappling the pond, and the trees thrust sharp, black shadows over the path. Nanu was walking toward her—so slowly!—in an old lavender sari translucent with wear. Once her grandmother had bathed her at this hour, holding her wrist so that she wouldn't slip on the slick, submerged steps of the pond. *Hold still*, she would scold, combing Amina's hair while she squirmed and complained. Then twenty years had slid away like water.

Her grandmother grabbed her arm and half buried her face in her shoulder.

"We thought you were gone forever. Like everyone else."

Amina couldn't help looking at the garden, where you could just see her grandfather's grave in the sun, between the beans and the tomatoes. Her uncles were deeper in the shade, under the mango tree. If they had lived, her grandfather would have taken that perpetually shady spot; by the time anyone else was old enough to die, the tree would've grown big enough to accommodate their tombs. As it was there had been two unexpected deaths so early that there was no good place for her grandfather when he passed at the appropriate time.

Her grandmother peered around her at the van, where the driver was still holding the heavy suitcases instead of setting them down in the dust, in anticipation of a tip.

"You didn't bring your husband," her grandmother said.

"He wanted to come. Only—"

"He was too busy at his job," her mother interrupted. "You know what Americans are like, always working."

"Your aunty cooked extra for him."

"But I told you he wasn't coming. Why would you do that?"

Parveen smiled. "So that you can tell him we did. Then maybe he'll be ashamed and come the next time." She and Nanu both laughed, and Amina couldn't help smiling. Her aunt and her grandmother were stubborn, but they were always completely themselves. You were never surprised by anything they did or said.

"You'll want to bathe," her grandmother said, taking her arm. "Then you'll eat." The smell of her nanu was so familiar that she wondered she hadn't once thought of it in America. Betel nut, rosewater, cook smoke, and something harder to classify, the mineral tang of pond water dried on your skin. If you took a little of each element in a Ziploc bag, she thought, you could keep it even in the pantry in Rochester, with the canisters of flour, sugar, and salt. It would be there forever to be opened, but you could also choose to keep it sealed.

She had wanted to get in and out of the pond before the news of her arrival reached the rest of the village, but it was too late. When Amina and her mother came out of the house with thin, checked towels over their shoulders, and the hard slivers of Lux soap her grandmother saved for occasions—ordinarily Nanu washed with clay—there was already an audience collected in the courtyard. She greeted Itee Nanu, her grandmother's elder sister, and her uncle Ashraf, who'd returned from town; she searched the faces in the courtyard for Micki, but her favorite cousin wasn't there. Her teenage cousins Trina and Mokti were standing shyly behind Itee Nanu, as if they thought she wouldn't remember them. Someone had even pulled an old string bed into the courtyard for her ancient great-uncle Sudir Haji, who was surrounded by a crowd of neighbors, servants, and children. There was a general cry of disappointment when it was clear that the American husband hadn't come.

"Maybe she was afraid to bring him. He likes Bengali women, and look at all these pretty cousins!" Itee Nanu laughed, showing a red mouth full of paan, and Amina was grateful for the distraction of her teasing.

"How is your health, Uncle?"

"*Alhamdulillah*, fine, fine. But you should be asking about the health of the village. We aren't well these days." Her uncle Ashraf was the tallest man in the village, and the most learned; he taught the oldest boys at the madrassa down the road. A dog had mauled him as a child, leaving a shiny white scar like a crescent moon on his neck— a mark from God, some people said. Now he switched to English to impress the crowd. "The water situation is very bad. Rainfall is less, even since you left. You must tell people. Go home to U.S.A. and tell your husband: there is not enough water in the Sundarbans of Bangladesh."

Her uncle wasn't finished, but he stood aside so that she could greet Sudir Haji, who was squatting on the string bed in a lungi, vest, and prayer cap. Her grandmother's pretty servant Kamla had fetched him a cup of water, but now she stepped back to whisper with a friend. Amina couldn't hear the words, but she could guess that the girl was disappointed. She'd expected someone dressed like the Western women in the glossy pages salvaged from magazines or calendars, which some of the poorer villagers pasted up inside their houses. Instead, here Amina was in an old shalwar kameez of her mother's, on her way to bathe in the pond.

Sudir Haji's voice had grown high like a child's. He stroked her head and asked if her marriage was a happy one.

"Yes, Uncle."

"Your husband is good to you?"

"Very good, thanks be to God."

"Engineer," her uncle said. "How much does he earn per month?"

"He wouldn't like me to say," Amina said. "Americans are different that way."

Her great-uncle laughed. "Does he eat our food?"

She nodded. "Only I can't cook it so well."

"Ah—your aunty Parveen killed a duck. He'll be sorry he isn't here." Kamla had disappeared, so the old man snapped his fingers at a child with a shaved head and kohl-rimmed eyes, naked except for a tiny cotton shift. The baby ran back behind the fence, where her great-uncle lived in a small concrete room, and returned with a glass jar: dried dates from his pilgrimage to Mecca fifteen years earlier.

"One for you and one for your husband. To keep the marriage sweet." He took her hands, then bent his head and prayed aloud. She could see Trina and Mokti slipping away, now that the excitement was over. She couldn't believe those children she had rocked and combed and wiped on twenty years of visits had been too shy even to say hello.

"Come, Munni," her mother said. "Before it gets too late," and they were finally permitted to continue on to the pond, with only a trail of small children in attendance.

"Where's Micki?" she asked her mother. "She didn't even come."

"She's in Khulna registering one of her boys for school—her father's taking him in. I think that eldest one is twelve already."

They passed under the archway and set their things down on the bench next to the steps. The pond was cool in the shade of the big mango tree, and a palm leaf screen further shielded them from the eyes of anyone passing on the path. Still Amina found it awkward, once they got in the water, to separate her wet clothes from her body in order to wash properly underneath.

"Three healthy boys, and she's only a year older than you are. She hasn't lost her looks either." Her mother sighed theatrically.

"And still here in the village," Amina said. She was hurt that Micki hadn't come, and she allowed herself to be carelessly cruel.

"Exactly," her mother said. "If they can manage here in the village, what is stopping you?"

Her mother was vigorously soaping her hair, working a lather from even the tiny shard of soap. She couldn't help watching for signs of madness, but so far her mother's behavior was perfectly normal. Her opinions came as directly and forcefully as they always had; there was no sign of the frightened, obsessive person Amina had been listening to on the phone for the past three years.

"Now you," she said, handing Amina the soap.

"I'll wait to wash my hair inside."

"There's no water at the indoor tap. Your uncle's right—this is a bad year."

"What does he think George can do about it?"

"He doesn't want to ask you directly," her mother said. "He's being polite."

Amina looked at her in amazement. "What could I do?"

"Give money, of course. For a tubewell or something else—some foreign solution, maybe." Her mother dipped her head in the water, and when she came out, with her eyes closed and her hair streaming down her back, for just a moment, you could see the beautiful girl she had been.

"Amma? You know George doesn't have money now. You understand, right?" She lowered her voice, in case any of the children were paying attention. Then she wondered why she bothered. Wouldn't it be better just to tell the truth, to say to everyone that George had lost his job, and that they might even lose their house? She could employ some of these children to run around the village, and then someone could go spread the news in Shyamnagar Bazar. She would lose face, certainly, but people would also welcome her more easily. Not only foolish Itee Nanu but all the rest of them would joke and tease her. Misfortune had that advantage. No one would envy or threaten them, and they would be safe again.

"I've been thinking of that apartment in Moti Mahal," her mother said, as if she hadn't heard the question. "Those weren't such bad times. Long Nose was kind, and your father sometimes had work from Omar. And you were funny at that age—very serious. Everything had to be just so, even your clothes. Do you remember that red-and-yellow dress I made, from the pattern you found? 'Tea dress.' And then you hung around in the hallway, waiting for the across-the-hall neighbors to see you in it—do you remember those people? I ran into them at Kaderabad Bazar just before we moved down here. The little boy was called Shajar."

They climbed out of the pond and stepped into a narrow shelter constructed from woven palm, open to the sky. Her mother was out of her wet clothes and into the dry ones almost instantly, without revealing anything—a trick Amina had never mastered.

"Shajar's mother was buying three hens at once, for a feast. She said she couldn't afford them, made all kinds of excuses, but I could see she was trying not to shame me. I had only vegetables in my bag."

"But you told me I sent enough. You told me more than enough!" It came out more fiercely than she'd intended, and her mother's face exhibited a familiar injured expression.

"Why would I buy three hens for your father and me? I'm only telling you—Shajar's family is doing well."

"And I'm only saying if you need money—tell me." The shelter gave the illusion of privacy, but anything they said would be overheard easily by someone standing outside. Amina struggled to keep her voice low. "Don't talk to others."

Her mother looked at her sharply. "Which others?"

She hadn't meant to repeat what her aunt had said. There was no way it could be true, and she was waiting to hear the truth from her mother unclouded by gossip.

"*Ai*, Munni!" Her aunt's voice came from the direction of the house, loud and teasing. "Have you gone back to America?"

"She wants to feed you," her mother said. She pulled Amina gently out into the open, but Amina hung back.

"What jewelry was it?"

Her mother spoke in an undertone. "Nothing valuable. Some wedding gold that belonged to your dadi—he said he wanted us to sell it in America."

"Dadu gave you the jewelry?"

"Of course. What did you think?"

Amina's relief came out as anger. "But you know you can't do that—I've told you a thousand times! You can't bring things in for business purposes, especially on the kind of visa you'll have. Why did you agree to take it?" She'd forgotten to lower her voice, and her aunt was watching them with interest from the porch.

"Your father knows all that," her mother said calmly. "He was only being kind. He said we could take it to a shop in Dhaka and sell it for your dadu there. He wouldn't know the difference."

"And then what happened? The jewelry was lost?"

"Stolen," her mother said. "Before we even left your dadu's house. We packed it in your father's suitcase the night before, and then Bhulu and Laltu came by late that night with whiskey. I told your father not to join them—but his own father and his cousins, how could he not? All the men sat and drank, and the suitcase was in the room. In the morning we left, and we didn't discover the jewelry was missing until we got back here."

"You never told me."

Her mother looked down, but a proud smile nudged the corners of her mouth. Amina wondered how many other things she'd been protected from.

"Does Dadu know?"

"It was a trick." Her mother's voice was electric with indignation. "Of course your dadu must've bragged about how we would sell his gold in America. Bhulu and Laltu knew we had it, and so they decided to take it themselves—so that we couldn't sell it at all."

She hadn't seen her grandfather since she was fourteen or fifteen years old. Their visits to her father's village happened only every few years, and she could remember the arguments Dadu and her father had once had—mostly over the land being sold and occasionally about the senselessness of spending all one's money on educating a girl. If they couldn't have sons, her dadu said, they might at least have held on to the land.

"Now those cousins are filling your dadu's head with lies. He'll never remember what that gold was worth. They're saying it's much more valuable than it really is—and that we stole it. They claim they're defending Dadu—defending! From us!"

"You mean they're saying we kept the jewelry for ourselves?"

Her mother nodded. "Your father told Dadu what he thinks happened that night, after they were all drunk. Bhulu and Laltu might have pretended to leave and then snuck back in and taken the jewelry from the suitcase. But they're the ones in the village with Dadu—of course he's going to believe them instead of us."

"So we send Dadu the money directly," she told her mother. "Let Bhulu and Laltu know we see through their tricks. How much are they saying it's worth? I have cash with me now, or George can wire me whatever it is."

"Ten thousand," her mother said quietly.

Ten thousand taka were about a hundred and fifty dollars. She wouldn't like to part with that much money, but if it would protect them, she could manage without it. She could tell George they had ended up staying in the hotel one night after all, omitting the jewelry, the drinking party, and Salim's violent history. There was no need to amplify an upsetting experience by turning it into a story.

"I have that much with me," Amina said. "Will that satisfy them? Will they tell Salim to leave us alone?"

But Parveen was approaching them from the house. "Come inside and sit," she said. "What are you chatting so much about? Around you your mother is a schoolgirl." She guided them into the house, handing Amina a spongy white round of pakan pitha.

"This is delicious, Aunty," Amina said. "Wait just a minute, while I get some things."

"Oh no," Parveen protested. "Why did you carry extra? Your bags must've been so heavy!"

Her nanu smiled. "You shouldn't waste your money."

"Come and help me," she whispered, and her mother followed her obediently into the room they would share, painted bright green, with an ornate Chinese-made Singer sewing machine in one corner. A large window opened onto the garden; at night you might latch the wooden shutters, but of course there was no glass. Already the garden was in shadow, her uncles' tombs white in the dusk.

"How fast can we get it to them?"

Her mother shook her head and put her finger to her lips. Parveen and Nanu were in the main room, and of course they couldn't close the door. Her mother's purse was on the table, and she reached inside and pulled out a pencil, along with a crumpled timetable, the type blurred where the ink had run; no doubt she'd been worrying it in her fingers all morning while she waited at the bus stand. She cupped her hand to make a writing surface and scratched something into the margin. Then she handed the paper silently to Amina. In the small white space above the timings, her mother had sketched a tiny symbol: $.

Ten thousand *dollars*. Amina stared at her. "You said that jewelry was worth nothing."

"That was before it was stolen," her mother said, her eyes on the floor. Then she took her daughter's arm and guided her back into the main room, where Parveen and Nanu sat her down on the bed and began to feed her the buttery, sugared sweets by hand.

6 She woke in the night and thought she heard a noise. The shutters were closed, and the wooden latch clicked gently in the draft from the fan. Otherwise the air was still. Amina reached for the miniature flashlight George had given her in preparation for the power cuts and checked her watch. It was before three in the morning, and her mother was sleeping soundly beside her.

She had always been frightened as a child in the village at night. She would fall asleep easily, watching her grandmother—at that hour usually engaged in the lifelong project of organizing her possessions—and listening to the sounds of Parveen finishing in the kitchen. When she woke next, it would be midnight, and Nanu and Parveen would've moved her so that she was close to the wall, just under the window. She hadn't been afraid of people then, but of spirits: a long, white arm attached to a pair of wings, something that would snatch her in its jaws and fly. She would turn from the window and burrow into her aunt's bulk, but it was not the same as being next to her mother; Parveen didn't have the same power. And so it was always better to turn and face the window, even if her stomach rose into her throat. At least she would be able to see the thing coming.

She would tell Micki nearly every day about how her parents were coming for her.

"They're only waiting until they earn enough. I'll go to a school called Maple Leaf, and my mother will come every day to fetch me herself."

"But my mother says your mother only gets piecework to do at home, and your father doesn't have a steady job either. They're living in a bad place, and she thinks they might as well come back here. Maybe you'll have to stay in the village forever."

The idea of staying in her grandmother's house, the only house she'd ever known, and having her parents there with her was not as unpleasant as Amina pretended. As much as she proclaimed her eagerness to leave, the idea of an English medium school in the city was frightening. There were things she'd heard her grandmother say to her aunt that made it difficult to discount Micki's version of her parents' life in Dhaka. And even though Micki had the tendency to repeat bad news, she knew that it was only because her cousin loved her. Micki didn't want her to leave any more than Amina wanted to part from her.

"If my father doesn't get a better job, then they'll come back."

"Nanu's house is big enough."

Amina shook her head. "We'll have our own house."

"Right next to ours."

"A concrete house, like Nanu's."

Having established what would happen in the real world, they would escape to an imaginary one. Their playhouse was in the most remote corner of the village, beyond Shoma Aunty's mustard field. The house had once belonged to a Hindu laborer and his family; they had fled to India during the war, but people in the village still called it by his name. Gopal's house had been so poor that no one but Amina and Micki had claimed it; the roof was gone, but there were some bricks from a long-ago courtyard and a stand of bamboo growing where one of the walls had been. They had built a little table with the broken bricks, and her grandmother had given them a jute mat too worn for any other purpose. The house became the one they would share once Micki had become a famous singer; Amina's profession changed daily—film star, air hostess, newscaster—but the two of them were always successful beyond their parents' wildest dreams. The game was rarely acted out but rather told:

This is our house in Dhaka. It has fourteen rooms and three indoor toilets, and the windows are made of glass.

Here is where your parents sleep—next to mine—and here's the room for

Nanu. Here's the refrigerator where we keep the ice cream, and here's where we put on our makeup to go out.

They had been playing this way for at least a year when Amina arrived at the house one day to find Micki there with a little boy. Ghoton was only four, a year younger than Amina, but Micki was on her knees in front of him, pretending to bathe his feet. Ghoton was telling her about the new Honda motorbike he was going to buy when he harvested the rice this year.

"You're the baby," Micki said to Amina, barely glancing at her. "Abba just came home, so you go and lie down. I'll feed you in a minute."

After Micki began including Ghoton in their games, Amina found herself less eager to seek out her cousin as a playmate. She had stuck closer to her grandmother and her aunt and had tried to focus her mind on the things that would please them. She made bargains with God, sitting still in school, and proving herself dutiful, even showy, about saying her prayers. She found she could do almost anything, if she imagined her fate was resting on it. In that way another year passed, and when her parents had finally come for her, just as they'd said they would, Amina had been more than ready to go.

In the morning they called her father. He was sitting at his old desk in her uncle's office, waiting for a package that might or might not arrive from abroad.

"No one is here," her father said. "So I can stretch my legs—I walk around and around. First I'll talk to you, then I'll walk for fifteen minutes. Then it will be time to pray."

"I can't believe you didn't call me," Amina said. "I was worried when there wasn't any answer."

"I knew you'd be angry if you found out I'd come to Dhaka. But you didn't know why—now your mother has told you."

"Moni Aunty made me promise we'd come there when we arrived. She said she was buying a bed."

"Nasir has also offered to host the three of us," her father said carefully. "I think it's safer. Salim knows exactly where Omar lives."

Amina thought the real peril was much more likely to lie at the consulate, where any erratic behavior on her mother's part could cost them the visas. Bhulu and Laltu had heard that Amina had a rich American husband, and so they'd sent their errant brother Salim to Dhaka to make threats and gather information. Perhaps they thought Amina and her parents would pay a bribe simply to be rid of them—something Amina would have been willing to do, had their demands been more reasonable. But ten thousand dollars? Because they'd been so arrogant, she was determined to give them nothing.

"Are you sure Nasir has room for us?"

"Yes, yes," her father said excitedly. Of course he would prefer staying with Nasir, who treated him like a father, to imposing once again on Moni and Omar, to whom they owed so much already. "He has three big rooms. He would be hurt if we went elsewhere. It won't be long anyway—less than two weeks. And then we'll be eight thousand miles away. No one will ever find us!"

There was a part of her, of course, that was eager to see Nasir and to have him see her. She was curious to know what his life was like—how did it feel to leave Bangladesh and then return here to live? She remembered their last meeting, almost four years ago now, and the way he'd lectured her about her marriage. Would he be different now that she'd returned, to all appearances a success?

"Did you tell my father about George's job?" she asked, when she hung up the phone.

Her mother nodded. "I know you told me not to say anything, but—"

Amina was suddenly ashamed. Her parents had kept the secret about her father's cousins to save her more worry. By contrast she'd concealed things out of pride. In spite of the bad news about George's job, her father had been cheerful on the phone; she knew he'd never for a moment lost his faith in her or the son-in-law he hardly knew. She thought of him performing his laps around the office, keeping himself in shape for an America he couldn't imagine—for her—and the strength of her emotion surprised her. If she were truly an American she would have wanted to hug them; as it was, she took her mother's arm in hers, drawing it close as if both her parents were somehow contained in that narrow, aging limb.

7   She didn't see Micki until that afternoon. Her cousin was still beautiful, but she'd gained weight and she was wearing a great deal of makeup. Amina complimented her on her clothing, a royal-blue shalwar kameez with gold embroidery, the neckline of which dipped slightly in back according to the new fashion. She was startled to realize that Micki had put it on for her.

"This village has become so modern," Amina said, but Micki only shook her head.

"You don't have to say that when it's only me. I know what a hole it is. I'd like to leave—maybe for Khulna, so we could all be together while the boys went to school. But Badal—my husband—he has the new auto shop in Satkhira." She hesitated for a moment, shyly. "Did you pass it?"

"Oh, yes," Amina lied. "So busy." She could tell Micki was pleased by the way her neck colored, just as it used to do when they were little girls.

"You look just the same," she said. "Your figure is so good! Did you bring pictures of your house?"

Amina had been looking forward to this moment for so long, but something had happened since she'd arrived. Her pride had evaporated, and what she wanted most was to confess to Micki the realities of her situation. Instead she went and got the pocket album from her room, which had pictures of her and George standing in the garden with the house and car in the background. She heard herself complaining to Micki in the same way she'd once deplored, when her students' wealthy parents did it.

"Actually I'd like to move to a smaller place. Now that my parents are coming, George says we'll be glad to have three bedrooms. But a big house is so much work—no wonder we haven't had time for children yet. My mother wishes she had a daughter like you."

"Not really." Micki dark eyes hadn't changed, still round and liquid. "She just wants you to have children. But she's so proud of you for going to America. And I heard that you're working in a bookstore. Badal has a friend who went to Texas, but he works in a restaurant."

"I work in Starbucks now," Amina said. "It's basically a restaurant.

Serving only coffee and snacks." But Micki was gasping at her wedding pictures.

"Like a model in a magazine." She guided Amina away from their grandmother's house, toward the path that led deeper into the village. "I was looking forward to a chat with you all these months. As soon as Nanu said you were coming. And I couldn't wait to see George—he's an engineer, right?"

Micki was looking at a picture of the two of them in the yard, Amina in the white dress and George looking proud, his arm draped casually over her shoulder. Her own smile looked naïve and silly to her now. If she'd truly wanted to give an impression of her life in Rochester, there would have had to be a picture of Kim, too—wearing one of her bright-colored kurtas, her long hair framing her beautiful face. Was she still in Rochester? Would she show up at the house now that Amina was gone, to say good-bye to George? It was infuriating to be jealous of someone who didn't actually want her husband—wanted only to gain his sympathy before she left forever.

Micki was shaking her head in admiration. "And I bet he listens to you—not like Bengali husbands." She hadn't relinquished the flip book; with her other hand, she held Amina's tightly.

"Sometimes he listens. But sometimes he can't understand."

"Men can't," Micki said, and laughed, showing the dimples Amina remembered from so long ago.

She hadn't been paying attention to the path, but all of a sudden it opened up onto a large field of dal. The farmer was using a hoe on the far side, in front of a row of banana trees, and suddenly Amina realized where they were. Gopal's house was long gone, crumbled into the mud and grown over with bamboo, but a part of the brick paving from the courtyard was still there.

"Listen," she said. "There's a lot I haven't told people. Have you heard that the American economy is terrible right now? George lost his job almost six months ago. If he doesn't find another one, we'll have to sell the house."

Micki stared at her. "But how much is an American three-bedroom house? If you sold it, you would have lakhs and lakhs of taka. You could come back to Dhaka and live like a princess. Maids, a cook and driver—you could have your babies here, and never have to do a thing!"

Here we are again, Amina thought, playing make-believe. Only she still believes that fantasy really exists.

Amina bent down to pick a stem of dal, and had the bizarre urge to put it in her mouth. The farmer stood up suddenly and shouted something Amina couldn't understand; she dropped the plant, startled.

"What did he say?"

"Insecticide," Micki translated. "He doesn't want you to get it on your hands."

"But they didn't used to use that, did they?"

Her cousin shrugged. "I don't pay attention."

"Do you remember that little boy you tried to make me play with?" Amina asked. "In the house—Ghoton?"

"I don't think we played together," Micki said. "But of course I know Ghoton. He went to Chittigong, to work for some shipping company. I heard he's done well."

"We did," Amina said. "He was the father, and I was supposed to be the baby."

Micki shook her head. "Remember how much *time* we had then? Just fooling around?" She put her arm around Amina. "I'm so glad I got to see you, even if I didn't get to meet your husband."

"Next time," Amina said.

"You won't come back, Munni." Micki laughed again. "Why would you?"

Amina began to speak, and then stopped. There was no breeze; the heat was trapped under the large, gray clouds. The farmer had bent over again, so you only saw the white curve of his undershirt in the middle of the field. For a moment the birds were quiet and the sky seemed to wheel above them.

Micki was talking again about Khulna: the new blocks of flats they were building on the outskirts, offered at cheap introductory prices. She had known so many people who'd left, and her cousin Munni was already in that category. There was nothing strange about it. It occurred to Amina that she was looking at this field the way George would, as if she had a camera, and that was what made it (an ordinary field of dal, dull green under midafternoon clouds) so beautiful. Micki's right: you'll never see this again, she told herself sternly. Say good-bye, before it's too late. The field waved listlessly, but the tears wouldn't come.

That night Parveen made a feast—duck and the tiny eggplants Amina loved from her grandmother's garden. The bread was hot throughout the meal, and the pulao was fragrant with anise and cardamom. The okra and the dal were so spicy that she thought Parveen might be testing her to see whether she'd gotten soft in America. There was a crowd of people, men in the courtyard outside the kitchen and her grandmother's female relatives in the house, but Amina ate first, along with Micki, who kept protesting to her mother that she wasn't a guest.

"We thought we'd have her husband," Parveen said. "Someone has to sit across the table from her."

She ate until she was so full that she thought she wouldn't be able to sleep. Then she excused herself and threaded her way through the assembled guests to call George. She ran into her uncle Ashraf talking with a visitor from a nearby village, an old man on leave from some government post. He considered himself an important local personage and buttonholed Amina for some time, telling her how he had gone abroad as a young man to stay with his uncle in Hamburg. He'd been most impressed by the autobahn, and it was his opinion that if Bangladesh had been colonized by the Germans rather than the British, many of the country's current problems wouldn't exist. When she finally escaped with the phone Omar had lent her, she went around the house to her grandmother's garden, where she crouched on a low wooden stool near the makeshift graveyard. It would be where her nanu sat, when she came outside to talk to the dead—her husband and her sons.

George answered after several rings. He sounded breathless. "Hi."

"Hi." The connection was perfect: she could hear water running and then the soft suck of the seal on the refrigerator door. "Where were you?"

"What?"

"Are you by yourself?"

George sounded confused. "Of course—I was just down in the basement."

He sounded sincere, and Amina had to admit that even if Kim were to stop by, it was unlikely to happen exactly at the moment she called.

"What's going on there?" she asked him.

"I had coffee with a guy I know at SL Associates. He does aeronautics—he doesn't know what they have in electrical, but I guess I'll send a résumé."

"You guess?" She could feel his hurt surprise, even before he spoke.

"Jesus, Amina—what's your problem? I'm doing my best here."

She'd almost given up on the fantasy that he would be employed again by the time they returned. It wasn't about the job—didn't he know that?

"Has Kim left?"

George hesitated. "How would I know?"

"You haven't heard from her?"

"No."

"Or from Cathy?"

"I think my mother said something about her leaving," George admitted.

Somehow she hadn't really believed Kim would go, in spite of all her talk at the dinner party. If she were in Bombay now, she and Amina were only a half hour apart, inside the same night, while George languished in the middle of a day that was already history here.

"Is she living with Ashok's family?"

"I told you—I have no idea," he snapped. There was a pause, and she remembered again their early conversations, when it had always seemed like there wasn't enough time to talk before the connection faltered. Now that they didn't have anything to say, the line remained surprisingly clear.

"There are some complications here."

"Take as long as you need," George said, obviously relieved to move away from the subject of Kim.

It wasn't about taking more time, of course. She had to be back in eleven days if she wanted to keep her job; given what her mother had confided in her, she thought it would be best to leave as quickly as they could.

"I don't know where we'll be staying, once we get back to Dhaka."

"Just let me know when you get there. Are you wearing your money belt? Make sure not to leave your passport lying around."

"Nothing would happen to it." She wasn't convinced that was true, but she resented George for making assumptions. He'd never been to any village, much less hers.

"Still," George said.

"They're having a party for me," Amina said. "I should go."

They said a stiff good-bye, but she wasn't eager to rejoin the party. She thought of her husband sitting in the near-silent kitchen in Rochester. She could hear the raised voices and laughter from the party, the wind scraping in the dry palms, and the call and response of a million insects. The men were singing a song with the refrain "O la la"—some new movie hit she didn't recognize—and she sat on her grandmother's stool for a few more moments, listening. As a girl she'd often imagined a sort of magic that could give her a glimpse of the person she would one day marry. The likelihood that he existed somewhere made this fantasy even more irresistible, and she could spend hours daydreaming about it in the opulent apartments of her students, waiting for them to arrive at the solutions to simple problems. How thrilled she would've been if she'd been able to see George then: a man already, hardworking and reliable, decent looking if not overly handsome, sitting at a computer in an American office. The desire to be sixteen again was suddenly so powerful that a sound escaped her, something between a gasp and a groan.

Her back was to the house, and all of a sudden she was uneasy. You were never alone in this country: there were so many warm bodies in such a small space that it was extremely unlikely to find a view without a human being in it. A ragged half-moon hung low above the grain shed; when a lizard chirped in the tree above her head, she nearly cried out. You were once afraid in Rochester she told herself, as she stood up and walked slowly in the direction of the courtyard—it's only that this is what's unfamiliar now. Her own bedroom window was open, but just as she put her hand on one of the shutters, there was a whooping sound behind her. She spun around and saw two pairs of eyes: two small boys, one in a pair of green shorts, the other wearing only a T-shirt with a cartoon character on the front.

Amina screamed, out of relief rather than fear, and the boys crept slightly backward into the trees, their eyes wide.

"What are you doing, sneaking around people like that? I nearly had a heart attack. Why are you out so late? Where's your mother?"

"Hello?" the bigger one said. "Howareyou?"

The little one giggled and hit his brother on the back. "I'm fine, I'm fine!"

"What is your country?"

"Bangladesh," Amina said, and the little boys laughed as if she'd made a joke specifically for their amusement. She switched to Bangla. "I was married in the U.S.A. In the state of New York. Can you say, 'New York'?"

The older one attempted it; his brother jumped up and down as if he had to pee.

"U.S.A., U.S.A.!"

"Clin-ton!"

"Osama bin Laden!"

Amina heard footsteps in the house behind her; Nanu had come to her bedroom window and was yelling at the little boys to get home before their fathers came out and beat them. The boys turned and ran with high, joyful strides, bare legs white in the moonlight.

"Uneducated people," her grandmother said. "Allowing their children to run around all night."

"They were trying to speak English to me."

Her grandmother hadn't carried a lantern into her bedroom, but there was light from the front room and the courtyard, where the singing continued. It illuminated the four-poster bed, where her grandmother and Parveen slept, and her grandmother's curio cabinet, which Amina had loved to look through as a child. She remembered in particular a box of Russian candies wrapped in paper printed with bears (how she'd once longed to taste them!); stern, individual photographs of her uncles and her grandfather in tiny silver frames; and trial-sized plastic bottles of Pantene shampoo. Now a Casio clock, displaying the correct time from inside its original cardboard and plastic packaging, hung above the cabinet. It was eleven thirty; one thirty in the afternoon in Rochester.

"Your mother is asleep," Nanu said. "She gets tired easily, especially in a crowd of people."

"We'll take her to the doctor when we get back to New York."

Nanu brushed that abstraction aside. "She says you won't stay with Moni."

"They don't make my father welcome."

Her grandmother tilted her head slightly in acknowledgment, her hooded black eyes glossy and sharp.

"My mother and I were talking about that time in Dhaka—when those men locked us in. I was thinking of how you invited him to stay that night."

Her grandmother took a hand broom from the dresser and began sweeping dead leaves off the sill into the yard. The skin on her hands was as creased and dry as the leaves dropping around Amina's feet.

"What did you think of my father, Nanu—back then?"

"A bad family. I never would have agreed to that match."

"But the first time you saw him?"

"I'd seen him before that."

"I mean, when you met him properly?" She expected Nanu not to answer, the way she often did when a question wasn't to her taste, and so she was surprised by the old woman's vehemence.

"Skinny. Dark. And a *watcher*—with his eyes on everyone all the time." Her grandmother's hair was white now, but her eyebrows were still pure black. It was hard to look away when she was talking. "But your father could talk to anyone—laughing and joking. Said he would share your Itee Nanu's bed, since Ashraf was in Jessore and she was all alone. We laughed all night."

"You liked him, once you met him."

Her grandmother frowned. "I opposed the match, and you see what bad luck has followed. Even that night—look what happened."

"My mother said they might have set the house on fire, but God protected us."

"Your grandfather might have kept the marriage from happening, but he was ill by then. And Khokon was gone. Still, I had Emdad.

When he died, I went to that wife of his. I said, 'Tell me you're expecting.' Stupid woman—she just sat there and cried."

Amina tried to picture her uncle's pretty widow, Botul, but the face
wouldn't resolve in her mind.

"Have children right away, Munni," her grandmother said. "Or you
might wind up alone like me."

"You have four living children. Eight grandchildren, and three
great-grandchildren. Four, once Rashid has his child."

"None for my house."

"I lived in your house."

Her grandmother looked at her curiously. It was hard to know
whether Nanu thought it was a foolish argument—Amina had lived
there, but then she had gone—or whether she simply didn't remember. It was possible that one granddaughter blurred into another.

"And Micki didn't leave," Amina added.

"Micki made a good match, under the circumstances. Parveen is
fortunate."

"And my match," Amina couldn't help asking. "What do you think
of it?"

She wondered if the two little boys had run back home, or if they'd
cut through the fields and doubled back around to the house, hoping
to sneak a sip of whiskey from one of the old men's flasks.

"Oh, who can say?" Her grandmother pulled her orna across her
chest, squinting into the shadows around the makeshift graveyard.
"God knows what will happen to you, all the way over there."

8 She woke up in Nasir's apartment on the morning of the visa
interview to the sound of her parents' arguing. The window was
open, and the noise from the lane was such that she couldn't believe
she'd slept as long as she had; the air had an unmistakable metallic thickness that would've let her know she was in Dhaka, even if
she hadn't opened her eyes. Nasir had given them his bedroom, in
spite of their protestations, and her parents had gone into the tiny
attached bath in order to talk without waking her. The door was shut,
but the knob was missing, and she could see a piece of her father's
hand through the empty hole.

"It's just a hen," she heard her father say. "It doesn't mean anything."

"And you're already selling its eggs!"

"You're overexcited because of the interview."

"I won't pass, I might as well not go." Amina could hear her mother opening the mirrored chest above the sink, selecting one of the neatly labeled tinctures. "I need something to calm my nerves."

"What if they test us?"

"Test us?"

"Urine test for drugs."

"Drugs!" her mother exclaimed. "Everything Mufti Huzoor prescribes is natural."

"I never thought you would follow that kind of nonsense. Your sisters or your mother, maybe—"

"My mother! Where would we have stayed, if not for my mother? Where would we have lived without my sister's husband? What would we have done all of these years?" Her mother burst out of the bathroom and glanced at Amina as if she were startled to find her there.

"Your father wastes our last taka on a hen for dinner. Before we've even got the visas."

"I'm only thanking Nasir for all he's done for us. Not celebrating yet."

"We have enough money," Amina said, as quietly as possible. "It's fine."

Her mother turned to face the wall. She started doing a frantic set of exercises, rotating her arms from the shoulders in circles and lifting her legs in a stationary goose-step. Her father stayed in the bathroom another moment, gargling loudly with water from a plastic bottle next to the sink, and then came out holding his wallet. He began shuffling through a stack of old business cards, as if there were someone he needed to contact immediately. Had these arguments between her parents started right away, when they were newlyweds in Dhaka, before she was born? Her father would have had no model for married life, barely remembering his parents together before his mother died, and her mother would've been living in a city for the first time, attempting to execute her wifely responsibilities as she'd seen them performed in the village. She thought they would have played these unfamiliar roles with painful awkwardness, relishing their time apart more than the time together—if only because it allowed them to relax into their familiar, singular selves. But wasn't that what it was like for all newlyweds? Certainly she and George had been no different. It felt strange until one day it didn't, until that abstract partnership finally seemed more solid than the lives they'd left behind.

She heard Nasir discreetly moving around in the main room, not wanting to disturb them before they were ready. There was another toilet, but it didn't have a shower; no doubt he was waiting to get ready for work until they'd evacuated the bedroom. She herded her parents into the main room, where her father announced that he was going out to buy the *Daily Ittefaq*. Nasir had just finished shaving and was standing at the sink holding a small green towel.

"Hello," he said. "How did you sleep?"

The bus had gotten in at ten the previous night, and Nasir had been waiting up for them when they arrived at his apartment a half hour later. She'd been remembering him the way he'd been when he came to bring *The Lawful and Prohibited in Islam*, with beard and prayer cap, and it was strange to see him clean shaven again, looking almost the way he had when she was a teenager.

"Munni," he had said, with mock gravity, but had paid most of his attention to her mother, asking about the bus ride and making her a Horlicks drink himself. Amina had been free to examine him, moving expertly in his tiny kitchen—his broad forearms beneath rolled-up white sleeves, the square, sharp line of his chin—and wished she knew whether he found a change in her.

"We'll make breakfast," her mother said now.

"I'll do it."

"Nasir loves Bombay toast—you won't do it right." Her mother laughed unnaturally, but at least she went into the kitchen, where Amina hoped a familiar task would calm her down.

"They're worried about the interview," she told Nasir, who nodded politely, although she was sure he'd overheard every word of her parents' argument. He was wearing jeans and a dark red T-shirt, and she wondered how he dressed around the house when he was alone. Most urban young men would wear shorts in this weather, but something about Nasir made her think he might put on a lungi like her father.

She waited for him to shower and change, and then sat with him while he ate breakfast. Her mother had made her a plate of toast as well, but the thought of the heavy fried bread made her stomach turn over.

"You remember we're going to your aunt and uncle's this afternoon, after the embassy," her mother said. "I promised we would. We've already insulted her by not staying there."

"Did you tell them we didn't know how long it would take?"

Her mother nodded. "We'll just call when we're on our way. Moni wants to show off her new furniture."

Nasir had eaten quickly. "She'd be horrified if she saw this place."

"This is a wonderful building," her mother said diplomatically, taking the plates to the sink. "Munni, have you seen what Sakina did to the roof?"

"It's a real garden up there," Nasir said shyly.

"Squash and peppers and everything!" her mother said from the kitchen. "You should see it."

"If you want to come up," Nasir offered.

"Won't you be late for work?"

"Our boss doesn't arrive until eleven. As long as I'm there at ten thirty." It was nine thirty, and the interview wasn't until two, so Amina allowed herself to be led up to the roof, where there was a surprisingly fresh breeze. Nasir's younger sister Shilpa lived on the ground floor with her husband and children, while Sakina had taken a smaller, one-bedroom flat on the fifth floor.

"She likes to be close to the plants," Nasir said. "I thought we'd find her up here, actually." Amina wondered if he were apologizing for the fact that they were alone on the roof together—a courtesy that seemed quaint to her now. Sakina's pots were arranged in rows; someone, perhaps Nasir, had built a long trellis at the southern end to accommodate runner beans, melons, and gourds.

"We shouldn't have taken your bedroom," Amina said. "I was so tired last night—I wasn't thinking."

"Actually I prefer the small room," Nasir said. "I would sleep there all the time, only it feels silly when I'm alone. Sakina Apu insisted I have this flat when she started looking for a bride for me. Little did she know it would take so long."

Nasir smiled down at his feet—in black plastic sandals, the kind of shoes George refused to wear because he found them feminine—and Amina saw that he was making fun of himself; he was so different than he'd sounded in his e-mails. Then again, she'd often winced when she reread her own saved e-mails, especially the first ones she'd sent to George. They seemed so labored and were riddled with the kind of tonal mistakes that you could only correct once you lived your daily life in the language in which you wrote. She wondered if the difference between Nasir on paper and Nasir now in person was the result of those same constrictions.

"You have time," Amina said. "A man always does. Better to wait and find the right person."

Nasir laughed. "Now you're the elder sister."

"I'm being strict with you." Amina smiled. "You were so strict with me before I left. I thought you'd become a mullah."

Nasir looked suddenly serious. "I was strict over there. I kept it up for a while after I got back, and then . . ."

"You were busy with your job," she supplied.

Nasir dismissed that with one hand. "That job pays almost nothing."

"At least you have one."

Nasir shook his head. "But it's not like abroad. Sometimes I still think about London—how if I'd just stayed long enough to meet some people outside the restaurant, what might've happened."

"The U.S. economy is in a recession right now—maybe even a depression. Europe's supposed to be next."

But Nasir brushed that aside with one hand. "It'll improve. It's always going to be better than here. The problem was—I couldn't stop thinking of home. It's like a girl. She's perfect while you're away, and then you come back and she's changed so much." He flushed and hurried on. "I mean, I used to dream about my mother's pulao when I was over there. In the dreams I would be a little boy in a tupi, going to the mosque with my father. Then we'd come home and eat."

"I dreamed about my parents in America," Amina said.

Nasir nodded. "And then you come back."

"And you've forgotten what they're like."

"I think I had forgotten they were dead." His voice wasn't bitter so much as lost, and she had to keep herself from touching his arm. "Sakina Apu makes pulao the same way, but it doesn't taste the same.

And I go to the mosque alone and see the beggars. I see how the tap doesn't work, the smell of all those bodies, everyone talking business, even during the prayers. It was easier to be strict over there. My sisters thought I should come home to find a girl, but even the women seem different to me now."

They were right at the edge of the wall, looking down into the narrow street, and it was exciting to be standing so close to him. On the roof opposite, two small boys were playing football; to the left an old woman in an abaya hung laundry, and several buildings down, construction workers were taking a break, eating in the spidery shade of a bamboo scaffold. A generator nearby roared to life, and she could hear voices from the street market down the lane, where her father had gone this morning to buy the hen. From this height she could make out the white and brown eggs separated into straw-lined baskets, but the chicks themselves were just a moving mass of gray and brown.

Amina could remember being a little girl on roofs like this one, the delicious fantasy of jumping. She felt that childish bravado now.

"You'll find a girl who hasn't changed."

Nasir looked as if he were going to speak, but she hurried on.

"Look down. There are so many of them. How about pink sari—there?"

"I hate pink," Nasir said flatly.

"All right," Amina said, cloaking her feelings in the pose of a bossy older sister. "Those two—getting out of the rickshaw. The one in green is too short, but the other is very graceful."

"Graceful is nice," Nasir said, getting into the spirit of the game, "but do you think she cooks?"

"Oh, I think she fries the best jilapi in the neighborhood."

"I'm not one for sweets."

"You're too picky—I pity your poor sisters, matchmaking for you. What's wrong with that one, bargaining for eggs? Don't tell me she's too plump for you."

"I do like them on the slender side." He smiled directly at her, knowing and wry, and suddenly she was back in the old Moti Mahal apartment, admiring his voice as he read aloud from her father's books after dinner. She had the same feelings, sweeter because they'd been dormant for so long, but her wish from that time had been granted: she was a grown woman, with everything she would need to attract a man like Nasir.

"Actually there is someone."

Amina felt the blood rush to her face. They had been flirting, but it had been harmless; now he was speaking seriously, and she had no idea what he was going to say. She knelt down to hide her face, on the pretense of examining some young coriander plantings.

"I haven't said anything to her yet."

The soil in the pots was wet, so someone must've been here already this morning. His sisters could come up at any moment and find them in the midst of this conversation.

"I think she lives right across the road—in that blue house, there."

Amina looked in the direction he was pointing. The combination of relief and regret was so strong that she didn't yet trust herself to speak. She wondered how she could have been so vain as to imagine he was talking about her. If he'd ever loved her, those feelings had long since passed; even if he had still been harboring a crush, he wouldn't have been so bold as to say it to a married woman.

"That one?" Amina said. "With the fancy grille?"

"I wasn't spying," Nasir said hurriedly. "I never tried to see inside. I noticed her going off in the mornings, to school or to work. They're simple people—she walks, or takes a rickshaw if it's raining."

Amina thought of her own days of going out to study and then to teach. She wondered if the girl had noticed Nasir, too. He was certainly tall and broad shouldered, but did his face have the same effect on other women that it did on her? She had never swooned over the newer Bollywood stars the way her girlfriends did; she didn't like men who looked like women. Something about the shape of Nasir's nose (it had been broken as a child), the square set of his chin and jaw, and those large, dark eyes—it was what she thought a man was supposed to look like.

"I don't know her name," Nasir admitted. "She was wearing a pair of yellow hair clips, the first time I really noticed her. Now you know my secret," he said, smiling. "I hope you're not going to tease me."

"I won't tell anyone."

Nasir considered her, and for a moment she was afraid he could see what she'd been thinking a few moments ago.

"I was surprised you agreed to come and stay here."

"I didn't think I could stand staying with my aunt again."

Nasir laughed. "How flattering."

"I mean, we all wanted to stay with you—only I was afraid my parents had been imposing too much. You've been better to them than their own relatives."

Nasir shrugged. "My parents are gone. You only realize what you had once you've lost it."

"Or when you're far away." Amina looked from Nasir to the street again, both hoping and dreading that they might see the girl he admired. "Even when they made me angry, I used to worry about something happening to them."

"And are you worried now?"

She'd guessed her father had confided in him about Salim, and now she was sure of it. Nasir had the kind of old-fashioned manners that kept him from bringing up anything unpleasant directly.

"Not now that we're here."

He nodded. "Still, it's good to be cautious. Perhaps stay inside unless it's really necessary."

There was a hint of the patronizing tone she'd resisted four years ago, and it made her own voice sharper. "The visa interview is necessary."

"Of course, but take a taxi." Anticipating her objections, he took a five-hundred-taka bill from his wallet. "Tell them your husband insisted."

"George would insist if he knew." She wondered why she felt she had to defend George to Nasir. Would she have done the same if he'd never brought up the girl with the yellow hair clips? Back in Rochester they would call them barrettes—a word she preferred for its glamorous, slightly foreign sound.

"Of course," he said again.

"Actually I can't tell him about Salim, because he'd worry so much."

Nasir nodded. He was still holding the money when they heard a noise behind them. She started, and then saw that it was his sisters, Sakina and Shilpa, coming toward them on the roof.

"Assalamu alaikum," Sakina said, looking her sharply up and

down, and Amina returned the formal greeting. Nasir's younger sister, Shilpa, smiled and embraced her; she was heavily pregnant and breathing hard from the stairs.

"Munni," she said, "you look so fashionable!" Amina was wearing a pale blue sundress she'd bought in Rochester with a pair of white shalwar trousers, and she'd neglected to put on a scarf. Shilpa may have admired such a modern outfit, but Amina could see that Sakina didn't share her sister's sentiment. Shilpa and Nasir had still been children when their parents died (Shilpa was eight; Nasir eleven), but Sakina was older than her brother by six years. An uncle had helped her manage the building until she could do it herself, and she'd taken care of her two younger siblings alone from the time she was seventeen years old.

Sakina noted the bill in Nasir's hand before he put it carefully back in his wallet. The white streak in her hair had gotten more pronounced. "We didn't know you'd arrived."

"We reached Dhaka only last night."

"Of course I want to pay a visit to your mother, but my little brother's been giving me orders about it."

"I only said not to sit chattering for hours. She hasn't been well."

"He's trying to keep you all to himself. And then we're off to Comilla next week."

"I remember you have family there."

"Oh—yes. But this time we have some business there as well." She gave Nasir a significant look.

"My sister's going along to help with the children," Nasir told Amina. Then he turned back to Sakina. "I have to get to work, and Munni's dealing with the visas for her parents."

"For America!" Shilpa put in: "It's so exciting."

Sakina ignored her little sister, fixing her gaze on Amina. Her eyes were an unusual hazel color, heavy lidded and intelligent. "How will they handle the change, I wonder. At this time in their life."

"The important thing is for us to be together," Amina said firmly. "That's how they feel."

"Of course," Sakina said. "Now that you've left."

"You'll be late, Munni," Nasir said, herding them from the roof, and Amina didn't hesitate. She thought of her aunt Moni, whose criticism always came from her own insecurities and could be dismissed as such; by contrast Nasir's elder sister never said anything dishonest or petty, even when she was deliberately trying to provoke.

"I'll visit your mother anyway," Sakina said, but she followed the three of them from the roof. Amina had been squinting, she realized, because her head hurt. All but the closest buildings were cloaked in a dense brown haze. And it would be much worse than this in the winter months; she couldn't imagine how she'd once ignored it.

They descended the narrow concrete stairs—Nasir ducking his head and holding Shilpa's arm to support her—until they were standing in the corridor outside Sakina's door. Amina thought he would be late to work, but he seemed unwilling to leave the three of them talking there together. He waited until his sisters had disappeared into Sakina's flat and then turned back to her. The collar of his shirt was dark with sweat.

"I won't see you until tonight. I hope everything goes well at the embassy."

"It'll be fine," Amina said, willing it to be so. "Americans are fair." It wasn't the Americans she was worried about.

They went down to the fourth floor, and he left her outside the door of his apartment. "Please take the taxi."

"Of course."

"*Allah hafez.*"

She returned the good-bye and then watched his oiled, dark head disappear down the staircase. When she got back inside his apartment, she went to the window. She could see the blue building, but not into the screened balconies. They weren't so much decorative, as she'd once thought, but functional—designed to hide the women inside while they hung their laundry, swept, or sat in the rare breeze to nurse a baby. She thought of Nasir's instructions and was annoyed all over again. Would he have told her to stay inside if she were a man? Salim had threatened her father, but she was the one Nasir had cautioned. All Deshi men were like that, she told herself again, no matter how open-minded and modern they appeared on the surface.

She took a corner of the homemade curtain between two fingers and tried to call up George's face. Instead she found herself remembering photographs: the first one he'd sent her, in coat and tie; the bleached-out childhood portrait; and the wedding picture that hung above the fireplace, in which he clutched her tightly to him but seemed to be looking at something slightly above the photographer's head. Across the street a square of sunlight hit the silver grille directly, picking up the dust from the road and giving the dark balcony behind it a hazy sparkle, as if there were some kind of hushed, interior paradise on the other side.

9 The embassy waiting room had changed in the nearly four years since she'd applied for her own visa. The paint had aged; there were stains on the carpet, and the plastic chairs struck her as unnecessarily uncomfortable. Even the seal with the golden eagle seemed to have grown smaller. The biggest change, however, was in the embassy workers she saw walking briskly in and out of the waiting room, talking to colleagues or on cell phones. There was something wrong with the way they were dressed, particularly the women, perhaps because of the challenge of conforming to standards of local modesty while wearing ordinary American clothing. Four years ago these embassy workers had seemed to her like angels, occasionally visible in a doorway or at the end of the hall, but clearly existing in another realm. Now, sitting in the first row of chairs with her American passport in her purse, she wondered if it had simply been the seductive legal fiction that this building existed on U.S. soil.

Her parents had been called into another room almost immediately, and there was nothing for Amina to do but sit and wait. She had squeezed her mother's shoulder before she went in; she'd seen the glazed expression on her face, the tremor in her hands, and hoped for a miracle. Her father, as usual, had been confident and self-possessed; he'd never had a passport before, but he carried the newly issued Deshi one as if it had already been stamped with the visa. If only they would let him do all the talking, she thought, but she knew that both of her parents would be required to answer questions. If her mother started rambling, about Mufti Huzoor's miracle cures or Kwaz, spirit of all waters, they would be politely escorted out. They could apply again in the future, but this denial and the reason for it would remain in the embassy's computers, and it was possible her parents would never get to America at all. For the first time since she'd left the country, she allowed herself to wonder about the value of the long journey that had led them all here.

She still remembered her snobbish seatmate on the flight to New York, and so as soon as she'd passed through the security check, she'd put her passport away in her purse. Both she and George had assumed she would have to give up her Deshi citizenship, but in fact she'd been allowed to retain dual status. The U.S. passport meant better treatment and shorter lines in both airports, however, so she'd gone to the trouble of sending it in to the consulate in Manhattan for a Deshi visa. Now the Deshi passports in evidence all around her made her think of her own arrival in the United States, of how many times she'd flipped through that old passport on the flight, checking that the visa was still there.

She'd been so jittery that the anxiety had finally spent itself, so the moment of arrival had been strangely still and calm. She had searched for George's face in the crowd and hadn't found it. This terrible possibility had occurred to her so many times that when it actually happened, it had almost failed to be frightening. She experienced a kind of peace in the face of her complete helplessness, a second infancy, and for several minutes she stood and watched the other passengers streaming around her. And then something had happened. An ear had appeared, between two other bodies, and she had known with absolute certainty that the ear belonged to George. She didn't call out, but waited for him to find and claim her, thinking how strange it was that she should recognize his ear.

She was remembering this moment when her parents appeared in the doorway of the waiting room. They looked smaller and thinner than they had been this morning, and their clothes—how had she failed to alert them?—only advertised the fact that they'd recently come from the village. The embassy had intimidated them into relative decorum at first, but her parents were now frightened enough to be completely uninhibited; her father massaged his forehead with his hand, while her mother waved frantically at Amina. Whatever documents they'd been given were in her right hand.

Amina hurried across the room to them. "What happened? You didn't get them?"

Her mother looked at her father.

"Oh, Munni," he said. "Oh Munni, I'm so sorry."

A uniformed guard began to usher them out, giving sharp directions to the exit. Amina followed her parents, aware that they were being observed by the other supplicants. Anyone else's case was interesting, with potential clues to the success or failure of one's own. She could remember watching four years ago as a girl her age left this room, near tears, and being ashamed of her own thought—that the girl represented one more visa they had left to give.

In the concrete forecourt of the embassy, Amina asked her father what had happened.

"I couldn't answer the questions," he said simply. "They gave me this." He handed Amina a blue sheet of paper on which she picked out the words "administrative processing."

She scanned the form, but couldn't make sense of the official language. "What questions did they ask?"

"Your wedding," her mother put in. "They asked him what day it was."

"I was thinking of the Islamic Center and city hall," her father said. "I didn't know which he meant."

"And then they asked him when you left."

"When I left Bangladesh? But you know that."

"I know," her father said. He slapped his hand against his forehead. "I know perfectly well. But the date—" He brushed his fingertips against his forehead.

"The thirteenth of March," her mother said. "I was thinking they might ask."

"Why didn't you say something beforehand?" her father demanded.

"I was thinking *I* would make the mistake. I wasn't worried about you."

It was maddening, but she couldn't be upset with her father. She hadn't prepared him, and she of all people should've known. Americans were fanatical about attaching numbers to days. Soon after she'd arrived in Rochester, she'd bought the first calendar of her life, so that she would be sure not to miss a birthday, holiday, or anniversary.

She turned to her mother. "And what did they ask you?"

"Easy things. About where you were born and where you'd gone to school. What was the name of your neighborhood in Rochester. I told them where you did your shopping, too, and how they have mangos even in the winter." Her mother looked pleased with herself. "The officer laughed."

"But they still didn't give it to you."

"They did." Her mother held out her passport. "But what's the use, if your father didn't get it?"

Amina turned the page to check, but her mother hadn't made a mistake: her information—names and dates, passport, case and registration numbers—were superimposed over a rainbow-colored image of the Lincoln Memorial and the Capitol Building. Beside Lincoln on his pedestal was her mother's startled face in blue-and-white relief.

10 She didn't realize how much she'd counted on the visas until they were in the taxi going to the apartment in Savar. It was bad enough to have to explain things to her aunt and uncle; it hadn't even occurred to her that Ghaniyah might be back from her trip or that she was as likely to be with her parents as she was with her new husband's family.

"Munni!" she exclaimed, when she opened the door. "It's so lucky! We were going to stay another four days, and then Malik had to come back for work. I just got home last night."

Ghaniyah was wearing an embroidered kameez over a pair of jeans and a great quantity of gold jewelry. The first place she looked was Amina's left hand.

"What's your news?" Her uncle came out of the living room, where the new furniture seemed to have just arrived. Amina could see the maid, Borsha, unrolling a large Persian carpet.

Her father shook his head. "Bad news. I wasn't approved."

"It's not final," Amina said quickly. "We don't understand the paperwork."

"What do you mean?" her aunt asked.

"My mother got her visa," Amina told them. "My father's needs 'further processing.' We have to do some research."

"I've heard of visas being delayed because you have a common name," her uncle said. "I thought 'Abdul Mazid,' but I didn't want to worry you."

"But I am Fatima Mazid," her mother wailed. "If I got it, how could he—"

Her aunt and her cousin exchanged meaningful glances, noting her mother's agitated mood.

"You are Fatima Areebah Mazid," Amina soothed her. "You were right to insist on using your full name."

"Never mind," said her aunt. "Let's celebrate my sister's visa." She shouted for Borsha and gave orders for snacks. "Maybe we'll get to keep you here a little longer while you wait for the other one."

"Don't say that," Ghaniyah teased. "Munni will miss her husband too much." Her cousin took Amina's hand in hers and pretended to see the ring for the first time. "All Americans have diamond engagement rings—isn't that right?"

"There's nothing all Americans do," Amina said. "Just like there isn't anything all Deshis do."

But she might as well have been talking to herself, since her aunt was ushering them all into the new living room. "How have I let you stand so long—come and sit. Most of the furniture is still covered with plastic, but you won't mind. Borsha will bring the food in here."

Her mother was complimenting everything while her aunt flushed with pleasure and pretended not to hear. She had begun complaining about Ghaniyah's mother-in-law.

"Now she's needling us about Gigi being here so much—but they were gone a month on this trip! Now she has the two of them *and* her younger son, and I have an empty house!"

Ghaniyah grinned at Amina. "You should have heard her talking about her own wedding. How she cried the whole time, and how girls today have gotten so bold. When I told her I was coming to Savar today, she looked as if I'd slapped her."

"Look at my son," Moni continued. "Rashid and his wife didn't stay a day with us—he had to go off and accept a professorship in Chittigong. And did I complain? I said, 'They're modern young people, they do what they want.' But my daughter spends one afternoon shopping with her mother, and she'll get a scolding. She wants her in the kitchen making samosas, I suppose."

"Has she tasted Gigi's samosas?" her uncle said mildly. "That might be the solution."

Ghaniyah rolled her eyes at Amina. "Let's go to my room, where we can really talk. I want to hear everything."

Amina's father was sitting on the edge of one of the yellow chairs, looking as if he wished he were anywhere else. He'd become silent in the taxi on the way, and she knew he was thinking about what it would be like to face her mother's family, having failed once again.

"Abba," she said quietly on their way out, "you ought to call Nasir. Maybe he could do some research about the visa at the office." She was trying to rescue her father, give him something to do, but she regretted mentioning Nasir a moment later. She could hear her aunt interrogating her mother about his apartment as they left the room.

"Handsome Nasir," her cousin said, once they were alone. Two red suitcases were open on the floor against the wall; obviously Ghaniyah was planning to keep some of her things at her parents' house. On the bookshelf was a collection of glass animal figurines that Amina had envied desperately as a child, a couple of high school textbooks, a framed photograph of the family at her brother's graduation from BRAC University, and a coffee mug that said LOVE 'EM OR LEAVE 'EM in neon English script; next to this souvenir was the pressed-tin robin Amina had left for her cousin.

"So tell me—is Nasir still as dreamy as before?"

"He's kind," Amina said.

Ghaniyah winked playfully. "And are you still in love with him?"

"Don't be stupid. Nasir's been good to my parents—they've stayed with him again and again."

"My mother's ashamed about that," Ghaniyah said bluntly. "She thinks she should've invited them to live here, after they decided to give up the apartment. She talks about it all the time." Amina had forgotten this quality in her cousin: she was indiscreet, not only about other people's lives but about her own family. It made it hard to be angry with her.

"They're all envious of you," her cousin continued, "Babli and Iffat and all that gang. They wanted to meet you while you were here, but I said you wouldn't have time. I wanted you all to myself."

"I would think they'd be envious of you. That big wedding—and Malik is so successful."

Ghaniyah shook her head. "But you have the dream life in

America—big house, no mother-in-law, no one pushing you to have a kid right away."

Amina looked to see whether her cousin was mocking her, but Ghaniyah was perfectly serious: she really seemed to believe that Amina's choices had been better than her own. Amina had an impulse to correct her, but nothing her cousin had said was untrue. She lived in a three-bedroom house alone with her husband, and no one but her own mother was nagging her about her failure to conceive a child.

"Are they pushing you?"

"They don't say anything about it directly—it's not the fashion these days. But I'll start working at my mother-in-law's office in a couple of weeks—there's no getting out of it. She loves talking about all the poor women she's helping in the villages. Then she'll take the trip to the big conference in Canada, and I'll be stuck answering her phone in the office all day with a bunch of chattering old aunties. And Malik works constantly, even at night. Having a kid is the only escape." Ghaniyah examined her hands, with their slender fingers and perfect French manicure. "I should've worked harder in school—like you. Then I'd already have a career."

"I had to work hard."

"And is it hard now? I mean, working and going to school and everything? Do you have a lot of housework to do?"

"It's easier for me there than it was here," Amina said carefully. "In a lot of ways. Once my parents come—"

"They'll do everything for you," Ghaniyah finished. "My mom asked me why you hadn't had children yet, but I told her of course you were waiting for your mother to get there."

"Munni! Gigi! Borsha's brought snacks."

Ghaniyah shook her head. "You never get five minutes' peace around here. India was like heaven—we hardly talked to anyone. We went to take our pictures at Ajmer and the Taj, and then we just sat around watching movies in the hotels."

When they went into the living room, her aunt was describing something that had happened several months ago, soon after they'd moved into the new flat. A bus driver had hit and killed a garment worker in Hemayetpur, and his fellow workers had staged a protest. Omar had been driving himself that day, since Fariq was visiting his village, and his car had been stopped in the jam at the barricade. He'd gotten out to use his phone, and he was standing on the side of the highway when a group of the striking workers began throwing rocks through the windows of his car. It had taken four hours before the army's Rapid Action Battalion had gotten the situation under control.

"Any excuse to leave their jobs for rampaging and looting," her aunt said. "That was why we needed the new car."

"We were going to get a new car anyway," her uncle said. "We just did it a little sooner than we thought."

"Blood," her aunt whispered. "All over the seats."

"They'd painted the rocks red," her uncle said. "It was a small protest, only about a hundred people."

Her aunt passed a plate of fried cauliflower. "Of course the conditions for these RMG workers are terrible."

"What's RMG?" Amina asked.

Her mother looked at her. "Ready-made garments," she said, as if Amina had asked the meaning of the word "carpet" or "chair." She thought of a bra she had ordered from the Gap soon after she'd arrived in Rochester—cream-colored lace with a rosette, more ornamented than she would have chosen if it hadn't been on clearance—noticing only after she'd tried it on that it had been made in Bangladesh. It had made her happy at the time, as if she'd received a friend in the mail.

"They have vandalism in Rochester, too," Amina said. "Troublemakers bash the mailboxes with baseball bats."

Her uncle looked confused. "Some postal fraud scheme?"

Amina shook her head. "They're just—" But she couldn't think of a Bangla equivalent for "joyriding." "They're drinking alcohol and driving around in their cars."

"These crimes are committed by people with cars?"

Her aunt gestured to her uncle to stop talking as Borsha entered the room. "Her husband belongs to one of those factories," she said in English.

"And anyway, we have to stop talking about depressing things, or they'll never agree to come to us." She turned to Amina, as if she were the decision maker in the family. "The guest room is all set up now, and you can sleep in there with Gigi. If we tell her in-laws you're staying, they won't make her go back yet."

"Please," her cousin encouraged her.

Her mother blinked uncomfortably, under pressure from her elder sister. "Nasir will be insulted," her mother said. "He'll think his hospitality isn't good enough for us."

"Oh," her aunt said, changing her tone. "It's too inconvenient for you. I understand—we never should've moved out of the city. And now we're so far from Gigi, too. I had a terrible feeling when we bought this place."

"This place is wonderful," her mother said. "Only perhaps dangerous for us."

Her aunt glanced at her husband and then gave her sister a meaningful look that Amina's mother didn't catch. "Munni thinks there's nothing to worry about, but I remember what Salim did the last time."

"I remember it, too," Amina said. "He scared us, and that's all."

"He did more than just scare that poor girl—*that* was before you were born."

Ghaniyah looked at her mother. "Who's Salim?"

Her mother flushed and began to apologize: "I didn't realize—"

"Some badmash from Kajalnagar." Her uncle waved his hand dismissively. "Not quite right in the head."

"But what does that have to do with us?" Ghaniyah asked.

"He's my cousin," Amina's father said. She always marveled at the readiness with which her father disclosed damaging or embarrassing information. She and her mother were proud, but her father didn't suffer from that fault at all; even when he was telling stories from the war, he gave the impression that what he relished was his participation in a just and victorious mission, rather than his personal achievements as a soldier.

"He's been in trouble his whole life, since he was a teenager," her father continued. "A girl's family rejected his proposal, and Salim attacked her with acid."

Amina's mother made a skeptical noise, and Ghaniyah's eyes got very big.

"Was she badly burned?"

Her uncle gave her father a look, as if to say that this wasn't an appropriate conversation to be having in front of his daughter.

"This was more than thirty years ago," Amina's father said quickly. "I'm sure he's no danger now."

Ghaniyah didn't seem reassured. "But he knows where we live?"

"Everyone in Kajalnagar knows us," Moni snapped. "How could they not? But we're perfectly safe. You can put it out of your head."

Amina's mother nodded darkly. "*You're* not in any danger."

Her cousin looked at Amina, clearly horrified. "But why would he want to hurt the three of you, if he's my uncle's cousin?"

"Gigi," her aunt said sharply.

But Amina was determined that they should all hear the truth. "They've made up a pretext," she said. "They say we stole gold jewelry—jewelry my dadu gave my father to sell. Now they're trying to extort a ridiculous amount of money. They believe we're rich, simply because we're going to America."

"Thank God we've never gotten involved with those people," her aunt said, but she didn't look at Amina.

"Don't be so dramatic," her uncle said. "They'll be fine."

"I'll have my nap, or I'll be a wreck by this evening," her aunt said. "You'll stay for dinner, at least?"

"We've bought a hen," her mother apologized.

"Come, Ammi," Ghaniyah said. "We'll lie down together." She turned to Amina. "We'll see you again, of course?"

"Of course," Amina said. She was grateful that the good-byes weren't belabored, the way they would be in America. If they were lucky and the problems with her father's visa were easily solved, there might not be time for another visit. It was still possible that they could leave in a week and a half; that she could keep her job; that everything would continue to go as she'd planned.

11 Fariq dropped them at the Kaderabad Bazar, where her mother bought another loaf of sliced sandwich bread for Nasir's toast. The sky was gray, and the air smelled like rain; people were rushing to complete their errands. While her mother was paying, Amina and her father took his phone to the Flexiload shop for more minutes; she and George had arranged to talk at half past six. They had just turned the corner to Nasir's lane when a man called her father's name in the

crowded street. Her father stopped, and her mother grabbed Amina's arm; but when they turned around it was only Long Nose, his distinctive profile half a head above the rest of the crowd. His gray hair had gone pure white, and he walked toward them with confident, long strides.

"Abdul Mazid." He put his palms together respectfully toward her mother. "And your Munni, too. How lucky this is." Long Nose and her father shook hands, and then there was a pause.

"How many years has it been?" Long Nose asked.

Her mother turned to her: "You were how old?"

"Twelve," Amina said.

"Then sixteen years!" Her parents shook their heads and smiled.

"And how are you?" Long Nose asked.

"Fine, fine," her father said. "Now that Munni's visiting from America."

"Wonderful." Long Nose looked at her a second longer than necessary, as if he saw something of her mother in her. "I heard you'd married there, but I didn't know where your parents were living. I would have liked to send a gift."

"No need, no need," her mother said. "You're too kind."

"And you? Where are you living?"

"In Savar with my sister," her mother said. "Things are still very hard. And now Munni's husband has lost his job."

She looked at her mother in wonder. Why would she tell Long Nose something they'd kept from even their closest relatives? Their arms were linked, and her mother gripped Amina's hard.

"U.S. financial crisis," her father said in English. "Thousands of layoffs everywhere."

Amina waited for one of her parents to mention the visas, but neither did.

"And how are your children?" her mother asked.

"Both married," Long Nose said. "Six grandchildren—four boys and two girls."

"You are blessed," her mother said. She put her hand out, palm up.

"It's starting," her father said, although Amina didn't feel anything. "We're going to dinner at my nephew's."

"Is his place nearby?" Long Nose asked. "I could walk with you."

"Nonsense!" her mother said. "It's a ten-minute walk in the wrong direction; you'll get soaked." She smiled. "But we're so glad to have met you."

Long Nose looked around uncomfortably; they were standing in the middle of the street. "Could I speak to you?" he asked her father.

"Right now?" her father said.

"Just for a moment," Long Nose said. "Perhaps the ladies would like to start back?"

"Go," her father said, speaking English again. "I will catch you." Her parents exchanged significant looks, and then her mother said good-bye to Long Nose. She had pulled her scarf over her head, nearly covering her face.

"Let's go."

"But Nasir's—" Amina began, but her mother was hurrying her in the opposite direction. They turned the corner and then doubled back around, approaching Nasir's from the other side.

"I didn't want him to see where we're staying," her mother said. "He's probably asking your father for money. Now George's job gives us an excuse."

They let themselves in the gate with the key Nasir had made for them and climbed the stairs. Amina flicked the wall switches without thinking, but the power was out. They moved around in the dim rooms, her mother putting away the bread and then going into the bathroom.

"Do you mean we never paid Long Nose the back rent?" Amina asked cautiously, once her mother was sitting at the table with the potatoes and onions to chop for the curry.

Her mother didn't look up from her vegetables, as if she were a small girl who needed to concentrate to work with a knife. "Let's see what your father says."

She could remember in elaborate detail certain pieces of the furniture they'd given Long Nose: the bed with a headboard stained dark to look like teak, a lamp with a patterned glass shade, and a pair of upholstered chairs, the antimacassars embroidered with spotted deer. She had begged her mother to save those, but one had to be left behind to cover a stain. At the time it had seemed as if they were losing untold riches—Amina hadn't been able to understand how seven months of rent could possibly equal all of that—and she would never forget the moment they'd stepped into the one-room flat in Tejgaon, the blistered walls, the cracked linoleum, and the roaches lazily arranged on the walls of the kitchen and bathroom, as if they were the flat's rightful owners. She had cried, and her mother hadn't smacked her (as she'd deserved, for that kind of behavior at twelve years old) but had taken her in her arms and pressed her face against her chest, so that she wouldn't have to see where they would live.

Now, suddenly, she calculated the relative values with adult eyes. That cheap furniture that her parents had brought as newlyweds from the village would have been worth at most two months of rent. Even if Long Nose didn't demand sixteen years of interest, they owed him perhaps six or seven hundred dollars—a small fortune at that time in Dhaka.

She and her mother both turned when her father opened the door. He didn't say anything, but his face was troubled, and he went directly to the sink to do ablutions. They'd missed the *duhr* because of the embassy, and it was almost time for *maghrib*.

Her mother sighed. "What are the chances, after all these years? Did he give you some number?"

Her father emerged from the bathroom. "Number? Oh, no—he didn't mention money."

"Only the debt," her mother said.

"Not even the debt." Her father brushed her mother's doubts aside with an impatient gesture. "I believe he's forgiven it." Then his face darkened. "But Salim was there—that's what he wanted to tell me."

Her mother put down her knife, startled. "What? At the market?"

"At Long Nose's building—the day after Munni arrived. Salim must've known we weren't at Omar's, and so he went back to the place he found us the last time. Long Nose said he told him he hadn't seen or spoken with us in years. Of course he never saw Salim the night he locked you in, but something about him made Long Nose wary—that eye unsettles people. And so he didn't tell Salim anything. But Salim kept haranguing him, asking for our phone number. Finally Long Nose said he'd call the police, but Salim just laughed at him." The set of her father's jaw was fiercely determined—for a moment, a soldier's face again. "He said he wanted to warn us, but he didn't have our number."

"And then Allah brought us together, like that," her mother said. "A miracle."

"I think the miracle is that Long Nose was so kind," Amina said. "Especially after how we've treated him." She was ashamed of herself. Six hundred dollars was three weeks at Starbucks, after taxes; not nothing, but certainly possible. Why had it never occurred to her that she might repay what they owed?

"If Long Nose wants to forgive an old debt, that's his choice," her mother said. "You'll insult him by offering money."

Amina turned to her father. "We should pay him."

Her mother looked up from the vegetables and spoke mildly. "What can *he* do?"

She didn't think her mother had meant it as anything but a statement of fact, but her father stood still as if he'd been hit. The light remaining in the apartment was yellow-green, and the rain had finally begun, a steady thrumming on the roof. Nasir's few possessions stood out in the gloom: a white refrigerator, a black plastic computer table, a dining table covered with a cloth printed with tiny Dutchmen holding apples—a loan from one of his sisters, Amina was sure, in anticipation of their arrival. The Dutchmen looked like corpses with their glassy, wide-open eyes.

Her father put his bare feet into a pair of black dress shoes sitting beneath the rack at the door.

"I'm going out."

"I'm sorry," Amina said. She bent down and touched his feet in the old-fashioned way. "Stay, Abba. I'll say the prayers with you."

Her father shook her off. "Get up, Munni."

"Nasir will be home soon. He'll have information for us."

Her father didn't say anything.

"Sit with me and read the form. I might need your help."

He looked to determine whether she was being disingenuous.

"Technical vocabulary," Amina said quickly. "I'm never good at that. I know the individual words, but I don't always get the sense."

For a moment he seemed ready to walk out the door, and then he softened. "Make some tea," he told her mother roughly. "If there's no power, at least Nasir should have something to drink when he gets home."

Her mother disappeared obediently to light the gas cooktop in the kitchen, and Amina and her father sat down to read the blue form. The room was warm and the air dead still. Eventually it became too dark to see even the apples in the Dutchmen's hands. Amina hunted until she found a flashlight in a basket on top of the refrigerator, and then they continued to work it out, line by line together.

12 Amina had been waiting, and she jumped when she heard Nasir's key in the lock. It was nine o'clock, almost dinnertime, and Nasir had been downstairs at Shilpa's, helping his nephews with their homework, since their father worked an evening shift. He went straight to the sink to wash, but as soon as they sat down at the table, he began discussing the visas.

"Your uncle is right," he told Amina. "It probably has to do with his name more than with the questions." Nasir ate the way her parents did, maneuvering the rice in neat balls to his mouth with his right hand. The nails on both hands were short and clean.

"But if I'd answered the questions," her father lamented.

"You still might not have gotten it. I talked to a friend of mine whose nephew goes to business school in the States—in Arizona. His name is Khuzaymah Menon, and his visa was approved right away, but he knows another guy, a Sylheti, who won an H1-B visa in the lottery. He was all set to go, and then they gave him this same blue paper. His name is Abdul Haq, so you see—it took them six months to approve him."

Her mother gasped. "Six months."

"You have to use the immigrant visa within six months," Amina reminded Nasir. "If we have to wait too long, my mother's visa will have expired—we'll have to start all over again."

"I did some research online," Nasir said. "I can do more tomorrow. It doesn't always take that long—sometimes it's only a week or two."

"Even two weeks," Amina said, thinking of her job.

"You can stay with me as long as you want."

"We'll go to a hotel," Amina said, more to see what Nasir would say than out of any real conviction.

"They would have security there," her mother said, but she looked doubtfully at Amina, obviously thinking of the expense of a hotel and George's job.

But Nasir ignored both of them, and addressed himself to her father. "Did something happen?"

"It was nothing," her father said. "We ran into our old landlord—the one with the building right around here. He said my cousin Salim had come looking for us there."

"He was threatening you?" Nasir's irises were dark brown with a black ring, exactly like her own. What would be happening right now, at this moment, if she had married him? The thought was pleasurably transgressive, and she could entertain it without consequences. She could pretend to be paying attention to her mother's paranoid fears, her father's empty assurances, and instead imagine the four of them sitting at this table as two couples, two generations of a family, just to see what it would be like. No one—not George, not her parents, and certainly not Nasir—had to know she was doing it.

"We can't put you and your sisters at risk," Amina said, but the sense of danger was less palpable than her curiosity about how much Nasir wanted them to stay and whether any of that was due to her.

"Don't throw away money at a hotel on their account. They're leaving for Comilla on Tuesday."

"Still," Amina said. "We don't know how long it's going to take."

"That's exactly why—" Nasir began, but her father interrupted.

"Munni—did you call George? It's twenty past seven."

She had completely forgotten the phone call. She took her father's phone into the bedroom and sat down on the yellow bedspread. There was enough light coming from the street, through thin, orange curtains, that she didn't need to turn on the lamp. She remembered the way she and her mother used to idle away the hours on the days she and George had arranged to talk. They would watch television or play cards, but they wouldn't go out within an hour of the call, in case he should be early and they should miss him. She thought of her last conversation with her husband and wondered if she should apologize now. But for what? Wasn't it right to be suspicious, after everything that had happened?

The dinner continued in the other room, her parents' voices mingling with Nasir's now that the food was finished. With George, of course, they would be shy, unlikely even to want to sit down at the table all together. George himself was inclined to go on at length—whatever his current preoccupation—but he would direct those monologues at Amina only, since her parents wouldn't be able to understand. Would they slip into some routine she couldn't imagine now, or would dinnertime be permanently awkward? She remembered how she'd dismissed these worries when they'd occurred to her in Rochester; only George had seriously questioned whether her parents would be able to adapt to life in the United States. How had he been able to see it more clearly than she had?

She let the phone ring six times, but there was no answer; when she heard the voice mail beginning, she had the impulse to hang up. Instead she left a businesslike message, explaining the problem at the embassy and asking George to call the free immigration hotline in Manhattan.

"It's decided," Nasir said, when she came out into the main room. "You'll stay as long as it takes."

"It will probably be only two weeks," her father said. "This friend of Nasir's is confident."

"Which friend?" Amina asked. "Khuzaymah or Abdul? Did either one of them actually get to the U.S.?"

Nasir looked down at his plate and smiled. He probably didn't share her father's optimism, but he'd managed to convince them to stay. The three of them had finished her mother's chicken curry, and her father was taking secret sips of whiskey and water from a glass Nasir had provided while her mother cleared the dishes and pretended not to notice. The alcohol was making him teary; Nasir had a photo album on the table, and her father had obviously begun reminiscing about his days with Nasir's father as university students in Rajshahi.

"Come look at this," Nasir said, and when Amina went around the table, there was a photograph she had never seen, of six stern-faced boys posing with rifles on a wooden porch. The rifles looked antique, like the one Aunt Cathy had mounted over her fireplace in Brighton, and several of the boys were wearing sunglasses. Her father apparently hadn't owned a pair, but his fashion sense was evident in a patterned shirt with an oversize collar, the points of which mimicked his widow's peak, pronounced even in his twenties. He glared fiercely at the camera as if it were General Yahya himself.

"We didn't know what it would be like," her father said. "We thought we were men already."

"How many in this group actually became Freedom Fighters?" Nasir asked, and Amina could see the eagerness in his expression as he leaned over the photo. How silly it had been for her to imagine that his hospitality had anything to do with her. Her parents were his last real connection to his own; her father was the only one who could tell him what his had been like as a young man, younger than Nasir was now.

"Four of us," her father said. "Your father and I, Usman, and Tariq. Yusef and Alamgir went back to their families first; they were planning to enlist from home."

"And what happened to the others?" Nasir asked gently.

"We survived, the four of us—isn't that incredible? We were all posted in different places except for your father and me—you know all this. We trained together at Dehradun and then went back to Khulna. I got this"—her father rolled up his pant leg to show the scar again, a white boomerang just below his knee—"near Paikgacha. Then your father brought me home to Kajalnagar—I wouldn't have gotten there without him. After it was over, we starting asking everyone we could find about Tariq and Usman. We found out Tariq had survived Boyra, and Usman got through the awful street battles here in Dhaka. When we heard we thanked God, and it didn't even occur to us to ask about Yusef until days later."

"What happened to Yusef?"

Her mother got up to clear the table. "Help me," she instructed Amina, but Amina lingered in the main room, stacking the plates and wiping the table with a cloth.

"Killed," her father said. "Massacred by those animals in his own home. You know his father was a lawyer, very successful, with a big house in Dhanmondi. His uncle was a poet—not very famous but well connected—and there would be gatherings at their place almost every night." Her father paused and took a sip of his drink. "We didn't know about the atrocities right away, but a family like that was doomed. His mother was raped in front of him, and his sisters were carried off to the cantonment, to be used by the soldiers. Then all the men in the family were murdered."

"Why?" Amina asked.

"Oh—they were important people, especially in the Language Movement. His brother and sister were at Dhaka University then, and his brother organized some of the student demonstrations. Those were the kind of people the generals were afraid of—intellectuals loyal to the nation." Her father stopped and corrected himself: "Not even the nation, because it didn't exist yet. They were loyal to the language." Her father got up suddenly, knocking the table, and hurried into the bedroom, where he retrieved one of the few books he had kept, an analysis of the Language Movement written by a Dhaka University professor. It was one he'd encouraged Amina to read—about how the 1952 student protests against the government's imposition of Urdu on the Bangla-speaking eastern wing of the country had given birth to the struggle for independence—and she was sorry now that she'd always put it off.

"You keep this," he told Nasir. "No point in carrying it all the way to America."

"I'm making Horlicks," her mother called from the kitchen. "Who wants some?"

"Oh no," Nasir said. "I couldn't—it's yours." But her father waved his protestations away, padding into the bedroom in his slippers. The three of them would continue sleeping in there, while Nasir took the small room without complaining. Now he sat at the table looking through the book, which she was sure her father had shown him several times before. Her mother placed two glasses of Horlicks on the table for them and then took another two into the bedroom.

"Sorry about this," Nasir said. "The power should be back soon." He turned the flashlight on its end so that it made a squarish spotlight on the ceiling and half illuminated a free calendar from BRAC Bank, featuring a photograph of snowcapped mountains. He looked suddenly shy, but whether it was the light or the fact that they were alone together, she didn't know.

"It hasn't been so long that I've forgotten power cuts."

"In England I found certain things very easy to get used to. Plumbing, electricity, clean water from the tap—it's much harder coming back in this direction. At work we have a generator, of course."

"How is your work?" It was exactly what she'd been accustomed to asking George every day when he got home, but she'd come to regret the habit after he lost his job. The same words to Nasir now felt like a small betrayal.

"It's fine—it's mostly making websites for small businesses. We use different templates, depending on the price, so it's the same thing over and over again. But my boss is good, and I get on well with my colleagues."

"Do they still think you're crazy because of those articles?"

Nasir looked blank for a moment and then he blushed. "No—I took them down. I'm surprised you even remember."

"I remember that e-mail very well. I was angry at you."

"I overstepped," Nasir said. "I don't know why I thought I could tell you what to do."

"You were being an older brother."

But Nasir shook his head adamantly. "I wasn't. I didn't think of you that way. When I was in London—when Sakina Apu talked to your parents—" Nasir colored and stopped abruptly. She'd hardly ever seen him struggle for words, and maybe that was why she failed to look down modestly, as of course she should have. She was too eager to know what he'd said to Sakina all those years ago—she would have been nineteen or twenty then—if he'd encouraged or simply tolerated the idea that they might one day marry.

Whether it was her boldness or his own caution, Nasir seemed to think he'd gone too far: he grasped the table with two hands, as if he were going to stand up and walk away. Instead he tilted his chair backward just slightly, like a rebellious child, and then let his weight return it to the floor.

"I mean, Sakina Apu always liked you. That's why she was hard on you back then."

"She still is."

He'd regained his self-possession and addressed her reassuringly, as if she were the one who'd crossed a line. "But she's that way with Shilpa, too. You should hear the fights they have."

Amina nodded carefully. She didn't know how they'd gotten onto the subject of his sisters, and she could feel her heart thudding against her ribs. Had he been about to say that he'd thought of her like a fiancée, rather than a sister? That he had thought of her in London and been disappointed to hear the news of her engagement? They both knew, of course, that a match between the two of them had once been discussed, but saying it out loud was something different.

"It's getting late," Nasir said, and just then the power returned: the ceiling fan ground into motion and in the bedroom the television came to life. A BBC broadcaster was reporting about the financial crisis in America.

"I was thinking I might fast next year," Amina said hurriedly, to keep him at the table. "It's been a while since I tried it."

Nasir smiled. "That's good."

"Think of what our parents' generation went through," Amina said. "And I can't even wait until sundown for a meal."

Nasir nodded, tracing the faded gold tooling on the album's leather cover with one finger. "You know, sometimes I envy them?" He glanced into the bedroom and then lowered his voice. "I mean when they were younger. Being part of the war and everything."

"How could you envy *that*?"

"Maybe it sounds crazy," he acknowledged. "But there was a purpose, then. Something beyond our own lives. It was much harder for my father after the war. He hated being a landlord—all the pressure when things broke down, and tenants always begging him for credit. My mother thought the anxiety was what gave him the heart attack—it doesn't run in our family. And my sister thinks our mother stopped wanting to live after he died. So you could say that this building killed them both—I think that story is as sad as Yusef's." He looked defiant when he said this, expecting her to be shocked again. "At least Yusef and his father died for something."

"What about his mother and his sisters?"

Nasir looked away and grimaced slightly, as if she'd used profanity. "I don't think your father meant for you to hear that."

"I don't see what's wrong with living quietly," Amina said. "We should be grateful for it. Why do we need to be part of history—what makes us so special?" She stopped short, embarrassed by the intensity of her voice.

"I think you're right," he said. "When I think about it. But sometimes I don't think."

"Like when you see the girl with yellow hair clips," she ventured, but that was the wrong thing to say. Nasir got up abruptly and took his glass to the kitchen.

"I shouldn't have told you that," he said. "Forget it."

"I'm sorry—" she began, but he'd already disappeared into the bathroom, where she heard him filling the buckets, in case the water didn't come in the morning.

Amina waited another minute, washing her own glass, but he didn't come out of the bathroom. Finally she went into her parents' room, where her father had fallen asleep on his back and was snoring loudly. Her mother moved to the center of the bed—Amina noticed how little space she occupied—and patted the place next to her. But Amina shook her head and indicated the pile of bedding folded in the corner, which Shilpa had lent in case Amina preferred sleeping on the floor. She unrolled the pad and quilts, not bothering with the mosquito net, and switched off the television and the light. Then she undressed and lay down at the foot of her parents bed, where her mother couldn't tell if she was awake or asleep. Soon she heard her mother's soft breathing in the intervals between her father's snores.

From the faint glow under the door, she knew the light was still on in the other bedroom. She would never be so bold as to knock on the door, but there was nothing wrong with going up to the roof. The heat felt oppressive to her, although people had been saying it wasn't as bad as usual this time of year—that she'd brought the cool weather with her from America. She listened to make sure her mother's breathing was still steady (her father never woke in the night) and then slipped on the same blue sundress she'd worn this morning. She considered the rough, white polyester trousers her mother had given her to put underneath the dress—conservative by Rochester standards, with its cap sleeves and calf-length skirt—and left them hanging over the chair: she was ostensibly going up to be alone. She noiselessly opened and closed the door to her parents' room, but once she was in the main room she was intentionally careless, walking with her normal tread and stopping to get a glass of water from the filter next to the refrigerator. They had drunk well water in the village, and she could remember sitting by a similar filter as a small child newly arrived in Dhaka, marveling at the shapes the air took as it burbled to the top.

Outside there was an occasional, gusting breeze that seemed to bring only more humidity; she thought the rain could come again at any moment. The roof was deserted, and Amina realized she'd forgotten the pleasure of going out after dark in light clothing, the softness of the air on her skin. The roof was divided in two levels: the upper, where Sakina's plants swayed gently in the dark, and the lower, where she went now, sitting down on the concrete next to a squat, domed black water tank, leaning her back against the brick barrier wall. The brightest part of the city was to the southeast, haloed in the smog. The roofs around her were mostly dark, although electric lanterns still burned at the construction site down the road; away from the lights, she knew the men who had finished their shifts had already unrolled their bedding to sleep. It was impossible to distinguish the building materials—stacks of bricks, bags of plaster and cement—from the softer clusters of human shapes collapsed outside the rings of the lanterns. Those men were dreaming of their villages, and Dhaka seemed as strange to them as Rochester once had to her.

When she heard his feet on the stairs, she covered her legs with her skirt. She turned to face the other direction and felt stupid, with the result that when Nasir opened the door to the roof she was looking right at him. He didn't smile, and she wondered if he was still angry at her for mentioning Yellow Barrette. She couldn't tell whether he noticed her clothing; if she'd wanted to please him, she might have put on the shalwar kameez she'd worn to the embassy, but even now she wasn't sure what her purpose was. She had been anxious lying in the room with her parents, and she'd known that the only thing with the power to relieve that anxiety was Nasir. Now that he was here, it was enough. She thought that she'd like to prolong this moment before they'd spoken to each other, that if there were a way to live a whole lifetime in this proximity, without the complications of speech or action, that was how she could be happy.

But he was walking toward her, ruining it, and she spoke from a nervous compulsion.

"I hope I didn't wake you—going out."

He stopped and considered her, sitting against the wall.

"You look like an advert."

"What?"

"Soap powder or packaged food or something. Modern conveniences for the modern wife."

She knew the type of ad he was talking about—in magazines or pasted up on hoardings in the roads. They were more present in Dhaka than they'd been when she'd left, which she took to mean that things were improving, at least for city people. The houses pictured in the backgrounds of those posters, affixed by men like the ones sleeping just across the road, were more perfect than any Amina had seen in America, or indeed anywhere but in the frothiest kind of Hindi movie. Here there was no room for verisimilitude, no humor—simply a shiny prosperity, desperate and false. The fair-skinned father and children (always an elder boy and younger girl) in sporty, Western dress, surrounded the mother, congratulating her on the sparkle of the glassware or the tastiness of a frozen pakora. Everything was modern except for the dress of the woman at its center, who would be sumptuously attired in modest, traditional clothes. In that sense, Nasir had gotten it wrong.

"In an advert I'd be wearing a sari."

"I mean you look out of place."

"These are the kind of clothes I've always worn," she reminded him.

"To be provocative?"

This was the kind of comment that might have infuriated her in the past, but she couldn't muster the same indignation. She felt as if she were looking at Nasir through a glass wall, which ensured they wouldn't get close enough to hurt or even touch each other.

"I preferred Western clothes even as a girl—I always covered my arms and legs. Even my hair sometimes—when the other girls I knew weren't doing it. My mother didn't have to encourage me."

"Why not wear our own clothes and save yourself the trouble?"

It was a question she'd been asked before, and she didn't have an answer. Why were some people attracted to what was unfamiliar, and others to what they knew? She thought it might have to do with how comfortable you were in your own life, how well you felt you belonged.

Nasir glanced at her ankles protruding from under the skirt, her feet in her mother's sandals. "You're not covered now."

"I expected to be alone." She was glad it was dark enough that he couldn't see her blush.

"You can't be alone," he said roughly. "Do you know what you're risking? Do you want to see pictures of what someone like Salim can do?"

She could tell immediately that he was serious, but the fact of the two of them on the roof together made it exciting rather than frightening. "You really believe that?"

He looked at her curiously. "You forget because you've been abroad. It's different here." He took the last few steps to where she was sitting, leaned against the wall.

"It's more dangerous, you mean."

"Everything's different," he said. "You know that." He looked away from her as he spoke, and she could see the smooth skin on the back of his neck, where his hairline had been neatly shaved. "Even men and women—the way they look at one another on the street there. It's okay to chat or flirt because it doesn't mean anything."

"Cheating means something though," she said. "Americans are obsessed with it."

"Americans in particular?"

"I think they worry about it more—so it happens more."

"Is it mostly the men?"

"Seventy percent of men and sixty percent of women."

Nasir laughed. "They keep records, then?" He dropped down suddenly next to her, rocking back and forth on his heels. She could feel the wall behind her through the thin fabric of her dress.

"You'll get your dress dirty," he whispered, and then he put his hands under her arms and lifted her to stand against him. For a moment he did nothing, just looking at her as if for some cue, and she couldn't believe what she felt, a charged readiness more intense than anything she'd ever experienced, except in dreams. Finally he put his arms around her waist, and she let her hands go up to touch that place at the back of his neck, softer than she'd imagined. He looked certain of what they were going to do, and she wondered about the women he'd been with before this. Her own promises and responsibilities were distant and indistinct, as if they belonged to a different person. At the same time she felt as if she'd entered herself again, the left-behind self who'd been waiting for her so long.

"Come on," he said, "let's go," and then he kissed her. How startling it was, the difference in the way two people could kiss. She had always resisted the feeling of George's tongue, the wet softness of it—intrusive and strange. Nasir kissed her so gently that she wanted more, found herself opening her mouth for him. His tongue had a slightly salty taste, as if he'd been swimming in sea water; his mouth was warm and rough and she wanted to go farther inside it. The idea that you might have a taste for certain people, just as you did for foods, was new to her.

He pulled her closer, and kissed more deeply, until she felt she had to pull away.

"Is this what you learned in London?" It was an unpleasant thing to say, and she regretted it as soon as it was out. She was delaying, she knew, because she was scared. She wasn't shy with Nasir, the way she'd once been with George, but she was afraid of what the consequences might be. Could they do this, and then go on as before?

"No. I told you—in London I spent most of my time off at the mosque." He ran one hand lightly up and down her back. He didn't release her waist, and she could feel his erection pressing against her dress. It was strange now to think all men were the same this way, in spite of their remarkable differences.

"Does George go with you to the mosque?"

She realized it was the first time she'd heard him say her husband's name. She didn't feel ashamed, or even vengeful—the world in which George and Kim existed seemed so far from this one that she doubted any one person could inhabit both. She had the strange thought that it might not be wrong to cheat with Nasir, just as long as they did it silently. She felt safer embracing him here than she had when they were talking at the table.

She hadn't answered his question, and he persisted: "He refuses?" His tone was light, not yet aggressive. He was gathering information.

"He would take me—but I've never asked."

"Not since the wedding," he corrected. A light went on in a window across the street, and Amina worried again that they could be seen.

"Not ever." She was close enough to see a small red pimple starting at his hairline, like a teenager. Even this endeared him to her. She moved against him, wanting to be kissed again. She would go downstairs with him now, be in his room.

But Nasir let go of her waist and took a step back. "Then where did you get married?"

She couldn't believe he wanted to talk about it now. "At city hall."

He shook his head impatiently. "I mean the Muslim wedding."

Something scuttered across the roof, a piece of tarpaper or a rat. The wind distorted the traffic sounds—now just below them, now far away.

"We told my parents we did it, but we didn't. We planned to do it at the ICR, and then we never got around to it."

"You mean, you aren't—"

"Legally we are."

"In America." Nasir was shaking his head, a strange animation lighting his familiar features. "You aren't. Not really."

"Marriage counts everywhere. Just because you travel doesn't mean you aren't married." But she thought of the way George had dismissed Kim's marriage in India—*some kind of ceremony*—and felt suddenly cold.

"We can go downstairs now," she said. "My parents won't wake up." But she could feel the moment was slipping away. Whatever pleasant dream they'd been existing in was gone.

"We can't," he said. "I won't. We have to be careful now—both of us."

As they descended the stairs Amina tried to convince herself that the thing clogging her throat was guilt. Simply because George had deceived her about his life before their marriage didn't give her the right to betray him now. What she was doing was worse: it was happening within the bonds of matrimony. Any impartial observer would take George's side.

But it was no use. Guilt was remorse for something you'd done, and she didn't feel that at all. She wished herself backward in time only so that she could act more decisively, and compound her crime.

When Nasir opened the door to the apartment, she turned to stand in his way.

"We could still—"

He shook his head, and together they listened for sounds from her parents' room. When he'd ascertained that it was quiet, he took her shoulders in his hands and kissed the top of her head.

"Get some sleep," he said, and then disappeared into his room, leaving her standing in the main room alone. The apartment was dark, but the power was on: the refrigerator hummed loudly, and downstairs she could faintly hear the drone of a television.

Did he believe they could marry? That would explain his behavior, but she couldn't imagine that he'd considered it clearly. Everyone knew about her marriage in America: she would have to get divorced, whether Nasir thought her marriage was valid or not. Even if he could accept the idea of a divorced woman for a wife, could his sisters? She thought again of how Sakina had criticized her mother for letting her marry abroad, and how her mother had said it was only bitterness. What were the chances that she would soften toward Amina now? Even if Nasir was determined enough to go against convention, there would be a thousand ways his sister could retaliate, with the support of a whole web of friends and relations. Amina imagined the way those women would look at her, when she walked down the lane to buy a phone card or eggs from the market. Could she stand to stay here under those circumstances?

She looked around the room and tried to picture it as a family home. She thought of the kitchen that had traveled with them throughout her childhood: the neat jars of rice, lentils, and spices, the bottle of cooking oil her mother wiped clean after each use. She'd complained about the waste of space in Rochester, the appliances she'd rarely used, but could she really do as her mother had done, planning and executing each meal in the narrow, cement galley, hovering around the table and replenishing dishes, clearing and cleaning, and then carrying plates up and down the stairs to the neighbors according to the complicated and necessary local rituals of politeness? Everything she and her parents had done had been to ensure she would have a different kind of life—what would it mean to give all that up now?

Of course her time in America and her fluency would yield her plentiful tutoring jobs; she would be able to secure a more prestigious teaching position at a school like Maple Leaf much sooner than she would the equivalent position in America. Her mother would do the cooking and the housework as long as she was able, so that Amina could work outside the home. But how long would Nasir expect that to last? He would want to observe the *'iddah*, the three-month waiting period before they were allowed to marry—a formality that ensured a divorced woman wasn't pregnant by her previous husband. That, at least, Amina could be sure of. The fact that she and George didn't have children yet would seem to Nasir a bit of luck, and perhaps even more evidence that the marriage itself was a kind of foreign fiction. It wouldn't occur to him that their childlessness was unintentional, or that the defect was on her side. After making such a painful concession, taking a divorced woman as his wife, how would he feel if he discovered that Amina couldn't conceive?

She made the reasonable arguments against it, and then she felt weary of thinking reasonably. She felt as if she'd been doing it all her life. She opened the door to the bedroom where her parents were sleeping, her father facedown on his stomach with his hands by his ears, as if he were praying, and her mother on her back, her head cradled in the crook of one arm. Amina hesitated a moment and then climbed in carefully, stretching out to her full length beside her mother so that she wouldn't disturb her sleep.

There was an electronic pinging from the room next door, and she knew Nasir was using his phone. Whom could he be calling so late? His voice a moment later was low and urgent, but she couldn't make out the words; he seemed to speak for a long time without waiting for the other person to respond. She forced herself to listen to the noise outside, to avoid straining for clues. The rain had started, and she could hear the persistent complaint of car horns in the bazaar. It muffled the construction sounds, almost as if she were listening over a long-distance line. Her mother rolled suddenly against her, her body warm and almost impossibly slight inside a bulky cotton nightgown. She could no longer hear Nasir's voice, but somewhere below them on the street—it came very clear—a man was whistling.

13 She reached George the next afternoon. She hadn't antici- pated it while she was dialing, but when he answered she was almost afraid to say hello. She thought he might hear something in her voice, as if that kiss on the roof could have changed the register or the accent.

"I'm sorry," George said right away when he answered. She was so surprised that she didn't say anything. "I overreacted when we were talking about the job. And the stuff with Kim—"

"It's okay," Amina said.

"She's gone," he said. "I checked with my mom—she left the week after that dinner party. No one's heard from her—she hasn't even e-mailed."

She'd considered the possibility, when she woke this morning, that what had happened on the roof last night might finally neutralize her jealousy, alleviate one betrayal with another. But the two poisons seemed instead to compound each other's effects.

"No," she said now. "I went too far. There was no reason for me to think she would be there."

"Of course not," George said. "Anyway, she's gone. I just wanted to tell you that."

"Thank you," Amina said. You couldn't be angry at someone for an expression you'd glimpsed on his face or a feeling you believed he'd had. That was the hardest thing about marriage, she thought—how could you continue to be kind, once you knew all of another person's secrets?

"And I talked to the hotline," he hurried on. "It's an additional security clearance, so it's just going to take some time."

"But what can we do?"

"You've just got to sit tight until someone reviews the application. You're depending on a human being, unfortunately—so it's com- pletely unpredictable. But don't worry—that's why we bought the open returns."

"What about Starbucks?" Amina asked. "Keith only gave me the days to be nice—since it was a onetime thing. If I'm not back a week from Monday, he'll find someone else to take my job."

"If you lose it, you'd get another," George said. "You should enjoy yourself. Who knows when you'll be back there?"

"I won't come back to Bangladesh." She was sitting on the bed in the room Nasir had given them, her knees pulled up to her chin. In the distance she could hear a loudspeaker mounted on a truck, advertising some political candidate over jangling music. "Not unless my father's request is denied."

"It won't be denied," George said, attempting to reassure her. "How are your aunt and uncle—still torturing you?"

"No," Amina said. "We're not staying there. We're at Nasir's now."

"Nasir?"

"He's the son of my father's oldest friend."

"Right." George hesitated, and in that silence she could hear her pulse in her ears. It was so loud she imagined he could hear it, too.

"I sent in that résumé," he said.

She hadn't realized she'd been holding her breath. "That's great."

Her enthusiasm seemed to encourage him. "I got a follow-up e-mail, and they want to set up an interview—it could be just informational, but you never know."

"Great," Amina said again. She was suddenly so lonely that she felt a tightness under her cheekbones. The loudspeaker had moved on, giving way to the familiar sounds from the street: the echo of hammering, metal on metal, horns, the whine of a siren somewhere in the distance. In the kitchen her mother was frying bitter melon, spiced with turmeric and cumin. How could she feel homesick again *now*—in the city where she'd spent most of her life, with her parents in the next room and her husband on the phone?

There was another pause.

"Well, call me when you hear something," George said.

"Okay," she said again. She was about to say good-bye and hang up, when he spoke again:

"Amina?"

She wondered if this of all times was the one he would choose to tell her he loved her. Nasir's yellow-and-orange curtain fluttered at the window, and through the open door to the main room, she could see the green towel he used for shaving, folded neatly over the side of the sink.

"Are you using the camera?"

"What?"

"Are you taking a lot of pictures?"

"Not so many." George's camera had remained in the bottom of the suitcase, where she thought it was safest. They would've taken hundreds of pictures in the village if he had been there, but with only herself and her parents, no one had suggested it.

"Take some for me," he said. "I want to see what you're seeing—once you finally get home."

She had eleven days. They still intended to leave on the thirtieth, and arrive in Rochester with a day and a half to spare before she had to start work again on the first. If the visas came through, they would try to leave even sooner. And then there was the alternative—that the visa would be denied, and they would be marooned at Nasir's indefinitely, a scenario that was as tempting as it was frightening. She didn't sleep well, and during the day she felt claustrophobic and on edge: not since childhood had she been in a position where she had so little control.

Nasir treated her as politely as he always had, eliminating only the teasing and joking that had become a part of their relationship since she'd returned. He paid her no special attention and showed no less solicitude about either the threat to their safety or the progress of her father's visa. Amina pretended a modesty she only half felt and made sure not to be in the room alone with him, and after a few days, with a sinking feeling, she realized that he was taking similar precautions.

Both Nasir and her parents insisted on the necessity of staying indoors, and at first she didn't take the trouble to disobey. But she spent hours thinking of what she would do if she had those eleven days to herself. She had no interest in the major sights, Lalbagh Fort or the National Assembly, but she would have liked to visit the places she and her parents had lived—to stand outside those apartments and let the particular sense of each time wash over her. She would have liked to walk to the war memorial by the river, as they sometimes had on cool nights in her girlhood, her father buying them newspaper cones of chanachur while her mother speculated about its probable contamination. She thought of trying to explain to her parents the way a walk like that would start to take on the drama and beauty of a favorite old film as soon as they got to America. But they seemed to exist in a kind of limbo between here and there, preferring each other's company and the silence of the apartment to the proof that life was continuing in the city without them. For once, they were united in their stubborn optimism about the future that awaited them, and she could hardly blame them: she had felt the same way herself.

She skipped three dinners with Nasir, on the grounds that she couldn't wait until ten o'clock after having become accustomed to eating before the sun had set in Rochester.

"But you ate at the normal time in Haibatpur," her mother said.

"I couldn't be rude to Nanu."

"But this looks rude to Nasir!"

"He doesn't care," Amina said. "He doesn't even notice—he's just so glad for your home cooking." Then she sat in the bedroom and listened to him talk with her parents, just as she'd done so many years ago. She remembered his passion, when the conversation turned to political subjects, and the way he gently teased her parents; what she couldn't have noticed then was how young he sometimes sounded, when he talked about his own prospects or awkwardly dodged her mother's prodding about his future marriage and family. That tone in his voice was the one that made her shut her eyes and try to conjure again the moment just before he'd kissed her on the roof.

On the third night after they'd been on the roof together, she rejoined them for dinner: her father and Nasir were having a conversation about a scandal in the Department of Agriculture, and she allowed herself to examine his face openly as he talked, a knot that appeared at the corner of his mouth when he was excited, as if he were manipulating a glass marble with his tongue. His eyes flicked up to her face and away, and the corresponding sensation in her chest made her afraid she should have stayed in her room. He and her father had been arguing about whether it was possible to be honest when you were surrounded by corrupt colleagues. Her father believed that Bangladesh could only be saved by another natural leader like Fazlul Huq; Nasir pointed out that Sheikh Mujib had been considered such a leader, until his Awami Leaguers had dragged the country even deeper into corruption and chaos.

"You can't rely on one man," Nasir said. At this point her father, who was prone to stomach troubles, had to rush to the toilet. Her mother commented that he had suffered from diarrhea on and off since returning from the village, and then went into the kitchen to replenish the fried okra. Amina's first thought was not that she and Nasir were alone together again but rather embarrassment about her parents and their manners—the unselfconscious discussion of bodily functions that would mark them as villagers no matter where they ended their lives. She was startled, then, when Nasir reached across the table and put a hand on her arm. Her pulse reverberated in her ears, and she could feel the heat in her face.

"Don't watch me like that—they can't know anything now."

She was still staring dumbly at him when her mother returned with the okra, speculating aloud about whether it would be possible to find the ingredients for the dish in America. Nasir looked purposely away. What had he meant? He had spoken English as a precaution, and that left his meaning open to interpretation. Could he have said *now,* and meant *yet*? For four days she'd been telling herself it was crazy even to imagine staying; they had to go, as soon as they could. But the following morning she woke up with a bright feeling of possibility, as palpable as a change in the weather and equally difficult to deny.

That was Saturday, exactly a week before their intended departure, and they still hadn't heard from the embassy. It took Amina two hours to convince her parents she might go to the university district unaccompanied to check her e-mail, and once she got into the street alone, the exhilaration was intense. She'd allowed her father to put her into a rickshaw; he'd carefully selected the driver, paying extra and barking instructions about the route, but as soon as they'd turned the corner she collapsed the flimsy hood and let her scarf slide down around her shoulders. The sun wasn't yet too hot on her face or her hair, and no one gave her a second glance. The shouting and the bicycle bells, the smell of fried snacks from the roadside vendors, and the air that got inside her clothing as the driver pedaled expertly through the stalled traffic were thrilling, as was the feeling—after five days hiding in Nasir's apartment—that she was taking a risk. Her parents had allotted her only an hour and a half, but more than once she thought of redirecting the driver and making a circuit through the city. She wasn't sure if it was the threat or simply her time away, but as they traveled past Dhanmondi and the Science Laboratory, south through the city to Fuller Road, everything they passed seemed to have acquired brighter colors and a more definite shape. She almost wished she'd brought the camera, as George had instructed.

When she logged on at the British Council, the first e-mail was from George, who said that his interview was on Tuesday. They'd told him there was actually a job open, and so he was hopeful; he wrote that he would call her after it was over, and that he loved her.

She was scanning the rest of her in-box, expecting only junk, when her eyes fell on the message as if it had been highlighted:

Dear Amina,

Well, I don't know if you're even reading this. I can see that you might not open it, if you saw it was from me. If you don't write back, I'll just tell myself that you were too busy seeing friends and relatives and things, and not that you hate me. I could understand if you hated me permanently, but I'm back in Bombay (going a little crazy) and I couldn't help writing now that you're so nearby.

I'm on the computer a lot these days, but I don't have too many people to e-mail back home. Ashok is working for his dad now and he's never here—they're making a movie about gangsters. When I ask what kind of gangsters (since isn't every Indian movie about them?) he says I wouldn't be able to understand since I'm not from here. I told his mother I was interested in getting a job, but she said no job I could get would pay enough to make it worth my while.

Amina, I've got to get out of here. I thought that maybe if I told them my girlfriend from home was in Bangladesh—maybe they would let me come and visit you? I thought I could say your parents were sick or something, and you needed comforting? I remember you said it would be difficult getting your parents' visas—could an American friend be helpful? If so, I would be so grateful to escape even for a couple of days. I could fly to Dhaka—or to Kolkata even, and take the Maitree Express.

I read on Wikipedia how the name of that train means "Friendship
Express." I guess you know there hasn't been train service between India
and Bangladesh since before the war, and it just started again in April.
I would LOVE to take that train, just for the experience. And to see you on
the other end would be fantastic.

Oh, Amina—I hope you're reading this! I think of you often and I would
love to hear from you. I hope everything is fine with your parents' visas,
and that it's nice to be back home for a while. Write soon if you can!

Love,
Kim

The message had just come yesterday, and Amina sat staring at it
for several minutes, assimilating the fact that Kim was really in India.
Then she ended her session and sat down at the table with *Time*,
determined not to respond. But it hadn't even been a quarter of an
hour before she was back at the computer. It was easy to picture
Kim arriving in Desh unexpectedly, dressed in a shalwar kameez or
in the strange, colorful pajamas of young European tourists—the
type you could occasionally find hanging around Lalbagh Fort or
Shankharia Bazar, suntanned and decorated with jewelry, their
mysterious possessions strapped in dirty packs on their backs. What
a disaster if Kim were to show up and call from the train station,
compelling them to offer some kind of hospitality. Amina imagined her unrolling a sleeping bag on her aunt and uncle's floor—or,
worse, on Nasir's—waking up eager to see the sights. With his mild
manners and conservative clothes, George had been enthusiasti-
cally welcomed everywhere they went—strangers assumed he was
a visiting businessman. But Kim was wrong if she thought a hippie
traveler at the American embassy could speed her parents' emigration.

Dear Kim,

We're having some difficulty with my father's visa (probably because
of his common name) and so now we must just wait. We don't have a
comfortable place for you to stay here, and so I'm afraid it isn't practical
for you to visit at this time.

I hope you will eventually be happy with Ashok's family. Indian families
are probably similar to Deshi ones—they like to keep visitors safe. Of

course you aren't really a visitor, but you look like one. Something I found out in Rochester is that it's hard for people to remember that you belong to one place when you look like you're from another.

Best regards,
Amina

She hit SEND and logged off, hoping that the brevity of her message would signal that she didn't expect to hear anything further from Kim.

They did receive two other visitors. Her aunt came twice, talking sternly to her mother about the lack of security at Nasir's building, the vicissitudes of foreign immigration policy, and the need to prepare for disappointment—advice Amina had to admit was sensible and that her mother clearly didn't hear. She smiled and nodded at her elder sister and then speculated to Amina once Moni had gone about what sort of gift they might send back to her and Omar after they were settled in Rochester.

And then on Monday, the day before she was to leave for Comilla, Sakina came to see them. Amina had gone out with her father to Kaderabad Bazar, to check on the tailor who was making George a wedding kurta of traditionally woven, bright-colored silk. Her parents believed that the ceremony had happened three years ago, but they still wanted to take the wedding photographs they'd talked about so long ago. Her mother worried about the safety of the market, even in the middle of the day, but Amina's primary concern was the wastefulness of the errand. She had tried to dissuade her father on the basis of the expense—George would resist such a showy, foreign costume, she told him, and prefer to be photographed in his own clothes—but her father had insisted. Now he wanted to determine that the tailor was making progress.

When she and her father returned from the bazaar, her mother was full of Sakina's news.

"They've been matchmaking for Nasir," her mother reported excitedly, coming in from the balcony where she'd been hanging laundry. "She says there are several candidates—one very beautiful girl in particular. That's why they're going to Comilla. If this girl is as promising as they expect, things should be settled very soon."

Amina took her mother's place and began helping to wring out the wet clothes in the bucket. Most children grew out of the notion that their mothers could see what was in their heads, but with her mother's reputation for clairvoyance, she'd never been able to discount the possibility entirely.

"What does Nasir say about it?" she asked, from the relative safety of the balcony.

"She said he'd be angry if he knew she was talking about it with us. I got the feeling that they disagree about the candidates. But she said that once her brother meets this girl, he'll fall in love—any man would, she said."

She suddenly saw why Nasir had been trying to prevent his sister from visiting them. Sakina had obeyed her brother's wishes to a point, but her pride wouldn't let her forget the alliance that had once been considered between their two families, nor the fact that Amina's parents had held out for something better. Now she was eager to demonstrate that no one in Nasir's family regretted Amina's foreign marriage, since an even more suitable bride had been found.

But what did Nasir think? He might not have been enthusiastic, but his sisters certainly wouldn't be proceeding with their negotiations without at least a grudging approval from the bridegroom-to-be.

"But Sakina is excited, of course," her mother continued. "With no family of her own, this match will mean a lot to her."

"I don't think Sakina wanted to marry," Amina said, and then dared to go further. "She didn't want a mother-in-law—she wanted to be a mother-in-law. She's just waiting for some poor girl to terrorize."

Her mother glanced up quickly, but then nodded. "That's true." She brushed a strand of hair behind one ear: a nonchalant, girlish gesture. "That's the only reason I wouldn't have been completely happy with him for you, Munni." Amina froze, her hands in the bucket of water, but her mother continued from the other room unaware of how closely her daughter was listening. "Otherwise Nasir is perfect—so handsome and so kind."

"And now that he's given up this religious nonsense . . . ," her father put in.

"And Sakina says this job has great potential. He doesn't make much now, but his boss is talking to foreign investors—you know eventually all this outsourcing will be outsourced again. It'll move from India right here to Desh!"

Amina couldn't help herself. She came back into the main room, an undershirt of her father's still dripping in her hand. "What are you talking about?" she demanded. "You're the one who kept telling me to write to America." She could hear her voice becoming shrill, and her mother looked at her in surprise. She turned to her father: "You weren't happy with him when he returned from London, unemployed and bringing us that book."

Her father raised his eyebrows and put up his hands. "I was always happy with Nasir. You're the one who wanted to go abroad. And now, you see, it's all worked out."

Amina went into the bathroom, because she was starting to cry. At least in the bathroom it wasn't strange to shut the door. She thought of the night they'd kissed each other on the roof, how Nasir had gone into his room and telephoned someone. Why hadn't she seen the significance of that before now? At his age, and with his parents dead, he wouldn't leave the selection of a bride entirely to his sisters. He would be pursuing his own favorite candidate in the modern fashion. The unceremonious way Nasir had begun that phone conversation she hadn't been able to overhear, hardly pausing for a response from the person on the other end, suggested that he'd been talking to someone he knew well.

The bathroom was painted an unpleasant shade of lentil green, and in the humidity the smell of sewage was unmistakable. The only relief came from a square vent in the wall to the outside, through the patterned opening of which it was possible to see jigsaw cutouts of the buildings opposite, including the blue stucco façade with the iron grille. She remembered how angry Nasir had gotten when she joked about Yellow Barrette that night at the table. Of course he wouldn't have reacted that way if she were just a girl he'd seen on the street. Could Amina have been a distraction from the stress of a genuine courtship, an outlet for the constraints inherent in wooing a truly virtuous woman? The other night at the table, she'd let herself believe they had a secret—one that they had to keep quiet for "now." But couldn't he just as easily have been trying to tell her to forget it? What had happened between them was the result of simple nostalgia, and she would ruin everything *now*—at the moment of his courtship—if she were to let it slip.

"Munni—are you all right?" her mother asked, and so she was forced to open the door.

"I'm fine," she said, brushing past her mother and going into the bedroom. The more she thought about it, the more obvious it seemed that Nasir was in love with Yellow Barrette, against the wishes of his sister. He might have amused himself with Amina on the roof, because she'd made herself available—she nearly groaned out loud, when she thought of how forward she had been—but he'd stopped them both at the crucial moment. Then he'd hurried to his room to call the woman he hoped to marry. The business with the yellow clips had been a pretence; Nasir would know not only her name, but probably her pet name too. If they were in the habit of talking so late at night, it was likely they had even arranged to meet alone. These secret meetings would happen in the entryways of buildings, at a stall in the market, or on the bus, the public nature of which would allow only longing looks, the exquisite accident of an occasional, glancing touch.

From the bedroom Amina could see the outer gate to the building, enclosing a modest courtyard. Eventually the girl would have to come or go from there, but Amina's parents would question her if they saw her standing at the window for hours. The angle would make it difficult to see the girl's face, and of course it would be impossible to be sure. If she wanted to see Nasir's beloved, she would have to cross the street and knock on the door. She sat there thinking for several more minutes—she could hear her parents moving around in the living room, no doubt wondering whether she was sick—and all at once a strategy came to her, so simple and inspired that it seemed to belong to someone else. It was as if she'd been deceiving people all her life.

14 On Tuesday morning, after Nasir left for work, she showered and dressed carefully in one of her mother's best shalwar kameez: a black-and-white print appropriate for Language Day. She wore her engagement ring (which she'd been keeping hidden since

the interview at the embassy, in an interior pocket of her suitcase) and tied her hair up in a twist. Then she came into the main room and told her parents casually that she was going to visit her old student, Asah.

Asah's family's apartment was even closer to Nasir's than it had been to their old Mohammadpur flat, but Amina's father still argued with her until she promised to go by rickshaw. Even then he insisted on accompanying her to the end of the lane—he would go on to the market to pick up George's kurta—and negotiating the fare before he would let her go. As soon as they had turned the corner and she was sure her father was on his way to the market, she told the rickshaw driver she'd forgotten something.

"Take me back around the other side," she instructed him. "The road that way is better." The rickshaw-wallah, a young man in a lungi and a threadbare black T-shirt with a picture of the Sydney Opera House in neon green, obeyed her, and soon she was back at the opposite end of Nasir's road. She paid the full fare and told him he didn't have to wait; he put his palms together to thank her.

It was the middle of the morning, and she expected Yellow Barrette to be at her university. She was interested to know which one it was: it wouldn't be Dhaka University or BRAC, certainly, but it might be one of the second-tier institutions—Jagannath or Jahangirnagar. She was also curious to find out how big the family was, where they came from originally, and of course to see Yellow Barrette herself. She would be pretty, but how pretty? If Nasir really preferred this girl, what was it about her that gave Sakina pause? It had sounded from his description as if Yellow Barrette were pursuing a master's degree, and so she was likely twenty-three or twenty-four—a reasonable ten years younger than Nasir. He'd said they were "simple people," and so they weren't likely to own the building as his family did. Still, Sakina had dismissed other families for being interested "only in taka." Amina was curious enough to feel her own heartbeat and her body temperature rise as she approached the entrance.

The apartment building was modest but respectable, similar to Nasir's, with a large courtyard half shaded by its cantilevered first floor. Behind a second gate, this one locked, was a set of stairs. She stood in the shade under the overhang and opened her purse, into which she'd put only one hundred taka and a book called *Conversational English*. This was one of the primers she and her mother had used, and her father said he'd kept it so that they could review before going to America. But she hadn't seen him open it since they'd been at Nasir's, and this morning when she'd proposed giving it to her former student as a memento, he hadn't argued. Now she took the book out and pretended to study it until she heard footsteps on the stairs above her.

She was lucky: it was only a fish vendor, a diminutive man of indeterminate age, dark skinned and southern in aspect, carrying an aluminum box on his head. The cooler would contain silvery-pink hilsa or plump, brown perch, and he would know which fish was preferred, and in what quantity, by each of the ladies in the building.

"Bhai, excuse me."

She put her hand on the gate before he had a chance to close it. The vendor misunderstood and raised a hand to his box, preparing to lower it to the ground for her inspection.

"Is there a young woman who lives here, a college student?"

The vendor looked slightly alarmed, as very poor people did when you made an unusual request. It was something she'd forgotten since going away. She reached into her purse to give him an incentive.

"I don't know every family."

She handed him a twenty-taka note; she was afraid it wouldn't be enough, but he pocketed it with a nod. "There's a girl on the top floor—her mother just bought a half kilo of hilsa."

"Is the girl at home?"

The man shook his head. "Only the older lady."

"Thank you," Amina said, and then shut the gate behind her as if she had every right to be in the building.

There were two apartments on the top floor, both with nameplates: Razzak and Rahman. Amina hesitated for a moment, listening. In Razzak she could hear a couple arguing mildly, but the fish man had intimated that Yellow Barrette's mother was alone. She chose the other and knocked.

The woman who answered was at least ten years younger than Amina's mother, and beautiful in a completely different way. While her own mother's looks had always been dramatic, with her sharp cheekbones, sunken eyes, and long, perfectly straight hair, Mrs. Rahman had a soft, childlike quality to her features, enhanced by naturally thick eyelashes. She had pinned her hair up in back, in an unsuccessful effort to control her curls; black ringlets escaped around her face. Her cheeks were flushed from whatever labor she'd been engaged in before Amina had arrived, and her feet, in white plastic house slippers, were tiny under the hem of her sari. Yellow Barrette's mother took in Amina's fancy shalwar kameez and the ring on her finger.

"Yes?"

"Excuse me, is your daughter an English student?"

Mrs. Rahman looked wary. "Yes. But we're not looking for a tutor. She helps the other students."

"Oh no." Amina smiled, switching to English and speaking fast. "I'm not looking for a job. I think your daughter may have dropped this outside the gate."

Her mother was flustered by the fluent English, as Amina had expected. She took the book, hardly glancing at it. "Excuse me," she said in Bangla. "I don't speak English well—it's only my daughter. You're very kind to return it. She dropped it in the road?"

"She was getting into a rickshaw," Amina said, taking a chance. She didn't know of a college within walking distance. "I was all the way down the lane, and by the time I reached it, she was gone. I used to use this book myself."

Mrs. Rahman frowned. "This was just now?"

"Some time ago," Amina improvised. "I had to stop at home first."

The woman shook her head, smiling. "Lazy girl—she could easily have walked. Please let me give you tea. Mokta's always been careless."

Mokta, Amina thought: of course. She smiled at Mrs. Rahman. It was impossible to know whether Mokta really was careless or if the criticism was a rote politeness. "No, I can't. I just wanted to return the book."

"You went out of your way," Mrs. Rahman said. "Please. Are you an English teacher?"

Amina shook her head. "I used to be, before I married. We live in the U.S.—I'm only here for a few weeks to see my family."

Mokta's mother gave her a frankly curious stare. "Do they live nearby?"

"We're staying with a friend just down this lane. Actually, I've come to bring my parents back to America."

"I've just put the water on," Mrs. Rahman said. "You'd do me such a favor to keep me company for a minute."

Amina finally agreed, as if hesitantly, and entered a living room, modestly furnished but with abundant light from two large windows. The room was immaculate, but Mrs. Rahman had been dusting anyway; a feather broom was hastily stashed beneath a small table. The table was covered with an embroidered cloth like the ones Parveen made; on top of the cloth was a fancy portable chess set, inlaid with mother-of-pearl, the pieces indicating an interrupted game. Amina looked around the room, but the only photograph she could see was on a chest of drawers in the bedroom, angled away from her. On the wall above the dining table was a small oil painting in a deliberately naïve style, covered with a sheet of protective plastic. The painting showed a village scene: a girl in a green sari bending over a palm-fringed pond to fill a copper jug.

"Is this a painting of your village?" Amina asked when Mrs. Rahman returned, apologizing for the plate of packaged biscuits. They sat in the two wicker chairs, facing two walls of bookcases. Amina was surprised to see that several shelves were devoted to mathematics, along with a collection of Russian novels, translated into English rather than Bangla; an *Oxford English Dictionary*; and many volumes of poetry, among which she recognized Tagore, Mukhopadhyay, and Nazrul Islam.

"Oh, that's just something Mokta did," Mrs. Rahman said shyly. "She's always amused herself with drawing and sketching. I like that scene because I think it looks southern, but our village is in Rajshahi."

Working within a simple idiom, Mokta had somehow managed to indicate the shadows of the palm trees on the pond, the light on the copper jug, and a faraway expression on the girl's face. Amina had noticed the painting because it reminded her of Haibatpur, but there was no doubt that Mokta knew how to paint.

"If only you'd come later," Mrs. Rahman said. "We would've had sweets for you. Mokta's stopping on her way home because my husband's bringing a colleague for supper."

"What kind of work does your husband do?"

"He's a mathematics teacher," Mrs. Rahman said with evident pride. "Do you know St. Joseph's School?"

"Of course." A part of Amina was surprised to learn that the family was so respectable—cultured, educated, and industrious—and again she wondered why Sakina wasn't more enthusiastic about the match. Why was she still considering other candidates, if this was the girl her brother admired? It occurred to Amina that Sakina might not like the idea that Nasir had discovered the young woman himself; she would want to exercise complete control, to select her brother's wife as she'd selected her little sister Shilpa's husband. Sakina was someone who'd been thrust into a responsible position at a young age, and instead of collapsing under it, she'd determined to execute her responsibilities to perfection, so that no one could find a single error. Some people mourned a loss like the one she'd suffered; others spent their whole lives defying it.

"He's also one of the chess instructors. They've graduated three grand masters"—Mrs. Rahman said the words in English—"though not while he was there. If only it were a school for girls, he always tells me. If Mokta were a boy, she might attend St. Joseph's for less."

"She's your only child?"

Mrs. Rahman nodded and squinted out the window, as if she were trying to make out something across the street.

Amina had asked the question innocently, but she was familiar with the way people prodded when you admitted to having only one. She'd watched her mother shrink under that question for years. "I'm an only child as well," she said quickly. "My mother had a complicated labor, and they decided one was expensive enough."

Mrs. Rahman smiled gratefully at Amina. "And now you're bringing your parents to America—how wonderful."

"If my father's visa gets approved," Amina said. "We're still waiting. My parents already gave up their apartment—we used to live in the Kaderabad Housing, not far from here."

"I know the building!" Mrs. Rahman said.

"We were going to be with my aunt and uncle in Savar, but it was too far from the embassy. And our host here is the son of my father's oldest friend."

She could imagine what Mrs. Rahman would think if she knew her daughter was already meeting Nasir in secret or talking to him late at night on the phone. They had only one child, but that didn't mean they had any less love than a family with three or four. It was simply intensely focused on this one girl, who would be likely at some point to break under the pressure. She might even jeopardize the future her parents had so carefully planned for her, just for the feeling of escaping their scrutiny for a little while. Amina felt angry suddenly, but she wasn't sure whether she was angry at Mrs. Rahman or at Sakina or at her own parents. She had the peculiar feeling that she wanted to do something for Mokta, something selfless and pure. If she were able to arrange a meeting, one that appeared to happen naturally, wouldn't that help forward a match that both Nasir and Mokta obviously desired?

It hadn't escaped her that in doing this she would be proving something to Nasir. He would see she hadn't been undone by what had happened between them and that she fully intended to go back to her life in America. She would also teach Sakina a lesson about the limits of even the most meticulous plan. You couldn't control your own life, much less someone else's.

She thought she must've had a strange look on her face, because Mrs. Rahman was watching her with concern, as if she thought she might have caused some offense.

She smiled to reassure Mokta's mother. "Where did your daughter go to school?" she asked.

"Oh," her mother said. "Just the local primary school."

Amina had been thinking of secondary school, but she didn't want to embarrass Mrs. Rahman, who might not have gone further than primary school herself. She could imagine evenings in the apartment, Mokta's mother cooking and then clearing away the dishes while Mokta and her father worked through her problem sets or enjoyed a game of chess. The pieces now standing at attention must be the remnants of one of those games.

"And your husband?" Mrs. Rahman asked. "What does he do in America?"

"He's an electrical engineer," Amina said. Mrs. Rahman would learn about Amina's marriage soon enough, but she wasn't going to be candid now. She had thought before she'd come that there must've been something wrong with Yellow Barrette or her family, but everything Amina had learned since she'd been in the apartment made the match seem equitable or even tilted in favor of the Rahmans.

"I would love for Mokta to meet you, if you have time before you go. She's always been interested in studying abroad . . . but, of course, the expense. Her father would like to try"—her mother smiled apologetically—"but I'm selfish. I can't imagine my life here without her."

There was no reason that she had to see the girl's picture before she invited her. If she wasn't pretty, Nasir would never have noticed her in the first place. Still, she was disappointed not to have a mental image of Mokta to take away from the visit.

"I would be happy to meet her," Amina said. "Perhaps the two of you could come to tea one afternoon before we leave. My parents and I are home all day."

Mrs. Rahman looked delighted. "That would be wonderful. If you promise you won't go to any trouble. You'll only embarrass me again about these biscuits."

"My father's friend passed away years ago, and his son and I grew up like cousins. But he's a bachelor and so his apartment is shabby. You see, we'll be apologizing to you."

Mrs. Rahman laughed. "I doubt that. Well, we'll call on you then. On Thursday?"

It was Tuesday now, and Amina considered the logistics involved. She would have to bring it up as soon as she got back and admit to her parents that she'd lied about visiting her student. When she finally met Mokta, she would have to act surprised that the book wasn't hers and speculate about how it had come to be lying in the street. And of course, sometime between now and Thursday, she would have to confess to Nasir that she'd gone to see the girl for herself. If he were angry, she could confront him with the facts she knew from her mother. Sakina was still considering other candidates; why hadn't he told his sister that he wasn't interested in the "very beautiful" girl she preferred? Amina would tell him he was being a coward—that his whole life's happiness was at stake.

"Come in the evening, if you can. You might as well meet your neighbor—our friend—since we'll be gone soon."

Mrs. Rahman nodded. "If Mokta's father is home early, he'll accompany us."

"I hope it's actually Mokta's book," Amina said. "How ridiculous if it turns out I'm wrong."

Mrs. Rahman was surprised. "You mean you didn't actually see her drop it?"

"I did—but of course I didn't know which apartment. The fish man said there was a girl on the top floor. I thought I might have knocked on the wrong door, but now that I see you, I think it must've been your daughter."

Mrs. Rahman nodded slowly. "Most people say Mokta resembles her father's family. But I have an idea—if you can wait just a minute?" She disappeared into the bedroom, and Amina couldn't help smiling at her success. She thought that Mokta would be a version of her mother, twenty years younger. She thought of black curls, round black eyes, and full scarlet lips. *Mokta*, she thought. A pearl.

Mrs. Rahman came back, flipping through a plastic pocket album and frowning.

"This was taken at Eid. You see—I made her clothes myself."

Amina found herself looking at the photograph of a young girl. Mokta had her mother's large, round eyes, but as Mrs. Rahman had suggested, the rest of her face didn't show a particular likeness. Her hair was straight—the barrette, this time, was white—but her skin was luminous and clear, and the smile at the corner of her mouth was playful, as if she had promised to hold still for only a second. She was looking at the photographer, who was probably her father, with an expression that combined innocence with absolute trust.

Amina turned to Mrs. Rahman: there had been a misunderstanding. "But this is from many years ago?"

"From last year. You see, she isn't like me—much more like her paternal grandmother."

"How old is Mokta now?"

"Sixteen. She'll graduate the year after next, and then her father hopes she might win a scholarship at BRAC. When I think that I was married by her age—things have changed so much since then." She paused, seeing Amina's confusion. "But I think my daughter isn't the girl you saw?"

"No," Amina said. Her hands were shaking. "I'm so sorry to have troubled you."

"No, no." Mrs. Rahman was eager to be gracious. She retrieved the English book from the table, where it had been sitting next to the plate of biscuits, and handed it back to Amina.

"I didn't think this looked like Mokta's. I can't read her books, but I certainly pick them up enough."

She was joking with Amina in order to put her at ease, but of course she couldn't begin to understand what was really the matter. Standing in Mrs. Rahman's door, she had to admit to herself that she was in love with Nasir for the second time in her life. She had been able to stand the idea that he might end up with someone else, when the someone else had been an accomplished young woman of twenty-five. It was something entirely different to think he was pursuing a girl who had not yet finished high school, even if he was prepared to wait for her. She was ashamed of how she'd suspected Sakina of sabotaging Nasir's happiness: finally it was clear why his sister would've been reluctant to approach this family.

As a girl Amina had been in the habit of dreaming she was in love. Although the dreams were different, she recognized the lover each time. Their history was so rich and complex that its residue would still be with her when she woke up. She would lie in bed running through the list of people she knew, sure that she would be able to identify him eventually. She refused to believe that her brain had the capacity to invent someone so palpably real. Now, as she stood in Mrs. Rahman's doorway, she felt as if she were mourning that phantom lover all over again. It was only in losing her idea of Nasir that she realized how much he meant to her; by showing her one photo, Mrs. Rahman had sucked all the brightness from her life. She had killed Nasir, or worse, she had somehow led Amina to understand that he'd never existed at all.

Amina put her old schoolbook back into Mrs. Rahman's hands. "Please tell Mokta to keep it," she said, and then she was moving down the stairs. She knew Mrs. Rahman was still talking to her and would be confused by her sudden rudeness. The woman probably would've liked to bring her daughter to visit them anyway, to talk about Mokta's prospects—a contact abroad was well worth an afternoon visit—but the thought of the girl in Nasir's apartment was suddenly repulsive. When she reached the bottom of the stairs, her phone was ringing. She looked down to see if it was George, calling about his interview, and then remembered that the interview was Tuesday morning Rochester time and hadn't happened yet. Her phone displayed a Dhaka mobile number she didn't recognize, and so she ignored it, hurrying out of the building in case Mrs. Rahman should take it in her head to follow her.

15 When she got home, her father wasn't back from the market, and she was startled to find Nasir at home in the main room. Her mother was fixing him something to eat in the kitchen, and he was sitting at the table with the newspaper open in front of him. He smiled broadly when he saw her, as if they could have no secrets from each other.

"Nasir took his sisters to the bus stand, and now he's eating something before he goes in to work," her mother said, as if this information would be of the utmost interest to Amina. "Did you see Asah?"

The name startled her: for a moment she'd forgotten the pretense she'd used this morning. "No," she said.

Her mother's brow immediately folded in on itself, in anticipation of another misfortune. "What happened?"

"I decided to visit someone across the street instead. A young woman." Nasir looked up mildly from his paper, and she could see that he really didn't know what she was going to say.

"Which young woman?" her mother asked. Amina addressed herself only to her mother, trying to keep her voice calm and even.

"Another possible match. I thought it might be nice to invite the family—for tea. They're very respectable. Her father teaches math at St. Joseph's."

"But how—" her mother began.

But Nasir interrupted: "Where did you go?"

"Don't worry," Amina said. "Mokta was out—at high school. She's only sixteen, so she won't start university for another two years."

"But that's too young," her mother protested. "And anyway—"

Nasir stood up from the table. She had wanted to unsettle him, but she was suddenly afraid she'd gone too far. He was looking at her as if she'd said something obscene. "You're joking," he said coldly.

"I was trying to help you. I didn't realize you'd thought of someone so young."

Nasir just stared at her, but her mother looked baffled.

"What's this Mokta? I thought she was called—"

"Munni misunderstood," Nasir said. "There was never any question of a girl across the street."

Her mother nodded, relieved. "Because Sakina seems set on this girl in Comilla. They're planning to finalize everything on this trip."

Nasir stared at her coldly. "You thought I was serious about a girl across the street?"

"You said—"

He exploded: "I said I admired a girl with yellow hair clips."

"Who lives across the street." But her face was burning, and she knew she'd made a humiliating mistake.

"Across the—who knows if she even lives there?" Nasir exploded. "Maybe she was just walking by. My God, Munni—I can't believe you went to see some stranger!"

"But why did you say there was a girl?"

"What if there had been? What gives you the right? You think you can just come back here and play with people's lives—and then disappear back to America?"

Her mother was looking worriedly from one of them to the other. "The girl from Comilla will be more suitable. Sixteen is way too young these days. I was seventeen when I married, and even then—"

"I'm not marrying any Mokta!" Nasir spit out the name as if it were bitter to him.

"I thought—" Amina began, but he was gathering up his things, shoving his paper in a messenger bag with a British label that was hanging over the back of the chair.

"Sorry, Aunty," he muttered, and then hurried past them out the door.

"He forgot to change his shoes." Her mother looked at the door, where Nasir's leather shoes were waiting neatly on the rack.

"He has a temper," Amina said, but it was no use reminding herself of Nasir's faults. She couldn't believe what she had done.

"Like your father." Her mother smiled, then immediately became serious again. "But I hope he won't tell Sakina. She'd be so angry if she thought we were interfering in this marriage business of theirs."

Her mother's cheeks were so sunken, you could see the shadows in them. Her hair was pulled back in a braid, and her clothes hung off her body as if they belonged to someone else. She rocked unselfconsciously from heel to toe, doing the television strengthening exercises that had become second nature to her. Apart from what she'd seen on TV, everything her mother knew about the United States was from Amina's description. Had she been honest enough? Or was her mother still imagining only another Desh, reputedly colder, where she would have to wear a sweater even in the month of April?

She hesitated, watching her mother begin to clear the table, using a cloth with one hand while she balanced the dishes in the other. "But is it really settled with the girl in Comilla?"

"Nasir hasn't said yes or no," her mother said. "It's very delicate. But Sakina is confident that once he sees—"

Amina's phone rang again in her purse, and this time she reached for it. It was the same unfamiliar number, but anything was better than hearing from her mother the attributes of the great beauty in Comilla.

"Hello," a man's voice came on the line. "Hello?"

There was noise in the background, as if people in a crowd were yelling at once. "I think you have the wrong number," Amina said.

"Hello! This is Amina—Munni?"

"Yes?"

"There's been an accident—at the bazaar. Your father's injured. We're taking him to DMCH."

"What kind of accident?" Amina demanded. "Hello?"

"It's bad," the man said. "Your father's been hit with acid."

16 No one could find her father at the hospital. They went to every floor, ward, desk, and waited in clusters of other anxious relatives. When a nurse finally deigned to look at them, her mother would say her father's name; slowly, a clipboard would be produced, pages riffled, and then a bland, faint smile, satisfaction of

a duty completed. "No, no—not on our floor." Amina fought back tears each time they got a no, but her mother remained firm and efficient, suggesting they call the number that had appeared on Amina's phone to see if the man had any more information about where her father had been taken after they'd arrived at the hospital. But no one answered, and Amina had neglected to ask even his name.

It was also her mother's idea to call Omar, and after what seemed like several hours, her uncle appeared. The nurses at the desk snapped to sulky attention at the sight of Omar's fine shirt, his large gold wristwatch, and his impressive girth. A male orderly appeared from behind the desk, called Omar "Sahib," and went to check with the OT nurses. He was back less than five minutes later, smiling broadly and saying that her father was in surgery. He had no information about the progress of the operation but asked whether they wouldn't please come and wait in a private room. Amina couldn't see how much Omar tipped him, but they were soon sitting on brown metal folding chairs in a small, unventilated supply room that smelled of formaldehyde and antiseptic. The bottles on the shelves were dusty, the boxes yellowing, as if the medicines and supplies they contained had been sitting there for years. Omar looked through the messages on his phone, and her mother began to pray:

> *A'uzu billahi minashaitanir rajim*
> *Bismillahir Rahmanir Rahim*
> *'Al-Hamdu lillahi Rabbil-'Aalamin*

Amina recited The Opening with her mother, but she didn't feel any calmer when it was finished. She longed suddenly to go into the hallway and call George, but it was the middle of the night in Rochester; she would have to wait until late tonight. Her mother hadn't wanted to call or text Nasir before they knew more; how strange to think he was at work, not even aware of what was happening.

If it was a punishment, it was meant for her. How careless she had been! She'd betrayed George with Nasir and then betrayed Nasir's trust as well. Worst of all was what she'd done to her parents. She'd felt invincible, going blithely on her invented errands, as if her passport were a shell protecting her from harm. Her father, of course, hadn't felt the same way. Perhaps he'd even guessed that something like this might happen, that as they got closer to their departure, Salim would have gotten bolder and more reckless. Salim's more clever elder brothers—Bhulu and Laltu—might have instructed him not to risk harming Amina, the one with the American bank account, and so he had attacked her father in a last, desperate attempt at extortion or revenge.

And yet her father had taken a needless risk—for what? For a gift he imagined presenting to his American son-in-law: a piece of silk George would look at once, pretend to admire, and then put away on the top shelf of a closet, along with the stained trousers he could no longer wear to work. When she thought of their conversation about Long Nose, she was nauseated to think of how she'd made her father feel. Abba often joked about his own failures, his gift for making the wrong decision again and again. Had they ever corrected him? Had he taken this chance because he valued his own life so cheaply, or was it because he thought they did, too?

Her mother had finished her prayer, and Omar stepped into the hall because he wasn't getting reception.

"I'm sorry, Amma." She pressed her face into her mother's shoulder. "It's my fault."

But her mother didn't touch her, or move to accommodate the embrace, and so Amina lifted her face. Her mother gave her a strange, distant look.

"It's God's will," she said. "It doesn't have anything to do with you."

"Let me go ask again," she begged. Her mother shrugged, but Omar stopped her at the threshold.

"That boy will inform us," he said. "Better to wait here." She could remember joking with her parents in the past about her uncle's worldliness. Her aunt would ostentatiously complain that she couldn't even send him to the market anymore, because his size and fine clothes led people to assume he was a *bideshi* and give him the foreigner's price. Now it was a shock to see how much more of an insider Omar was than she herself. The way he failed to make eye contact frightened her, as if he knew something about her father's condition she didn't. The pictures she had seen in newspapers and on TV over the years came back to her: faces misshapen and caved in on themselves;

a child's mouth shrunken down to a tiny O; a woman with one eye missing, simply swallowed up by flat, white skin. And those were the ones who survived. She tried to picture her father's face as it had been this morning, when he'd put her into the rickshaw, but what came to her was a much older memory—of a childhood visit to her dadu's village. She was living with her parents in Dhaka then, so she must have been seven or eight. They'd gone down for one of their rare visits to Kajalnagar. Amina had wanted a coconut—the young, green variety that grew in clusters from the skinniest palms—and her father had said he would show her how to climb it. She'd never seen him do that, and she'd watched in amazement as he rolled up the legs of his city trousers, put his glasses on the ground at the base of the tree, and began to climb, hand over hand, closing his feet adeptly around the trunk. When he was almost at the top, he grinned down at her and, without grabbing the nut, started his half-scrambling, half-sliding descent.

"But you didn't get it," she'd said, disappointed, and her father had said:

"Now you try." He'd given her a boost, holding on to her feet while she tried to pull with her hands. She had been frightened but excited, and eager for the prize at the top. She thought now that there was no way she could have made it that high, but her father didn't stop her; it was her mother who came out of the house, her orna pulled over her head as it almost always was in her husband's village, yelling at her father and demanding to know if he was crazy.

"She's a little girl," Amina remembered her scolding him: "What will people say? You want her to grow up to be a coconut seller?" She also remembered the way the smooth-looking bark had made long, thin scratches in the soles of her feet, and how her father had bent down to whisper, as they followed her mother back to the house:

"You were almost there—next time."

Her mother knew how to plan for every contingency, and Amina had always been able to execute those plans. But her father was the one who'd had the inspiration for their boldest ventures—the only one of the three of them who knew instinctively how to hope. If she'd accomplished anything, she saw now, it was because her father had made her believe that she could.

It was another forty-five minutes before the orderly returned to say that her father was being brought out of surgery. They left the airless little room, and Omar took out his wallet again: there were no beds in the ward, but Omar spoke to the orderly in private, and when they returned, it turned out that one would become available as of that evening.

When the trolley boy wheeled him toward them in the corridor, her mother finally started to cry. Amina was crying, too, and it was a relief to see that he was sleeping. Her father's neck, shoulders, and chest were bandaged, as well as the upper portion of his arms, giving the forearms an exaggeratedly sticklike appearance. They'd covered his legs with a blue blanket in spite of the heat, and his chest was rising and falling under the bandages.

"This can't just be *allowed* to happen," Amina said. "We have to report it!" Her mother and her uncle exchanged glances, and her mother patted the air, motioning for her to lower her voice. It wasn't only that her father was sleeping, but that there was, of course, no privacy in the corridor.

"Salim knows how to disappear," her uncle said. "We could press charges—but it would take years to come to court, you understand. And by then, hopefully you'll all be settled in America."

She saw the logic of what her uncle was saying, but it was impossible to let it go. "But what about the man who sold it? Isn't he responsible as well?"

"Of course," her uncle said patiently. "They're supposed to have permits. But who would go to the trouble of getting one if the police never bother to check? Even if they did check, the price of the permit would buy them off."

Her father's surgeon came soon after the orderly left and said that her father had been fortunate compared with many survivors of acid attacks. He guessed that the attacker had used a small jar, perhaps in order to conceal it more easily, and his aim had been less than perfect. (Later her grandmother would say that the attack had been carried out with the ineptitude characteristic of her father's family.) The doctor noted that the worst wounds were to his father's chest, but the skin graft had been successful. The men who'd rescued and brought him to the hospital had known enough to flush his wounds with water; the doctor explained how the acid could burn through tissue in minutes and, in cases when it wasn't neutralized immediately, even melt human bones. Her mother had been standing behind Amina, mesmerized by the doctor, but now she gasped audibly. The doctor didn't look up from her father's chart, but remarked that they were lucky the acid hadn't hit his eyes.

"Or his hands," Omar said.

Amina looked at him.

"They've already taken his fingerprints," her uncle said matter-of-factly. Then he turned to the doctor. "My brother-in-law is in the process of emigrating. Once his visa arrives, when will it be possible to travel?"

"That depends on his progress. The nurses will show them how to change the bandages." He glanced at Amina and her mother, then turned back to Omar. "And then he'll come back for my assessment." The doctor suggested that if her father recovered as expected, he might be moved as soon as Friday. There was no hope, she realized suddenly, that they would leave for America this weekend.

The doctor left, followed by Omar, who promised that Fariq would drop off a package of supplies in a few hours. Her mother whispered her gratitude, but her uncle shrugged off the familiar thanks: this was what family members did for one another. As soon as Omar was gone, a young nurse appeared to show them how to change the bandages. Amina had to force herself to look. The skin was gone, and the human meat underneath was sizzled and charred, dark blisters swollen with blood and areas of fluid, yellow pus. She tried to concentrate on her father's sleeping face, which was paler and older than usual, but otherwise the same as the one she remembered from those mornings of her childhood, when she'd woken up first and watched her parents sleeping. Especially just after she'd been reunited with them in Dhaka, she had liked to examine their faces, compare them with the ones she'd held in her memory during the time they'd been apart. Was there something she'd forgotten—an unfamiliar mole or crease? Her mother always leaped out of bed the moment she awoke, to begin the morning's tasks, but when Amina was still small enough, her father would put his feet together in the air, hold her hands, and lift her up so that she could pretend to fly.

"She won't do it again," her mother said, once the nurse had gone.

"Why not?"

"They don't like dirty work," her mother said. "And they hate everyone to see them treating men. We'll have to do it ourselves."

Two women in the next bed who had been staring at her father started talking audibly, shaking their heads at the novelty of a man suffering a fate usually reserved for young women. Amina wanted to tell them to shut up, a laughable notion amid the babble of voices in the corridor: wailing, haranguing, coughing, arguing, laughing. She had remembered to secure her engagement ring in a zippered compartment of her purse, but she was aware that her clothes—the dressy shalwar kameez she was still wearing from her visit to Mrs. Rahman—made her look both more and less prosperous than she was. Instead of her parents' daughter, newly returned from America, she looked like something much more recognizably enviable: a woman like her cousin Ghaniyah, expensively dressed and educated, married but not yet burdened with children. She felt apart from the hospital's commotion and fraudulent at the same time.

As the evening came, her father slipped in and out of consciousness, once opening his eyes completely and attempting to speak before going back to sleep. There was a sense of anticipation in the hallway as new relatives arrived with tiffin carriers full of food, and the smells became even more intense. The upper half of the walls was peeling, and the green paint on the lower portion didn't obscure the brownish-red stains where people had spit paan. Amina felt as if she might vomit, especially after she used the hospital toilet, pulling her trousers up above her knees before she squatted over the rank hole. Her father had a bedpan, which her mother emptied matter-of-factly, hurrying back afterward to his bed. There was a large crack along the bottom of the wall, in which you could see ants and brown cockroaches scavenging for the bits of food that dropped from the improvised picnic dinners on each of the patients' beds.

Her father woke up at seven thirty and asked for water. They propped the pillow under his back and got him into a half-sitting position; her mother tipped the bottle gently, so that the water trickled into his mouth. Amina went downstairs to the nurses' station to ask what her father could safely eat; her aunt had provided a mild and nourishing yellow dal, but she had to stand there for fifteen minutes before one of them acknowledged her. (She had noticed that the nurses sat and chatted until someone approached; then they were suddenly busy with the stacks of blue clipboards.) When they finally approved the dal, she went down and found her father refusing her mother's attempts to feed it to him.

"What can I do, Abba?" she asked, but her father shook his head and then winced suddenly.

"Don't smile," her mother scolded. "See how that pains your neck." She fed him three spoonfuls of the dal before he regurgitated it onto the bandages.

"I can change it," her mother said. "I watched them carefully. Then I'll help him with the bedpan. You go for fresh air." Amina started to argue and then saw her father's expression: it was bad enough to have to suffer all of this in the hallway, without having his daughter watch as well.

She went to stand at the window in the stairwell. Outside, the hospital's grounds were still muddy from all the rain. The sky was pink above the coconut palms, but the street outside the gate was artificially dark beneath the heavy acacias. A pair of young men passed, arms interlinked, their heads bent together in secret confidence. Crows wheeled above them, crying, and landed in the rinsed black leaves. She watched until she was overcome by a sense of her own uselessness, and then she went to find the doctor.

She had planned to rail at him in the officious style of her Devil Aunt, until he acquiesced and moved her father. She finally found him examining a boy on a bed in the second-floor hallway, the agitated relatives hardly giving him room to move. The family didn't look like they could've paid anything in bribes, but the doctor was kneeling on the floor by the boy, taking his pulse. Amina noticed the dark stains on the front of the doctor's shirt—the hallway felt airless, even with all the windows open—and she simply stood there watching him.

It was after eleven when they finally moved her father to the ward, which was cleaner but as crowded as the hallway, with tiled walls and a scrubbed concrete floor. The ward boy who appeared told them matter-of-factly that the saline drip the doctor had recommended would cost seven hundred fifty taka; Amina paid without protesting, although the machine looked decrepit, and she was surprised by the speed at which it whirred to life. In addition to the food, her aunt had sent Fariq with a package of extra bedding and two mosquito nets. Her mother set up a pallet on the floor next to the bed and invited Amina to lie down, but she'd been waiting until it was late enough to call George. She left the ward and went into the stairwell, where she stood on the landing between two floors. A window was open to the humming night, and she took her phone out of her purse; the reception was good, but there were no messages. When they hadn't shown up tonight, Nasir would have called—but she was still using the phone Omar had lent her, and she didn't know if he had the number. He would call her father's phone, but of course that was turned off. For a moment she considered calling him herself, and then dialed Rochester instead.

It was the morning of his interview, and George had just gotten out of the shower.

"My father's been attacked with acid," she said, and again she began to cry. Her voice was so garbled that she thought George wouldn't be able to make it out. "He's had surgery already."

"*Acid?* Sweetheart—what?" The sound of his voice was an enormous relief, as if it somehow carried America inside it.

"Amina?"

She got herself under control. "He's all bandaged—his arms and his chest. He's barely awake, but they say the operation went well."

"But the acid," George said. "I mean, who—?"

Amina hesitated for only a moment. "A stranger," she said. "Some crazy person. It missed his face, thank God."

"Was it hydrochloric acid?"

"It's usually sulfuric—when you read about it in the newspaper. But I didn't ask the doctor."

"Christ, Amina—is he all right? What does it look like?"

"It looks like a picture in the newspaper."

"Where are you?"

"At the hospital."

"Is the hospital okay? Are the doctors—"

"It's crowded and dirty."

"Are *you* okay—Amina, tell me, do you need me to come?" He stumbled over the words, and for a moment she considered what he was offering. She imagined him bringing not only the strength and size of his physical person, but that whole antiseptic newness along with him: she pictured her father in the kind of recovery room she and George had seen a hundred times on *ER*, in his own curtained enclave, with a pristine plate of unappetizing foods, separated and sealed with plastic. She and her mother would use a toilet in a clean, white bathroom, with a sign above the sink reminding them to wash their hands; they would take turns sleeping on chairs that reclined to become beds and complain about discomfort in the morning. Doctors would come in and out in white coats, their reassuringly unfamiliar names stitched onto their pockets—she longed suddenly for Jessica's awful husband, Harold—making jokes while they checked an array of sophisticated machines.

But George couldn't bring America with him. He would be appalled by the conditions at the hospital and unequipped to help them with even the simplest errand outside. He would have to be checked into a hotel, where he would be able to do nothing but wait.

"No—" she said. "No, but thank you. It's not great, but basically . . . basically, we're fine. We've bribed the staff for better treatment."

"Jesus," George said. It struck her that this was the thing that seemed most to shock him—although that was probably unfair; there was so little of this that he could actually imagine.

"We'll shift to Moni and Omar's now—as soon as my father is discharged. It could be as soon as Thursday."

"Where were you before?"

"At Nasir's. He's my father's—" She beat back a crazy urge to confess everything, to beg for his forgiveness.

"Relative," George supplied. "You told me. So this is still the best number to call? If you're okay, I have to go to this interview now—but can I call you afterward?"

"I'm okay."

"But will you call me if anything changes? I mean—you can call anytime, you know that, right? I won't turn the phone off."

She didn't want to hang up, as if there might be a risk of permanently severing the connection. If she could just get her parents away from here, everything would be all right. Once they had their Social Security numbers, her parents would be eligible for Medicaid; if her father needed care outside of what those benefits provided, they would find a way to pay for it. The care would be better in America, and so of course that was where they had to go. There was a kind of relief in realizing her choices had become so simple.

"George?" she said.

"What is it?"

"I'm sorry."

"Sorry for what?"

"For everything. For—that things aren't better . . . I mean, between us."

"Amina—please. It was my fault, and it's over now. This is going to be a new start for us. We just need to get your father well."

"Okay." Her voice sounded foreign and unsteady, even to her.

"Are you really?"

She nodded, forgetting he couldn't see her. "Good luck at the interview. Did you have to prepare anything?"

"Never mind about that," George said. "I know you're overwhelmed, honey—but remember to tell your father I'm thinking of him, okay?"

When she got off the phone, she saw that Nasir had sent her a text: *just talked to aunty . . . call me.* She stared at it for a moment and then buried the phone in her purse. Her mother would have told him everything; she could only embarrass herself by calling now.

When she got back to the ward, her father was obviously in pain. His bandaged arms rested on top of the blanket her aunt had sent, which her mother had immediately changed for the hospital's. Now that he was fully awake, his face was gray and exhausted; he looked at her and then closed his eyes, as if by resting one organ he might save his strength for another.

"Did you reach him?"

She hesitated for a moment and then understood he was talking about George. "He was very upset. He couldn't believe it—he asked if we wanted him to come."

"They don't have acid throwing in the U.S., do they?" Her mother's tone was curious and detached, as if she were asking about events in a book.

"Of course not," Amina said, although she didn't know for sure. It would be something to ask George.

Her father spoke again: "What did he say exactly?"

"He says he's praying for you."

Her mother smiled, pleased by this, but her father blinked in an irritated way.

"Praying!" he said. "Didn't you tell George how lucky the doctors said I was?"

17 As her father recovered, he was able to tell them the story. He and Omar guessed that Salim would have bought the liquid and the jar for fewer than fifty taka at Tantibazar, where it was sold to the jewelers and leather workers, and carried it to Mohammadpur, where he must have hidden himself somewhere in sight of Nasir's apartment. He had waited until he'd seen her father passing, on the way to pick up George's kurta, and followed him to the Kaderabad Bazar. At that point an accomplice, whom her father described as a thin, very young man, overdressed for the weather in a formal shirt and trousers, had told him that the shop immediately behind the one where they were standing was selling phone cards at a deep discount; not being able to resist a bargain (and imagining there might be many more calls to Rochester before his visa was secured), her father had followed the young man into the narrow alley between two rows of shops, where they had heard the chugging of a scooter and paused to let it pass. The scooter had instead stopped right in front of them, and the young man had jumped on the back; in spite of the cloth pulled across the lower half of the driver's face, there was no mistaking Salim. The acid had felt for the first few seconds like water, but her father had known what was coming: he said it was as if whole minutes had passed while the scooter roared away and he waited to feel the fire on his skin. He said that now he knew what it must have been like for the Hindu widows who were thrown into the flames of their husband's pyres.

Her father had spent another three nights in the hospital, and then they'd moved to her aunt and uncle's. Omar called the men who'd saved her father, but they never answered their phone; her father and uncle thought it was likely that they were afraid to be involved, in case Amina and her family asked them to be witnesses in court. It was ironic, Amina thought, that they'd spent thousands of taka on bribes in the hospital, while the men who'd actually saved her father's life wouldn't even allow them to say thank you. Her mother frowned when Amina said this out loud. She said that those men were true Muslims, who hadn't done it for her father but for God. Their reward was waiting for them, and they wouldn't ask to be repaid on earth.

It wasn't until they were settled at her aunt and uncle's that her mother thought to check the messages on her father's phone. On Wednesday morning, the day after the attack, the embassy had called and left a new number. When Amina called back, a young Deshi man with a convincing American accent said that her father's visa had been approved and that he or his agent might bring his passport to receive the stamp at window number 3 any afternoon between two and four.

Her father had immediately begun worrying about the bandages, speculating about the possibility of removing them for the trip, and so Omar had gotten in touch with a lawyer friend. The lawyer had said that Abdul Mazid would be examined at both airports in New York and that he should say it was a "workplace accident."

"Then you can explain that he's had a skin graft," Omar instructed Amina. "But be sure to say he doesn't require any further surgery. All that's true enough."

"Nasir also believes it will be all right," her mother reported, as if Nasir were a high authority on U.S. emigration. Her mother had called Nasir as soon as he was home from work that evening, and—Amina couldn't help having noticed—just when she'd left her father's bedside to call George. Nasir had told her mother that at first he'd thought they might have gone to a hotel, because of his quarrel with Amina, and it was only after he'd failed many times to reach them that he'd started to worry.

"But you'll all have to stay indoors until you leave," her uncle added now. "Nothing but the trip to the embassy, and Fariq will take you there."

Amina didn't need encouragement. Ever since the attack, she'd been having nightmares. Several times she and her mother were in the old apartment at Long Nose's—or in the very similar Mohammadpur apartment they'd had when she'd first started e-mailing with George—watching as flames licked the walls. Once, however, she'd found herself in the Rahmans' apartment, waiting to see the photo of Mokta. While Mokta's mother was in the other room, Amina sat down in one of the two empty chairs by the chess set, next to an open window framed by heavy, green drapery. She knew the window was dangerous, but she longed to look out; when she stood up she saw that the view wasn't of the alley in front of Nasir's building but of the pond in the village, where Micki was bending to fill a copper pitcher. She called out to her cousin, but just then the wind ruffled the drapery, which moved to reveal a man's bare foot in a plastic sandal protruding only inches from her own. That time she jumped so violently in bed that her mother had to shake her awake to calm her.

Her aunt had made her father's bed in a small, bright guest room behind the kitchen, where Borsha prepared special foods: biryani, korma, and the sweet lassis he'd always loved. Ghaniyah had gone back to her in-laws, and Omar was at work all day, so her mother and her aunt spent most of the time her father was asleep in the kitchen, talking to each other in low voices. Her aunt was one of those people who was electrified by tragedy; their residence in the apartment gave her a sense of her own generosity. The attack had cast a prescient glow on both her aunt's and her mother's sense of impending danger—as well as her parents' desire to leave Desh, which was even stronger than before.

The night before she went to get the visa, she sat down at her uncle's computer, and IM'ed with George until they found the best fare. She and her parents would leave in ten days, provided her father's doctor gave permission, flying Emirates with a six-hour stopover in Dubai. She'd already accepted that the Starbucks job was gone, and she tried not to think about how long it would be before her parents were independent enough that she could begin to look for a new one. She checked her e-mail on her uncle's computer several times a day: she was corresponding regularly with no one apart from George, but there were long, empty stretches of time while her father was asleep,

and her mother and Moni were together in the kitchen. She hadn't
had so much time to do nothing since she'd first arrived in Rochester,
and perhaps it was that feeling—the day stretching drearily in front
of her—that made her go back and reread the first messages Nasir had
sent her. Floating in the strange limbo of the last days before their
departure—now six, now five, now four—she returned especially to
the e-mail in which he'd compared the "past and present Munnis."
She felt she was on the verge of another transformation, but of course
she couldn't rely on Nasir to tell her what it would be.

Her aunt Parveen once told her that if you spent a great deal of time
waiting around to hear from one person, another, less desirable one
was sure to show up in his place. And so the e-mail that came three
days before they left had the air of the inevitable.

Dear Amina,

**Oh well. It looks like it wouldn't have worked anyway. Now I'm under
a kind of house arrest—even worse than before. I'm not sure if you'll
believe me when I tell you the reason, but here goes. I'm pregnant—for
real this time. So it turns out that not only am I not allowed to get a job,
I'm not allowed to go ANYWHERE, especially places that might be dirty
or unsafe. They laughed when Ashok brought up the idea of a trip to
Bangladesh.**

**Of course I know Desh is perfectly safe. I might have fought with them
if you'd said okay. But since it doesn't work for anyone, I'll give up my
little Friendship Express dream. I guess there isn't really any friendship
express—I've thought a lot about how I might prove that I'm your friend,
and I hope that someday I'll find a way to do it.**

**With love,
Kim**

Amina wondered what it was that made Kim write to her now. She
didn't think it was simple cruelty (though the word "pregnant," she
discovered, still had the power to rip a jagged seam in her chest). Kim
had exactly what she wanted, and if things went as she planned, there
would be few opportunities in the future for the two of them to meet.
And yet Kim had pursued a friendship with this desperate intensity
from the beginning, as if there was something she hoped to get from

her. What fascination had she held for the American woman, beyond her exotic provenance? Men, she thought, could make a clean break with a woman, could leave in the way Parveen's husband had, or could even be left, like George, and determine to make a life another way. It was women who longed to retain ties and connections, to mix things up in complicated ways. She thought again of her visit to Mokta's apartment, and felt a creeping shame.

There was no trouble at the embassy, but when she got back with her father's passport, her parents hardly looked at it. They examined it for a moment, her mother turning the pages for her father to see the immigrant visa, exactly like her own, before quickly returning it to Amina for safe keeping.

"Nasir came to say good-bye. This was the only time I told him not to come—I knew you'd be out—so we were surprised to see him. He said he'd wait until you got back, but then there was an emergency at his office." Her mother watched her curiously as she said this, and for the first time Amina was afraid that she guessed something about what had happened between the two of them.

"We forgot to give back his extra key," her father said. "But you'll want to go see him again."

"And leave some kind of gift," her mother said. "You and I will go together—we'll be safe with Fariq."

"Why go all the way back there?" Amina asked. "You've said good-bye. Fariq can drop off the key—it's simpler."

She felt she'd successfully clothed her feelings in irritation, but she was sorry when she saw the way her father looked at her; she hadn't spoken to him that way since the attack. There was a part of her that was relieved Nasir had managed the farewell for her, and she thought she might have done the same if the situation were reversed. Still, it was painful to think about the lengths to which he'd gone to avoid her, leaving work in the middle of the day and then inventing a premise to flee. He would have had an obligation, as well as a genuine desire, to visit her father and say good-bye to both of her parents. She thought of him getting on his scooter with a quick backward glance, his relief in feeling that he'd fulfilled his obligation.

She resolved to forget everything to do with Nasir, but her parents couldn't stop talking about him. Both her mother and father were especially concerned about how they were going to manage an appropriate parting gift, now that there couldn't be any more trips to the bazaar.

"If only we'd known how much we were going to rely on him—you could've brought something special from over there."

"What about the watch?" her father said. They were sitting in the guest room. Her mother had sent Fariq to Savar Bazar as soon as they'd gotten back from the hospital, with instructions to buy four ready-made shirts for her father to wear in Rochester; her father had joked that with his bandages, he finally required a large. But he was saving the new shirts, wearing one of the old ones unbuttoned to give them easy access to his bandages, which slowly acquired a rust-colored tinge until they needed to be changed. Borsha had dragged two of the living room chairs into the room, so that whoever was watching her father would have a place to sit, but her mother was pacing the floor instead.

"That old watch is worth nothing—except to you. Keep it."

"I have a travel alarm clock and some socks," Amina said. "And a New York Yankees baseball cap."

"That will have to do," said her mother. "Someday we'll meet someone who's going back, who can carry something else for Nasir. Something electronic." She glanced at Amina. "I mean, when things are better."

And then, as sometimes happened, a casual prediction of her mother's became reality right before their eyes. Amina's phone began to tremble on the table, as if it were cold, and the home number in Rochester scrolled across the screen.

"Amina—can you hear me?" The signal was clear, and it would've offended her parents if she'd moved to another room, and so she told George she could hear him and stayed where she was.

"How's your father?"

"He's the same." She made the mistake of looking at her father, who frowned.

"Tell him how much better I am today," he said. "Tell him how much I've been eating."

"I have good news and good news," George said. "Which do you want to hear first?"

"What?"

"I got the job at SLR—the better job. They had two positions open—I thought I was interviewing for the other one, but it turns out they had me in mind for the more senior one. I'll be managing a team on a new data center in Gates—it'll take at least five years, and they're big enough that layoffs shouldn't be a risk even after it's done. We haven't discussed compensation, but Ray—that's the guy I know in aeronautical—he thinks it's probably going to be more than I was making at TCE."

"That's wonderful," Amina said. It was everything she'd been hoping for in the months before she'd come to Desh. She thought it must've been her fear for her father that kept her from feeling the expected joy and relief.

"The nice thing is, they're a Rochester company, and they only work in the region. There's no risk of transfer the way there was at TCE."

Her parents were looking at her inquisitively, and so Amina fixed her eyes on the window. "What's the other good news?"

George laughed. "Well, you're not going to believe it. I almost thought I should wait until you got home, but then the job happened and I had to call you."

"What is it?"

"I hope you're not going to mind that I opened your mail, but I saw it was from Starbucks."

"Do I still have my job?"

"Better," George said. "You're the grand prize winner."

"Winner of what?"

"*You* know what," George said. "I thought you said you were too busy to write another essay."

" 'Reach for the Stars'?"

"I can't believe you didn't tell me."

Her father turned to her mother, whispering loudly, "What did they win?"

"Ten thousand dollars' tuition," George said. "That's more than a year of MCC."

"But I didn't—"

"You don't have to be modest anymore—you won! I'm so proud of you."

She looked around at the empty, bright room, the bed and chairs islanded on the gleaming marble floor. Of course there was only one person who might have written five hundred words about Amina's life and entered it for a prize. She remembered the pointed way Kim had inquired about the contest that awful rainy night at Cathy's house.

"The letter said it was going to be published on the website," George said. "I'm not surprised—it's really great."

"You read it?"

"They included it. You have to sign something before they publish it. The stuff about the ICR's right on—even if it's not exactly true. You almost made *me* believe we had the wedding there." Amina was still processing the idea that Kim had sent in an essay about her. She must've done it right after they'd seen each other last, just before she went to India. It was shocking to think that Kim had won, out of all the people who must have entered—what on earth could she have written?

"It made me glad we're going to do it," George continued. "I even told my mom I was planning to convert."

"What did she say?"

"She's says it's okay with her—if that's what makes me happy. Cathy's going to be another story, though."

Amina found she was hardly listening. Ten thousand dollars was really very little money in Rochester, when you counted up the years it would take her to finish her education: she would be at least thirty-five by the time she got her teaching certificate. She couldn't picture herself teaching American children in a classroom, and she no longer cared about the diploma for its own sake. She looked at her father, watching her hopefully from the bed, his hands frail and inert on the red coverlet. What good was ten thousand dollars now? She wanted to throw the phone across the room.

"My father bought you a fancy kurta," she said instead. "To wear for our wedding pictures."

"Oh, God," George said. "Can he return it? Can't you tell him I'll just wear a coat and tie or something?"

Amina's mother was sitting on one of her aunt's new upholstered chairs, watching Amina and holding the Yankees cap protectively in her lap. She wished she could go back to the moment, almost five years ago now, when they'd first agreed she would write to George, to remember who had said what. Had it been her mother encouraging her, or the other way around? Even if her parents had wanted this, had they known enough to decide? And now that she knew, wasn't she the one responsible for their happiness—for making the right choice for them as well as for her?

"Amina?" George said.

"Yes."

"That essay—it made me think of those e-mails we used to write. It sounds like you—like the way you talk." He hesitated. "I miss you."

"My parents are right here."

"You can't even say you miss your husband in front of them?"

"No."

"That's good for me to know. Cultural differences—" He laughed. "Hey, do you realize it's only four more days?"

Amina found that she couldn't speak.

"I'm having trouble hearing you," George said. "If you can hear me, I'll see you at the gate on Tuesday."

He waited a moment and then gave up. "Bye, honey."

"What?" her mother said, when Amina hung up. "George got a job?"

Amina nodded. "A good one—even better than he expected." She had the strange feeling she was lying, even as she told her parents the truth.

"Thanks be to God," her mother said. But Amina was thinking of how her parents wouldn't be able to drive themselves to the grocery store. How unhappy her mother would be to depend on her or George every time she ran out of something in the kitchen.

"You see," her father said happily, "things are working out."

"Here, look—you forgot these." Her mother had found the box of tin birds, empty except for the wood thrush, the sparrow, and the cardinal, and was squatting on the floor in the village style, examining them. "We can drop one off for Nasir before we leave—maybe this red one. His wife will like it, when he marries."

Amina had left the other two in the box because of their dull, brown coloring, but she'd been pleased not to have to give up the cardinal. At one time she'd been annoyed at the real bird; now she felt nostalgic for his crazy determination—his stubborn belief that there was something through that window for him.

"Not that one," she said, replacing it. "I think the clock and cap are enough." Her parents exchanged glances but didn't argue, and her mother purposely changed the subject:

"But what did you win? You didn't tell us."

A part of her wanted to conceal it, but she'd never been good at lying to her mother. "A scholarship," she said. "Ten thousand dollars toward my tuition at MCC."

Her parents gasped, and for a moment she thought they were struck, as she had been, by the irony of that particular sum.

"Ten thousand dollars for university," her father said. "My daughter!"

"It's just a community college," Amina said.

"American scholarship," her mother said in English. "For real this time." Her mother's eyes, listless and dull before the phone call, had taken on a familiar sparkle, and both her parents were looking at Amina in a way that made it impossible to contradict anything they had said.

18 The day before the flight, Fariq drove Amina back to Nasir's to deliver the gifts. She was afraid she might run into Sakina, whom her mother informed her was back from Comilla, but that Monday afternoon Amina was lucky. It was Nasir's younger sister, Shilpa, who called her name on the stairs as she blinked in the sudden darkness of the stairwell. It was the hottest part of the day, and most people who weren't at work would be either eating or napping indoors. Shilpa met them on the stairs and insisted on serving Amina a cold drink in her apartment while Fariq loitered uneasily inside the door. She seemed eager for the company; she said she'd been sitting on her balcony hoping for a breeze when she'd seen Amina get out of the car. Shilpa's two boys were in school, and the apartment was calm and relatively cool, with the fans going and all the curtains closed.

"How is your father?"

"*Alhamdulillah*, he is recovering," Amina said. "We've been staying indoors, of course."

"Of course. My brother told us as soon as we got back—we're praying for you." Shilpa put a hand on her enormous belly, stretched taut. Now, so near the end of her third pregnancy, Amina thought that bearing children must seem like the most normal thing in the world to Nasir's sister, hardly to be remarked upon, requiring no special luck or skill.

"We didn't know you were back," Amina said.

"Thank God we are," Shilpa said. "You think it's hot here? It's like an oven down there, and those people are so used to it, they don't even notice. I could hardly remember everyone's name—my brain was cooking the whole time."

"Is it a large family?" Amina asked casually.

"Enormous," Shilpa said. "The girl is the youngest of nine, everyone's pet. I thought she might be spoiled, but my sister was right. She's very quiet and sweet—the kind who's embarrassed about being so pretty. She made all the food herself. You could see her fingers were still stained with turmeric. We were all impressed."

"Wonderful," Amina said.

"Their children will be frighteningly beautiful," Shilpa went on slyly. "My poor Shabu and Lallu won't be able to compete." Then a recent scrapbook was pressed upon Amina, who was forced to disagree. She admired pictures of Shabu and Lallu in their school uniforms; at a mathematics competition (Shabu had failed to distinguish himself, but Lallu had placed third in his age group); and in front of the tiger cage at the Mirpur Zoo.

"Do you have pictures from the trip?" Amina asked, but Shilpa shook her head. "They sent a portrait of the girl, but I think my sister's given it to Nasir already."

"So it's all settled?" Amina asked, as casually as she could manage.

Shilpa gave her a candid smile. "Well, now they'll have to meet. But I think the families agree. You won't get any argument from the girl—she's very obedient. She'll be lonely here without her family, though."

"Your brother will be kind to her."

Shilpa shrugged. "If he agrees to meet her. Who knows with him? He called Sakina the other night—it was so late, but I sometimes sit up with her, watching TV. She said he sounded crazy, talking about how he couldn't marry—how we shouldn't make the trip. But when my sister asked for his reasons, he wouldn't tell her."

"When was that?"

"Oh, I don't know," Shilpa said. "A few days before we left. My sister ignored him, of course—the trip was all planned. And my brother gets worked up so easily."

Amina felt her face flushing in a way she thought Shilpa couldn't help but notice. If she'd made a mistake about that phone call, and he'd really been talking to Sakina, what did it mean? Had he seriously considered breaking off the negotiations with the family in Comilla? If he had preferred her, even briefly—and then she'd gone across the street and tried to interfere in his life? After all that, he couldn't help but be disgusted with her.

The apartment felt hot and close, and Amina was dizzy. She sat down on a chair, expecting to have to make excuses to Shilpa—it was embarrassing, given the other woman's condition. But Shilpa's attention had wandered to the plastic Home Depot shopping bag Amina was holding, which she'd used for packing. She'd forgotten the exotic cachet such things had here.

"I just brought something from my parents for your brother. I'll leave it in the apartment, with the key."

"I can take it up," Shilpa said.

"I wouldn't make you climb all those flights," Amina said, and then, before Shilpa could protest: "I'm afraid my mother left something behind in his apartment—a tonic for her eyes. She's obsessed with these herbs from the village."

"Our mother was the same way," Shilpa said. "That's the way we Deshis are—we complain and complain in the villages, and then take us out and it's all we can talk about."

"Aren't people that way everywhere?" Amina said. "I mean, when they lose something?"

"Are they?" Shilpa laughed in a self-deprecating way. "I wouldn't know."

Nasir's apartment was hot, although he'd left the windows in the bedrooms open. Fariq followed her inside and watched as she set the gifts on the table; clearly he didn't think much of them. He looked at his phone in a way that implied he would be glad when her troublesome family was no longer his responsibility. Amina had to remind herself she owed her uncle's servant no explanation. Still, she went into the bathroom as if she were looking for her mother's medicine. Water dripped from the tap onto an overturned plastic bucket, and through the vent in the wall she could hear children calling to one another outside.

Nasir, she thought, only the thought was like speech: she seemed to hear her own voice as if it were coming from the other side of the wall. She went into Nasir's bedroom—he still hadn't moved back to the larger room—with the vague idea that she was searching for the photograph of the girl in Comilla, but of course it wasn't lying out on any obvious surface. There was a thick cotton spread on the bed, a green-and-gray pattern, and a dresser with a photograph of his parents in a gold frame. The only other piece of furniture was a nightstand with an empty eyeglass case sitting on it, a five-taka coin, and a book— a Tagore novel, *The Home and the World,* which she'd neglected to read in Bengali Literature at Maple Leaf. The room was very still, and she had the strange thought that she could be visiting the bedroom of someone who had died, preserved by the bereaved relatives as a memorial.

She stepped out onto the balcony, where several of Nasir's shirts were drying. One of his sisters must've washed them for him after he went to work this morning, and they were hanging against the iron grille, making a wet curtain between herself and the street. She touched the sleeve of a white shirt and then pushed it carefully to the side, as if she wanted to look out. In fact her mind was so full that she found herself simply staring at the wall of the building opposite, adjacent to the one where the Rahmans lived. She thought she must have stood there for a long time, and gradually she became aware of the people passing in the lane below, on foot and in rickshaws. The apartment was so similar to the one she'd left three years ago that she could almost imagine she was back there, waiting eagerly for the first glimpse of her husband-to-be. But instead of George it was a girl she saw, wearing her uniform shalwar kameez and carrying a heavy bag of schoolbooks on her back. She paused in front of the gate, searching through her bag for her key, and then let herself into the courtyard of the blue building. Her hair was loose around her face, but Amina knew very well who it was.

She peered through the grille, stifling a peculiar urge to call out. Once she had thought there was a girl who'd stayed back to hold her place for her, but that was just another one of the illusions that came with distance. The balcony was small, the view obscured, and Amina was alone.

19 They arrived too early to go through security, and so they were forced to wait near the baggage claim, on orange plastic chairs that her mother insisted on wiping with a napkin before they sat down. No flights were coming in, and several of the ceiling lights had burned out; they sat in the gloom while other, larger families coalesced and dispersed around them, flush with the busy self-importance of air travel. It was afternoon when they entered the airport, but it seemed like dusk inside. Her parents continued peering through the tinted glass to the parking lot, and Amina wondered if they weren't already regretting how little time they'd spent saying good-bye.

Halfway around the world, George was just getting out of bed. It was a new one, a box spring and mattress they'd ordered online just before she left, much cheaper than the fancy bed frame they'd looked at in the store. What had George said that day, about her and her inflexible plans? She'd thought he wasn't being fair, that he couldn't understand her, but was it possible he'd been right after all?

She looked at her parents—her mother with a green woolen sweater already draped over her shoulders against the terminal's mild air-conditioning, and her father in an oversize shirt that tented out around his bandaged chest. When she'd gone alone, she'd been able to adapt, and because she had no one to talk to about the things that were shocking or offensive or odd, they'd slowly grown to seem less so. But with three of them there, it would be different. Her parents would unwittingly begin taking over the house—little touches like the slippers by the doorway, the smell of spices in the furniture, the language itself—until not only George but even Amina herself would feel like a stranger there. This was the moment she'd imagined: when she was supposed to have fulfilled her obligations as a daughter. She was handing her parents a gift, the magnitude of which dwarfed the modest television she'd once presented. They had watched the safety and security of life abroad on that tiny black-and-white screen for years and believed they had seen the future. Now, just when she should have felt the weight of responsibility lifting, she seemed to have grown even heavier, burdened with three people's fates, each of which was being irrevocably changed because of her.

It should have been obvious that her parents were waiting for someone, but she realized it only when she saw him coming through the double doors. Nasir was dressed for work in a white shirt and gray slacks, carrying his briefcase under his arm. He'd clipped the bottoms of his trousers in order to ride the motorbike and forgotten to undo them when he dismounted; there was something that touched her about the plastic clips and the strip of black sock revealed under the cuff. He had already spotted them, and gave a brief, familiar wave, as if he were the final member of their party arriving to travel.

"Jams everywhere," he said. "I couldn't have gotten here without the bike." He had been avoiding her eyes, but now he turned to look at her directly. "Do many people ride scooters in America?"

"Not in Rochester," she said. "It's too cold."

Nasir nodded, as if this were vital information he'd been seeking for some time. He took in the crowd at security, less a line than a heaving throng. "What time can you go through?"

Her father glanced at her mother and then maneuvered his arm painfully to reach into his pocket for the watch, which he handed to Nasir. He looked exhausted already, and she couldn't imagine the toll the long flight would take on him.

"Please keep this," her father said. "It's nothing—it was my father's. He gave it to me before I went off to university, just before I met your father. Your father used to admire it. Back then it was quite fashionable."

Nasir was shaking his head. "I can't."

"Someone will give you a new watch when you marry," her mother said. "The bride's family. Take this old thing until then."

Amina could see that they'd agreed her gifts weren't sufficient and had settled on this course of action last night before her father slept. She had been next door in Ghaniyah's room, waiting for her mother to join her, but they'd still been bickering when she'd fallen asleep. Their concerns were always shared; they only differed on how best to address them. She almost envied them their perpetual quarrel—the way it tied them together, more securely than any marriage contract. This morning she'd woken to find that her mother had spent the night in the chair beside her father's bed.

The two of them went back and forth with Nasir about the watch until he finally accepted it. He was just able to fasten it around his much broader wrist; he would have to make another notch in the leather strap. Both of her parents were beaming, relieved and pleased, and of course Nasir now got out his own gifts, secreted in the briefcase.

"The one I should've given you years ago," he said, handing her father a book of poems. There was attar for her mother, from his sisters. "Less than three ounces—so they won't think you're trying to blow up the plane," Nasir joked. Then he handed Amina a small white box, fastened at the sides with tape.

Her parents were watching her closely, and she was forced to look at Nasir simply to avoid their identical, inquiring expressions. They wanted her to open the box, but she was suddenly afraid of its contents.

"I should apologize," Amina said. "It was wrong of me to meddle in your affairs."

Nasir nodded, acknowledging that fact. "I confused you, talking about that other girl." He was looking at her as if they were alone, and she realized that he was just as comfortable with her parents standing there as he might have been without them. She remembered George's distaste for "dirty laundry," and she knew there was no business Nasir could have with her that was secret from her parents. The thought made her fear the white box even more.

The intensity of the conversation was beginning to disturb her parents, who were shifting uncomfortably on their feet, glancing at the security line. Surely they would be allowed to pass through now. Her father was still worried about the suspicious bulk of the bandages under his shirt and had told them several times that they would have to allow extra time for him to be checked by hand.

"Open your gift, Munni," her father said. "Then we have to go."

Amina fiddled with the tape on the side of the box. Such a small box could only contain jewelry, but she couldn't imagine what Nasir would think appropriate to give her. Because she didn't know what else to do, she slid her nail under the tape on the side of the box and lifted the lid. Inside, nestled on a white cotton square, was a pair of enameled yellow hair barrettes, with a pattern of intertwining white leaves and branches—the kind of trinket you might buy at a stall in the bazaar for twenty taka.

"I made up that girl," he said suddenly. "I was embarrassed—you bringing up my marriage directly like that. That's because you've been abroad so long."

She stared at him. One of the broken lights above their heads buzzed suddenly and went on.

"Only two hours until the flight," her father said. "Imagine if we missed it."

"You never saw Mokta?"

Nasir shook his head as if he were disgusted. "I didn't even know there was a girl living there." He was looking at his gift as if he regretted it. "When you were young, you used to wear clips something like that. At least, I believe you did."

"She did," her mother confirmed. "Exactly."

"It was so long ago—but I thought these might remind you of home."

That was another thing about the kind of proposal she'd dreamed of receiving. It happened unexpectedly, and you didn't hesitate for a moment in your answer. Nasir was looking down, and his lashes were so long that they touched the darker skin underneath his eyes. He wouldn't ask; she couldn't accept. The seconds were grinding down to nothing right in front of them.

"Yes," she said, too loud. "Yes—I'll remember every time I look at them."

"It can take an hour and a half just to get through the line," her father was saying. "I've heard that. And then we have to find the gate."

"I have something," Amina said. "Hold on." It wasn't in the first suitcase, and so she had to open the second. Down at the other end of the row of chairs she noticed another woman opening another suitcase, unburdening herself to her relatives, as if she'd only now realized the difficulty of future exchanges. The cardboard box was at the top of the suitcase, where her mother had carefully surrounded it with a nest of clothing, and when she opened the lid she found all three of the birds intact. She removed the red cardinal, along with one of the metal fasteners, which you were supposed to use to bind the feet to the branch of an evergreen tree.

"One came to the yard—" she began, and couldn't continue; instead she held it out to him. Was this brush of the palm when he took it the last time they would touch? Did that occur to him, too? There was no clue in his expression.

Nasir frowned. "Is it really this red?"

"Redder," Amina managed. "It doesn't look like something you would find in Rochester. But you do."

"Your wife will like that someday," her mother said happily. Now Amina could see that she felt the gift exchange had been equitable. "Be sure to tell her it comes from abroad."

She and her mother each took the strap of one rolling suitcase. Across the departures hall, the line had begun to move.

"Let me take those," Nasir said. He had wrapped the cardinal carefully in the same paper he'd used for her mother's perfume and put it in his bag. It would ride back downtown with him to his office, bumping against his side. In the evening he might rediscover it, unwrapping and setting it on the folding table (would Sakina or Shilpa have taken away the cloth with the red-cheeked Dutchman?). The bird would stay there, observing him each morning and evening as he took his meals, prepared on alternating days by his sisters up and down the stairs. One day soon he would get married, perhaps even to the girl in Comilla. But it wouldn't be like him to lose or throw away her gift. It would live with him forever in this city, which she was very likely never to see again. At once she felt a yearning for this object so strong that she might have reached into his bag herself to touch it if they hadn't already been moving toward the security barrier. She hadn't known it was possible to envy a molded piece of tin.

"We'll send you an e-mail," her father said. "Let you know that we've arrived."

"It would still be good to send something more later," her mother whispered as they joined the line. "If we can find someone who goes back and forth."

"Which of you is traveling?" demanded a guard in green, and Nasir had to return the suitcases. Her mother offered their documents while her father watched helplessly, looking at this airport functionary as if he expected him to reject them on a whim. Instead the guard grunted and returned them, then blocked Nasir with an outstretched palm.

"Step back, step back," he said. Nasir glanced at the box she still held in her hand—and then turned away so quickly that it was difficult even to fix a final image of his face. Instead she watched his broad back passing through the tinted glass and into the parking lot, where he was abruptly drained of color, taking on the antique distance of a figure in a black-and-white film.

"Keep moving," said the guard, and they did.

❖

Reach for the Stars

In my native country, Bangladesh, it is difficult to get an education. When I was thirteen, I had to leave school because my father—a decorated Freedom Fighter in our Liberation War with Pakistan—couldn't support us. I couldn't stand the idea of falling behind my schoolmates, and so my mother helped me study on my own for my college entrance exams. We would check out books from the English library and look up all the words we didn't know. My relatives, who had more money than we did, shook their heads and used a Bengali proverb, saying that my parents and I were "sleeping under a torn quilt and dreaming of gold." Maybe so, but we didn't give up. Five years later, I passed my exams on schedule.

I dreamed of going to college abroad, especially in America, but that was too expensive. Instead I became an English tutor for wealthy children, traveling to their houses by rickshaw. Many of those families had their own computers, and it was on one of those computers—practicing my written English in an international online forum—that I met my husband, George, an American.

As a woman in Bangladesh, I was rarely allowed to enter a mosque, but here in America I can worship freely. My husband and I were married at the Islamic Center of Rochester, in a hall with light streaming through the stained-glass windows. I wore a red sari, which is traditional in my country. As I listened to my husband repeat the words of the *shahada*—the Muslim declaration of faith—I looked at our witnesses from the congregation. There was an Egyptian, a Saudi, and a Pakistani: people who would never have met if they'd stayed in their own countries. At the ICR I have met determined people from all over the world, struggling to make better lives for themselves here in Rochester.

What I love about working at Starbucks is getting to know my customers. They tell me about themselves, and they're interested in my story as well. I believe that getting to know your customers and anticipating their needs are the essence of good service. It's what makes Starbucks not only a coffee shop but a center of our community. When I'm not working, I take courses at Monroe Community College. I'm pursuing a degree in education because I'd like to teach English to others like myself one day. I would like to help my students become as comfortable in English as I am when I speak to our customers. I believe that it is only by sharing our stories that we truly become one community.

By: Amina Mazid Stillman
Barista: Starbucks, 1914 Monroe Avenue
Rochester, New York

ACKNOWLEDGMENTS

I wouldn't have written this book if not for an extraordinary person I met six years ago on an airplane. Farah Deeba Munni opened her life to me, sharing her two homes, her sense of humor, and her memories, while giving me the freedom to make something entirely different from them. A writer couldn't ask for a more valuable gift, and I'm deeply grateful for her trust and her friendship.

The hospitality of Farah's parents, her grandmother, and her extended family, both in Dhaka and in Haibatpur, exceeded even extremely high Bangladeshi standards. Farah's husband, David Butler, was an invaluable resource for all things Rochesterian, and I'm grateful to him for his patience with this project. I owe thanks also to Omar Shareef and Shahriar Kabir and their families for welcoming me into their homes in Dhaka, and to Betsy Hartmann for discussing her experiences in Bangladesh.

At a time of sparse funding for the arts, I'm indebted to the Guggenheim Foundation and the Dorothy and Lewis B. Cullman Center for Scholars and Writers, which provided financial help as well as a genuine community of writers, a rare thing. I'm also thankful to Deborah Treisman at *The New Yorker,* and to David Bezmozgis, Emma Freudenberger, and Fatema Ahmed for their thoughts and suggestions about early drafts of the manuscript.

Robin Desser is the kind of editor who isn't supposed to exist anymore, both sympathetic and exacting, and this book is much better for her hand in it. I always feel lucky to have Binky Urban for an agent—this time in particular for convincing me to keep going when I thought I was really stuck. And this book is dedicated to Paul, who supports me in ways I couldn't have imagined when we were only newly wed.

He just wanted a decent book to read ...

Not too much to ask, is it? It was in 1935 when Allen Lane, Managing Director of Bodley Head Publishers, stood on a platform at Exeter railway station looking for something good to read on his journey back to London. His choice was limited to popular magazines and poor-quality paperbacks – the same choice faced every day by the vast majority of readers, few of whom could afford hardbacks. Lane's disappointment and subsequent anger at the range of books generally available led him to found a company – and change the world.

'We believed in the existence in this country of a vast reading public for intelligent books at a low price, and staked everything on it'
Sir Allen Lane, 1902–1970, founder of Penguin Books

The quality paperback had arrived – and not just in bookshops. Lane was adamant that his Penguins should appear in chain stores and tobacconists, and should cost no more than a packet of cigarettes.

Reading habits (and cigarette prices) have changed since 1935, but Penguin still believes in publishing the best books for everybody to enjoy. We still believe that good design costs no more than bad design, and we still believe that quality books published passionately and responsibly make the world a better place.

So wherever you see the little bird – whether it's on a piece of prize-winning literary fiction or a celebrity autobiography, political tour de force or historical masterpiece, a serial-killer thriller, reference book, world classic or a piece of pure escapism – you can bet that it represents the very best that the genre has to offer.

Whatever you like to read – trust Penguin.